The Cockscomb Legacy

JAMES LEE PATIENCE

The Cockscomb Legacy

Matador
9 De Montfort Mews
Leicester LE1 7FW, UK
Tel: (+44) 116 255 9311 / 9312
Email: books@troubador.co.uk
Web: www.troubador.co.uk/matador

In this work of fiction, the characters, places
and events depicted are either the product
of the author's imagination or they are
used entirely fictionally.

ISBN 1 905237 36 7

Cover illustration: Andy Clarke

Typeset in 11pt Stempel Garamond by Troubador Publishing Ltd, Leicester, UK
Printed by The Cromwell Press, Trowbridge, Wilts, UK

Matador is an imprint of Troubador Publishing Ltd

PART 1

The Demon Landlord's Demise

Chapter 1

Juliana had always been a restless child. Now, on her sixteenth birthday she was sitting on the lawn in front of her parents' caravan, as she always did on this special date, wondering what better presents she might have got if only they lived in a house. To one side of her was a paddling pool, half filled with water but unsplashed in; on the other a remote controlled sports car, probably of a German marque but equally ignored. Behind her were a dolls house in the style of a Palladian villa, and a Monopoly board game.

These were not this year's presents, of course. She was much too old for all of them now, but as she had grown from a child she had kept those birthday gifts that reminded her of what she would most want when she grew up; and she would bring them out again each year to test her resolve. As a child she had always brought her toys onto the lawn to play, because her bedroom was so small and there was no space to play in any of the other rooms either. And over the years her resolve had grown and grown: "I'm not going to put up with this. I'm going to marry a builder and he'll have to build me a big house ... with lots of big bedrooms, and a swimming pool outside, and a long drive with electric gates at the end" ... and such like.

On Shottington Ridge, beyond the fields to one side of the caravan park, there were lots of big houses. Juliana liked to look from one to another and pick out the ones she thought she would most like to live in, and then imagine how she would improve and extend them if she had the right husband to help her. The villagers didn't actively despise the people in what they called "the shanty town at the bottom of the hill", but they likewise sought to not really encourage them. The Parish Council distributed its newsletter on the park, not so much as a goodwill gesture but more to let the caravaners read about all the things they weren't encouraged to join in with, so that they wouldn't want to anyway.

The village's Millennium commemorative book, that was also distributed on Cockscomb Park, said: "There is a detached mobile home estate of 110 homes off the Lower Road, but to participate in village activities means a long and hilly walk or the use of a car." Most people on the park got the meaning. How all this, and the smallness of everything around her, frustrated the growing Juliana who was a bright and confident girl and itching to broaden her horizons.

This was not to say that their home was a particularly small caravan. As caravans go it was actually quite large, but second bedrooms in caravans are nevertheless always very small and Juliana's was no exception. The manufacturers were building bigger and bigger ones to sell for more and more money to even more retired people than already lived at the park with Juliana's family. They were even starting to call them "park homes" so that people living in them wouldn't think they were in caravans at all. But outsiders still always thought of them as caravans, and so did the children at the village school who liked to look down upon Juliana, and called her "Gippo".

They were just ignorant of course, but Juliana still cried sometimes when she thought about it. Her parents had always been happy to live in a caravan, and saw no reason why she shouldn't be content too. Since they rarely went out themselves they seldom took her anywhere. To their daughter's constant complaints they countered that there was plenty she could find to amuse herself with on the park, and that meeting boys could wait until she was eighteen and responsible for herself. Juliana just couldn't wait. What life was this for a girl of spirit and ambition, and who could she turn to, to get her out of it?

They were a funny bunch who lived at the park, pretty much. Juliana had heard that people in Wales were all called Jones, Davies or Evans and so were identified by their jobs: Jones the farmer, Davies the baker, Evans the postman, etc. Here it seemed that almost everyone was called Brian or Bryony, except for Mr Scrote the warden, and the landlord Mr Dellsey whom everybody hated but few dared say so to his face because they were all afraid of him.

There was brain dead Brian next door, who spent all his time wandering around the park in a trance, like a lost soul in torment. Some people said it was to help his circulation because he had a weak heart, but others just thought he had nothing better to do. Brian the fish keeper wasn't much better. Except for when he was feeding his fish, he did nothing all day but watch the skies for Herons and Red Kites, and would fly into a panic whenever he saw one. He thought that any bird bigger than a Pigeon must be after his fish, having nothing better to do either.

Brian the jogger seemed to display a similar lack of ultimate purpose, though people assumed that his incessant criss-crossing of the park itself and the fields up to the ridge and back at least kept him fit. "It makes me feel tired watching you!" one or another old grumbler might call out as he passed by on his daily rounds. There were too many people around her like that, Juliana thought. All they do is argue about each others' sheds and fences, complain about the roads and the drains, and most of all about the landlord; but they never do anything to make things better for themselves.

One of the strangest residents of all was Brian the pony tail. He was never seen by day but his Cuban heels could always be heard clicking home at the dead of night. What puzzled people most was how he managed to get out in the first place. From time to time his neighbours would mount a watch on his door, but no one ever saw him leave. It was thought that he was a brilliant computer techie at the car factory in town, but nobody knew for certain because he didn't speak to any of them. What everybody did know was that he never cut his grass or painted his caravan, and that once while he was away it flooded and he hadn't changed the carpets afterwards. How much it must have stunk inside kept people talking for weeks.

Next door to Brian the pony tail lived body bag Brian, who was stranger still. He always wore a heavy overcoat, even on the hottest summer days, and carried a large sack over his shoulder. Imaginations ran riot as to what was in it, but he didn't tell a soul. Like Brian the pony tail, his curtains were always drawn but his loud television could often be heard, drowning out what people dreaded to think. Some of the older residents said the park was full of characters, but Juliana just wished there were some other people her age there who she could go to town with and meet boys, and find out which ones were builders.

Last but not least, there was Brian the tree feller who had been done for by Sheralee, the white witch. Sheralee lived two rows away from Juliana with her Dad, Brian the undertaker. Their caravan had broken gutters, and holes in the walls and leaks in the roof, and they would be seen coming and going at all hours of the day and night in his old black hearse. But most importantly where park gossip was concerned, there used to be five old oaks on their particular corner, but not any longer because Brian the tree feller cut them down. The last named liked to spend his spare time, when he wasn't fishing in the River Isis that flowed through the nearby town, loping around the park with his familiar stooping gait, staring up at the ever dwindling ranks of mature oak and ash with a knowing and doubtful eye. And whenever he met anyone who lived close by one of them he would proclaim anew: "That'll blow down on your caravan if we have a storm, unless you let me do something about it. They're all diseased you know."

Only one long since rotten tree had ever actually blown down, but the moaning and groaning old caravaners nonetheless liked to complain about autumn leaves and being pooped on by the Pigeons almost as much as about the roads and drains; and Mr Scrote hated having to sweep up the leaves more than anyone. The invariable outcome was that tree after magnificent old tree had disappeared from the skyline of Cockscomb Park, Brian the tree feller maintained a modest retirement income, the warden took his own cut of the proceeds, and the landlord thereby got out of having to prune them properly himself. Brian the undertaker defended his five old oaks to the last, but eventually the tree feller persuaded Mr Dellsey instead to let him butcher them too, thinking he would be paid though the landlord was not in the habit of paying anyone.

Up until what then happened to this particular Brian, everyone had thought Sheralee was a bit crazy and all talk. On the morning that the tree feller came to cut down the oaks, he found a note saying: "Bad luck will befall he who damages these trees".

Not thinking anything of it, he just handed the warning to Mr Scrote who stuffed it through the letter box of Brian the nature lover nearby then bawled him out the next time that he saw him. Imagine the widespread consternation when the morning after Brian the tree feller had finished cutting down Brian the undertaker's five old oaks ... his goolies fell off!

People said they couldn't have been much use to him at his age anyway, but nevertheless acknowledged it must have been an uncomfortable experience. Worse was to follow: Brian the tree feller was also an angling pundit on the local TV channel, and in the next three programmes that he appeared in he caught only scrap metal. Then, on the point of being sacked by the producer and fortunately off camera, a riverside willow fell onto Brian's head after which he remained in an even more persistent vegetative state than previously. Sheralee had thereafter enjoyed a certain reputation.

Thinking through all the other Brians and Bryonys who lived around her on the park, Juliana couldn't imagine any of them being of much use. "Why is everyone so old?", she would cry as so many times before. "And why are they all so dull?" Now that she was sixteen, the problem would be getting suitable young builders to come to the park from which to make her selection. She knew the village boys would hardly consider it because their friends would call them "Gippo" too. And anyway they were all snobs and more likely to want to be lawyers or accountants, or singers in the local opera.

That meant town boys, but Cockscomb Park was so out of the way and there was only one bus a day. And the usual sort of town boys only came in the middle of the night to steal people's motor bikes, or their plant pots to sell in boot sales, and break into the landlords' workshop. They had even stolen Bryony the Christmas light queen's reindeer, but she still won the local TV channel's best lights award that year. Three nights later the whole lot disappeared, but Bryony vowed to be back the next year with a better display than ever. Outsiders just had no respect, but why should they? It was just a caravan site to them. That's what it said on all the local maps.

Juliana was a very pretty and personable girl and knew that if the right sort of town boys could be attracted to the park, they must surely all fall in love with her. But what if they only saw caravans? Then the realisation struck her. If she could persuade Sheralee to cast a spell to bring lots of young builders to the park who would think they were seeing big houses, once they were all besotted and fighting over her she would be able to pick out the most clever and ambitious one. Then he would want to build a bigger and better house for her than all of those he thought he was seeing before him. By the time he had finished, they would be married and even if he should find out that she had grown up in a caravan he wouldn't mind at all, because they would love each other so much.

The trouble was, Sheralee was so weird. Could she be relied upon to cast the right spell? She was always walking around asking people if they wanted spells put on others who had annoyed them, but was she up to the particular subtleties of a love match? The witch could probably be trusted not to run off with the best prospect, because though she was the second youngest person at the park after Juliana herself, Sheralee had never shown much interest in getting married. There had been young men from time to time, but they had all been frightened off in the end by her weirdness.

Weird or not, Sheralee was Juliana's only hope and she resolved to go and see her that evening. Just as night fell, she turned the corner where the five old oaks had once stood. Sheralee was sitting on one of the stumps, setting up an astronomical telescope with which to survey the night sky. Juliana looked sadly at the poisoned stumps, with the criss-cross chainsaw marks across them, and wondered if the little shoots sprouting on all sides of them would ever grow into tall, strong tress again.

"Hello Sheralee," she said. "Like the telescope!" Juliana knew that with Sheralee and her Dad there was always some new enthusiasm, and that getting on with them meant taking an interest in whatever it was. One week it might be an electronic organ, the next an easel and stock of oil paints, or a deluxe picture framing kit.

"Yeah," replied Sheralee. "It's something I've always wanted to do."

"Do you still play the electronic organ?" Juliana enquired.

"No, that's Dad's. He plays it sometimes, but he's doing an aromatherapy course now", came the reply. There was always an earnestness about Sheralee, whatever the current enthusiasm might be; though Juliana wondered why they didn't spend some of the money on fixing their roof, and the holes in their walls and broken gutters. It wasn't any of her business, she decided.

"That must come in handy living across the way from Brian the pony tail," she then offered. The white witch laughed politely, but knew for sure that aromatherapy actually had nothing to do with stinks.

It being not quite dark, and with a little cloud still lingering in the otherwise moonlit sky, Sheralee finished setting up the telescope and started to pay more attention.

"Need any spells putting on people?" she then asked.

At that, Juliana could hold it in no longer and poured out all her woes to the white witch, who being a kindly soul immediately felt sympathy with this young girl who had no chance of finding friends of her own age and whose parents didn't take her anywhere. She listened to Juliana's tale intently and then, as the night sky began to clear, said that she would search all of her best spell books in the morning and see what she could come up with.

"Thanks, you're a pal," conceded the young girl; then she enquired: "Have you always been a witch?"

At that, Sheralee's earnest expression assumed a little more studied tinge of weirdness as she intoned softly and almost to herself: "No … There was an ancient power in these oaks that called me to it … and it's still there beneath the stumps. I can feel it. All the trees were here for a purpose that talks to me inside my head sometimes." The speaker then drifted off into a reverie, before the moon burst fully from behind the last vestiges of cloud cover in the skies overhead, and she turned back to her telescope.

Juliana recalled other caravaners having spoken of this peculiar belief of the undertaker's strange daughter, and some of them mocking her companion for it; though none of those detractors could now deny the ultimate fate of Brian the tree feller or the forewarning that he had ignored. She could see that Sheralee's interest had drifted away once more and so, casting a sideways glance at the broomstick that was propped up against the battered walls of the caravan, thanked the witch again and said that she would see her soon.

"God, she *is* crazy," the young girl thought to herself as she made her way back to her parental home. Several times she returned, but her new friend's attention always seemed to be elsewhere; either on the night sky, or a new oil painting, or stacks of frames for pictures to cover the holes in her Dad's caravan walls.

Then, one evening Sheralee suddenly said: "Think I've found a good spell. Want to try it?"

They walked back around the park to Juliana's parents' caravan. Sheralee suggested that her young friend laid out all the past years' birthday presents across the pitch. So Juliana placed the toy sports car on the parking space, and the dolls house beside the front door, and left the paddling pool where it was on the lawn.

Not being able to think of what the Monopoly board game could be turned into, she took it indoors. She came back outside again and said to Sheralee: "Ready!"

The white witch raised her arms and spoke for two or three minutes in a language that only she understood.

"That should do it," she then pronounced, and flashing Juliana an enigmatic smile walked off back to her Dad's caravan and her telescope on the tree stumps outside.

"Thanks, Sheralee," thought Juliana. "Hope it works."

Chapter 2

The following morning Juliana made her hair look nice, put on one of her most alluring crop tops, and waited to see what would happen. It being the school holidays, she had time on her hands. At around about 11am she heard the unmistakable sound of a diesel engine approaching. Looking out of the window her heart leapt into her mouth as she saw a pick-up truck laden with sawn timber moving slowly towards their caravan, its windows so dirty that she could hardly see inside. Walking out onto the lawn in as nonchalant a fashion as she could affect, she called out: "Oy mister, are you a builder?"

The pick up's passenger window wound down and the driver replied: "Not exactly, love. Do you know who wants this load of wood?" The excitement drained from Juliana's face at once; the man was old enough to be her father.

"No, sorry," she said. "I thought you were someone else."

At two or three caravans' distance away, the air began to turn blue. Mr Scrote the warden was walking towards them, carrying a big bunch of drain rods under one arm, while he waved another of them furiously in his free hand.

"No parking on the road! And no reversing," he bellowed, with many expletives. "Don't you know there's a 5mph limit here? I'll have you banned from the park!"

George Oliver Scrote (most people said the initials really stood for Grumpy Old) was Mr Dellsey's agent on the park, and hence his eyes and ears, and not to be trusted. This was not to say that people who knew how to handle him couldn't enjoy some advantages, since the cantankerous old warden was as big a double dealer with the residents as his boss was with the local authority. Aged nineteen, George Scrote had had to drive a DUKW ashore in the Normandy landings, over the bodies of the fallen front rank.

"Terrible it were," he would say. "Jerry was mowin' 'em down." People assumed that the experience at such a tender age must have had a profound effect on him, because it seemed to have moulded his approach to most things in life ever afterwards. At seventy-nine, he was showing no sign of mellowing.

Having lived out a normal working lifetime in which he hadn't been in charge of anyone, Mr Scrote had suddenly been elevated by Mr Dellsey to the position of park warden at well past the usual retirement age. He had previously been engaged as a mere labourer. Ever since the warden had regarded Cockscomb Park as his personal fiefdom.

"It's OK. Just slip him a fiver," whispered Juliana.

"Don't worry, love," replied the pick-up driver. "I know how to handle him."

Mr Scrote had reached them now, and the man pulled out his wallet and offered him a crumpled five pound note.

"Be more careful in future," the recipient muttered, and started to walk away again, glowering darkly.

Just as he was out of earshot the bank note suddenly whizzed back through the air on a gossamer string of elastic, landing back neatly into the pick-up driver's wallet to which it had been attached all along. Juliana and the driver exchanged knowing glances. Every delivery man, and taxi driver, and various other people whose business regularly brought them onto the park, knew this trick. The residents had seen it over and over again, but never tired of witnessing it one more time.

The amazing thing was that Mr Scrote didn't ever seem to notice it himself. He was in any case so much more interested in showing just who was in charge than the small pickings involved. If he rummaged in his pockets and couldn't find any money he would assume that he had lost it on the horses; and besides he was earning much more from the contraband operation that he ran with long distance Brian the HGV driver, or by selling building materials from the park workshop behind the landlord's back.

The contraband operation was one of the park's best kept secrets from outsiders, second only to the notorious contents of Bryony the schoolteacher's shed; neither of which even Mr Dellsey knew anything at all about. It was the thing that made Mr Scrote's job most worth doing, since the landlord paid him but a pittance, when he paid him at all. Long distance Brian would smuggle in van loads of liquor, cigarettes, jewellery and anything else that could be sold on at a decent profit as often as he could get away with it. He had once been known as Brian the Intercontinental, but kept getting called upon by local authority health visitors looking for the park's more senile residents.

Long distance Brian, as he had since decided to be known, lived in a very old caravan with his partner Bryony the peace activist. She regarded the scam as a smart way of beating American multinationals at their own game, and insisted on a percentage to donate to the many good causes that she supported. Being as she was an idealist, that percentage didn't turn out to be very large. No business being allowed on the park, and to prevent the landlord from finding out and demanding a cut too, the contraband was mostly stored in a big hut in the garden of Mr Scrote's council house in town. From there, he distributed it far and wide via his many contacts, as well as through customers on the park.

Juliana and the pick-up driver laughed once more as the blue mist faded into the distance, then her visitor drove off to look for his customer. She hung around for the rest of the day, but nothing else happened. It was clear that Sheralee's spell had not yet worked. Day upon day passed, all through the school holiday, without one suitable suitor appearing. Then an ugly, ill-favoured looking motor mechanic turned up, who said that his name was Darius. Juliana got rid of him, but one or two residents let him look at their battered old vehicles that they couldn't afford to maintain in the usual course of events.

When this Darius found so much wrong with their cars that he said needed fixing at such great expense, those people were very worried at first. But remembering what had happened to Bryony the schoolteacher, who had given a man money to buy aluminium to fix her caravan's roof then never saw him again, they decided to call in Mr Scrote to see if they were being fairly quoted. The warden could be seen a short distance away, delivering a couple of bottles of contraband to Brian the taxi, who was currently unwell as he was known to be from time to time. During such episodes his fellow drivers from the town would all refuse to take him to the supermarket, out of sympathy. Mr Scrote had no such qualms: "They're the last two bottles! I could get double that price for them," he was heard saying.

Flushed with the success of such an easy and inflated transaction, the grizzled old reprobate sauntered across the road, stuffing the proceeds into his breast pocket. As he reached the small group that surrounded the two geriatric cars, Darius was confidently diagnosing ever more serious faults that he said were not worth repairing; though he could take them off their hands, at a price.

"Don't listen to him!" thundered the warden. "He's just trying to get his hands on more old cars to convert into bangers and race at the stadium on The Lees."

"That's defamation of character," countered Darius. "You'll be getting a letter from my solicitor!"

"Balderdash!" shouted the warden, or words to that effect, and the mechanic began to stalk off back towards The Lees – the bad estate on the edge of town where police patrols only went in pairs and ne'er do wells from all over town liked to race stolen cars and then burn them out. A village joke said: "There's four easy steps to finding your way to The Lees. One, look for the police helicopter. Two, head for it. Three, wind down the windows and inhale at intervals. Four, when the predominant smell is of burnt out cars, you're there."

It seemed that knowledge of the elastic bank note trick hadn't yet penetrated all parts of The Lees. Mr Scrote pulled a twenty pound note from his back pocket and stroked it covetously between his gnarled thumb and forefinger.

"That bugger even paid me to come on here today," he chuckled, then he walked away in a swagger. He had had a good day on the make, and the gathered throng hoped it might improve his humour at least for the time being.

As the warden reached the lay-by in front of Bryony the schoolteacher's battered yet beloved old "van" as she always called it, a furtive and fair-skinned man with a little tuft of nose-tip facial fur was busily concealing two cartons within the boot of a shabby saloon car. The passer by glanced briefly towards the accomplice who was closing the decaying door of the infamous old wooden shed to the rear of that particular pitch. Then as the diminutive yet nonetheless daunting figure of the part-time rock of Our Lady's, who parents all revered and no child dared to defy became framed in her doorway, the warden looked to the ground and hurried on by. Not even George Oliver Scrote, the scourge of Cockscomb Park, dared to demand a percentage of this sinister trade.

The school ma'am was holding a beautiful little great niece to her left, while she extended her right hand and demanded: "Pounds if you don't mind, or Euros with a handling charge. None of those obsolete punts, this time!"

One of the men shuffled forward nervously and thrust a wad of notes into the outstretched palm, but the recipient was not to be fooled.

"*And* the money for the fuses," she then boomed, as the child at her side intensified her own disapproving gaze. "That only covers the detonators. Your side knows exactly what our bargain is. Try to profit again yourselves and it'll be the drill for you my fine lads, just like that rogue who didn't repair my roof."

The visitor audibly yelped before surrendering the hitherto concealed contents of his own inside pocket and beating a hasty retreat to the vehicle that with his companion at the wheel sped away.

"Bejayzuss, but she's scary ain't she?" one man exclaimed as they swerved out of the park.

"Saints prisoorve us!" affirmed the second.

The episode of the motor mechanic dominated park gossip for some days to come, almost as much as Brian the pony tail's stinking carpets had in their day. But it was not, of course what Juliana had been hoping for and she cried herself to sleep that night. The school holiday was almost over, and she would soon have to fend off the stuck-up village kids' taunts once more.

Throughout the holiday, Juliana had been round to see the witch on most evenings, who she pestered unrelentingly with her hopes and ambitions, and beseeched to come up with more and better spells. The two had become passably good friends, and though she felt a little irritated by the young girl at times, Sheralee basically liked and tried to sympathise with her as much as she could. Eventually, though she snapped.

"For God's sake, girl. Don't you ever stop?" she flared angrily. "What's wrong with it here anyway? I've lived here most of my life and I don't care what those stuck-up villagers say about me."

"Yes Sheralee," replied Juliana, carelessly. "That's all very well, but you're so…" Then she bit her lip. Her friend's face was starting to turn quite red.

"What?" screamed the witch. "What am I? Go on, say it.

Weird! That's what you think isn't it?"

"No!" protested the young girl. "Of course not. Oh, I'm sorry … it's just that …" But she was interrupted by a blinding flash; then everything fell silent except for the sound of a few Crows and Pigeons that crashed out of the trees in fright, and the distant bark of a dog over on the ridge.

"Must've been a spell. Hope it works," said Sheralee. "We still friends?"

"Yeah, course," replied Juliana. Then they made it up and both went back to their separate caravans.

Juliana felt pleased in a way to have roused her friend's famous temper, because the witch's reputation was of a better success rate with her spells when angry. During that night itself, nobody really noticed what was happening. Some people said they had felt a slight shuddering sensation as they slept, but that was about all. Juliana arose rather later than usual the next morning, and went to the front door to breathe in some fresh air. Her bedroom was so small and stuffy that she often did that. She saw a lady in nurse's uniform speaking to the very old man who lived in the caravan opposite theirs.

"Brian the Intercontinental?" he was saying, indignantly. "There's nothing wrong with my bowels."

"No," the nurse tried to explain. "I want to buy a couple of bottles of brandy, purely for medicinal purposes of course." It was no use, she just couldn't make herself understood.

"Bandy? There's nothing wrong with my legs either. You won't be getting me into a home."

Juliana recognised the visitor as bedridden Bryony's community carer, and called out: "The old one near the entrance, or ask the warden." Then she smiled encouragingly and shrugged her shoulders.

"Oh God, not him," said the nurse, and then she walked away downcast.

Looking around, Juliana became aware of the small groups of caravaners who everywhere seemed to be standing in groups, staring and pointing. Then she noticed something seemed to be different about the old man's home … and the one next to him … and brain dead Brian's next door … and their own! She touched the wall next to the open front door and her heart leapt as she realised that she was feeling … bricks and mortar! She rushed into the road and looked around further. All the caravans had tiled roofs, and brand new uPVC windows, some with criss-cross leading in the glass, and brightly coloured doors in the latest styles. They had all turned into … houses!

And it wasn't just her parents' caravan that had changed. On the parking space where she had put the toy sports car the first time that Sheralee had tried her spell, there stood a gleaming new Porsche convertible. Even the paddling pool had changed into a garden pond, because there wasn't room on their pitch for the full sized spa with sauna and sun bed that Juliana had asked Sheralee for. When Brian the fish keeper saw the new pond he immediately flew into a lather, saying it would bring in even more Herons and Red Kites. Then, oblivious to all the other changes around them, he rushed off to borrow Brian the nature lover's binoculars to scan the skies with, even more earnestly than usual. Brain dead Brian just carried on wandering around just as he always did, apparently unaware that anything had altered at all.

Not being able to contain herself, Juliana began a little dance, squealing: "Oh Sheralee, Sheralee, I love you so much. Friend, friend, friend! Did I ever really doubt you?"

Then, a rather tempering realisation began to descend upon her: "They weren't actually … very … well, er … big houses!" In fact they were mostly no larger than the caravans they had replaced. As her spirits began to sink again, Juliana remembered that the caravans had only been meant to look like houses to visiting suitors … and that the illusion was supposed to have been one of very big houses indeed!

"Oh, Sheralee," she sighed, "Why do your spells always go so wrong?"

Chapter 3

Within days, eviction notices from Mr Dellsey arrived through the doors of every home on Cockscomb Park. They cited unauthorised alterations that changed the nature of the homes, and thus contravened the park licence. They were much too well phrased to have been sent by the landlord himself, so the residents' committee knew at once that his lawyers and accountants were involved; and that hence he was onto a serious money making venture. It was obvious what that was: he wanted to repossess all the houses and sell them at a vast profit. An emergency residents' meeting was scheduled at once, and the caravaners gathered at the next village's hall at the appointed time. It wasn't that they weren't allowed to use the hall in the village on Shottington Ridge across the fields by the park, but they weren't really encouraged to either. Things were always that way.

At the top table sat Bryony the chair, flanked as always by Bryony the treasurer and Brian the secretary. Once everybody had arrived, the last named banged on the table with a little wooden hammer and began to introduce the proceedings. Knowing how long it took for Brian the secretary to say anything, the audience busied themselves with passing around cups of tea and biscuits, and waited for him to come to the point. Then, sensing their inattention, Bryony the chair cleared her throat and the room fell silent. There was a particular emphasis in the way that Bryony the chair cleared her throat that always made people sit up and take notice.

"Fellow residents," she intoned sternly. "You all know why we are here. This Rachmann-like man is proposing to cast us all out from our homes onto the streets, and we mustn't let him succeed. We have taken professional advice on what he is proposing to do and it is illegal. If we all stand together, we can beat him."

"Yes that's right," said Bryony the treasurer, who always agreed with Bryony the chair and also liked to repeat certain things that she said in case anybody had missed the point. Bryony the chair referred to the landlord as "this Rachmann-like man" more

18

often than she did by his own name. People would say that when she was really up for a fight she was in "full Rachmann mode." She certainly was on this night, backed by her committee colleagues; and the whole room full of caravaners became swept away by the enthusiasm of it all. Brian the secretary tried to speak from time to time, but Bryony the chair would succeed in stopping him, seeing that there had never been such a response as was now taking place in all the history of the park. After some two hours discussion, during which even the most timid people present were rallied to the cause, it was decided to face down the enemy at the earliest opportunity.

A meeting was set for 2.30pm on the next rent day at the park office. Rent day was a monthly ritual that was always played out in precisely the same way. Though a multi-millionaire, the landlord would nevertheless make the long round trip from his country estate, Dellsey Manor to collect the rent in person. He had no liking for things such as direct debits or automated cash transfers, and in any case couldn't use a computer, regarding this as a sign of good breeding. He was by no means thought of as well bred himself by the county types in his own part of the world, but being so wealthy he knew the ways of the gentry and tried to imitate them as much as possible.

He considered it much more befitting his family's self-made status if the caravaners were forced to pay their rent into his office, like tenants on a medieval manor walking up to the big house with their groats and begging sire's pardon. This the mostly elderly residents would endure every first Friday morning, queuing at the door whatever the weather while Mr Scrote entered the payments slowly into the landlord's book, bawled out anyone that he might have some petty grievance with, and took orders for contraband from others.

At 12 o'clock prompt, the greatly feared William Dellsey himself would arrive in his top of the range multi-purpose vehicle, the most expensive on the market that rivalled for size and opulence even some of the most over the top four wheel drives on the local school run. Mr Scrote would then be despatched to round up anyone who had forgotten what day it was.

Once the last few stragglers had been dragged to the office to the tune of many curses and expletives, the warden would take all the cheques, and envelopes stuffed with cash, into the landlord's inner chamber and set them onto his big oak desk. Mr Dellsey would then open his briefcase, with it's gold-plated locks and his diamond-encrusted initials set deeply into the leather in one corner, and take out a pair of silk gloves. Putting them on he would pick up and inspect each of the cheques individually, and match them to Mr Scrote's entries in his book. He would covet each one as he did so, between his gloved thumb and forefinger; and then count the cash to make sure that the warden hadn't put any of it to one side for himself.

Finally, he would put all the cheques and cash into a sterling silver box, that Mr Scrote had to polish up each rent day morning and leave in the top right-hand drawer of the desk. Locking it tightly with a bright silver key that he would draw unfailingly from his breast pocket, he would then snap shut his book with a sound that could often be heard over much of that end of the park. Both treasured artefacts were then concealed in his vast leather briefcase, ready for the journey home.

Everybody knew that the rifle shot sound of the book closing was the signal for his tour of inspection, the most dreaded part of rent day since woe betide anyone who might be found to have infringed the landlord's many park rules. Word would spread to the far end quickly and many of the caravaners would hurry indoors and put the kettle on. Some would half draw their curtains to peep from behind as their lord and master passed.

Mr Dellsey would then drive around the park slowly in his luxury MPV, looking for misdemeanours like a headmaster keeping an eye on his naughty little charges. He was probably the only person who could keep a vehicle to the regulation 5mph limit, because his had been fitted with a special speed limiter to heighten the intimidating effect of this tour. If he spotted anyone that he knew was afraid of him he would lower a window and threaten them with eviction for not cutting their grass, or letting their plants grow to more than one metre high, or laying a gravel path on their pitch instead of the regulation slabs; or whatever other petty violations he could identify.

The landlord never knocked on any door. Instead, letters would arrive in the post over the ensuing week, setting out the infringements and the required remedies, usually at some profit to himself. The presentation would always give away whether these had been dictated by Mr Dellsey to one of his succession of brow-beaten, lowly qualified secretaries, or whether they had been drawn up by his accountants or lawyers. The badly spelt and phrased, typewritten ones were taken less seriously by those in the know, because this was mostly sport to their tormenter and he rarely followed them up. But the well prepared, computer generated ones could suggest some more sinister purpose, and should thus be referred to the residents' committee.

The landlord's lack of consistency in applying his park rules was one of the biggest causes of grievance amongst the caravaners. Like all bullies, he could be stood up to, and those who knew how to play him could get away with things that others might have been told were eviction matters, or causes for urgent work by Mr Dellsey's labourers at more expense than they could afford. Some time was therefore set aside each first Friday afternoon for residents with one grievance or another to air it with the landlord in his office. Whether he actually saw them or not would depend on his mood that particular day, but the outcome was always the same. The bruised complainants would retreat to their caravans muttering that he always had all the answers.

No such time had been set aside on this rent day, because of the meeting with the residents committee. Mr Dellsey took much longer than usual over his tour of inspection, knowing that the chair, treasurer and secretary would be waiting for him at the park office. Eventually he returned, ignoring them as he walked in and summoning in a newly arrived accountant instead. After a further delay, Mr Scrote ushered the three committee members into the landlord's inner chamber, where Mr Dellsey was sitting behind his big oak desk that he always kept between himself and the world. His eyes were closed and his hands were clasped behind his head, as he leaned back in his chair listening on his rather dated walkman to a piano concerto by Rachmaninov, his favourite composer. At one side of the desk sat the accountant, busying himself with some papers and a laptop computer.

Bryony the chair knew from long experience that there was no point in provoking their adversary. She busied herself with papers of her own that she had brought just for the purpose, as did Bryony the treasurer; while Brian the secretary resumed that day's

Times crossword. They would have to play along with his little game, letting him think he was in control. Some twenty minutes passed like that, then Mr Dellsey opened his eyes, took off his headphones and looked each of them slowly up and down.

"Rachmaninov, you know," he said. "A good concerto always relaxes me before doing business."

"How very appropriate," sneered Bryony the chair, relishing the battle to come. "My favourite is Prokofiev, but I don't always manage to say it properly."

"Oh, very droll," countered Mr Dellsey, who aimed one of his most malevolent smiles at her, showing just a flash of his many gold fillings. The accountant continued to rustle his papers and tap on his laptop.

Brian the secretary then put down his newspaper and roused himself to speak. Seeing the look of alarm on the landlord's face, as he reached for his headphones again, Bryony the chair spoke up: "OK, Mr Dellsey ... I'll be brief. We have taken professional advice, and the action you're proposing to take to evict us all is illegal."

"Oh really?" countered the figure on the other side of the desk, drawing himself up in his huge leather chair and pushing the walkman to one side. "I would be interested in discussing that with your lawyers."

He was paying attention now, being a man that ate, slept and breathed litigation. It was the second greatest passion of his life after making money itself, and rumour had it that he was currently engaged in hundreds of lawsuits. He looked upon it as a fitting hobby for a wealthy man, and another indicator of his status. And the taking part was always of much greater importance to him than the outcome, since he regarded the legal fees involved as small change and much more worthwhile expenditure than wages for his staff or payment to his suppliers.

It was fully five o'clock when the committee were eventually shown out, past the glowering Mr Scrote who had been waiting all that time to lock up. They felt victorious in their way, having never gained the landlord's interest for so long before, and knew he must be up for the fight which was the most important thing where he was concerned. One or two caravaners were still hanging around the outer office, hoping to get Mr Dellsey's ear about some small matter or other, but he just swept contemptuously past them and out to his MPV, where he immediately started to make phone calls. Mr Scrote bid the stragglers begone in his usual fashion, then locked up and headed home to his garden hut to sort out the day's contraband orders.

Chapter 4

It was shortly after this that Juliana met Samantha and Bethany. The news about the caravans that had turned into houses and the impending law suit had caused quite a stir locally; and sometimes townies would come out to the park to see for themselves. One Saturday afternoon the two friends, who were both eighteen and highly attractive, came driving round in Beth's trendy sports off-roader. Juliana being the only young person that they saw, they stopped to talk to her.

The vehicle's number plate was A1 BET, which impressed Juliana; and there were huge scratch marks along either side that intrigued her. Beth tried to say that the deep scratches were a cool design feature, but Sam laughed and said her friend just couldn't help bashing into and scraping against things, and there would be no point in mending it because she'd only do it again.

"At least I know how to park it," retorted Beth. "It's not me that all the neighbours call 'Skewiff', like you down your street."

"You wouldn't want to park down my street anyway," hit back her friend. "There aren't any double yellow lines. I mean, we all have our little bumps and bashes, but all along one side on your own gate post? On the way out? How sad is that?"

Sam had a way of tilting her head back slightly and shouting that amused the young caravaner. "Yeah, I'm a shoutaholic," quipped the town girl, reading her mind.

Juliana immediately liked them, and jumped at the chance to get talking. They soon began to ask her about where the houses had come from, and Juliana sensed that the pair (who seemed both streetwise and rather gullible all at once) would not be the type to believe in witches and spells, but could nevertheless be led on. She hoped most earnestly that Sheralee would not appear while she was talking to them.

As they chatted, Juliana could tell the town girls were trying to find out if there was a decent scam to be learnt here, that they could pass on to their boyfriends who they said were both builders. Her heart jumping a beat at the mention of that, she said that her own boyfriend had bought the park from Mr Dellsey at a knock-down price, then built the houses after getting planning permission through his particular contacts, to sell them at a suitable profit. She couldn't, of course let them know that she didn't yet have a boyfriend. Seeing they were impressed, Juliana continued that her boyfriend had then done another deal with Mr Dellsey enabling him to recoup some of his losses in return for evicting all of the residents without letting them know about the planning permission or change of ownership.

"Nice car!" said Sam, who didn't have such a head for business, and had just noticed the Porsche.

"Yeah, that's one of his. He's got several like that," Juliana replied. "He lets me keep it here though I'm not old enough to drive it yet." Her two new friends looked more impressed still. "Trouble is he doesn't think as big with houses as he does with cars. By the time I'm eighteen I want a husband who'll build me the biggest house in that village over there, ('and then let those stuck-up kids at school look down on me' she thought to herself, but couldn't say so.) I don't think he's the right type, really. I want to ditch him."

Now Sam and Beth sensed action. They told Juliana that though they had steady boyfriends, they still went on a girl's night out every other Friday to play the field at night clubs in town. They had gone last night, so the next time would be the Friday after next, and they invited the young girl to go with them. Juliana was ecstatic but managed not to show it. She said she would see what she was doing and got their phone numbers.

The next thirteen days passed in a blur. Juliana could hardly contain her excitement and didn't know what she was doing half of the time. By the middle of the second week, Sheralee realised that she had not received one visit from her young friend as usual, and wondered why. On the Thursday she went round to see Juliana, who not being able to keep it in any longer, indiscreetly blurted out everything. Being a witch, Sheralee managed to hide her feelings well at first, but inside she felt abandoned, used and intensely jealous. After all, if she hadn't turned the caravans into houses in the first place, Juliana would never have met these new friends. And as everybody at the park knew by then, when Sheralee got angry, strange and drastic things could happen, things that were not always intended.

On her first trip to a club with the town girls, Juliana felt carried away by the glamour of it all. Two bucks sipping vodka and coke's were the first to play their hand, both eyeing the newcomer because they knew that the other two, though attractive had a reputation as teasers.

"You a builder?" Juliana asked the first one, coyly.

"No, I'm a plumber," he replied.

"Too bad. I only go out with builders."

"I'm a builder," said the second one, sensing his chance.

'He's not bad,' thought Juliana. "Oh yeah? What ya building at the moment, then?"

"An extension."

"Hope it's bigger than that one," she quipped, cocking her head at the bulge in his trousers. Behind her, the more seasoned campaigner Beth snorted wickedly. This was the sort of sport that she and Sam most loved, but the bucks seemed to be encouraged. Juliana sensed it too and led them on further. "You ever built a house?"

"Might've"

"How big was it then? " ... and such like.

Driving home from the club in the early hours, the orange glow on the horizon seemed to be growing in intensity. Still intoxicated by her evening's many triumphs, Juliana at first only half noticed it; but as more and more fire engines, police cars and ambulances raced past, sirens wailing, the three friends realised they were all going their way and in the direction of ... "The park!" screamed Juliana, "It must be the park!"

When they arrived, a scene of utter devastation lay before them. It was obvious what had happened. The bulk gas tank at the near end of the park had blown up, taking half the houses with it. But they weren't houses any more; they had all turned back into caravans, and many of them were burning. Fortunately, Bryony the schoolteacher had sold on her entire stock of plastic explosive earlier that same day, and at a tidy profit; so there had been no second blast once the conflagration reached her shed. Still fire fighters, police officers and paramedics were everywhere; with dozens of stretchers laid out on the ground, some of them covered completely by blankets.

Juliana became hysterical. "No Sheralee, no! You couldn't have done that," she screamed. "You couldn't have meant to! . . . I'm sorry.... I didn't mean to.... I only wanted..." And then she passed out. She regained consciousness in her mother's arms.

"Thank God you're alive," she heard. "We didn't know where you were."

At that her Mum eyed Juliana's two friends suspiciously. "We searched all over the park for you, and were at the other end when it happened."

Chapter 5

The coroner's verdict was one of accidental death on all of the residents who had died. To the authorities that could be the only explanation, since the police investigation had found no evidence of arson, and after all it was only a caravan site and safety standards were known to be lax in such places. The surviving residents nonetheless knew the fact that the houses had turned back into caravans as the tank exploded meant it must have been Sheralee's doing, whether or not she had meant it. But the witch was their secret, and they weren't about to share it with outsiders.

Sheralee herself had disappeared, never to be seen at Cockscomb Park again; and her Dad left soon afterwards, unable to bear the shame or to repair his burnt-out home. He was seen thereafter from time to time living in his old black hearse in lay-bys and on wasteland across the county. He had converted it into a camper van, it being just the right size and shape to sleep in, with a little room left over for a stove. Caravaners driving past would toot in recognition, but Sheralee was never seen with him.

Mr Dellsey bluffed his way through the investigation by saying he had made the caravans look like houses himself to try to get housing development rights on adjacent land. Then when his advisers assured him that the planning application would fail he took down all the facades because renting the land to caravaners would still be the best way to make money out of the park. Like all pathological liars, he was good at that sort of thing, always having all the answers as people said, and he usually seemed to get away with it.

Then, sensing a further profit opportunity, the landlord began to clear the land and lay bases for big new park homes that he could sell to index-linked pensioners moving out from the town. Any remaining trees were cut down in the process, by his own labourers. He also laid new gas mains so that he could pipe in natural gas on a big margin, and milk the new pensioners for all they were worth. He said mains gas for the surviving caravans at the other end would have to wait, and allowed the owners to use bottled gas again, but only from the supplier with which he had an agency and at a suitably large mark-up.

The residents' committee said there should be some kind of memorial garden for those who had lost their lives, but he just grinned malevolently in his usual fashion, then squeezed in an extra concrete base just to spite them. Bryony the chair wrote to the local constituency MP as on many previous occasions, but as usual he couldn't care less and just sent the bland reply that Parliament demanded. Then, Mr Dellsey built himself a new office where the gas tank had been, with an armoured vault below it that doubled as a nuclear shelter, just to fill the crater that the blast had caused.

Slowly at first, Juliana's confidence began to recover, and then more quickly. After all, the explosion hadn't been her fault. She couldn't help it if Sheralee's spells kept going so uncontrollably wrong. All she had wanted was to find a husband to build her a big house, and until she met Sam and Beth, Sheralee was the only person who could help her in that aim. Sheralee was fifteen years older than her and not so interested in husbands anyway; and don't all seventeen-year olds, as she would soon be, go clubbing to meet boys? Yes, she could hardly blame herself, but she still wondered sometimes where Sheralee was and would have liked to thank the witch for what she had done for her, no matter how weird and accident prone she might still be.

They had moved to another caravan at the far end of the park from the explosion, which was bigger than their previous one but still much too small in Juliana's eyes. It was nonetheless all her parents could afford, and they told her she would have to put up with it until she found this husband that she so wanted. Some residents couldn't bear to live at the park any longer, and so applied to the district council for sheltered housing for which they were given priority in view of the disaster; and then they sold their caravans to people who had lost theirs.

Mr Dellsey insisted on taking the full ten per cent commission to which the law entitled him on all the sales and increased the rent as homes changed hands, saying that he was incurring a lot of expense in clearing the other end of the park which would need to be passed on. He naturally overlooked to include in his calculation the fifty per cent margin that he would make on the new homes, but everybody knew about that anyway, apart of course from the pensioners who were going to buy them.

Having absolved herself in her own mind of all blame for the gas tank explosion, Juliana revived her arrangement with Sam and Beth and went clubbing with them every other Friday. Her parents came to cautiously approve of the friendship, since it at least stopped their daughter from complaining to them quite so much. Anyway, they reasoned, if she did find this mythical husband, he might in the future build a cottage in the grounds of the biggest house in the village that she so wanted, in which they could live out their old age. It could at least be worth encouraging her in that ambition. Then they would no longer be dependent on Mr Dellsey, unlike so many of their neighbours, some of whom had actually sold houses thinking that they were opting for a much nicer way of life.

The problem for Juliana now was that the boys she was meeting at the clubs in town were consistently such morons. And since they all seemed to know what she was looking for by now, they mostly lied to her to try to get their way. Sam and Beth didn't mind what sort of boys they flirted with on these nights out, because they already had steady boyfriends and just went out together once a fortnight to persuade themselves that they weren't really involved, when actually they didn't want anything else. It dawned on Juliana that they possibly might enjoy seeing their younger companion taking things so seriously, and hence might realise that she didn't have a boring boyfriend of her own after all, with a fleet of performance cars and a property portfolio, but who just wasn't the right type to marry.

After all they had both seen that all the houses at the park had become caravans again on the night of the explosion. She still rather envied them for having builders as boyfriends, as they assured her they did. But she wondered, since she had not yet been allowed to meet them, whether their men would really be her type, and thus whether Sam and Beth were so worth knowing after all. In her frustration, Juliana was coming to regard her girlfriends from town as possibly rather shallow, and resolved to broaden her horizons further and look for a husband elsewhere.

It would soon be the summer holiday, and she wanted to get a job. But the only place do so locally was at the supermarket by The Lees, and she knew that all the kids from school would be working there too. Villagers were usually preferred over kids from The Lees itself, who were not generally considered trustworthy. Thinking over her options, which were limited, Juliana decided on the most daring one. She would ask Mr Dellsey for a job at his country estate. She had heard that he was always extending his great manor house and having new cottages built, so she reasoned that there ought to be some nice young builders about the place,.

Next rent day, the crafty young girl walked right into the landlord's inner chamber, past the protesting Mr Scrote who had been looking at the topless models in the Daily Star and hadn't noticed her until it was too late. Shutting the door on the warden's foot and ignoring his many curses, she said: "Are there any summer jobs going at your estate, Mr Dellsey sir?" The landlord barely looked up. He reached into one of his desk drawers and pulled out an eighteen page typewritten document, with "Contract of Employment" written in felt tip on the cover in large bold characters.

Opening it at the last page and laying it on the desk before her, he said: "Sign there."

"Can I read it?" Juliana enquired.

"No," came the reply. She signed anyway, knowing this was standard drill with the landlord.

"You can start on Monday," her new boss informed her.

"How much will you pay me?" the young girl ventured.

"We'll talk about that at the end of your probationary period," Mr Dellsey replied, tapping the contract of employment slyly before slipping it into his briefcase. Showing her a brief final flash of his gold fillings, he then called for Mr Scrote to show her out, which the warden did with many dark mutterings.

Turning a corner back towards her parental home, Juliana waved to bedding plant Brian, an affable character who always produced some of the park's best floral displays. As he reached for his watering can, a small group around a nearby caravan's steps burst as one into a pointing, fist waving chorus of: "I'm subsidising you!", their minds having turned at once and as always to the metered water supply.

"Disgusting!" "It's *his* dirt," and "You'll not catch me putting anything into Dellsey's dirt," the girl heard these surly scrutinisers muttering as she walked by the scorched and weedy patch of grass about which they were seated. Then she turned and shot a glance back at the gardener, who merely looked skywards briefly and filled his can once more.

A little further on, a supermarket home delivery van's driver was asking an anxious looking old gentleman standing guard by his heavily fortified garden pond: "Have you seen the big bird?", as the speaker liked to refer to his customer.

"What?" came the inevitable response. "That'll be after my fish!" Then Brian the fish keeper scuttled off towards Bryony the schoolteacher's to attempt to purloin an Uzi sub-machine gun or perhaps a Stinger surface to air missile launcher. The delivery man chuckled to himself and then winked at the teenager as she passed, before unloading big Bryony's copious weekly delivery of sticky cakes and chocolate treats and taking them to her own specially widened door.

"Oh well," thought Juliana. "At least I'm getting out of here for a while."

Chapter 6

In the morning, Bryony the chair walked over and asked Juliana if she could speak with her in her own caravan. They crossed to it and Bryony showed the young girl into the small home office in her second bedroom, then went to make some coffee. Juliana looked around at the several shelves of files, and the suite of office equipment that was of a fairly recent vintage. On the wall above the desk there hung a portrait of Sir Winston Churchill, below which was a framed transcript of his most famous wartime speech set out in old-fashioned italic script.

The caravaners champion walked back in and put coffee and biscuits on the table. "The whole park knows what you've done," she began. Juliana hadn't supposed it would be any otherwise, and didn't need to guess what people would be saying about her either.

"I just want to get away from those stuck-up village kids for the summer," she protested. "There's no-one my age here, and I thought there might be some nice young builders about his estate. I want to find one to marry."

Bryony the chair knew about the girl's ambitions and frustrations, and smiled kindly. "Well I hope you find someone suitable, my dear" she replied. "Though I fear you might need all the friends you can muster in that dark place." Then she drew herself up in her chair and, glancing at the portrait on the wall, began: "I want to bring down this Rachmann-like man, finish him once and for all. For years we have suffered at his hands ...", and then she recounted a catalogue of the landlord's malpractices and wrong doings. "Perhaps you could help me. Would you?"

Seeing that Bryony the chair was into full Rachmann mode, and not wanting to be thought of as a turncoat or a wimp, Juliana shrugged and said: "If I can."

The chair looked encouraged and leaned forward. "I would like you to find out as much as you can about how he calculates the electric, gas and water," she continued. "And about the blocking of sales, and his dealings with local authorities, and most of all about his other parks," at mention of which the older conspirator shuddered slightly.

It was rumoured that Mr Dellsey owned at least fifty other caravan parks, but nobody knew the exact total for sure. Juliana, wondering how much time all this might leave for her own particular mission, smiled and said; "I'll try." Sensing the girl's unease, Bryony the chair relaxed more and said: "Well anything you can tell me will be most welcome, please do what you can." Then she asked: "Do you have a mobile phone?"

The electric, gas and water were added onto the rent by Mr Dellsey each month. He enjoyed monopolies on the supply of all of them, buying them in from whoever he pleased and billing them out for whatever he liked. Aside from the fact that they were being grossly overcharged for all three utilities, nobody knew for certain how the figures were arrived at, because the landlord wasn't in the habit of producing accounts. The resident's committee needed something concrete to present to the district council, the local MP or the various layers of authority to which they campaigned constantly to get something done about it. None of those worthy public institutions were particularly concerned though, because after all it was just a caravan site and such things were known to go on in those sorts of places. Caravaners were nevertheless required to pay the full rate of band A council tax.

Every Wednesday afternoon, Mr Scrote would read the gas and electric meters. There were fewer people about than usual at this time since it was also when various of the park's more discerning gentlemen attended Bryony the dominatrix's strict supervision classes. These enjoyed a widespread local repute, even in the village on the ridge and notwithstanding the space constraints within that lady's caravan, as a most effective cure for many everyday aches and pains; and so were always well supported.

The warden had never himself sought such solace: despite being almost an octogenarian, the hardy old soul would have to don his knee-guards and whatever the weather, enter the readings from the meters on all of the parks's 120 pitches onto the landlord' s gas and electric sheets. The air would assume the deep blue tints of a tropical lagoon, each of the 240 times this most vexed of veterans had to bend and kneel and straighten himself again through the proceedings; struggling with the waterproof covers that would sometimes snap shut on his wrinkled fingers.

Most people would avoid him, especially if his gout was playing him up; though the occasional wag might call: "Don't go adding any noughts," through the window. At this the sufferer would rant and rave and raise his clipboard at them in a fury. Then he would have to phone all the readings over to the office at Dellsey Manor, since his boss regarded fax machines as another sign of ill breeding; and then go through them all again one by one to check he had been heard properly. Lastly he would put the sheets in the post. Why the meters were read four times for each monthly bill was a mystery, other than it being an obvious scam; and exactly how the various readings were aggregated together and where the noughts were added nobody knew for sure.

The water was another major bugbear for the sorely tested caravaners. The residents' committee knew that, like the roads and the drains, the park's water mains were in a state of total disrepair. Much of the metered water supply was simply leaking away under the very ground that they lived on. In response to their constant complaints, the landlord would just phone the water supply company, that would send its emergency call out team to drive quickly around and then out of the park again, because it was just a caravan site. Their bills would be added to the next month's water charge, suitably marked up.

Last, but by no means least, there was blocking of sales. As residents aged and needed to move into sheltered housing or nursing homes, their families would often try to sell their caravans to help pay for the expenses involved. First they would go to Colin the caravan seller in town, who had all the best contacts and would therefore quote the highest sales values; next they would find a buyer, and lastly the law required them to get the landlord's approval for the formalities involved in a transfer of ownership.

At this point, Mr Dellsey's tactic would be unerringly effective. To the many enquiries of this sort that he received at the Manor he would respond: "Oh," with a sharp intake of breath. "I think I would have to insist upon a structural. And … to be honest with you... I don't think it will pass."

Only the landlord's approved surveyors were allowed to carry out a structural, and no matter how well maintained caravans might be they would always fail. The families would then have no choice but to sell to the landlord for a pittance, and pay for their aged parents' care themselves. If anyone attempted to get around this either by fair means or foul, he would simply frighten the prospective buyer off.

Having bought in caravans in this way, Mr Dellsey then had two options. He could either rent them out for a just a little less than the smallest available properties in town, or move them to his other parks and put bigger caravans or big new park homes in their place. Colin was, of course in league with the landlord, though he thought of him as the meanest man that he had ever met. The salesman would keep Mr Dellsey informed as to who was in the market, how much they were worth, and whether they were selling a house or not. For this reason, the landlord regarded Colin as one of those very few who might be worth paying; a rare accolade though he still didn't pay him very much at all.

If a good prospect was identified, repossessed caravans would be whisked away one morning by Mr Dellsey's giant low loader and taken to one of those of his other parks that Bryony the chair so wanted to find out more about. Then the diggers would move in, tearing up the loving retirement's pastime of some ageing soul and replacing that garden in an afternoon with the regulation pitch of the park rules. Any trees that obstructed this process would be felled as if they had never existed, just as the gardens over which they had once reigned would be consigned to skips. The saddest thing of all was that index-linked pensioners moving out from town so consistently seemed to fall for it. After all, it was just what they wanted, and they were prepared to pay good money for it.

That was why the landlord got away with it. He had the caravaners by the goolies so much in all of these respects that more than a few people had envied Brian the tree feller when Sheralee had caused his own to fall off. To Bryony the chair's question about having a mobile phone, Juliana replied: "Yes, but not a very good one. I'd really like one of those new picture phones." (Inside, she thought: "Who would I talk to anyway, those village kids? And nobody here's got one.") Her parents saw no practical use for them, saying there was a perfectly good telephone indoors that she could use if she needed to.

Bryony the chair reached into her desk and picked out an old, black cash box, with an adhesive label on the lid that bore the felt tip inscription: "Association Funds." She opened it and found just a few crumpled notes and a small array of coins. Resigning herself to the inevitable for the umpteenth time, she reached for her own cheque book and took Juliana in her car to the supermarket by The Lees. There the young girl picked out one of the latest picture phones with internet and many other cool features, saying it was important to have the best.

At first her older ally protested, but she quickly realised the potential of such an "ill-bred" device at Dellsey Manor, in the hands of an agent who knew how to use it. "What about a digital camera?" Juliana then offered, turning to the display next to the phones. "This one here's got …" Bryony the chair stopped her saying she couldn't afford that as well, but agreed it would be useful too and said she would try to get some money from the "national association".

They returned to Bryony the chair's caravan and Juliana demonstrated how the phone worked. Then the first-named reached into her desk again and produced a second device that she also handed to her young accomplice. It was a portable e-mailer that could be plugged into any telephone socket. "All the members have several of these," Bryony said. It's top side bore the House of Commons crest. Juliana turned it over and saw a brushed metal plate on the underside on which was engraved the name The Rt Hon Milton Lawson MP.

Her work on behalf of the caravaners had brought Bryony the chair into contact with counterparts on other parks throughout the country. They had formed a National Caravaners Protection Association and through their tireless campaigning had eventually prompted the formation of a "Parliamentary Sub-committee on Caravan Park Reform". The uphill task of inspiring this worthy body to get its act together (as they say in Parliament) had become a further *cause celebre* for Bryony.

Mr Lawson was nominally the committee's head, but there were many other more pressing concerns that occupied his time. The group met from time to time, usually when the deadline for claiming expenses was approaching; but even when it came up with some reasonably debatable proposals, Parliament never seemed to have time to actually debate them in its current term. The government's all consuming domestic priority was after all the ongoing class war through which it aimed to supplant permanently those older-moneyed, gentrified ranks that it had succeeded in replacing in power some several years previously. So for an ambitious politician to identify himself with such a lowly minority amongst his party's one-time grass-roots support as mere mobile home dwellers was hardly a career enhancing strategy; and the said Milton Lawson was steadfast in his own desire for the highest future office.

Bryony the chair had often beseeched her fellow residents to write *en masse* to this MP and even the deputy prime minister to try to make something happen. But the park's assorted malcontents mostly regarded that sort of thing as "getting involved", and would much rather complain amongst themselves about the roads and the drains and most of all the landlord without actually crossing that line. The chair even considered a petition to the prime minister himself, but he always seemed to be out of the country. Given the government's indifference, she had next joined forces with Bryony the peace activist to forge huge numbers of letters from supposed caravaners on parks spread far and wide. They loaded them all into long distance Brian's big green van that he brought the contraband home in, and travelled the country posting them in small batches in the hope of making them appear more authentic. Still nothing happened.

Eventually, Mr Lawson sacrificed one of his personal, portable e-mailers for the sake of a little peace and quiet, and made it plain that his tormentor should not get back to him until she had "something concrete." The device had remained unused in Bryony the chair's desk ever since. She now reasoned that making it available to Juliana could be her best option.

"Report back to me whenever you can, dear" she coaxed. "If you need anything else, let me know. I'll find out from Steve the delivery man from The Lees who it is who brings the catalogue shopping down there, and then we'll smuggle it in to you that way."

"Send me a builder," thought Juliana. "Please God, just send me a nice young builder!" But she felt that she owed a debt of gratitude to Bryony the chair, as all the caravaners did, and resolved to help the cause in any small way that she could.

"Don't let Him see it," Bryony the chair went on. "I don't suppose it matters about the mobile phone. He'll probably just think it's a teenaged affectation."

"Thanks!" thought Juliana, then she replied: "I don't suppose he'd know what it is anyway."

Chapter 7

Mr Dellsey arrived at Cockscomb Park early on the Monday morning to supervise some surveyors who were laying out the new bases. He surprised Juliana by driving her down to his estate himself in his very expensive MPV. He didn't speak a word to her the whole way, spending all the time talking business on his high-end in-vehicle communication system, or listening to Rachmaninov on his ageing walkman. When he was on the phone, Juliana was required to wear ear plugs to stop her from overhearing his business. He didn't speak to her even then, just tapping his own ears each time the phone rang or when he keyed a new call, so that she would know what to do. He clearly wanted her to be in awe of him.

Juliana would pass the time by listening to her much cooler iPOD, pretending to send text messages on the mobile phone so that her boss would think she had lots of friends, or just watching the scenery fly by. At 11 o'clock, he stopped at a roadside fast food restaurant, locking her in the vehicle while he went inside. She could see him through the window devouring the all day mega breakfast and talking into a remote link to the in-vehicle communication system, that flashed and buzzed and clicked on the dashboard in front of her. She wondered why he didn't consider that device to be "ill bred", and whether the author was being quite consistent in his portrayal of the character. When he finished the breakfast, he ordered a second one and devoured that too, though more slowly.

Over an hour later, by which time Juliana was beginning to suffocate in the hot sun, he walked back out and gave her a packet of crisps and a lukewarm can of 7 Up. Then he tapped his ears again. Even when she had the ear plugs in, Juliana could hear a lot more than her boss realised, and she greedily consumed the many interesting titbits that she could pick up. She wouldn't have dared inform on her boss in his presence, but saved up all the information for later, only pretending to send texts when he had his earphones on. And so the time passed.

Eventually they reached the great gates of Dellsey Manor, and Juliana's spirits soared as she saw a line of builders' vans waiting outside. She counted at least six of them. As they approached she could see an especially burly man collecting sheets of paper from all the others who were gathered there. As the MPV drew to a halt, this man strode across and thrust the invoices through the window that her boss was lowering. Looking Mr Dellsey squarely in the eye, the man demanded: "When are these going to be paid?"

Mr Dellsey, who couldn't look anyone in the eye himself, was nevertheless practised at evasion in such circumstances. Assuming his most nonchalant air, but with a touch of seriousness to keep his creditors guessing, he inspected the various documents and slipped them into his briefcase, making sure that the sun reflected off his diamond encrusted initials into the man's face. "I'll pass them to my book keeper tomorrow morning," he pronounced. Then reaching down and tapping a code into the gate entry console, he sped into his personal kingdom.

The estate seemed to stretch as far as the eye could see. Juliana couldn't have imagined how long the drive would be, and resolved there and then to have a longer one herself some day. There was a lake with a jetty, follies and gazebos here and there, a mock Greek temple on a hummock; and a huge walled garden to one side of Mr Dellsey's massive manor house. On the horizons, woods seemed to stretch in all directions. Her boss stopped besides a group of estate workers who were burning wood in a brazier besides the drive. After issuing some instructions, he pulled the builders' invoices from his briefcase, dropped them into the brazier and drove on to the house.

There he summoned his chief housekeeper, introduced Juliana to her, then disappeared into it's vastness. For the first week, the newcomer was put to work in the kitchen, or helping the maids, or working on the estate with the grounds men; wherever she was needed. Juliana quickly made friends with various of the female staff and gained admirers from amongst the younger men. Her first conquest was Mark, the kitchen boy who very soon worshipped the ground that she walked upon.

Mark came from a travelling family who had been found trespassing in Mr Dellsey's woods. He had taken the boy into his employ in return for not prosecuting the family, who in any case said that they could not afford to support him. Before her first week had passed, Juliana had similarly captivated Dennis the gamekeeper's apprentice, Tom the junior grounds man; and Melvin the delivery man who brought Mrs Dellsey's catalogue shopping, and who though somewhat older than Juliana was still rather dishy.

The last named enjoyed a certain reputation in the area with ladies of all ages, and Mrs Dellsey was a very big orderer having little else to occupy herself with. "In his dreams," Mark would think, as he watched his idol through the kitchen window, signing the parcel manifests in the tradesman's entrance doorway, while inclining herself to maximum advantage in her alluring crop tops. He vowed to become a master builder himself, if only he could release himself from Mr Dellsey's indentures and get his hands on some back pay with which to put himself through college. His employer had never allowed him to go to school, and Social Services were unaware of his existence.

Over the coming weeks, Juliana would entertain her various suitors whenever time allowed. She would regale them with stories of her glamorous boyfriend at home, with his property portfolio and fleet of performance cars, and wonder out loud how terribly he must be missing her. Having arranged with some of her friends amongst the maids to receive texts during these conversations, she would sigh at Bryony the chair's mobile phone, look lovingly into the middle distance and then pretend to return them, before resuming. The trouble was, she couldn't see much evidence of builders about the place, and wondered whether her boss owed them all so much money that they would do no further work for him until they were paid.

On the second Monday, Mr Dellsey summoned Juliana to his study and said that she was to become his secretary. "Have I completed my probationary period then?" she asked. "No," came the firm reply.

The master of Dellsey Manor was simply not capable of keeping a secretary. All the employment agencies in the district knew how he would insist on their using typewriters instead of computers, and constantly set traps so that he could find fault with their work. Then he would use the fact that they left so quickly, often in tears before completing their first day, as an excuse to not pay the agencies' fees. Hence, they never sent anyone decent along in the first place.

Juliana didn't realise any of this yet but would find out her bosses intentions towards her before so very long. At first, she quite warmed to the idea, and sent a text to Bryony the chair that evening informing the caravaners' champion of her progress. As she settled into her new role, Mr Dellsey set many traps for this new secretary as he had with all the others; but she would invariably outsmart him with clever manoeuvres of her own while acting dumb and compliant to put him off his guard. After all she wasn't one of those no hopers that the employment agencies sent.

Juliana could tell that her boss was actually quite impressed by her abilities, but he didn't once acknowledge it or offer her a single word of encouragement. Over the school summer holidays, he took the young girl to various of his parks. The rent day routine at all of them was pretty much the same as at Cockscomb Park. At the smaller ones that had no warden, he would drop her off in the morning to collect the rent and enter it in his book, before returning later.

At some of the larger ones, she would have to sit and take notes while he saw off those tenants who might have some small grievance or other to air. During these conversations he might turn to her and bark things such as "Make a note of that for my lawyers," to terrify the elderly supplicants who just hoped to get this or that done at last, and thought that anything remotely connected with lawyers must amount to "getting involved". It usually had the desired effect of seeing them back out of the door.

Mr Dellsey would also sometimes take his young protégé on his tours of inspection, on which she would witness the same routine of bullying and intimidation that her parents' neighbours were so familiar with. Juliana also discovered that an occasional diversion of his, in the quiet season of August when not much other sport was to be had, was to detain children who had been found trespassing in his orchards, and then call a meeting with the local village parents association to negotiate their release.

One day, on which he seemed to be peculiarly unoccupied, her boss ordered her to hire the village hall, as he always did for this purpose. At the appointed time Juliana watched through the window as three vehicles drew up and were equally badly parked on the pavement outside. The village Mums all travelled in giant four wheel drives and liked to compete with one another over the best number plates for them. The grass verges by the school were a complete morass, and at rainy times all of the double yellow lines in the village would be obliterated by the mud from it.

Mr Dellsey would refer, sarcastically to the parents association committee by their number plates instead of by name. On this day, as every summer CLA 1R the chair, MAZ 10K the treasurer, and SAN 34D the secretary filed into the room. The ladies sat down and passed the time by chatting about the new autumn catalogues that Melvin had just brought, while they waited for the master of Dellsey Manor to take off his headphones. He then attempted to make them beg and cajole and plead for the children's release.

Juliana could see that this had become a rather tired routine. Since many of the villagers had moved out to those parts from London, and commuted back there to work over-long hours each day for the sake of their careers and the mountains of debt that supported them, they didn't know what their children were doing most of the time anyway. These parents naturally expected local activities to be arranged, but left that sort of thing to "people who had time for it"; namely the Mums who worked part-time locally or the few who didn't work at all, whose representatives were now in that room.

Some of the smarter village kids would get themselves caught deliberately, so as to witness the horrors that Dellsey Manor was reputed to conceal, and then during the rare moments when they met their parents at weekends, negotiate for the latest computer games or mobile phones in return for staying away from the place in future. Juliana could see that her boss realised there was considerably less sport to be had here than if the detained children had been the committee members' own, and that they in turn were merely toying with and not afraid of him at all. He returned to his personal kingdom in an especially malevolent humour, summoned his head gamekeeper to prepare the shotguns, and then stalked off to kill things in his woods instead.

On the final day of the school holidays, Mr Dellsey told Juliana that she now knew so much about his business affairs that he couldn't allow her return to Cockscomb Park, and that she would have to stay at the Manor permanently. She asked him once more whether she had completed her probationary period, but he said that he had been incurring a lot of extra expenses recently so she would have to work for her keep. "Just like Mark," his secretary thought. "No way, mister!"

All too aware that she hadn't so much as caught sight of any young builder, never mind a suitable one over the whole six weeks of the school holiday, Juliana called Bryony the chair that evening to demand to be got out of there. But for once, the older conspirator put her own interests ahead of others' and persuaded her agent to remain.

"You'll only be more unhappy back in that village school," she reasoned. "And you can always finish your education at the college in town. I've heard there's a very good building construction course there, that parents from all over the county send their sons to."

The indignant young girl was eventually swayed, and two days later Mel the delivery man brought a brand new digital camera. Before going down to the office that morning, she determined to persuade her boss to invest in a computer for her, and miraculously, so she thought, succeeded. Having done so, Juliana knew that she must be of some value to Mr Dellsey now, and waited to find out in what way that might be.

Chapter 8

The longer she was in Mr Dellsey's employ, the less wary he seemed to be about revealing to Juliana the true extent of his business interests. She still habitually acted dumb and compliant with her boss, while also seeking to impress him with her many advantages to him. He in turn was becoming ever more confident of his hold over the girl, and began to take her with him to the sites that the old caravans were taken to on his great low loader. These were the ones that Bryony the chair most wanted to find out about because she thought there might be "something concrete" there; the ones where the foreign migrant workers were housed.

Juliana learnt that her boss was a major supplier of grey market labour to farms, forestry interests, abattoirs and sweat shops of all kinds. To her, the run down caravan sites that the decrepit old coaches took the men out from each morning and brought them back to up to eighteen hours later, seemed like the most dismal places on earth. These camps were all much the same: rows of geriatric caravans, some verging on the derelict, with bright orange gas bottles attached to their sides. Electricity would be provided by battered generators that often broke down, and the only water supply was usually from two or three standpipes.

The camps were all staffed by surly guards, though if women were housed there as well there would also be one or two equally sour-looking matrons. Mr Dellsey was actually quite straight-laced in such matters. Twice, she had seen new coach loads of workers arriving, to be searched by the guards, given a number and then entered into the landlord's camp book. Anything of value that they brought with them was confiscated. On the second occasion she had compiled the inventory of valuables that her boss always insisted upon.

When one or two new arrivals were found to have nothing worth purloining on them, Mr Dellsey said: "Do a physical," in the same tone with which he would require structurals from callers to his office back at the Manor. His guards then pulled on pink latex gloves and dragged the offending men to another room. Once on arriving at one of the camps a guard at the gate had fingered Juliana's security tag that she had to wear around her neck, while still wearing the gloves. She had recoiled at the smell, knowing that he couldn't have been rodding drains like Mr Scrote back home, because none of these places had any.

She wondered what things must be like for these men in their own countries if this was the better option, and whether they were ever paid any money to send back to their families at home. But try as she would, Juliana could find no evidence that her boss was actually dealing in illegal immigrants, and could not therefore give Bryony the chair anything concrete to pass to the Parliamentary Sub-committee.

Then one day Mr Dellsey said they were going to "the transit station". He warned her with a deadly gravity not to breathe a word of what she saw there to anyone, otherwise she would end up in "one of the transit stations abroad". The young girl didn't know exactly what that meant yet, but was nonetheless impressed by the extra special malevolence with which her boss had made the threat.

The MPV pulled up at the entrance to what looked more like a prison camp than a caravan site. It was at the end of a long track through what remained of a forest that her boss owned. This had once been the country's last remaining nesting site of the Two-barred Lesser Woodchat Shrike, but Mr Dellsey had felled much of it for matchwood and sited repossessed caravans in the trees' place. Few outsiders ventured there now.

Juliana had been here two or three times before, but her boss had always locked her inside the vehicle while he went about whatever business he had inside. Left to herself, she would call Bryony the chair on the mobile phone, who felt instinctively that if "something concrete" was be found then it must be here. There was a perimeter chain link fence inside which a tall conifer hedge completely hid whatever might lie behind it. To one side of the heavily padlocked entrance gates there was a small wooden guard house. More than once Juliana had seen battered minibuses drive in, and thought that she could make out anxious faces behind their blackened windows.

On those previous visits, there was something about the chief guard here that had always made Juliana feel ill at ease. As she watched him from a distance through the stained guardroom window, slavering into what she guessed must be an internet picture phone, she had felt there was something familiar about his ill-favoured face. But as she could only half see him, she couldn't tell what it was. Today, as the guard walked out to Mr Dellsey's summons and climbed into the back of the vehicle, she recognised him at once. His face had been all over every newspaper in the land two school summer holidays previously, and as Juliana recalled, on several other occasions prior to that. The young girl's flesh began to creep.

Once inside the compound, her boss parked besides a prefabricated building that housed a kitchen, canteen and shower block. These were the only amenities on the site. She counted eighteen very old caravans, none of which were connected to gas, electric or water; and some of which seemed almost too dilapidated for anyone to actually live in. Mr Dellsey beckoned Juliana to follow him and his surly lieutenant, then they walked across to a two-tone grey caravan that was covered in green mould and stepped inside.

A group of girls, most of whom looked a little younger than the secretary herself though one or two were barely out of puberty, sat huddled around an inadequate paraffin heater. They all had dark hair and almond coloured eyes, and were very pretty though also very frightened looking. Juliana counted sixteen and guessed that they must be Albanians. Her boss moved from one girl to another, examining their teeth as if they were new calves on one of his farms or checking their hair for lice. "Looks like a good batch," he eventually pronounced.

Then he demanded the valuables inventory from the guard. "None of 'em had nothin' on 'em, boss" the man replied. "D'ya want me and the lads to do a physical?"

Mr Dellsey read the man's mind at once and, jabbing a finger close to his leering face, snapped: "No! You know the rules here. Fresh produce gets to market fresh. Lay a finger on any of them and I'll turn you all in. My clients will know." Juliana, feeling something concrete hardening in her mind, wondered who the other "lads" might be; since she remembered every detail about this guard now.

Her boss and the guard continued to talk about various

matters, while she tried behind their backs to aim comforting smiles at the frightened girls. She sought to take in the squalor in which they were standing, the girls' predicament and her boss' indifference to it. Then she heard him say: "There's a consignment of Kurdish orphans coming in on Friday. I want them fed, washed, dressed and then shipped straight to the studio."

Juliana retched. Her boss glared over his shoulder at her and she managed to smile back: "Sorry, just a little tickle in the throat," feigning dumb compliance as always.

"Make sure they're fresh too," Mr Dellsey sneered to the guard. "If my clients say they're not I'll take you back to that God forsaken town you come from myself, chain you to the gates at school time, and leave you there when the number plates arrive."

Juliana was practically swooning by now, but managed to retain her composure as she considered the chemistry between the two men. The guard's mix of subservience and loathing towards probably his only benefactor said that he knew his 'guv'nor' would carry out the threat if he transgressed. She considered whether Mr Dellsey was tantalising this reptile, keeping him so close to what he most wanted but denying him access. But she quickly dismissed the notion, knowing that her boss was not that subtle.

The way in which he so habitually referred to mothers as "number plates" particularly chilled Juliana. She wondered what his own mother must have been like, and whether he had broken her heart. She had long since realised that anyone was a number on a balance sheet to her boss, and that all people were just a resource to him, as his own father must have taught him. Whatever it was that bound his more captive employees to him, just made them a more valuable resource. The guard's past crimes were unimportant: Mr Dellsey viewed the fugitive from police custody with the same cold indifference as all of his subordinates, his secretary included.

"These girls will all have to be photographed for the catalogue," her boss then said, "And it had better be quicker than last time."

Juliana seized her chance. "I could do it with my digital camera, sir" she ventured. "It's much faster than a film one. I can print the pictures from the computer and have them on your desk in the morning."

Her boss at first feigned a mixture of gentrified amusement and mild disgust at such an ill-bred notion, but agreed to give it a try, saying: "It had better be good." The concrete in her mind had just set hard.

The Albanian girls were then herded over to the shower block, where two sour looking matrons were summoned to supervise their washing and dressing. Mr Dellsey sent the guard to recover the hidden valuables and the regulation inventory, to keep him out of the way. He passed the interval until the girls had been made presentable barking into the remote link to his in-car communication system. Juliana, who had decided to help the matrons with dressing the girls, twice more thought she heard the word "fresh" as well as "guaranteed". The first was such a simple, everyday word; but from that day forth she could never hear it again without a slight shudder at the memory of that place.

The girls were ready now, and Juliana showed them back into the room where her boss sat. The guard had returned with the confiscated valuables, and Mr Dellsey was checking them against the inventory. There were various items of jewellery and other trinkets, few of which looked very valuable; but Juliana could only guess at what they must have meant to these abandoned souls. She noticed an exquisitely crafted locket, in which was a tiny portrait of what must have been one of the girls' mothers. She thought she caught a brief sight of a longing glance towards it, but her boss just inspected it coldly before dropping it into a black velvet bag with the rest of his loot.

Suddenly he seemed aware of the female presence in the room. "Oh proceed, carry on, carry on," he said dismissively.

Juliana began to photograph the Albanian girls, darting them little smiles of encouragement and trying to find a way of saying: "Don't worry, I'll have you out of here soon," but none of them spoke English. Just as she was finishing, she noticed over her shoulder that her boss and his chief guard were standing very close to one another. She spun suddenly round and captured several frames.

The guard tried to snatch the camera from her in alarm, but she side-stepped him and tapping it several times said: "There. All deleted again, sorry I slipped!" Mr Dellsey thought nothing of it, regarding the device as just an ill-bred, teenaged affectation that was not worthy of his gentrified consideration. He was already looking forward with relish to the morning's trap that he assumed he had sprung for his secretary. "Yes!" every fibre of Juliana's being yelled inside of her as she slipped the camera back into her bag.

The guard had no more chance to protest, because his 'guv'nor' was already ushering Juliana from the building. "The fillies go to market on Friday too," he barked over his shoulder as they left, and then added. "Fresh, mind," one last time with a final jab of his finger. Juliana felt exultant. Her boss ignored her as usual all the way back to the Manor, but did he realise that he had just stepped into concrete galoshes? - she thought not.

When they got back to the Manor, Juliana said she would have to get working on the photographs, but went straight to her room instead to call Bryony the chair and tell her everything. Then she pleaded with her older accomplice to get her out of there before her boss discovered her treachery. Later on she went down to the office to process the digital pictures on her computer, and e-mailed Bryony the chair the best picture of Mr Dellsey with his accomplice. The caravaners' champion recognised the guard at once. She drove to the police station in town, held up the picture at the counter and said: "I know where this man is and who is sheltering him."

Lastly, Juliana went to find Mark the kitchen boy to tell him she would be leaving very soon. The youth, who she had come to regard rather like a younger brother, cried and begged her not to go. She said that she had to and asked him why he didn't leave too.

"I don't have anywhere else to go," he replied. "And I have no legal status in the outside world."

Thinking of the migrant workers and their guards, Juliana sighed and thought: "So what's new?"

Chapter 9

There were two more working days before the Kurdish orphans'
arrival at the transit station and the fillies' shipment to market, and
Juliana wondered how she would get through them. She felt like a
coiled spring, but fortunately her boss was away for the whole time
and she was glad at least to be out of his company. She wondered
what worthy clients he might be doing business with now, and then
thought of the caravaners back home with their moans and groans
about the roads and the drains, and why their neighbour could have
a fence when they had been told it was against the park rules.

She hoped that the Albanian girls were safe from the attentions
of the guards, and wondered where their parents were and how they
could abandon them so. Would those grumbling old caravaners,
retreating from the park office on rent day afternoons, feel that their
lot was quite so bad after all if they could have seen those frightened
faces in the mouldy, smelly, paraffin heated atmosphere of that
room; and heard their hated landlord talking about shipping fresh
produce to market unsoiled? And so the interval passed.

Friday morning duly arrived. As the world prepared for it's
coming day's business, a determined young figure was walking
through the vastness of Dellsey Manor, from the kitchen towards
the office of its master. At Cockscomb Park a woman in nurse's
uniform was enquiring after long distance Brian, speaking to a
trance-like wanderer who simply replied: "Not me, I don't want to
get involved," whilst an only slightly more purposeful figure
jogged on by. At the migrant workers' camps, the day's shifts were
being roll-called and the buses loaded. And outside of the transit
station, a battered black minibus with smoked cellophane-lined
windows was moving slowly towards the guard house.

The man inside disconnected his internet picture phone, wiped
the slaver from his lips and walked out to unlock the gates. As he
swung them back, the air became suddenly filled with the sounds
of many shouts, and barking dogs, and screeching brakes, and the
whirr of rotor blades. Squads of armed police officers leapt out of

the conifer hedge through the gaps in the chain link fence that had been cut in the night. The vehicles that had raced up the track behind the minibus disgorged many others, while more descended from the skies into the compound itself.

"Hallo, Stan," said a chief superintendent, as his officers handcuffed the frightened fugitive. "So this is where you've been hiding. Let's go inside and see what you've been up to here, shall we?"

The police had been investigating the people trafficking operation for a long time, but until Juliana and Bryony the chair's revelations they had lacked any concrete evidence. On this momentous morning, dawn raids were being conducted at locations across the south of England, and two police armoured vehicles were also drawing up at the gates to Dellsey Manor. The previous evening Juliana had received a text saying: "Coming 2 get U O O there. No go down 2 office AM. Regards HM Police. PS wots entry code?"

Juliana watched from her window as the vehicles raced up the long drive to the house, one screeching to a halt by the outer door to her boss' office, while the other headed for the tradesman's entrance to rescue her. As the first team beat on Mr Dellsey's office door, they heard a gunshot from within. Then they broke down the barrier and beheld a frightened young man standing over the bulk of his former lord and master who lay dead on the floor. Mark the kitchen boy had walked in from the inside door moments before them and boldly demanded his back pay. On being told to "Go back to the kitchen where you belong and never dare set foot in here again," the "Gippo" had pulled out a revolver and shot the master of Dellsey Manor between the eyes.

The sequence of events from that morning on dominated the newspapers and television news bulletins for days. The re-capture of such a prominent national hate figure as Stanley Brooke, the chief transit station guard, and its association with the plight and dramatic rescue of the pitiful Kurdish orphans and the cruelly abandoned but oh so pretty young Albanian girls, seized the public imagination and refused to let go. As more and more lurid detail emerged about the people trafficking operation, and the nature of its clients, and the late Mr Dellsey's role in it all, the story ran for weeks to come.

Juliana became a national heroine for a while, appearing on television many times, and the Daily Mirror serialised her story. She eagerly fed its ghost writers with many fine embellishments about the dark goings on that she had witnessed at Dellsey Manor, the migrant workers' camps, and most of all at the transit station; and also supplied picture exclusives to other newspapers from the stock that she had compiled behind her former boss' back. Another tabloid took up the cause of Mark the kitchen boy, demanding that all charges against him be dropped and that he too be declared a national hero instead.

Juliana even came second in a broadsheet's personalities of the year poll, in the category of "person most worthy of canonisation". It was the closest anyone had ever finished behind Tommy Pilkington, the rugby icon who won that section every year. At every opportunity during this period of fame, the reluctant heroine would emphasise that all she really wanted was to marry a builder who could build a nice house for their children, because her schoolmates had looked down on her for living in a caravan and called her names. Mail bags full of offers were redirected from newspaper and TV channel offices to her parents' door. Eventually, the government itself identified a re-election strategy.

Concerned at the unpopularity of the country's involvement in so many foreign wars, the Ministry of Public Deception and Unmandated Agendas needed a domestic feel good factor with which to woo back the electorate. That body had been set up to secure the government's third general election victory and was afterwards retained to run the country, freeing the prime minister to attend to more pressing concerns abroad. The full weight of the department's spin machine now fell behind the grievances of the National Caravaners Protection Association, and the Rt Hon Milton Lawson MP's Parliamentary Sub-Committee on Caravan Park Reform was ordered to draft a bill that could be debated at length throughout the final Parliament of the current term.

The prime minister himself actually returned to Downing Street and stayed for three days, the longest anyone could remember him being in the country since his re-election. On the second day it was announced that he would address the nation live from the House of Commons, just before prime minister's question time. In anticipation of unprecedented public interest in actually being able to see him at the seat of government, giant video screens were set up in city centres across the land. The caravaners all filed into a pub in the next village to watch the address on its live footie screen. It wasn't that they weren't welcome in the pubs in the village on Shottington Ridge across the fields by Cockscomb Park, but they weren't really encouraged to go there either.

A reporter was speaking from outside Parliament as the caravaners took their seats, and then the cameras switched to inside the building. There, actually in the House of Commons was standing the Rt Hon Sylvester Schwarzenorris, as the prime minister had rebranded himself early in his third term of office. He was wearing his customary flak jacket and red military beret. On the floor to one side of him lay a large canvass kit bag, covered with sewn on patches bearing the names of the many places to which his travels took him. Two of his favourite Simpsons videos, the ones in which he himself appeared, could just be seen protruding from the top of this bag. On the front bench seat behind him was a bulging rucksack bearing many more patches, and his favourite Kalashnikov assault rifle was propped up against the despatch box.

On the great leader's right, as always sat the Rt Hon Alasdair Handelson, the Minister of Public Deception and Unmandated Agendas, over whose shoulder the Rt Hon Milton Lawson MP could just be seen straining to get on camera. "Fellow citizens," the prime minister began. "Never again must the disadvantaged and vulnerable on the margins of our society be allowed to be concealed from our view in the unregulated environments of which we are now aware. The noble actions of my Rt Hon friend in sending that brave young woman into the unknown has revealed a teeming underworld of unscrupulous landlords and criminal gangs." He looked around for Mr Lawson, but not actually knowing who he was turned back towards the TV cameras.

"Bastard!" thought Bryony the chair, recognising the inevitably of the MP eventually taking most of the credit for her own years of dedicated toil. Juliana wondered if she herself would be likely to meet the great statesman, but the readiness of the kit bag and rucksack suggested not. "These activities must be brought under strict centralised control," the prime minister was saying, nodding towards his Rt Hon friend the Minister for State Interference and Indirect Taxation. He spoke for a full three minutes more and then prime minister's question time was announced.

On the benches opposite, the shadow Secretary for Unelectable Alternatives nudged the gently dozing figure beside him. The leader of Her Majesty's opposition shook his head, rubbed his eyes, and slipping on his barrister's wig rose to speak.

"May I first say how very flattered we on this side of the house are to find the Rt Hon gentleman, the member for Barking back in our midst," he began, to a chorus of jeers from his back benches. "Is the Rt Hon gentleman aware that..."

But the prime minister was already gathering up his kit bag and rucksack, and slinging the rifle over his shoulder. Filming was due to begin in Hollywood of the new blockbuster Simpsons movie, and he needed to be on his way. The Rt Hon Alasdair Handelson rose to field the opposition's questions, as he always did. The pub landlord brought out trays of sandwiches, and the caravaners ordered more rounds of drinks.

The prime minister's such unprecedented attention to a domestic policy issue ensured that caravan park reform remained a hot topic in the media for some time to come. All of the late Mr Dellsey's business affairs were thoroughly investigated, and hundreds of creditors sued his estate. The Kurdish orphans were all fast-tracked through the adoption process, as were the younger Albanian girls; while the older ones mostly became models or dancers or TV game show host's assistants.

The Department of Public Deception made sure that every step of these unfortunates' integration into the new vision of society presented in its general election manifesto gained maximum media exposure. This was designed to enhance the feel good factor being created by the deliberately drawn out progress of the Caravan Parks Reform Bill through the final Parliament of the government's third term. To avoid any public opinion backlash at such a sensitive stage of this re-election strategy, Mark the kitchen boy received a suspended sentence; and then he went to college to start a building construction course.

Juliana enjoyed the attention of her own brief spell in the limelight, but soon felt it was time to get back to the real business of finding a husband. She began to sort through the mailbags that seemed to half fill her parents' caravan, picking out the more promising suitors and sending them detailed questionnaires asking each one what they had built, how big it was, and what their hopes and ambitions were for the future. When the replies came she set about compiling her shortlist.

Chapter 10

Juliana got married on her eighteenth birthday as she had always wanted to. The newly weds bought a house in town with the money earned from her TV appearances and newspaper serialisation, and then another and another. Her husband would improve and extend each of them before selling them on at a suitable profit. She had clearly made the right choice, but then as she would tell people: "He's got a pushy wife."

Our heroine eventually settled with her husband, Alex and their three children, none of whom were named Brian or Bryony, in the biggest house in a nice village on the other side of town from Cockscomb Park. Alex built it himself in the style of a Palladian villa, and added a row of garages for their several performance cars, that Juliana would still sometimes drive through the village on Shottington Ridge across the fields from the park, just to say: "Hi everyone, I'm back!"

They also put a swimming pool in their garden, and electric gates at the entrance to their long driveway, that they lined with gilt statues. Having learnt well from her experience at Dellsey Manor, Juliana planned to eventually own the whole village and let it to tenants before moving to a bigger country estate than her former employer's. Some things, it seemed never changed. Her parents stayed at the park in one of the big new homes, where they would as always insist: "Never get anything on tick."

Life there carried on much the same as in the past, with Brians and Bryonys coming and going and forever having the same old moans and groans; but the park became much better managed. This was not solely because of the Caravans and Park Homes Reform Act that was passed in the first Parliament of the re-elected government led by the Rt Hon Alasdair Handelson MP, prime minister, following its landslide general election victory. Mrs Dellsey had inherited everything, and put it in trust for their only son, Emlyn pending his coming of age.

Freed from the boredom of her married life's endless routine of catalogue shopping, she assumed control of the family businesses. Those of her late husband's parks that were not closed down under the new Act of Parliament or sold to pay off the many creditors who sued the estate after his death, were placed in the hands of a management company, including the one where Juliana grew up. The residents all waited apprehensively to see whether "son of Dellsey", as they called him, would be an improvement on his father.

Mr Scrote eventually departed for the great contraband operation in the sky, though taxi drivers visiting Cockscomb Park at night said they still saw his ghostly form, bawling and cursing and waving his drain rods at them in rage. A few still kept their elasticised bank notes ready in their wallets, just in case it was really him. Still some residents said they sometimes saw a strange blue mist around the place, even on the hottest summer days, and half-heard the sound of distant expletives on the wind as it blew off Shottington Ridge.

Sam and Beth both married their boyfriends and had children. Their giant four wheel drives - SAM 100H and A11 BET - remained a constant hazard parked badly on the pavement outside corner shops and sub-post offices, and muddying grass verges in front of schools all over town. Juliana would still bump into them now and again, and laugh about old times. She never saw Sheralee again, though she heard that Brian the undertaker had won the lottery and felt sure that he would know where his daughter was and see that she was all right.

No longer having Mr Dellsey to have a good fight with, Bryony the chair became a district councillor and took up many worthy local causes. Having also been a leading advisor to the Parliamentary sub-committee that prepared the reform bill, she eventually received an OBE for her contribution. It's chairman became Sir Milton Lawson MP in the first term of the new Parliament, and was then promoted to a senior home office ministerial post. Bryony the treasurer continued to help Bryony the chair, and agreed with her at meetings of the many organisations that they supported; while Brian the secretary still did the Times crossword on most days.

Finally, Mel the delivery man at Dellsey Manor, finding it increasingly difficult to focus on his job, began to spend his days dreaming up naughty satires featuring players in whom any resemblance to his best celebrity customers would be entirely coincidental, and various locations and characters suggested by the different communities through which his lone daily wanderings took him. And so, some seventeen years in the future, the second part of this history became set to unfold.

PART 2

The Gremlin's Wrath

Chapter 1

Juliana sat cross-legged on one of the several sofas in the lilac reclining room at Great Donnington Manor, holding a gold plated home comms link to her ear, while with the other hand she key-padded the range of trigital mail order consoles that were set out all around her. Further afield were cast many tabloid newsprints that all seemed to bear her name and picture, and some of the free TVDs that inevitably fell out from them. It would soon be her 34th birthday for which a lavish party was planned, and she was getting to the end of a very big order indeed, having reason to be especially pleased with herself. "Oh, and about the titles I ordered yesterday," the caller concluded. "I don't really think they sounded dynamic enough, upon reflection. Could you change that to Lord and Lady Goldendawn? … Thanks!"

It was possible to buy titles by mail order in the 2020s, as the King had a few years earlier abolished the birthday and new year's honours for everyone except politicians and rugby coaches; though senior civil servants still received them as a condition of service upon attaining certain grades. Knowing the new monarch's view that the old system was rather too pretentious and elitist, the government had made "Honours for All" a central plank of it's most recent re-election manifesto. "Oh, and could you ask the courier to push them right through the letter box," Juliana added. "Don't want them to get wet, do we? ... Byeee!"

Throughout the sixteen years of her married life so far, Juliana had always indulged her love of mail order shopping. Now she was the country's most famous catalogue shopper of all, having three days previously won the reality home cinema show: "I'm a Home Shopper. Get Ordering." What had particularly captivated the public about her success was that in the final she had beaten Kelly Pilkington, the ex-pop star wife of Sir Tommy, the England rugby coach and former playing icon. As a result, Juliana was embarking upon her life's second major period of celebrity, and by the estimates of the renowned publicist Jack Gifford stood to earn at least three million from it.

Lady Goldendawn and her husband Alex had enjoyed successful careers as property developers since their earliest ventures funded by Juliana's first brush with fame. Aged sixteen, she had brought down the evil empire of William Dellsey, the demon caravan landlord and people trafficker, and inadvertently inspired a successful general election campaign. The HC audience in 2021 had as then warmed to the unaffected, outgoing personality of the good natured now mother of three; and as the show progressed had increasingly favoured her over the country's foremost but rather ageing celebrity shopper.

Juliana remembered finishing second to Kelly's husband in a newsprint personality pole those seventeen years previously. Not having finished second in many things in life since, she felt determined to see off the media's golden couple on being cast for the show, and employed all of her subtlest arts to that end. Tommy and Kelly never finished second at anything, so imagine the female partner's chagrin on eventually being abandoned by her hitherto adoring public for this upstart property developer's wife who had grown up in a caravan. The ensuing war of words had sold new record numbers of tabloids over the previous two days, and the Daily Mirror had begun serialising Juliana's story for the second time in her life.

That life story had gone something like this. The new Lord and Lady Goldendawn still lived in the biggest house in a nice village on the opposite side of town from where Juliana had grown up. Alex had continually improved and extended the original Palladian Villa design, and added more and more garages for their growing collection of new and vintage performance cars. Since Juliana's girlhood caravan home had been known in the trade as a "Donnington", they had eventually renamed their marital abode "Great Donnington Manor". They also owned and let several other properties in the village, and many more in town, as well as various holiday homes abroad. At one time Juliana had aspired to moving up to Hogs Hill, the exclusive belt that lay between her village and town; but she and Alex had fairly quickly abandoned the idea.

The peculiar geological feature that was Shottington Ridge across the fields from the caravan park of our heroine's youth, was dissected by the great river Isis that flowed through town and on towards London, and on this side spread out in three directions. It was all very old money up there, and pretty much a closed world to outsiders. Self made wealth or "trade" in any conceivable form were simply not to be tolerated on the Hill. It became plain to the young couple that Juliana's childhood persecution by the stuck-up kids that she had gone to school with would pale by comparison with being looked down upon by the Hogs Hillites. They decided to stay in their nice village where, though the female partner might still suffer scorn out of envy from some of its shallower, more ineffectual London commuters' wives, she would invariably get the better of them.

Almost all of the houses on Hogs Hill were very old, very big and totally un-modernised; since the residents regarded that sort of thing as vulgar and indicative of ill breeding. There were only two exceptions, and Juliana knew both their mistresses well. One was Gina Day, the furniture tycoon's wife with whom she had become tolerably good friends before Gina's children had gone away to private schools. The other was Elronda d'Oriel, whose husband was big in the fashion and cosmetics worlds, and who was also Juliana's deadly local rival. Both these upwardly mobile Hogs Hill couples shared the Goldendawns' love of extending and modernising their properties, but Elronda always seemed to display the infuriating knack of managing to keep one step ahead of the others. Gina herself managed to stay out of such rivalries, since though sharing Juliana's good nature she lacked her friend's competitive streak (leaving that side of things to her husband); but the house that Gina kept and its extensive grounds were still very beautiful indeed.

Alex viewed Hogs Hill as a potential goldmine, as any property developer would on beholding its scores of vast old piles that simply ached for improvement but whose incumbents steadfastly refused to renounce the former age that they represented. In their early years in the village, he had often ventured up there himself to make very good offers for some of these relics, that in his hands could quickly be turned into hotels or conference centres, apartment blocks or homes for millionaire sportsmen or showbiz personalities. But he had always been rejected out of hand, to many dark mutterings concerning "trade" and "ghastly *nouveau riche*."

Alex next tried the subtler tactic of finding out when people had died and sending in his appointed agents, but they also would end up negotiating the latter half of Hogs Hill's many long and often winding drives with the dogs at their heels. Having had such fusty, dowdy, stuffy upbringings themselves, the next generations to whom the properties were always handed down simply remained as impervious to outside influence as their parents had always been.

Virtually the only outsider who enjoyed any degree of toleration was the current mail order courier, the postal workers union having declared the district off limits years previously; but the only person who ever gave this courier a Christmas tip was Gina Day. The Days were certainly not accepted, though allowances were made to an extent for the d'Oriels, since Elronda was known to come from very good stock despite her latter day more "vulgar" inclinations.

Having been frustrated at every stage of attempting to exploit this opportunity on his own doorstep, Alex had reached something of a crossroads in his business life and he was currently casting his nets more widely in search of new challenges. The Goldendawns were tolerably wealthy according to the standards by which Juliana judged such things, but much of it was tied up in property and having come from humble origins besides having a growing family to consider, they felt wary of attempting unduly risky new ventures. The cash injection that Juliana's HC success now stood to earn them would change all that, since it would amount to serious investment power indeed.

"I'm a Home Shopper" was the brain child of the media mogul James Lee Patience, who had got the idea whilst working as a mail order courier himself, during a period of demotivation following the collapse of his public relations business earlier in his career. Juliana remembered the raconteur, wit and all round good egg as Mel the delivery man, who had brought the catalogue shopping at Dellsey Manor whilst she was employed there in her youth. He in turn had always remembered the alluring young girl with her equally alluring crop tops, who had fascinated him so at that time. James Lee, as he subsequently reinvented himself, went on to become a best selling novelist and then got into home cinema. By its third series "I'm a Home Shopper" would be rated the most successful reality HC show of all time, and anticipating this James

Lee had pressed his producers to cast Juliana in it.

The show's format certainly proved a ratings winner. Twelve celebrity shoppers were confined for two weeks to an empty four bedroomed detached, equipped with just one change of clothes, rudimentary cooking and eating utensils, and an array of the latest trigital mail order consoles. They then had to furnish and equip the house and order quantities of clothes from which to select an outfit for each day. Most of the major catalogue retailers participated, regarding the exposure as excellent publicity and an opportunity to establish brand dominance. The exception was "Foremost", that didn't wish to stand comparison with what it regarded as down market competitors.

The all day dialogue on the various catalogues' contents, and the competition and chemistry between the participants, made compulsive viewing for millions who deserted HC shopping channels in their droves. The carefully scripted characters of the several, constantly calling couriers - there was a dishy one, a rude one and a lecherous one, naturally enough - created rich scope for innuendo. To counter that side of things with a comfort factor, other couriers were nice homely ladies who liked to stay and join in the chat; whilst the tantalising possibility of seeing the celebrities with their kit off during the incessant clothes fittings further enthralled the audience. The clever camera angles that were employed so effectively in home and garden makeover shows were likewise used to keep viewers in a perpetual state of readiness for something to drop right out; though in the event, of course, nothing ever did.

Each evening, a panel of fashion writers and media style gurus would enter the house to discuss the contestants' selections with them, and assess them on good taste and fashion consciousness. The audience would then vote on the various contributions, and the lowest scorer would leave the house. At the beginning, Kelly Pilkington had of course been the bookies' clear favourite to win, since she and Tommy were never out of the newsprints. Juliana, whilst remembered fondly for her heroic deeds as a sixteen year old, was considered a relative outsider; but she steadily made up ground as the show progressed until her by then renowned bickerings with Kelly were put to the final test.

The show's third series eclipsed all previous viewing figures, and looked certain to generate significant turnover increases for the participating catalogue retailers. It was certainly successful in keeping people's minds off the war, and the war itself out of at least the tabloid newsprints. With an hour still to go to school time, Juliana slipped one of her free "I'm a Home Shopper" TVDs into her player and settled down to enjoy the triumph one more time. Having watched it so often already, she dozed off towards the end. When she awoke, the mortified countenance of Kelly Pilkington had been replaced on the home cinema screen by the familiar, bright yellow features of Sir Sylvester Schwarzenorris, the supreme Western Coalition commander. He appeared to be droning on as usual to the sparsely populated and mildly snoring ranks of the Divided Nations Insecurity Council.

On his retirement from British politics seventeen years earlier, the former prime minister and Rt Hon member for Barking had become secretary-general of the Grand Western Coalition for the Total Elimination of Funny Foreigners, as he had re-branded NATO following his appointment. From that day hence that fine democratic institution had gone about the remit of its title with a hitherto unmatched zeal of biblical dimensions. Successive British governments, led first by Sir Alasdair Handelson, then Lord Lawson of Milton (as they now were) had naturally felt obliged to back their trans-Atlantic cousins against the world-wide forces of non-English speakers who might not like burgers.

"Barking Schwarzee", as the tabloids would dub him on the rare occasions when their attention might turn towards the global conflict, had since risen to become supreme commander in the War on FuFos, as the coalition campaign was renamed for brevity's sake. The present government was showing no signs of wavering, and the broadsheets remained as preoccupied with the international war effort as the red tops currently were with the domestic rivalry between Juliana and Kelly Pilkington. The local victor listened momentarily to the great world statesman, but on concluding that she was just hearing the same old guff for the umpteenth time, set off instead to collect her children from school.

Chapter 2

Silence suddenly engulfed the main group of Mums who were gossiping alongside the morass at the village school gates, as Juliana's red Ferrari disgorged its owner. "Don't let me stop you," our heroine thought, whipping out her mobile comms link and proceeding to transmit pretended messages to who know's who's trigital mailboxes. After a few moments, a particularly sly voice intoned: "Well, if it isn't Lady Golden-Orbs, the Queen of the Cybermall. How very vulgar!"

Juliana recognised the offender as snooty Sharon, a former schoolmate from the village on Shottington Ridge, across the fields from Cockscomb Park where she had grown up. This class swot had married a stockbroker and then moved across town into a house near the top end of this village, that was also the second largest behind Juliana and Alex's. After producing two children, Sharon had rarely seen her husband since, because he was always working in London.

Lady Goldendawn had heard from the man who brings the catalogue shopping that Sharon liked to set traps for him, by giving Foremost misleading information about where she would leave her returns. Then when he couldn't find them she would "make a complaint", as she constantly threatened, hoping he would be sacked; but he never was because nobody else wanted his job anyway. London commuters' wives never seemed to realise that.

Sharon's habitual bile had intensified when she had once been forced to take her returns to the errant courier himself, and actually discovered that he lived in a caravan! Then, on proclaiming that she presumed he would have had the sense to find the returns himself, he had calmly retorted that he was quite happy as he was and didn't think in terms of large detacheds. Juliana thought anew of her friend James Lee's habitual irreverence, and wondered whether the two men might be related, or indeed variations on the same character. It was obvious to her what Sharon's problem was: unlike the many other village once-a weekers, she didn't see her husband even on Saturday mornings any more.

The new media heroine settled against the front wing of her Ferrari and keyed a number on her mobile. "Hi, James Lee," she trilled. "It's me, Jules. There's just one or two things about the new contracts. Give me a bell when you've got five. Ciao!" The small throng of village Mums' indignant silence deepened further as the object of their hostility slipped the comms link back into her pocket and gazed triumphantly into the middle distance. Then the gathered ladies turned to more mundane concerns. "I wish the council would do something about this mud," said one. "It's hardly very healthy for the children, is it?"

"No. Here, let me have that," said another, taking a disposable nappy from a friend who had been changing her baby in the back of her vehicle, and stuffing it into a litter bin mounted on a lamp post by the school entrance. The smart Mum's preferred mode of transport had evolved during the first two decades of the 21st century from the most giant of four wheel drives into vehicles not dissimilar to armoured personnel carriers. All things warlike had become fashionable in the current world political climate, though Juliana herself still preferred performance sports cars. Manufacturers were now offering armour-plated, radiation and blast-proof APCs, with inevitable consequences across the nation for school grass verges and double yellow lines anywhere in the vicinity.

A short distance away from the main group, a smaller number of Mums were chatting amongst themselves. These were the ones who merely drove cars, with non-personalised plates, and hence were regarded as lower in the village pecking order by the APC owners. Slightly further away again, so as to be just out of contagion range, stood the forlorn and familiar figure of Janet Bates, the village child minder. She was dressed as always in her bright green germ warfare suit, since she regarded all children as being highly infectious. Several of the tiny charges that she brought to the school gates each day for collection were clinging to her latex gloved fingers. Two of these were kicking up a terrific din that only Janet seemed unaware of, her ears being tightly plugged as always inside her all enveloping suit. Through its Perspex visor, her anxious, impatient eyes could just be seen searching out the clients who would soon relieve Janet of her daily burden.

The only time the child minder took off the suit and gloves during her working day was when the courier brought her catalogue shopping, since she couldn't keep her hands off him. All the part-time working Mums wished that somebody rather more sympathetic was available to fill Janet's role, but nobody else wanted to do it so they just had to make allowances for her little eccentricities. Suddenly spotting a fairly new Jitsuhishi Battlebus (the current APC market leader) with shattered headlamps behind its buckled bull bars, and deep score marks along the length of both its sides; Juliana waved and called out: "Hey, Beth! It's me, Jules. Great to see you."

Her old friend, who had moved to the village and was equally unconcerned at the main group Mums' pretensions (and hence also despised by them) sauntered across the road from where the child minder was standing. As she lovingly wiped the reddened cheeks of her youngest, who had stopped crying immediately upon being reunited with her mother, Beth felt relieved at avoiding the familiar complaints that: "These kids have all got something, you know. I'm beginning to feel funny already."

"Oh, hi... loved the programme!" Beth beamed, as she greeted her kindred spirit. "I'll never forget the look on that Kelly's face..." and such like. The children had now emerged from the school gates and most of them became engaged in the daily rituals either of splattering each other with the mud or falling headlong into it themselves as they fought their way towards the waiting vehicles. It having rained heavily overnight, various of the main group Mums were sinking in up to their own knees as they attempted to supervise the stampeding throng; while the separate gathering of mere car drivers simply smiled at one another as their own kids side-stepped the melee and walked scornfully past. Juliana and Beth, after seeing their particular protagonists score many vital points off the main group kids, gathered them up and with a final, triumphant high five took them home.

As they raced back along the lane, Juliana recognised Elronda d'Oriel's Bentley parked in a lay-by, waiting as usual for the main group APCs to disperse. Elronda always beseeched her own children to "wait inside until Mummy comes". They in turn would much rather join in the mud fight at the end of each school day, but knew that doing so would mean being confined to their rooms for the evening without supper. The subtler fascinations of the adventure playground that their parents had provided for them in the rolling grounds of "d'Oriel Dale" would always carry the day.

On spotting her adversary, Juliana flashed her Ferrari's headlights at the vast bulk of Beth's damaged APC on the road ahead. (She never dared take her own life in her hands by letting her friend follow her.) That was the pre-arranged signal for Beth to slam on her brakes, then accelerate violently, causing a wheel spin that splashed the remaining mud from the APC's tyres along one side of the idling limousine. A protruding end of Beth's mangled bull bars just managed to scratch the Bentley's' front wing, with a pinging sound that echoed in Juliana's ears as she lowered her own window and stared exultantly into the occupant's fair skinned, fragile and furious face. She noticed that it seemed to be disfigured with several dull green blotches, and knew full well why.

Elronda was considered a great beauty, and also appeared regularly on the local HC channel as a fashion and style pundit, though she didn't as yet seem to court national exposure. Anticipating the likely public interest in "I'm a Home Shopper", the local channel had enlisted her punditry throughout the show's two weeks' duration; such was the renown of the many fashionable parties that were hosted throughout the summer months at d'Oriel Dale, to the gentrified disdain of its neighbours. Elronda, the biggest Foremost customer on the Hill, had throughout favoured Kelly Pilkington over Juliana; though as the likelihood grew of the latter winning, her criticisms became ever more subtle. Her conclusion after the upstart property developer's wife's triumph was that the show appeared to be moving down market so as to appeal to the type of viewer that it attracted; thereby inviting a future contract from her own favourite catalogue.

Juliana had learnt of this from her family immediately upon returning from the "I'm a Home Shopper" house for a few days' rest before the new contracts were sorted out. Once, when the courier had still been finding his way around Hogs Hill, he had brought one of Elronda's deliveries to the Goldendawn's house, since up there he had merely been told: "Oh, that big new vulgar monstrosity." Having discovered her rival's customer account details, Juliana would thereafter on occasion order things in Elronda's name to an alternative delivery address, then substitute them for various messy tricks that she would acquire from the joke shop in town and keep a stock of just for that purpose.

She knew that the courier worshipped the ground that Elronda walked upon, and so would give him the booby traps for on-forwarding, since he would if necessary camp outside her rivals' great iron security gates for hours at the end of his day just to catch a glimpse of her. Juliana had bid her elder son the previous evening to select an especially vile joke (a task at which he proved only too adept), then ride up the hill on his bike to deposit it in the cast iron mailbox besides the entry console outside d'Oriel Dale (a further task he had fulfilled with relish).

Juliana sniggered to herself for hours at the sight within the Bentley of her arch critic looking greener than all of the assembled main group Mums between them. When she got back to Great Donnington Manor, and after sending her energetic brood to the shower suite by the pool, to wash off the day's other little victory, she saw that Sir Sylvester was still droning on, on the HC screen that she had neglected to turn off. The mother recoiled at the sight of his cosmetically altered, bright yellow skin; and wondered whether Mrs Schwarzenorris might also set traps for her delivery man on Saturday mornings, just as snooty Sharon at the far end of the village did. Remembering that the person in question was a barrister, she concluded probably not, but shuddered again anyway.

The great statesman had effected the makeover some two years' previously, to celebrate winning a lifetime's achievement Golden Raspberry in the category of "Worst real-life person to be depicted as a cartoon character". Not appreciating Simpsons' movies had thereafter become an annihilation offence in the Grand Western Coalition's eyes, on a par with not speaking English or not liking burgers; and the wily old politician knew full well on which side his own bun was buttered.

Then the comms link rang and Juliana switched the HC off. "Hi, darlin'. James Lee asked me to call ya myself," intoned the cheeky cockney accent of the publicist Jack Gifford, that was well-known to the listener from a thousand news channel bulletins. "Ave I got some nicc little earners lined up fer you! Can me and Jimmy come raa'nd in the mornin'?" He presented a brief résumé of some of them, and his newest client's head began to swim.

Chapter 3

Juliana lay awake for most of that night, as she turned the past few weeks' events over and over in her mind and tried to somehow take in the myriad opportunities that Jack Gifford had outlined briefly to her. As Alex slept soundly by her side, she thought back to the many nights as a teenager that she had lain awake in the cramped, stuffy second bedroom of her parents' Donnington, determining to find a better life but wondering exactly how. Eventually she began to doze fitfully, but was roused at some time before 4am by the sound of Jimmy McGrouse's milk float negotiating its erratic way through the many gilt statues that lined Great Donnington Manor's long gravel drive.

"Oh my God," Juliana started awake. "I've forgotten to put his money out." Then she leapt out of bed and rushed downstairs. The Queen of the Cybermall distantly recalled the habitual bawling and cursing of George Oliver Scrote, the former warden at Cockscomb Park across town, and knew (like everyone else in her village) that it would be as nothing compared to the unsocial hours' hullabaloo if Jimmy the milkman should fail to find his week's pay on the doorstep at the appointed hour. She reached the door in the nick of time to prevent him from waking the children, not to mention half the neighbourhood.

The Goldendawns' village being in the same post code district as Hogs Hill, the Dairy Products Delivery Operatives Association had declared the area off limits some years previously, just as the postal workers' and most other trades unions had all done at some time or other. So in much the same way that the villagers were forced to make allowances for Janet Bates the child minder's eccentricities, so they had little choice but to accept the curious routine of the only non-union milkmen who were prepared to work the Hill.

Jimmy McGrouse, or "Too Much Grouse" as he was almost universally known locally (the exception being Snooty Sharon who simply called him 'that even more dreadful man'), awoke unfailingly at 2am each morning and would then set out to work at once. Never mind that deliveries would invariably be frozen on the doorstep in winter by the time their customers awoke, and curdled in summer; he and his cousin Jock Crabbie (who assisted Jimmy) always got around before even the earliest London commuters were up and about. Then the pair would head home to their council flat on The Lees estate across town, via its 24-hour multi-mart "Dellsey's", and spend the remainder of each day living up to their reputation; interrupted only by necessary visits to the chippy or the Chinese take away. Lots of people on The Lees lived like that.

The financing of this peculiar lifestyle relied upon the collection of a certain amount of cash each morning, since Dellsey's didn't encourage tick. Elronda d'Oriel and a majority of residents on the Hill had always been used to paying milkmen and such other trades people on Saturday mornings; but the only person aged under fifty who did so in the village was Snooty Sharon, since she herself had little else to do at that time. The last named had set every possible trap and complained endlessly to the non-union dairy, but nobody else wanted Jimmy and Jock's jobs. London commuters' wives never seemed to appreciate that. The majority of village families had therefore come to a collective arrangement whereby the continuity of the milkmens' service could at least be relied upon, since sufficient money would be left out for them on each weekday. Those few with electric gates had even given the dubious pair their entry codes.

Juliana opened her front door just as Jimmy raised his hand to smite it. Much as she had recoiled some twelve hours' previously at the sight on her HC screen of Sir Sylvester Schwarzenorris' cosmetically altered, bright yellow features; so she did now on beholding the milkman's pallid grey complexion, his bright red eyebrows and sharp little teeth. She also took in the livid red features of his cousin Jock, who was leering through the gap behind the milk float's cab. The tired, worried mother imagined momentarily that her adversary was raising a drain rod to strike her with, but Jimmy was merely placing three bottles of platinum top onto her doorstep. The Goldendawns only drank the best.

"I almost forgot about you, Mr McGrouse. Please don't wake the children," said Juliana, thrusting a little extra into his nicotine-stained hand.

"Nae bother, hen," came the reply, grey dust issuing as always from Jimmy's mouth and ears as he spoke. "Saw ye on the telly. Ah'l ne'er fergit thae minging look on tha' wee malkie Kelly's face, see you."

The milkman walked away, shooting a mischievous glance over his shoulder at the sleep deprived figure in the doorway; while his assistant on the back of the float gave a rousing thumb's up. The only person who had ever tipped them previously was Gina Day.

Juliana felt wider awake than ever now, and so sat down in front of the HC system and began to flick through the channels. Her attention was eventually arrested by a vehicle commercial. A top of the range Dreisler Buttkicker, the subtly branded American competitor to the Jitsuhishi Battlebus, was parked at a crazy angle on the pavement outside a beauty salon, its front wheels at eighty degrees to the wings. Inside were two beautiful little girls, who looked about two years apart in age, each with masses of elaborately coiffed blonde curls. They both tilted their heads back slightly and called in unison: "Mum!" Then there was a massive explosion, laying waste everything around the APC, but the vehicle itself was left unscathed and the little girls safe inside. Lastly, their mother walked up to the vehicle that towered above her and drove nonchalantly away.

"I didn't know Sam had gone into modelling," thought Juliana, recognising she and Beth's great friend from their teenaged years. "I'll have to give her a call." Then she thought: "Why does everything have to be so warlike these days? Doesn't anyone else like nice sports cars?" Eventually she nodded off, to be awoken a little later by Alex who was urging: "Come along, love. Get moving. Jack Gifford'll be here soon."

At around 11am, Juliana and Alex activated their electric gates and watched as a silver Rolls Royce made its way slowly up the driveway to their front door. A chauffeur stepped out and opened a rear passenger door from which emerged the sharp suited and trinket adorned figure of the renowned publicist. From the other side, the much more casually dressed, laid back persona of James Lee Patience seemed to half stumble out. He had in any case selected his *nom de guerre* as an irony, and couldn't be bothered to wait for the chauffeur to get around to his side, being less concerned with appearances than the Roller's owner.

"Allo' darlin'," said the publicist, stretching out an immaculately manicured hand, every finger of which seemed to sport chunky, nine-carat gold rings, in some of which large diamonds were set. "Jimmy here's told me all about ya. I 'ave to say you're even more allurin' in the flesh."

"Thank you, Mr Gifford. This is my husband, Alex," Juliana began.

"Pleased to meet ya, Al," Jack responded, stretching out his palm sized goldmine a second time. "Luv'ly spread ya got 'ere. I've got several meself."

"So have we," Alex retorted, feeling not entirely comfortable with the publicist's familiar tone towards his wife.

"Hi, Milady, remember me?" James Lee cut in, waving casually from slightly behind his co-conspirator.

"Of course," replied Juliana. "Would I ever forget? Got any parcels for me to sign for?"

"Not these days," came the reply. "You wait till you hear the package that Jack here's got lined up for you now."

They all went inside, and Jack Gifford proceeded to present many glamorous money making ventures, for each of which he would produce a contract from a large leather briefcase and ask Juliana to sign it. Sometimes as he did so, the pale, diffused sunlight that was shining through Great Donnington Manor's leaded glass windows would reflect off the diamonds in his chunky gold rings, casting little patterns on the ceiling or walls. "Can I read them first?" Juliana would enquire. "Just trust me, darlin'," always came the firm reply. James Lee would then nod over the publicist's shoulder, at which she signed anyway, knowing that she could at least trust him.

Lady Goldendawn wasn't quite sure whether she liked the famous publicist, wondering more than once who he rather uncomfortably reminded her of; but she nevertheless realised these were far too good opportunities to miss. Behind her, Alex was almost beginning to blink with a "tch-ching"-ing sound as he imagined being able to develop holiday apartment complexes abroad, hotels, shopping malls and entertainment complexes with the sums that Jack Gifford was discussing. He very soon began to nod in unison with James Lee, who as always seemed rather distracted and in a world half of his own. Juliana just assumed that her old friend was dreaming up his next blockbuster novel, or smash hit HC series after the unrivalled success of "I'm a Home Shopper", and the satirical social commentary "Builders' Wives."

Eventually the publicist finished, and after gathering up all the various contracts said that a limo would call for Juliana at 7am on Saturday morning, two days hence. The campaign was to begin with a grand launch at one of the smartest hotels in London, followed by major catalogue promotions in each of the West End's major department stores, at which Juliana would be present to autograph new subscribers' personal copies. Stretching out his gold encrusted palm two final times, the great man then strode back out to his Roller from the Goldendawn's hitherto exclusive realm, followed at a slight distance by the ever pensive James Lee Patience.

Saturday morning duly arrived, and shortly before the appointed hour a short procession could be seen moving slowly towards the far end of the village, past the invariably drawn bedroom curtains of its London commuters' homes and the giant APCs parked on the drives below. At the head was the milk float, since Jimmy and Jock would arrive on that side of the Hill later than usual each Saturday, having already had to gather all of their money up there from the end of its numerous long drives. Next in line was an old, unmarked white van, inside which the latest grey market moonlighter to be assigned to the post code district was searching for a house that some Foremost customer had insisted on giving a name to in a long numbered sequence.

The latter at least felt grateful that the milk float was proceeding so slowly in front of him, so that he himself couldn't be blamed by the three executive saloons that were flashing and hooting and revving their engines behind him. These were local commuters, heading into the office for their unnecessary Saturday morning stints, to create the right impression since that was what all their rivals on the promotion ladder also did. The milk float eventually pulled in by a large house in which all of the lights were blazing and a peevish figure was frantically polishing her windows from the inside. "Nae bee'un seen tae, as usual," Jimmy said over his shoulder to Jock, "Wud ye?" Jock leered back through the gap behind the cab, but both men knew that the drink had long since rendered such a possibility unlikely.

Jimmy placed two bottles of semi-slimmed and four yoghurt

pots on Snooty Sharon's doorstep, then searched all of the usual places in which she might have hidden his money. He found nothing and walked back around to the front of the house, where Sharon thrust a little brown envelope "oot the wundae".

"Sorry ah cannae oblige ye, lass," Jimmy muttered as he snatched it from her grasp. "Ah need to be gettin' hame."

"How dare you!" Sharon began, but then she saw the new courier approaching from behind the milkman and relished this unexpected opportunity to try to put somebody down. "About time too!" she pronounced in her shrillest tone. "I've been waiting for three days."

"Oh really! So how do you expect anyone to find an address like this?" bit back the courier, pointing to his crumpled manifest. "And if you've got some returns, why don't you just call me instead of that call centre in Rawalpindi?"

"I want to know that they'll send somebody. I'm the customer," Sharon insisted sniffily, then added: "They're by the back door."

The courier walked once around the house, then returned to Sharon's window and declared: "There isn't a back door."

"Then you'll just have to work out which one I mean, won't you," his customer replied. "I've got a big house and you haven't. So there!"

The irritated new courier stalked away empty handed, and Sharon rushed to pick up the comms link and complain to Rawalpindi (or Bombay or New Delhi, or wherever UK calls were being directed on that day), her tone becoming shriller and shriller as the operator failed to understand her. Most mail order catalogues had long since switched Sharon's accounts from their own couriers to the Royal Mail, and the workers at the sorting office in town all knew it. They would throw all her deliveries into a separate cage, then report them missing and take them home to their own wives and children, leaving Sharon to contest the claims. But Foremost still regarded such behaviour by its customers as being indicative of their upmarket status, and Snooty Sharon believed it too.

When the courier got back to his van, he beheld a tractor extracting two of the executive saloons from a ditch on the far side of the road, since all three had attempted to overtake at once when the milk float and van had pulled in. Both the losing drivers were frantically making calls on their mobiles and tapping palm tops by the road side, just in case any competitors' local commuters should pass by and see them. The milk float was still there, since on encountering any such little dramas on their travels, the ne'er do wells on board would love to jeer and cat call in their unintelligible accents until it was all over.

"Hasn'ae bin seen tae fer months," Jimmy called across to the departing courier. "Wud ye?"

"No!" the courier spat back, then climbed into his van and sped back towards town and his PAYE day shift. Lastly, the milkmen themselves tired of goading the farmer on his tractor, and made their way back to The Lees.

Elsewhere in the village, the school caretaker was getting out his heavy iron roller to give the morass by the gates its weekly flattening, and two ladies in nurses' uniform could be seen checking the opening times on the off licence door. Just up on the Hill, an early party from the riding school was passing the great iron gates of d'Oriel Dale; whilst on the Town side the effigy on the gibbet at the head of the Days' long drive, that served as a warning to all roaming salesmen, swung gently in the early morning breeze. Back at Great Donnington Manor, a platinum-plated stretched limo was drawing up to collect Lady Goldendawn and whisk her off to London.

The limo disgorged two of the burliest minders from Rick Nicey's Heavy Hire Agency in town, one of whom walked up to the Manor's front entrance, while the second held open a car door for its departing mistress. Within the confines of the limo, three of Jack Gifford's PRs were keeping up an appearance of frenetic activity on the in-vehicle communication system and their state-of-the-art palm top computers. Then the Queen of the Cybermall herself emerged into the morning light, kissed each of her husband and children in turn, and was whisked away from her village home to embark upon a 24/7 round of untold fame and fortune that seemed set to change their lives forever.

Chapter 4

The next nine months of Juliana's life passed as a continuous social whirl. There were countless promotions to attend in High Street stores across the length and breadth of the southern half of England, new fashion range premieres in the smartest London venues and major department stores, personal appearances at sporting and social events, photo-shoots for magazine and poster advertising campaigns, merchandise launches, HC advertisement shoots, more HC appearances on quiz and chat shows; even cameos in some soap operas. All of the participating "I'm a Home Shopper" catalogues experienced healthy turnover increases, but still none of them outsold Foremost which remained the clear market leader.

Foremost's PRs rightly calculated the Queen of the Cybermall's shelf-life to be no longer than the interval before the show's next series, or less if they could themselves find a way to derail the phenomenon in the meantime. They as always played upon the "up market" affectations of that portion of their customer base that believed in their own PR, and so enlisted the bruised Kelly Pilkington as their figurehead. Foremost initially reasoned that the seasoned celebrity status of an enduring national sporting icon's wife must endure over the short term phenomenon of the upstart HC reality show winner. But Kelly had taken her defeat at Juliana's hands very much to heart, and as the war of words in the tabloids continued, her behaviour became progressively more erratic and unpredictable.

Five months into the "I'm a Home Shopper" campaign, Foremost therefore launched Elronda d'Oriel as a second string to their own bow. The last named, having been concerned that her deadly rival's burgeoning if temporary fame should not be allowed to undermine her own reputation locally, had begun to seek national exposure for herself. She implored her husband, Armando to use his extensive influence in the fashion and beauty businesses to secure her the contract with Foremost that she so desired.

Foremost were very impressed with the presentation from Armando's PRs, that highlighted his wife's sophisticated punditry on the local HC channel, her great natural beauty and his own widespread association with all things representing style and good taste.

Kelly and Elronda were seen to work well together at first, but being very aware of the deepening fragility of Kelly's state of mind, the cuckoo in the nest progressively engaged all of her own subtlest arts to push the senior partner over the edge, just as Juliana had outwitted her in the original HC show. Kelly herself could never be described as a particularly subtle personality of course, and as it transpired could easily be undone by clever tactics from others. The former pop star was simply not capable of adjusting to a lower degree of public adulation than she had always been used to.

Fuelled in part by Jack Gifford's PRs, the exchanges between Kelly and Juliana in the red tops seemed to become more acrimonious by the day, until one morning their headlines all screamed the hitherto unthinkable: TOMMY AND KELLY TO SPLIT. The national icon's days as an A-list celebrity were over, and Foremost dropped her; Elronda becoming their sole standard bearer while they waited to see who would be cast in the reality HC show's next series. The mistress of d'Oriel Dale had as always displayed her infuriating knack of keeping one step ahead of the game, since with Kelly's removal from the equation public interest in the "Queen of the Cybermall" phenomenon immediately began to wane.

After all, neither Juliana or Elronda had ever been pop stars, nor their husbands sporting icons; and the absence of any scandal concerning either woman's life meant the tabloids quickly lost interest. Rival celebrities' agents all upped their clients' own scandal factors to regain the column inches. Attendances at "I'm a Home Shopper" promotions and participating catalogues' turnovers were both seen to have peaked; and Foremost secretly paid Armando d'Oriel a substantial sum in return for his brilliant strategy that had upheld their market dominance whilst also maintaining his adored wife's public face. Foremost didn't pay their delivery sub-contractors' couriers any extra, naturally enough.

In the meantime, back at Great Donnington Manor, Alex had

put most of his previous business interests on hold, while his wife amassed the millions that would secure their immediate futures. He still collected the rent, maintained their many let properties, and dealt with his tenants' moans and groans; but devoted more and more time to managing and investing the substantial sums that Juliana's contracts with Jack Gifford were bringing in. He had concluded that despite the publicist's "sign here, just trust me darlin'" approach, and his diamond rings that had cast such unsettling little patterns onto their walls and ceilings, they were nevertheless being fairly dealt with. He likewise felt thankful that Juliana had so captivated the enigmatic James Lee Patience in her youth.

Alex felt less comfortable about Jack Gifford's obvious and all too pervasive influence, and that of the tabloid ghost writers and showbiz PRs that his wife was now mixing with, upon the good natured and unaffected person that he had married aged eighteen after giving all the right answers on her detailed questionnaire. His wife's natural competitive streak, he thought was being honed at the expense of those other good qualities, and especially in relation to the other players in the drama. The intrusions into their privacy at the Manor were a further bugbear, though Alex realised this was a natural downside to the rewards of fame and fortune that they would have to put up with.

The sight-seers and souvenir hunters who would creep around the Goldendawn's marital home at all hours of the day and night, quickly became an intolerable nuisance. Alex was forced to build an unsightly security fence around their property, and hire two heavies on a permanent basis from Rick Nicey's agency in town to deter unwanted visitors. The property developer and security agent met a few times through their dealings and got on well, in part because the latter also felt that he had reached a crossroads in his business life.

Rick was by far the county's foremost provider of heavies for night clubs, sporting and social events and celebrity protection assignments. Visiting high-profiles from London, not least amongst them Jack Gifford, would always call upon Rick for his "gentlemen minders" who were all selected for being as adept with the charm offensive as they were with the baseball bat. The local security agent steered clear of the murkier worlds of debt collection or score settling heavies, but knew full well how to get into that side of things if he wanted to. But his business now largely ran itself, and his general manager took care of most of its day to day formalities.

Rick preferred to work from home, so as to minimise his overheads and so finance his passion for the latest and most expensive Mercedes cars. He still did his own invoicing and accounts, and sent in the heavies himself if people didn't pay him (rarely more than once); but sometimes it seemed to Rick that he spent most of his day answering the door to the constantly calling couriers who brought his wife's catalogue shopping, since Jenny Nicey was one of the biggest orderers in town.

Just like Alex, immediately prior to Juliana's current fame, Rick Nicey was casting his nets more widely for challenging new business opportunities. What he really wanted to get into were the higher profile markets tied up with the many targets - such as airports, hotels, public transport networks and buildings of high office - that the government constantly counselled were under the threat of attack from funny foreigners. But there were already established and highly successful operators in those areas, so Rick would need to carefully select the opportunities to gain a toehold in those lucrative fields.

When he wasn't attending to his temporarily scaled-down business interests, the Queen of the Cybermall's other half doubled as a part-time house husband, since he appreciated that Juliana must necessarily be away from home through much of her reign. Being a man, Alex managed to largely disregard the gossip at the school gates and the rivalries between the various grades of vehicle owner. The assembled protagonists in turn mostly ignored him, though some of the car drivers might have a few words now and again and ask after his wife. He similarly managed to keep their children out of the daily mud fight for much of the time. In any case, it seemed to Alex that most of the talk seemed to be about somebody called Sharon and not Juliana, at which he also felt relieved.

Elronda d'Oriel had not been the only woman locally whose subsequent lifestyle had been altered by Juliana's own success. Whereas most of the London commuters' wives had managed to move on from their initial envy, since the whole nation was after all being fed a perpetual Queen of the Cybermall diet that was difficult to ignore, Snooty Sharon had at once become gripped by an all consuming resentment. At the thought of the fame and fortune that had befallen her teenaged peers' former scapegoat – now the Ferrari driver at her own childrens' school gates who seemingly always got the better of her latter day put downs – the neglected wife felt a deep mortification that gnawed at her very soul and refused to let go.

Sharon couldn't help but contrast Juliana's glamorous celebrity schedule with her own daily round of keeping house and raising children without ever so much as a supportive word, or even less a 'kind deed' from her absent husband. She therefore resolved once and for all to broaden her horizons, much as Juliana had done as a teenager, and break free of her indifferent spouse's yoke. If she was honest with herself, Sharon would admit that most of the tradesmen that she so unrelentingly baited also seemed to rise above her various put downs with ease. So she further resolved to be more nice to them in future, particularly since in secret she thought the new courier to be rather dishy in a rough sort of way, and certainly a great improvement on "that awful man who lived in the caravan".

One fateful Friday night, nine months into the Queen of the Cybermall's reign, the campaign reached crisis point. Not one HC fashion or style guru attended what was intended to be a make or break new range preview, while most of the women's and teenaged magazines sent only junior reporters, some with little or no knowledge of their subject. But, unbeknown at that point to the "I'm a Home Shopper" winner herself, some national newsprints were running extensive picture features on the newly launched "Elronda's Guide to Good Taste in Home Furnishing" in that weekend's colour supplements; mainly featuring Foremost product lines of course.

Travelling home early that Saturday morning, a restless and anxious Juliana was turning over in her mind how Jack Gifford's PR's had all seemed to be keeping up an even more frenetic front of hyperactivity than ever as they strode excitedly around the launch venue shouting into their mobiles and almost assaulting their palm tops. Then they had all disappeared into a meeting, still gushing as always in their habitual marketing-speak. Lady

Goldendawn herself had been left to kill the wee small hours in the Ritz's coffee shop, fielding the attentions of its many jet-lagged American and Oriental businessmen, until eventually the welcome sight of the platinum-plated stretched limo had drawn up to take her home. The passenger had never had the vehicle all to herself before, and as it headed out of London she began to feel uncomfortably alone.

At around 7am, the limousine sped into the Goldendawn's home village from the far end. The weather forecast had been of storms, and the first peals of thunder were beginning to be audible in the distance away to the west. "Oh, hello. Sharon's got a new Dreisler," Juliana observed sleepily, before starting fully awake on noting the old, unmarked van that was parked beside the APC for anyone to see, and that the lights in the house were all switched off. "Well I never! Who would have thought it?" the Queen of the Cybermall smiled to herself; not realising that her recent absence from village society had rendered her possibly the only person other than Sharon's own husband who did not know that the workaholic stockbroker's wife was now taking regular comfort with the new courier.

But the passenger in the limo quickly thought also of how little she was seeing of her own family, and how she always seemed to feel so very tired these days. Then she wished more than ever to get home. The worrying split that Alex had noted in her personality had also been tugging from both sides at Juliana for some time. The wife and mother in her was almost looking forward to the end of her reign, a return to normality and a still better life from the fortune that the fame had generated. But the competitive, sharply honed persona that Jack Gifford and his showbiz PRs had so adroitly shaped as a foil to the now much troubled Kelly Pilkington, nevertheless felt reluctant to give it all up.

A little louder rumble of thunder seemed to half echo off the Hill on one side of the road, as the limousine passed the familiar sight of the milk float that was moving very slowly in the opposite direction; trailed as always on Saturday mornings by its small procession of hooting, flashing, revving executive saloons. Juliana thought this strange apparition from The Lees seemed to be almost completely enshrouded in grey dust, as its occupants engaged in animated discourse about something or another in their odd, unintelligible accents; in between bouts of shouting and gesticulating towards the frustrated local commuters that they prevented from passing them by hugging the centre of the road.

Another faint thunderclap sounded momentarily, then the chauffeur turned off the road and summoned Rick Nicey's two resident gentlemen heavies to activate the security gates of Great Donnington Manor. "You didn't tell me about Sharon," Juliana yawned as she walked back into her marital abode.

"What, that one they all talk about at the school gates? What about her then?" enquired Alex, who was preparing a mega breakfast fry-up in the kitchen for the minders at the gates, with rather smaller portions for their own family.

"Oh nothing," replied his exhausted wife, flopping into a convenient chair.

"Er, are you forgetting anything?" the male partner enquired, standing invitingly in his apron before the sizzling range, with his arms spread wide.

Juliana thought for a second then jumped back up again. "Sorry!" she declared, kissing her husband and giving him an extra big, long hug. "God, I feel so tired." Then, as a slightly softer growl of distant thunder echoed briefly around the Manor, she went off to find and cuddle their children.

Shortly after lunch-time, Juliana having grabbed some welcome sleep in the interval, Jack Gifford called to say the "Queen of the Cybermall" promotion was being wound up. The sky outside was now almost black as the storm clouds prepared to unleash their burden, and the indignant Juliana demanded to know why she was being dropped.

"The cat'logs all think the punters 'ave lost int'rest naa that Kelly's in the Rect'ry Clink, and the only ones 'oo still care 'ave got more int'rested in Elronda than they are in you," came the all too direct reply. "And ya know 'oo she works fer. Ya saw it yerself last night darlin', no-one important turned up. That's showbiz!"

The "I'm a Home Shopper" producers were beginning to cast the show's next series, and the participating catalogues were all demanding the most scandal-prone possible line-up of pop stars, glamour models, soap actresses and other tabloid self-publicists who could hold the public's attention for a full twelve months.

"Can't we get the punters back on our side?" Juliana enquired, rather naively.

"Ya cud be pictured leavin' a footie player's 'ouse at 7am," the publicist mused. "Delroy Tork's agent called me just yest'day. That model 'e's bin 'umpin's gone back to 'er toy boy. Might just giv' us anuther cup'la weeks on the Cybermall thing!"

"No way!" cut in Alex, on his remote comms link.

"Oh, 'allo Al... luv'ly loyal wife ya got there," the great publicist retorted, rather sarcastically. "Trubble is they don't sell newsprints!"

From high above Great Donnington Manor a lightening bolt struck one of the gilt statues along the drive, and the pregnant skies began to release cascades of storm water. The gentleman heavies sheltering in its gatehouse cast their eyes about them uneasily, as they imagined the sound of long lost curses and expletives blowing off the Hill; then a manhole cover burst open. Juliana herself briefly sensed an eerie childhood memory of drains backing up and glanced uneasily towards the downstairs loo.

"Mind you, I 'ave to say that Elronda's one gorgeous, smart cookie," Jack Gifford added.

"So am I!" Juliana almost screamed into her comms link.

"Yeah, I know ya are," the publicist replied. "But it's a fickle public aa't there. Look, I'll come back to ya if I get somethin' fresh, OK?"

Shuddering slightly as she always did at the sound of her own personal "F-word", but more so in these particular circumstances, Lady Goldendawn threw her comms link to the floor. "That woman!" she exclaimed, as another thunderclap resounded in the skies overhead. A second lightening bolt had just struck the great gates of d'Oriel Dale, freeing its cast-iron mailbox that seemed to half make a cackling sound as it tumbled carelessly downhill towards the village below, startling a line of nervous ponies whose young mounts were coaxing them back towards the riding school.

"He's right ya know," said Alex, lowering his remote comms link and trying as best he could to select his words carefully; faced as he was by an adversary whose countenance seemed to almost match the raging storm outside. "Look ... you've had a good innings, and we've made three and a half mill from it ... And that Elronda's ..."

"What?" demanded his wounded wife, her face blackening

further. "What is she? Don't you dare say it!"

But the male partner simply protested: "… bound to have to make way for someone else before long. Blimey, love! What did you think I was going to say? … What's happening to you?"

"Oh, I'm sorry! This has all got me so wound up," Juliana conceded.

Then Lord Goldendawn gathered up his Lady in his arms: "Look, it'll soon be the school holidays," he coaxed. "Let's take the kids and go all round the holiday homes. Then we'll think up how to spend all that lovely loot … we don't need 'em, eh?"

"No, course!" came the reply.

"Ya don't sound too sure?"

"Course not, I'm a celebrity!"

"Love ya."

"Love you too."

Then Juliana noticed a small package lying on the coffee table. "What's that?" she asked.

"Oh, the courier brought it yesterday," her husband replied. "Seemed to have a big smile on his face … dunno why."

"It must be that new mobile I ordered," reasoned Juliana, tugging carelessly on the package's sealing strip. Then: "Aagh!!! … Yeuk!! … It taste's foul! … What a stink! … Oh my God, it's all over the walls … and the ceiling, and the new suite!! … The bitch!!! … Are you laughing at me? … You're not laughing are you Alex Goldendawn?"

"Course not, love!"

"You just get that cleaned up, d'you hear! … Aagh!!! … That woman!! Yee…euk!!!" The retiring Queen of the Cybermall stalked off towards the shower suite, while the thunderstorm rumbled on outside. Then Alex searched the Trigital Pages on his mobile comms link, and found the heading "Chemical Spill Specialists – Domestic".

"Ah! Sandy's Plagues and Stinks Solutions, that should see to it," he decided. Fortunately, Sandy's wife Mandy was not for once on the customer hotline to Foremost (being one of town's biggest orderers), and Alex got straight through. Sandy said he'd have someone out within the hour, or even sooner should the storm subside.

Chapter 5

The Queen of the Cybermall's reign had been followed avidly throughout its ascent and eclipse by Emlyn, son of William, on the several, high-end, wall-sized home cinema screens of Dellsey Manor; at two counties' distance from the Goldendawns' own village. The heir to the family fortune at that time when the teenaged Juliana had become a national heroine through laying bare his father's people trafficking empire, entertained an antipathy towards our heroine that might possibly be described as "hatred", were it not for the younger Dellsey's ultimately cold, calculating and ultra-logical character.

For several years, Emlyn had consistently been listed amongst the country's wealthiest residents. He invariably finished ahead of the old money figures such as the Dukes of Westminster, Cornwall, Cumberland and even Old Tork; but likewise some way behind the succession of foreign émigrés who always seemed to claim, then as quickly relinquish the top spots. But mud stuck, and whenever he periodically made the news through some clever technological innovation or audacious takeover bid, the tabloids would always tag him "Emlyn the Gremlin". Even the broadsheet newsprints would attach the label "son of the notorious people trafficker", or such like, unfailingly on these occasions. And if the red tops reported Emlyn's wife Greta's occasional incursions onto the London social scene, they would dub her "Gremlineta".

When the infamous child murderer Stanley Brooke had been released on parole a few years' previously, the massed media corps had immediately camped outside the great iron gates of Dellsey Manor; from where morning and nightly bulletins were broadcast speculating as to the national hate figure's most likely whereabouts; conveniently just at the start of the school summer holidays. Baying mobs of vigilantes from all of the south of England's worst housing estates inevitably followed. This was hardly good for business since "Dellsey's *Fresh* 24-hour Multimarts" were located in all of those estates' run down local shopping centres.

Thankfully, most of these local communities' concerned parents' own dependencies, outside of the very early shifts when they might actually work, nevertheless ensured a continuity of custom. Stanley was eventually traced to a secure police station in the west of England, to which both the media ranks and the attendant mobs likewise dispersed. The family name had nevertheless been besmirched anew, and its current head determined as never before to one day wreak a fitting vengeance on the perpetrator of so many slights to his forbears' honour.

The family businesses had grown in value many fold under the stewardship of the management companies appointed by Emlyn's mother, now the Dowager Dellsey. On assuming control of them, the adored only son had sold off his late father's more "gentrified" concerns such as farming and forestry, and invested heavily and with great success in high technology. The Dellsey Housing Corporation, the Dellsey International Labour Corporation, and the Dellseys multimart chain all remained in the hands of appointed management companies, under the Gremlin's strategic direction.

Though he displayed all of the elder Dellsey's insatiable greed, avarice, bullying nature and innate cruelty; Emlyn certainly did not share the former's "gentrified disdain" of technology, being all too aware of the part that affectation had played in his father's eventual downfall. The son had excelled in science and electronics at both school and university and went on to become one of the country's leading young technology sector entrepreneurs, patenting numerous clever tricks some of which had become indispensable everyday aids to millions of consumers. Then he turned his attention to the development of rather more clandestine and fiendish technologies in the wider, war-ravaged world.

As he entered his thirties, "Son of Dellsey", as he was still called by the native minority that still inhabited the family housing corporation's many park home estates, headed a secretive, global technology empire that masterfully exploited the international order of the 2020s. Over the first two decades of the 21st century, the world had pretty much separated itself into clearly defined zones. On opposite sides of the planet, the Grand Western and Oriental zones generated all of the wealth and developed most of the clever technology. Between the two lay the Funny Foreign zone, in which the impoverished locals had the hell bombed out of them by the Grand Western Coalition, when they weren't busy killing one another themselves. On the southern fringes, in the Antipodean and Latino zones, people still carried on partying much as they had always done. Nobody knew for sure what went on in the Siberian zone of the far north, though the occasional emergence in western society of mysterious figures loosely termed "Russian billionaires" suggested fortunes could be made there by those in the know.

The Grand Western zone comprised America, it's offshore subsidiary and loyal servant Britain, and the United States of Europe. But whereas British governments always backed their trans-Atlantic masters' FuFo zone adventures to the hilt, their wilier USE peers would always prefer to nod and agree and make all the right noises without actually getting over involved. American and hence most British industries largely ignored their Oriental counterparts due to America's (and so Britain's) traditional aversion to all things "not invented here." That in turn suited the Oriental zone's legions of inscrutable businessmen, since they could develop all the cleverest tricks and most fiendish devices themselves then export them to the other zones, and especially the Funny Foreign one behind the Grand Western Coalition's back.

Emlyn Dellsey had become something of an exception amongst western technology entrepreneurs, having fairly early in his career moved his own research, development and manufacturing functions into partnerships with the most inscrutable of all Oriental high-tech enterprises. This maximised his scope for developing the endless stream of clever tricks and fiendish devices that his immense natural talent for such things so consistently generated, without anyone else in the West knowing about it. Hence when the Funny Foreigners eventually won the war, through the technology that would be developed and supplied by Emlyn's Oriental associates, the Gremlin would achieve his grand vision of world domination. That ultimate goal was still some years in the future, however.

Back at Dellsey Manor, Emlyn switched off the home cinema system on learning that the Queen of the Cybermall's reign had prematurely imploded, and picked up a second device that looked very similar to the HC remote control. He pressed a button and two doors on the opposite wall slid apart. Then he pressed another and from within the recess emerged Mark, the elder Dellsey's former kitchen boy and eventual assassin, who was now one of the son's most lethal cyborg captains.

"Who do you serve?" the Gremlin enquired.

"I serve only you master," replied the automaton, as the figure before it pressed more buttons that sent it into a series of painful contortions.

"And who will you bring me today?"

"Any enemy that you desire, master."

One of Emlyn's cleverest achievements had been to escape any implication concerning the decease or disappearance of so many business rivals or people who had crossed him in one way or another over the previous five or so years. A small number had simply been found dead in circumstances that would always be attributed to natural or accidental causes. Juliana's former mentor Bryony the Chair for instance had been discovered one morning in her caravan besides the similarly expired form of her loyal life partner Bryony the Treasurer; but the inquest concluded that the deaths were due to a carbon monoxide leak. Despite the Caravans and Park Homes Reform Act of 2005, safety standards were still considered to be less than ideal in such places.

Certain members of the Parliamentary Sub-committee that had drafted the bill, the then National Caravaners Protection Association, and various other public servants who had investigated the late William Dellsey's affairs were likewise despatched. But no wrong doing was ever proven, such was the convincing lack of evidence of foul play in all these cases. Some of the worst offenders in Emlyn's eyes were confined to the dungeons below Dellsey Manor itself, where its master would enjoy a little sport with them in its torture chambers whenever the mood seized him, which was frequently.

But as the electronics genius had advanced his pioneering knowledge of cyborg development in collaboration with his inscrutable Oriental associates, he would simply kidnap anyone who annoyed him and then ship them out to his secret Siberian production facility. There the miscreants would be converted into mindless automatons who did only their master's bidding, and cloned in the required quantities. On their return, the cyborg stocks would be put into hibernation mode and stored in hidden cellars beneath the Dellseys multimarts on the south of England's worst housing estates, though a certain number were kept at Dellsey Manor itself. From these locations they would be despatched whenever they were required to carry out Emlyn's most deadly and sinister bidding, whatsoever that might be.

The captains were all selected from the most lengthily confined inmates of Dellsey Manor's vile dungeons. Once these unfortunates had been suitably desensitised by the brutality they either witnessed or suffered themselves at the Gremlin's hands, they would be ripe for the special programming that would enable them to lead their lesser cyborg peers. Mark had been apprehended some years previously, very early one morning in a Dellseys multimart, having failed to adjust to life in the outside world after abandoning his building construction course. As one of the longest enduring and most brutalised recipients of the Gremlin's wrath, he had eventually been turned into possibly the most effective cyborg captain of all, almost a commander though of course he wasn't actually in command of anything.

Emlyn's ultimate goal was to create a vast cyborg army of funny foreigners from that zone's unfathomable resource of brutalised, de-sensitised young men who knew of no way of life but war and killing, and were unsuited to any other livelihood. Then he would set about realising his grand world vision, but that was still some years in the future since cyborg research and development would have to advance considerably before he and his inscrutable Oriental associates could consider taking on the military might of the Grand Western Coalition. The master of Dellsey Manor picked up another remote and a large plasma screen lowered itself from a slot in the ceiling before flickering into life. Then a hefty keypad console rose from the floor in front of him.

File after file on people the Gremlin considered to have crossed him proceeded to appear on the screen. Several other cyborg captains had by now made their way from the dungeons and into this control centre, and their master interrogated them in turn over their progress in bringing these various targets to him. Then he issued the captains with new orders and sent them back out to raise their subordinates from the multimart cellars and carry out his dark and dangerous business wherever in the world it might take them.

When he was quite alone again, Emlyn brought onto the screen an old TV broadcast from 2004 in which a bright and pretty sixteen year old girl was being interviewed outside the great iron gates of the revered ancestral pile in which he now sat. Then he idly flicked through various more recent images of the same person in womanhood, many of them taken from recent tabloid newsprints. He curled his lip sneeringly as he did so, to reveal just a hint of his growing collection of platinum fillings, had there been anyone else in the room to see them. Of all his many perceived enemies, the Gremlin was saving up Lady Juliana Goldendawn for last, and her planned unspeakable fate that he would constantly refine in the most evil recesses of his clinical mind would be his *piece de resistance*, to be supplanted only by his grand world vision itself.

Emlyn Dellsey's extensive interest in cyborg development was by no-means the only fiendish, world threatening technology that he and his inscrutable Oriental associates were working day and night to perfect. Whenever the Grand Western Coalition bombed the hell out of new FuFo zone countries, for offences such as setting import quotas on Simpsons TVDs or banning the wearing of baseball caps in schools, it would always claim that the FuFos were building naughty, illegal bombs of their own; or developing creepy plagues and messy stinks with which to booby trap western politicians who might have annoyed them.

But once those countries had been pummelled into compliance, the Coalition would become so busily preoccupied with plundering their natural resources and allocating "redevelopment contracts" to American multinationals, to build fast food outlets or new call centres to serve Western service industries, that they would never find the time to actually locate the offending weaponry. If they did occasionally look for the bombs, plagues and stinks, the FuFos would by then invariably have hidden them all over again where they couldn't be found.

Emlyn Dellsey knew exactly where all the bombs were, not to mention the creepy plagues and messy stinks. So he should, because early in the global conflict his own inscrutable Oriental associates had taken control of the moving and hiding process; after which they themselves began to develop the considerably more lethal bombs, plagues and stinks with which they eventually planned to win the war through their FuFo proxies. The Gremlin's substantial personal input had contributed to the perfection of new "Tricron" bombs that had the destructive capacity of older nuclear technologies but without emitting harmful radiation. The time to conduct limited tests of these devices, that were being manufactured in volume in hidden factories of the Arctic tundra, was drawing nigh; as America's offshore subsidiary and loyal servant Britain was soon to discover.

The Dellseys multimart chain provided a very effective channel through which Emlyn could import, re-export and stockpile those quantities of clever tricks and fiendish devices that might be required for whatever purpose. Since the working locals only frequented the convenience stores during the early morning rush hour, and would generally not feel inclined to walk back at those later times of day whenever hunger struck, the estates' chippies and assorted other takeaways would invariably operate farther out from the long outmoded local shopping centres; and offer home delivery services to anyone who might not by then be able to walk at all.

So for the rest of the day, nobody really paid much regard to what went on in the centres, since the trickle of state pensioners that might call at odd times were after a lifetime in these environments not generally capable of noticing much at all. The multimarts had therefore become the only surviving business there, and Dellseys would buy up all the other empty shop units and convert them into secure lock-ups. The multimart delivery trucks, that came and went in their familiar "Dellseys *Fresh*" livery were hardly likely to attract unwanted attention.

The exception was benefit day, a weekly ritual that was always played out in precisely the same way each Friday. The denizens of these estates liked to make up names for their children and spell them in any way that they liked; or else name them after the places where they had been conceived, after the fashion that had emerged at the turn of the century but which by now survived nowhere else. As the morning rush hour subsided on benefit days, legions of late-teenaged Cuylees, Joolyas, Raychulls, Bekas, Wotfuds, Inadich's and Effnos would begin to assemble in long queues at the multimart doors.

The managers would summon two or three cyborgs from the cellars to man the entrances and shout "Far Queue!" at anyone who attempted to effect a premature entry or walk up the line. "Far queue an' all, mate!" an occasional, particularly belligerent offender might dare to spit back, before being manhandled to the back of the line. The air outside would turn progressively more blue as the young estate Mums failed to supervise their many unstimulated yet hyperactive little charges, who would run aimlessly and noisily around any colourful local characters who might already be lying comatose upon the pavement. The melee would be viewed from particular corners by small loitering groups of street drinkers, who liked to jeer and catcall the whole while in their incoherent slurred tones.

At 9am when the multimarts' sub-post office counters opened, the claimants would begin to make their slow progress forward. On receiving their cash, each would walk over to a table at which the various runners for the estates' money lenders were all seated. After entering the repayments into their separate books, these agents would write out a chit for the coming week's advance and the recipients would walk around the store. First port of call was usually the tobacco kiosk, since most would by now be desperate for a puff. Next they would browse the shelves and select from the ranges of unhealthy processed foodstuffs that the big supermarkets refused to stock, but which Dellseys purchased in bulk at very low rates then sold on at the highest possible margins. Last of all they would queue at the off licence counter for their partners' supplies of super strength, since those were the heaviest items to carry.

The cyborgs guarding the exit door allowed no-one to leave until the full value of their chits had been accrued. After the last of the long lines of claimants had filed through the store, the managers would calculate their percentage from the recovered chits and retrieve it from the runners, on pain of the Gremlin's wrath. This mutually beneficial arrangement ensured that both parties' business was permanently assured, given the never changing cycle of everyday life on the bad estates. If any overly ambitious local money lender occasionally attempted to disturb the system to his own advantage, he would simply disappear just like anyone else who crossed Emlyn Dellsey.

Benefit days were the only time that the law enforcement agencies might observe the multimarts' activities, since they could sometimes afford an opportunity to arrest some local miscreant or another. All the rest of the while, they too paid little attention to what was going on there. So in the summer of 2022, after the Goldendawns had retired to their holiday homes abroad as the school holidays began, the unusual build-up of incoming and outgoing delivery traffic at the local shopping centres on The Lees and its bad estate counterparts across the southern half of England, went largely unnoticed.

Chapter 6

One Tuesday morning towards the end of summer, at around 7.30am soon after the local night shifts had changed, the northern half of England became the scene for simultaneous, co-ordinated and unprecedented attacks that razed vast swathes of inner city housing into oblivion. The British government and its Grand Coalition masters alike were totally mystified as to what unknown technology could have caused such wide scale destruction, and how such a brilliantly conceived and devastatingly executed assault could have been set in place and then mounted behind their own so complacent backs. The targets' seeming lack of strategic importance was a further puzzle, though the government was naturally very relieved that it was the industrialised north rather than the affluent south that had been hit.

In the event, large numbers of funny foreign migrant workers had simply walked away from their factories when the night shifts ended, and at a pre-agreed time set off Dellseys-issue Tricron bombs that had reduced everything within a given radius to little piles of grey dust. Millions of their peers had perished, but the perpetrators had thought nothing of such killing since it was what everyone back home had always done, just like their forebears and their forebears before them. One of the great paradoxes of Coalition policy had always been that whereas funny foreign culture was simply not to be tolerated in its native regions of the world, the migrant denizens that nevertheless flocked to the West in search of a better livelihood were more than welcome to do all of the dirty jobs in Britain and America. The thought that these emigrés might one day be so bold as to bite the hand that feeds had simply never occurred in the corridors of high office.

Like his father, the younger Dellsey was still a major player in the migrant labour market, though he had always carefully steered clear of the greyer areas that had brought about his sire's ultimate downfall. The placing and priming through the Dellsey International Labour Corporation of so many willing martyrs, in locations that could collectively bring about the total razing of the target housing areas whist leaving the factories that they served mostly intact; and their subsequent arming with the required quantities of Tricron bombs via the Dellseys multimart distribution chain, was Emlyn the Gremlin's greatest feat of strategic planning to date. Both he, and the inscrutable Oriental associates who had backed him at every stage, considered the beta-testing of their apocalyptic yet radiation free technology to have been an unqualified success.

The Tricron devices came in various sizes, and stockpiles of all of them had been imported and then stored in the shopping centre lock-ups on the southern bad estates, before being redistributed to the FuFo carriers across the country's north. Tricron pellets, the smallest devices, all came wrapped in silver foil and packed into Dellseys own brand, mint crisp chocolate boxes. The mid-range pocket propelled grenades (or PPGs) were likewise disguised as chocolate oranges; while the full-scale Tricron bombs themselves passed for tins of red kidney beans, all with ring pulls that acted as their detonators. The ring pulls also distinguished the hidden bombs from the standard issue Dellseys red kidney beans that could be placed on the multimart shelves.

"Blimey, love!" declared Alex, as the Goldendawns followed the unfolding drama on the HC at their holiday home on the Algarve. "That's an awful lot of houses that'll have to be rebuilt."

"Oh Alex, how could you?" his wife retorted. "What about all those people who've died?"

"Aah, they're only foreigners, aren't they."

"Honestly! You sound just like that barking Schwarzee. What about their families back home?"

"Naah, there's plenty more where they come from who want to come over here. Things'll soon get back to normal."

"I don't believe I'm hearing this!" … and such like.

Over the first two decades of the third millennium, the historic "north-south divide" of the later 20th century had evolved into a virtually "two-tier Britain" as members of his majesty's opposition, the rebranded Unelectable Alternatives Party, would constantly carp on without ever actually going up north to take a look themselves. Successive governments had steadfastly resisted Britain's entry into the United States of Europe, where living standards were higher and the cost of living likewise much lower. This stance had always served to preserve the essential feudal character of British society, that forever safeguarded the interests of the "haves" at the expense of the "have nots"; and hence ensured the Ruling Party's repeated re-election.

So throughout the 21st century's second decade, skilled working labour had all headed off to sunnier climes, while their unskilled counterparts mostly succumbed to the aforementioned daily and weekly cycles of the bad estates. The management ranks had likewise migrated south, on being faced with drying pools of exploitable "human resource" in their former northern domains. By the time of this drama, the urban areas between the affluent south and the great distilleries, internationally renowned golf courses and stunning if rain-soaked provincial parks of Chilly Jockoland, had become a vast, southern administered industrial belt where all the "dirty industry" was concentrated.

Other than the regularly commuting factory managers and local authority administrators, the only time most southern Brits might occasionally venture north was on corporate hospitality outings to the footie stadia whose contests were broadcast at great profit to adoring, pay-per-view millions in the Oriental zone. The national sport of Rugby, together with it's genteel summer counterpart Cricket, were by now played entirely in the south.

Service industries were also all located in the south, served themselves by the remote FuFo zone call centres of the Grand Western Coalition redevelopment contracts. "Local operatives" who would be duly tolerant of long hours in return for low pay, would naturally still be required for the dirty industrial work. But the eager legions from the USE's newer entrants were hardly likely to consider life in the little offshore fiefdom, with its separate currency that was designed to keep local living costs artificially high; and all opted for the far richer pickings on the mainland itself. So the only available resource to Britain's latter day feudal overlords had become the much maligned FuFos themselves, and in his grand world vision Emlyn Dellsey had exploited this localised blip in as masterful a fashion as his grasp of the wider global order.

Since the Tricron bombs left no incriminating traces as to their origin, and all of their carriers had perished in the attacks, the

Grand Western Coalition remained totally at a loss to explain who could be behind this affront to its dignity. Its solution, as always was to bomb the hell out of new FuFo zone regions that had been identified as ripe for the plundering. The juiciest Coalition campaigns were always shown live on American prime time HC, with commentary by the reigning Coalition Secretary of No Sense, and studio analysis by retired military brass and HC news channel correspondents who would mull over the slow motion replays and reverse angle shots. Operation "Trash and Gore" was no exception and drew the biggest audience ever recorded for a live HC warfare show.

Successive Coalition Secretaries of No Sense had all been reputed to eat only minced beef casserole with lots of added chopped tomatoes, and were known to invent a jargon of their own with which to explain the finer points of the action. As the British HC audience beheld some distant metropolis burning under a relentless airborne assault, the sharp suited and forever smug persona of the present incumbent Ronald P Donspeake could be seen standing at a podium in one corner of their screens, pointing out various details of the unfolding drama with a long white cane.

From time to time he would crack one of his famed dry asides at the FuFos' expense, turning momentarily towards the camera as he did so in a way that always made people at home feel he was looking them directly in the eye. At these moments, "he who rules the world" would appear to be saying "Ya see what happens if ya cross me?" which of course was exactly his point. The studio anchorman would then read out the best incoming emails and trigitexts from viewers at home, which the No Sense Secretary either fielded himself or referred to the punditry panel.

"Do we have to watch this?" asked Juliana, as the Goldendawns viewed the syndicated repeat showing at their villa above St Tropez. "That Donspeake's just as barking as Schwarzennoris, and he always reminds me of William Dellsey."

Alex flicked through the channels, and his attention was eventually caught by a current affairs show in which another studio panel was discussing the more localised issue of how the razed areas of the north of England would be redeveloped. This debate grumbled on in the citadels of Whitehall for a further two weeks or so. Then the government announced that the destroyed inner cities would be replaced by vast park home estates for the new stocks of migrant workers, since its available budget for "proper houses" was all allocated to the ever burgeoning demand for new executive homes in the green belts of the south.

Nobody in high office appeared to query the Gremlin's housing and international labour corporations' remarkable state of preparedness in presenting such an apt remedy. So relieved was the government at this solution of its thorny little problem, that it even agreed to Emlyn's lobbyists' request to waive the politicians and rugby coaches rule and endow him with a proper title (not one of those mail order ones) when the reconstruction was nearing completion. "Oh no Ron Don baby!" mused the younger Dellsey, sitting before the plasma screen in his control centre at the Manor. "You're not half as clever as you think. When I rule the world, I'll turn you into an economy grade cyborg."

Migrant worker accommodation had already become the prime market for new park homes by the 2020s, since the index-linked retireds who had previously favoured them by now invariably opted instead for the expatriate colonies of the Mediterranean USE, where their pensions went so much farther. The market in "big new ones", as older school caravaners always called them, had long since dwindled and more modest units had become the norm once more. The manufacturers had nevertheless become stuck with large stock piles which the Dellsey Housing Corporation now bought in at rock bottom rates, before placing bulk orders for many thousands more new units.

Once this Dellsey family enterprise had rebuilt the destroyed areas, to house the new workforce that would be brought in by its international labour counterpart under the latter's lucrative government contract; the Gremlin's coffers would become swelled even further by the vast rental income that had previously all gone to private landlords, most of whom had also been wiped out in the Tricron attacks or clandestinely removed thereafter. "Who is the cleverest of them all?" Emlyn asked of a cyborg captain as it did a little dance to the tune of his key pad. "You, oh great master," came the inevitable reply. Then "he who must rule the world" turned his brilliant mind back towards the prime concern of his electronics businesses, and the perfection of ever more clever tricks and fiendish devices that would help him accomplish his grand world vision.

As the full might of the Dellsey Housing Corporation swung behind the reconstruction effort, one or two new entrants were nevertheless tempted into the market. Amongst these, the newly formed Goldendawn Housing Association secured the contract for that part of any new housing development programme that was still always allocated to "affordable homes for rent" at the behest of the public sector; and partly to puncture any possible censure from his majesty's opposition. On learning of the government's decision, Alex recognised or so he thought, the new business opportunity that he had been seeking. "Great!" he had enthused to Juliana in his home office at Great Donnington Manor. "Why don't we go into park homes and take that Emlyn Dellsey to the cleaners."

"Are you sure?" counselled his wife. "I don't think I'd really like to get involved with that family's business interests again. You didn't know his father. They're not normal human beings like you and me. Why don't you go into the expatriate colonies instead?"

But Lord Goldendawn was not to be dissuaded. "Naah! Everyone's doing that. There's too much competition. This is an important new opportunity. If we get it right up north, the government will start doing it down here as well. You know how they always want to save money." His lady reluctantly rested her case and, imagining a barely heard stream of invective on the wind that was blowing off the Hill outside, waited a little apprehensively to see what would transpire.

The younger Dellsey chuckled long and loudly to himself on reading of the Goldendawn Housing Association's intent. He would not of course reveal himself by using the Tricron technology itself against his hated enemy's spouse, and the other upstart market entrants that were daring to challenge him. But there were suitably large stockpiles of many and various older generation creepy, yucky plagues and messy, sticky, gooey stinks in the multimart lock-ups, through which he could enjoy a little sport with them; not to mention outright arson itself. So in the early autumn of 2022, the curious surge in delivery vehicle activity at the bad estate shopping centres again went largely unnoticed. And when the stocks in question and certain numbers of cyborgs had all been redistributed, Emlyn the Gremlin decided to send the Goldendawns a little indicator of his intent.

Chapter 7

Alex pressed ahead assuredly with his new enterprise, ordering the units for his first four "affordable home parks for rent", recruiting the required labour via his various contacts, and arranging to hire all of the necessary plant. On the late October morning when the convoy of trucks and vans that had assembled at a convenient location in town was due to head north, various London and local commuters' wives between Great Donnington Manor and the top end of the village could be seen on their brick or gravel parking areas angrily shaming the names of Jimmy McGrouse the milkman and his cousin Jock Crabbie.

As the sun hoisted itself hesitantly over the Hill to the East, only snooty Sharon remained unaware that the usual, half-frozen bottles of semi-slimmed, pasteurised or platinum top were not on the doorstep; the carelessly parked, old unmarked courier's van being in its familiar spot beneath her own bedroom window. Juliana herself made her way between the gilt statues to the Manor's gates and started as she beheld the milk float tilted at an odd angle to one side of the entrance. Having eventually questioned the wisdom of letting the dubious pair inside, she had altered the entry code and provided a little wooden box in which the milkmen could deposit her own platinum top and yoghurts; and where she in turn would leave their money.

The intrigued Lady Goldendawn moved closer and started for a second time as she beheld the still form of Jimmy himself, lying besides his rusting vehicle; and the bolt upright but nevertheless equally motionless figure of Jock leaning forward in his customary pose through the gap between the cab and the float deck behind it. Their familiar sallow grey and livid red countenances had each assumed a deadly pallor, with a curious stained wrinkling effect that suggested the action of some unknown plague or stink; and a small quantity of grey dust appeared to have frozen in mid air. But the departed reprobates nevertheless wore a rather peaceful expression that seemed to declare: "Aye … tha's go'a hell'o'a kick tae't."

Alex by now had almost reached the gates himself, and on recognising what he thought must be another booby trap incident, rather casually observed: "Oh no, love! ... Who've you been annoying now?" His wife spun round and retorted angrily. "I wouldn't be so sure it's me that's upset someone ... They're dead!"

Then she stalked back up towards the house and as she did so a party of Rooks crashed out of a nearby tree, and one of them swooped down towards her. The peculiar albino markings of this particular bird's head suggested a wrinkled bald pate, and Juliana half-imagined that it turned towards her and cawed in a familiar voice from her childhood: "I told that bugger so!" Her husband leaned down and examined the remains of a charred package that lay beside Jimmy's nicotine stained right claw, then looked inside the milk box and found the unopened little brown envelope containing his money.

The coroner's verdict was one of death by misadventure, since there was no apparent evidence of foul play. The obvious conclusion was that both non-union milkmen had succumbed to alcoholic poisoning after a particularly heavy day, since there were several such cases on The Lees each year. One benefit to the villagers was that the unionised dairy, given the local publicity that had surrounded this case and sensing an opportunity to create goodwill, added them to a round that had previously covered certain other villages to the immediate north and west; though the Hill itself remained firmly off limits. At first the service was seen to improve dramatically, but the new arrangement meant that its somewhat younger and undeniably rather more wholesome (if still a little rough) franchisee entered the village from the top end; and hence his first call was at Sharon's. So before so very long had passed, the village's dairy produce began to be retrieved from the doorstep in as frozen a state in winter, and as curdled in summer as it had ever been.

Meanwhile in the wet and windy north of England, the willing workforce of the Goldendawn Housing Association began to lay concrete bases, then site new park homes in regimented rows and landscape the grassed and paved areas in between, in accordance with the Department of Housing's strict standards. Lastly they laid out the compulsory play areas that these regulations demanded, even though the future residents' children would all still be living overseas. Alex came home to Great Donnington Manor for the four week commercial extravaganza of the annual Midwinter Festival break with an air of great confidence in his new venture, but when he returned to it in mid-January 2023 a wholly different picture awaited him.

At all four parks, those still standing units that were not charred and blackened shells had all been doused in a range of concoctions that when summoned, the public health inspector immediately identified as highly toxic industrial waste that would render the sites uninhabitable for years to come. The realisation hit home on Lord Goldendawn that he had possibly got into a rather dirty business, and his wife again urged him to reconsider. They both suspected that Emlyn Dellsey must have been behind the sabotage, and even began to fear that he could have had a hand in the original razing of those same inner city areas that his Corporation was now so busily redeveloping.

But Alex had never been a quitter, and did not feel ready to be intimidated. Instead he called up Rick Nicey, who upon hearing the former's appraisal immediately sensed a chance to gain the exposure that could get him into the high profile security markets where he so wanted to be. Alex signed up Rick as his security chief, then for plagues and stinks expertise they turned to Sandy Tiller, the local specialist who had cleaned up so effectively after Elronda d'Oriel's booby trap of the previous year.

When the three men met, Sandy was at once enthusiastic. "I have to say I do get a bit frustrated working from home," he confided in Alex and Rick. "Sometimes I think I spend half my day answering the door to my wife's catalogue couriers."

His prospective business partners smiled and exchanged wry glances. "Know the feeling, do you?" Sandy enquired.

"Oh yes!" his co-conspirators answered in unison. So early in February, Rick Nicey erected a large plastic bunker to one side of his marital home, with a sign saying JENNY'S STUFF; Sandy Tiller provided a similar facility for Mandy's stuff, and the three local businessmen ventured back up north, to build more new affordable home parks for rent and repel the worst that the Gremlin's wrath could conjure.

The ensuing weeks' battles in what became dubbed the "Great Park Home Turf War", as reported daily in the tabloid newsprints and evening HC news bulletins, soon captured the public imagination. "Rick's gentleman heavies and Sandy's green suits, armed only with baseball bats and spray guns", against the might of the "Gremlin army" and its fiendish array of creepy plagues and messy stinks; this was the stuff of legend. The three wives had met one another during the formation of the new partnership, and upon recognising their great common interest had quickly become friends.

As the battles in the north raged on, they would discuss at their regular coffee mornings how very involved men inevitably seemed to become in such little contests, before turning to the more serious business of browsing the latest catalogue supplements. "Had a nice week of boys' games, dear?" Lady Goldendawn would enquire as her Lord walked back through the doors of Great Donnington Manor each Friday evening, covered from head to foot in who knows what putrid concoction or vile infestation; but still the husband would not be deterred.

Emlyn Dellsey as ever deflected all suspicion of any deeper involvement on his own part. Given the temporary lack of FuFo human resource, he had included in his original tender an appropriate sum for the rather risky procurement of labour from both Chilly Jockoland to the north, and the Republic of Provonia across the Welsh Sea to the west. Such minor local skirmishes as were now taking place were known to be commonplace between the gangster barons who controlled both provinces, and neither the law enforcement agencies nor the government itself showed any desire to become involved.

Getting the distant and restive Celtic realms off Whitehall's own books had after all been the whole point of devolving provincial rule in the first place, back at the turn of the century. If pressed, the Gremlin's spokespeople would merely protest that the fighting was an inevitable consequence of the unfavourable position in which his Housing Corporation had found itself, in order to rescue Britain's offshore economy and keep it out of the dreaded USE.

The cyborg stocks that were deployed in this particular operation had all been altered cosmetically so as to present either the livid red faces, redder eyebrows and orange hair; or very fair skin and little tufts of nose tip facial fur that typically identified construction workers from the respective provinces; at least in the minds of affluent southern HC viewers. In the absence of the favoured FuFo scapegoat, this rather older and very convenient stereotype was seen to fit the bill in its place. The ongoing turf war continued to entertain the public, and the "Three Amigos" acquired a certain celebrity in their own right. The trouble was the Goldendawn Housing Association wasn't actually completing any affordable home parks for rent, and was falling behind in its contractual obligations to the northern local authorities.

Back in the village, it seemed to Juliana and her peers at the school gates that a second little turf war was being conducted in their own midst. The growing number of cowboy tradesmen that were targeting their pleasant semi-rural community were becoming an undoubted nuisance. Their old, dirty white vans and pick-up trucks would churn up grass verges and muddy the roads, and some of these invaders would stake out the village pub; spoiling the carpets with their boots and frightening the children at weekends with their coarse talk. Whenever doorstep enquiries about this or that work were rejected, the supplicants would respond with: "And is there anything *else* I can do for you today, madam?" with a look that left the village wives in no doubt as to the implied meaning.

As the root of the problem's experience of men had broadened beyond her husband and only previous lover, via the new courier and milkman, this person had discovered that the rougher they were the more she enjoyed them. After all, snooty Sharon's absent spouse had never been particularly refined in the bedroom manners department himself, nor her own father towards her mother. Talk was by now circulating concerning various further recipients of the workaholic stockbrokers' wife's favour; but as the latter's repute had grown, more over-long hours' working London commuters' wives had begun to almost envy the way in which their former scapegoat had taken control of her own life.

One or two had therefore felt tempted to sample the forbidden fruit for themselves, and then one or two more. Word spread through the more down market bars and working men's clubs all over the county, and an increasing number of punters had begun to seek a slice of the action for themselves. The social hierarchy at the school gates reorganised itself less on vehicle ownership lines, and more into the respective ranks of the "Haven'ts" and "Might'ves"; since no-one admitted to being a "Have", naturally enough.

The suspect group would nevertheless delight in inciting their more numerous counterparts on the far side of the lane with an assortment of coy glances, lip smacking smiles and finger licking gestures that collectively served to suggest: "Don't let us stop you!" Janet Bates was especially peeved by this state of affairs, since the more daring new diversion itself and the dangerous levels of gossip surrounding it had both adversely affected attendances at her village Fran Winters parties; and the child minder was therefore made more reliant upon her main job with its ever present risk of infection.

In the higher profile turf war to the north, the pendulum swung as the "gents and green suits" would enjoy some minor success before the Gremlin army clawed back their own advantage. After one particularly messy, gooey, yucky, stinky, sticky setback, Rick Nicey summoned reinforcements from an associate in the debt collection and score settling sector, Mick Nasty; and the ongoing battles became fiercer still. At this point, Emlyn Dellsey learned from his own inscrutable oriental associates that the newest generation of re-clonable super cyborgs was ready for beta testing, and a secret batch was smuggled in through Scousepool Aerodrome for the purpose.

When Juliana saw the pictures of the next day's particularly fierce clashes in that Friday's Daily Mirror, she shrieked out loud. The new cyborgs had all been cloned not as Jocko or Provonian labourers, but in the image of the 19-year old George Oliver Scrote whom she remembered from a browning monochrome photograph in her childhood caravan park's office. Now she felt convinced that her own and her new friends' husbands were in mortal danger.

"It's Dellsey whose doing this, I know it is!" pleaded Lady Goldendawn, pointing to the day's newsprint coverage when her Lord walked in that evening. "It's nothing to do with Provonian gangsters. Who else would have suddenly conjured up all these young Scrote-alikes, and what are they anyway? ... And if he can do that, who's to say it wasn't him that nuked everything in the first place? Get out for God's sake, while you're still in one piece!"

"I'm not quitting, and that's an end of it!" her battle-soiled and exhausted husband shouted back, before adding: "Er ... are you forgetting anything, love?"

"Not until you see sense!" came the vehement reply. "Honestly ... men! ... Why do you always get so involved in things like this?"

"Oh, not like you and that Kelly then, and Elronda?" protested the bruised combatant. At that, Juliana drew herself up, placed her hands firmly on her hips, assumed her sternest expression and retorted a little indignantly: "No, not a bit like that ... Girls go about things altogether differently!" Then the couple laughed, made it up and Alex got his extra big hug after all.

But unbeknown to Lady Goldendawn, nature had already intervened. When Sandy Tiller had arrived home that evening, Mandy informed him that she was pregnant with their third child. This was after a gap of several years, and she then astounded her husband by saying that he should settle and close her Foremost account, "because we'll have to save up". The equally delighted and dumbfounded plagues and stinks specialist thought things through over that weekend and then called Alex to say that it had all been great fun, but that he now felt more conscious of the risks involved.

Rick Nicey was by this point getting feedback from within the security trade that the recent exposure was gaining him a reputation as a smart operator who could clearly handle conflict-related business; and he too began to waver. So at the end of March, Alex Goldendawn cut his losses and returned home from the rainy and windswept north for the last time. "I'm sure it's for the best, dear," Juliana consoled him. "You'll think of something better to do soon. You always do."

As they spoke, a lone and ancient figure at one of the highest points on the Hill above was surveying Great Donnington Manor through an antique military telescope. The mind of this mysterious spy was not the only one in which thoughts of the Goldendawns were uppermost. In his control centre at Dellsey Manor, Emlyn the Gremlin having enjoyed the past weeks' sport immensely, was considering that the time had perhaps come to progress towards his *pièce de résistance*. As he did so, over on The Lees, Cuylee McGrouse, niece of the late Jimmy, was lifting two long frozen bags of Dellseys own brand, former EU offal mountain minced beef from a multimart cabinet; cuffing her restive little Kowlea about the ears as she did so and turning the air blue.

The young mother walked over to some nearby shelves and selected a tin of garlic and herb flavoured chopped tomatoes; then she asked a new junior if they had any red kidney beans. The girl said she would "have a look out the back", feeling relieved at having been noticed since the manager and stock controller were both at a head office briefing and no-one else seemed to know why she was there. She walked into the storeroom but could not see what she sought, then she noticed a door in the far wall and went through it, and then through another door again.

Eventually the junior reappeared in the shop and holding her trophies aloft pronounced: "Just the two left." The irritable Cuylee snatched them from her grasp, progressed to the off licence counter and then the check-out.

"How much?" she was heard to exclaim.

"They're the last two tins," came the reply. "We could get double that price for them!"

The fuming estate Mum was forced to surrender two cans of super strength, then she was let out of the store and wheeled her trolley home.

Chapter 8

One fateful morning during the Easter school holiday, when Alex
had taken the children out for the day, Juliana received a call from
Beth who said their old chum Sam was having a party at her beauty
salon in town to celebrate her own thirty-seventh birthday. She
asked her great friend to go along with her, and the invitee jumped
at the chance to see Sam again after what must have been at least
five years. She now looked back on the teenaged threesome's
carefree clubbing with some fondness, as most thirty something
mothers probably did without actually recollecting how awful it
had all really been at the time.

Just after 2pm, Lady Goldendawn drew up on Beth's wide
front brick patio, in the recently acquired green classic Aston
Martin roadster that Alex had always wanted to own but knew, as
ever that he would not get the chance to drive himself until the
newness had worn off with his wife. Appreciating that her friend
was never quite ready no matter how late she herself might arrive,
the driver took a little time to glance around. She imagined how
much nicer the property could look if only it had front garden
walls and iron gates, or flower beds or grassed areas; all the things
Beth's exasperated husband, Paul had long since been forced to
remove in favour of the stark brickscape that now lay in their place.
Shaking her head as she always did at the sight of the battered and
scratched APC nestling in one corner, Juliana eventually sounded
her horn impatiently and Beth bounced out of the house.

"Wow, nice car!" said the slightly older Mum.

"Yeah, he's always wanted one of these," replied the driver,
turning the key in the ignition and gliding off the patio.

"You're so lucky! Mine would never let me have a car like
this."

"Really, how unfair!"

"Can I have a go on the way back?"

"No!!"

"Oh, go on."

"Honestly, Beth, no."

"Why does everyone think I can't drive?

"Don't they? Surely not..." and such like.

As the vintage sports car sped out of the village at the far end, Beth looked to one side and upon noticing three carelessly parked and variously laden pick-up trucks observed: "Oh, hello. Sharon must be having a new extension. Can't see many builders actually on the go." Then she added with one of her wickedest snorts: "At least outside the house, eh?" The Aston sped on, and as it crossed the open countryside towards town, the two friends exhausted anew their full repertoire of Sharon jokes.

Meanwhile in the subject's own kitchen, three shaven-headed, tattooed men wearing brick and plaster dust encrusted tee-shirts, jeans and heavy boots were seated around the table, sipping from mugs of tea. Peering over the top of their open copies of the Sun and Daily Star, they were busily raising eyebrows and exchanging wry glances while they monitored the swelling cries that were echoing all round the village's second largest house. "More! ... Harder!! ... Rougher!! ... MUCH rougher that that! ... Yes!! ... oh YES!!!" Eventually, peace reigned anew, the door opened and their foreman walked back in. Making a final adjustment to his belt on it's buckle and straightening his tee-shirt, he announced: "Likes it rough. Who's next?" A second man then rose from the table and ascended the stairs to Sharon's chamber. "Keep yer boots on," called the foreman.

As Juliana and Beth turned into the elaborately traffic-calmed street in town where Sam went about her daily beauty business, the towering hulk of the birthday girl's Dreisler was immediately visible parked at a crazy angle across the only two parking bays (one of which was for disabled badge holders only) that the salon was by law allowed. As the Aston edged closer, every square inch of footway, raised brick obstruction, chicane and traffic hump seemed to be dominated by equally badly parked Jitsuhishi Battlebusses, more Dreislers and even some older-fashioned giant four wheel drives. This was clearly a town Mums' gathering *extraordinaire*, and not a single dash of double yellow paint was visible within some three hundred yards of "Sam's Beauty Emporium".

Fortunately, a resident permit holder pulled away just as the visitors passed the salon itself, and Juliana reverse parked the roadster at as crazy an angle as she could effect, since she always liked to fit in with any new group. The two friends knocked on the beauty parlour's door, on which hung a notice proclaiming "Private Party Only Today", and were greeted by two beautiful little girls about two years apart in age, each sporting masses of elaborately coiffed blonde curls. The children both tilted their heads back slightly and in unison called "Mum!", then Sam herself appeared behind them. "Jules!" she beamed. "Great to see you me' darlin'... Loved the programme! ... I told Beth to make sure she brought you, or else!"

"They're so gorgeous," Juliana enthused, looking again at her old friend's two little daughters who she herself hadn't seen since they were tiny. "So like you ... it's uncanny!"

"Yeah, ... we're all shoutaholics," came the reply. Then the beautician winked and gave the new arrivals a falsied thumbs up. "Cheers me' darlin' ... come on in and meet some of the girls." Beth beamed again into Lady Goldendawn's delighted face, and the three friends sauntered inside.

A great time was had by all throughout the birthday afternoon, then at around 4.30pm the local courier arrived to a rousing chorus of cheers, particularly as he was laden with the eagerly awaited new Foremost summer supplements. He naturally welcomed the opportunity to not only distribute so many of these at once, but also to half empty his van of that day's deliveries in a single call. Juliana recognised the man as the irreverent former Hill and village courier who Sharon had always called "That awful man who lived in the caravan", prior to discovering someone more to her own particular liking.

Then the courier himself noticed the former customer that he had then liked to tease the most, who was trying to remain incognito amidst the assembled throng of excited, plastic bag ripping or new catalogue browsing town Mums. "Beth!" he called. "Great to see you again. Pranged your husband's Jag recently?"

"Oh, don't!" came the only half embarrassed reply. "It's only a little scratch now and again. Why does everyone keep picking on me?"

"Can't imagine," smiled back the courier, winking over Beth's shoulder at Sam and Juliana who were trying to keep a straight face behind her. Then the last named enquired: "Do you know about that Sharon?" The courier guffawed loudly and assured the three friends that everybody at the depot knew all about the errant village wife; then he added teasingly: "And that one who came to the door in her jimjams just after New Year and stood under the mistletoe."

"Really!" cut in Beth, knowing full well who he was referring to and sensing the chance of a little revenge. "What did she do then?"

The courier replied rather archly: "Showed me all round the downstairs of her new house ... then said she'd show me round upstairs when her husband and kids weren't there."

"No!" chorused Beth and Sam in unison, digging each other in the ribs mischievously as Juliana reddened a little at the thought of the "Wha, ha, heys" that this anecdote must provoke whenever the various drivers at the depot compared their rounds' assorted bath towel moments and scanty incidents. Eventually the courier went on his way, but not before getting a big birthday hug from Sam herself; an opportunity that when available he never missed since according to some of her town friends, he worshipped the ground upon which the tiny, dishy beautician who was always in a hurry, walked.

Briefly recalling Elronda d'Oriel (which she latterly tried to do as little as possible), Lady Goldendawn wondered how many other customers this man might also worship; and whether he indeed was James Lee Patience in disguise. After all, it seemed that she and Beth were doomed only to suffer incessant teasing at his hands, though they had to admit he was always naughty but nice. Snooty Sharon had been the only person who hadn't rather liked him, and he was still the subject of his share of jokes at Janet Bates' Fran Winters parties, where all gossip about fellow females was strictly banned.

The party eventually broke up at around 7pm just as dusk was beginning to draw in, and the two village Mums decided to head home over Hogs Hill, rather than take the longer route by which they had come. There were three ways over the Hill from town. Most non-residents took the "main way", since it was the quickest and widest and the one that the intolerant Hogs Hillites themselves preferred intruding "through traffic" to keep to if it "had to be there in the first place at all".

The "middle way" branched off from the main way at the "first divide", winding up to and becoming increasingly narrow as it reached Barney's Tump, an artificial mound that had been raised at the geological feature's highest point centuries previously. This local landmark afforded past Hillites the most pleasing views over the infant town in the great Isis valley below; before it had latterly become disfigured by the tower blocks of The Lees on the far side and the many towering conifer hedges closer to home. Immediately after that point, the middle way became almost impossibly narrow, and hence was a favourite ambushing point at which unwanted visitors could best be apprehended by the diehards of the "Hogs Hill Preservation Trust" and made an example of.

This route widened again just at that spot where the respective great gates of the very old money "Hogs Hill Hall" and the 'vulgar' new wealth "d'Oriel Dale" seemed to square up to one another from either side of this ancient thoroughfare, their ever empty cast iron mailboxes eyeing one another sceptically all the while. From that point onwards it would be plain sailing for any brave travellers that might have successfully negotiated the middle way's preceding nuances, so long as they remembered to look out and slow down for the continually ascending and descending ponies from the village riding school.

Last, but by no means least, there was the "back way", that few outsiders ever dared to enter beyond the "second divide" where it split off from the middle way at a certain distance between the first divide and Barney's Tump. Tales were still told of past postal workers, dairy product delivery operatives, bin-men and diverse other despised "trades people" who had unwisely braved the back way never to emerge again; and the dogs up there were reputed to render the infamous rotties and pit bulls of The Lees mere poodles by comparison.

As the classic green Aston climbed uphill towards the first divide, the distant towers of that estate were still visible to the rear. Juliana and Beth were both feeling a little light headed from the afternoon party's wine. But since the first-named had surreptitiously refilled the latter's glass a couple of times, so as to have a good reason for not letting her friend drive back, Beth was by now busily engaged in recalling the various courier jokes from Janet Bates' most recent party; at each of which she would snort a little more wickedly than when entirely sober. Trying to find a way of changing the subject, the driver eventually offered: "Do you know my friend Gina? They've got a gallows at the top of their drive to scare off door-to-door salesmen. It's really funny. Want to see it?"

Sensing her friend's ultimate lack of interest in the undeniably rather tired courier jokes, Beth replied that she'd love to see the gibbet; and so Lady Goldendawn turned into the first of Hogs Hill's many mysterious private lanes and drew the roadster to a halt before the edifice in question. Since the Days owned the sprawling property at the top of this particular by-way, the intruders fortunately needed to venture no further into its rather foreboding and impenetrable depths. The dusk was now deepening slightly and a little chill wind was causing the great banks of foliage that towered above the village Mums to rustle with a sound that seemed to suggest rather menacing whispers of: "No traaaa ...yde" and "Ghaaaasssst...leeee nouveau reeee...ssh".

Before them, just as Juliana had promised, guarding the open-gated entrance to a long tree-lined drive, there stood a tall but slightly leaning wooden gibbet on which the stuffed form of a scarecrow dressed in what had once been a sharp suit, was swinging gently in the cooling evening breeze. On the gallows pole slightly beneath it a small square notice was mounted that bore the dire warning "SALESMEN KEEP OUT". Beth, who a little wine always made rather giggly, made one of her characteristic snorts and pronounced: "Hey, that's really cool. I wonder if Paul would let me have one." Then, sensing the inevitability of another driving joke from her friend, she added: "We could put it right in the corner at the front. Just out of the way, eh?" Then she giggled again.

Suddenly there blew a stronger gust of wind that triggered a further baleful chorus of sinister whispers in the trees overhead. Juliana shrieked out loud and turned, so it seemed to Beth, quite pale. "Hey, what's wrong Jules?" her friend enquired. "Nothing. Come on, let's get out of here." The driver threw the Aston into reverse gear, and turned back out into the broader and rather lighter thoroughfare of the main way. As the errant gust had briefly caused the effigy to sway a little more agitatedly on the gibbet, Lady Juliana Goldendawn had imagined that it leaned down and swore at her: "Bugger 'em!" And in that brief instant she had beheld the livid and fuming face, and furious, half-glazed eyes of the long departed George Oliver Scrote!

Resolving not to poke fun at Gina's gibbet again, since in the past these little Scrote premonitions had never heralded good fortune, the driver sped on up the hill towards the first divide. When the village Mums reached it they encountered a barrier bearing a sign that pronounced "GAS LEAK ROAD AHEAD CLOSED". A small group of workmen was just visible a little further on. The breeze was by now becoming steadier, and the trees around the first divide seemed to be whispering: "Onward, onward, never feeeee …er." There was no alternative. Juliana turned the Aston into the middle way and Beth began to shudder slightly beside her. The workmen walked back towards the junction, dismantled the barrier and its sign, then melted into the trees.

At the second divide a very old but nonetheless suitably sized heavy goods vehicle, a late 1950s or early 1960s Bedford by the estimation of Lady Goldendawn's limited expertise in such things, was sitting squarely across the already narrowing middle way; with no sign of a driver or any other attendant. "God, this is getting scary," whispered Beth, who by now was sobering up fast. "Come on, let's go back down and then home by the top way." The muffled sound of rotor blades was just audible, somewhere in the near distance between the village and the higher points of the back way, provoking in turn one or two outbursts of ominous barking and vindictive howling from the many formidable dogs in the immediate vicinity.. "Oh, it's just the Hillites … you know what they're like," said Juliana, who wasn't so easily discouraged. "Come on … I want to get home."

But unbeknown at this moment to the mistress of Great Donnington Manor, her beautiful, lovingly created marital abode simply wasn't there any more. At precisely that instant when she had steered the Aston Martin into the middle way, a PPG attack from the air had consigned the biggest house in the village to a little mound of grey dust. Only the blackened and grotesquely distorted remains of the gilt statues along the former driveway still stood as a now defiled testimony to its former grandeur.

"It's really creepy up there," Beth protested. "Are you sure?"

"Yeah, course. Haven't you ever been?"

"No, what's it like?"

Then the braver partner steered the classic roadster into the dreaded domain of Hogs Hill's back way, past the rotting wooden notice board whose flaking paintwork proclaimed in old-fashioned copperplate script: PRIVATE ROAD • NO THROUGH TRAFFIC • STRICTLY NO TRADE • BY ORDER OF THE HOGS HILL PRESERVATION TRUST.

Just beneath the mouldering sign was mounted a rusting 15mph speed limit plate. The washed out and pock-marked red paint of its perimeter seemed to aptly round off the faded character of the entire dire warning. Juliana progressed at as slow a speed as it was possible to keep the powerful old sports car to, in an attempt not to offend the locals, but it very soon became abundantly clear to the intruders that there was no chance of escaping detection. Immediately upon their entering the forbidden realm, the first of the back way's countless fearsome dogs began to yowl.

As the apprehensive women ventured more deeply still into the ancient, darkly forested but nevertheless traffic calmed interior, their progress would be announced to the resident diehards within at every step. From time to time they would catch a glimpse of flaring canine eyes in the gloom to one side of the lane or another, or a hint of slavering jaws. At particular little intervals amidst the more prominent chorus of barking and howling, strange little cries of "eHeh, eHeh, eHeh, eHeh, Go bek. Go bek. Go bek, Go bek. Go bek." (the territorial call of the Red Grouse) would issue from within the massed depths of the gnarled old oaks, dense conifers and acidic rhododendrons.

Even the loitering spirits of long since made away with, unsocial hours visitors from The Lees seemed to be intent on issuing their own peculiar counsel. At these outbursts, Juliana would half picture little emanations of grey dust from one side of the lane or the other, and more than once sensed the attendant echo of more familiar curses and expletives filtering through the glowering trees. It seemed that the ghost of Mr Scrote had a little difficulty in mastering the particular pronunciation "pharque" that was preferred on the Hill.

By this stage, Alex had arrived back at the site of the home that he had left with the children that morning. "That bastard Dellsey," he muttered under his breath, surveying the moonscape that lay before them. "Doesn't he ever know when to stop? ... I'll have to build another, better one now ... What *is* his problem?" "What's happened, Daddy?" enquired his little daughter. "Oh, we're going to build a bigger and better one, love," he replied. "You'll have to go and stay with Nan for a while."

"Blimey, Dad! Looks like a bomb's hit it," observed his elder, young teenaged son.

"Shuttup!" retorted the father. What he most wanted to hide from the children was his all too natural concern as to whether their mother had been at home when the attack had occurred. Alex attempted to call Juliana on his mobile several times, but always got the unobtainable signal. Hogs Hill was a well known black hole in all the trigital cellular networks, since the residents had for years past unflinchingly vetoed the installation of the requisite masts; but Alex didn't know that his wife was being lured there. Then he called his own parents, to ask them to take the children while he decided what to do next.

"Wow! These houses are all so old!" observed Beth, looking from side to side at those that were visible as the Aston Martin forced its inexorable way forwards along the now progressively darkening back way. "Oh my God! ... Look ... there's another gibbet ... and another one, over there!"

"Go bek. Go bek. Go bek, Go bek. Go bek," coaxed a little burst of grey dust from one side of the lane slightly ahead of them.

"So this is where Gina got the idea from," mused Juliana. "The old dark horse! Sometimes I wonder whether she might just be one of them after all."

Then an especially virulent bout of barking interrupted Lady Goldendawn's reverie from one side of the lane, while a sudden strong gust of wind from the other flank sent the many twisted boughs of the ancient trees overhead into a renewed, shadowy fervour of sinister whispering and condemnation. One or two more half-heard, Scrote-like invectives seemed to ascend on the temperamental breeze from the great Isis valley to the East, as the classic green Aston's engine suddenly cut out and resisted all the driver's attempts to restart it. They were sitting at the entrance to "Blackcroft", the largest and most mouldering of all the Hill's many ancient piles; the personal fiefdom of Maj-Gen (rtd) Grenshaw, honorary and honourable chair of the Hogs Hill Preservation Trust.

Then the sports car began to roll gently forward of its

own accord, through the ruined gates of Blackcroft and along it's multi-pot holed entrance lane; the longest of all the many long and winding driveways on the Hill. The two women exchanged glances in alarm, not quite knowing what to do. It was as if they were in the grip of a powerful traction beam, which of course they were. "I've had enough," announced Beth, trying to climb over the roadster's door, but finding it impossible to raise herself from her seat. It seemed the vehicle had become surrounded by an invisible force field, which of course it had. "Oh, I'm scared," whimpered Beth in the early stages of panic.

The village Mums' carriage was drawn ever onwards until suddenly the lane emerged from the tree cover, and the vast, decrepit old mansion with its high central tower became visible at the summit of the rising ground ahead. Just as on the eastern side, many of Hogs Hill's ancestral relics had been sited so as to enjoy the most spectacular views over the lower ground to the west, towards the rolling escarpment in the far distance. But none enjoyed a wider panorama than Blackcroft, the family seat of the fabled Grenshaws, who had fought in all of the most noble military campaigns of the past three centuries.

"Wow," sighed Beth, in the hushed tone that she had adopted ever since first penetrating the back way. "Imagine living up here. You can see everything." Blackcroft and a few other of its peers were visible in all their faded grandeur from the road through the village below, and that settlement was likewise all too readily observable to the nonagenarian Trust chair from his own vantage point above. As he and his committee colleagues' lack of useful occupation had intensified ever more steadily with their greatly advanced years, these local worthies had spent more and more hours each day spying on the villagers through bygone army telescopes, in the hope of identifying and then if possibly removing any miscreants who might be deemed guilty of "favouring change".

The occupants of the "big new vulgar monstrosity" at the village's heart had naturally risen up the Trust's wish list, as the husband had first committed the unpardonable sin of attempting to purchase the very sanctity of the Hill itself with a view to "modernisation"; then the wife had inexcusably generated so much unwanted "through traffic" consequent upon her only too apparent, "very vulgar" appetite for celebrity. So when Mark the cyborg captain had requested some local assistance in bringing the object of their ire to his master, the committee had immediately and unanimously agreed.

Eventually the classic green Aston Martin roadster drew to a halt before the great, stained oak doors and rust-despoiled, heavy iron door furniture of Blackcroft itself; and the silver metal box at the drive's end rumbled into idle mode.

"What do we do now?" whispered Beth in a more hushed tone still.

"Knock on the door, I suppose," replied Lady Juliana Goldendawn.

Chapter 9

The bolder of the two women advanced purposefully towards the grand old doorway and attempted to raise it's huge, half-oxidised relic of a heavy circular knocker. She managed to lift it about half way then a whoopsie from a lone Crow perched high on the guttering two storeys above narrowly missed her left shoulder and slightly splashed her shoe as it landed close besides on an already despoiled stone slab of the entrance way. Juliana started as the bird cawed loudly and flew away from the vast but crumbling old mansion that seemed from that close quarter to stretch as far above and away from them as the stranded village Mums could see; but this time it didn't remind her of anyone, or so she thought.

The iron ring fell doorwards, half dislodging the falsie from it's assailant's right index finger as it did so, then it landed with a thud that was largely absorbed by the damp and lichen-covered surface on which it fell. "Look, there's a bell pull," whispered Beth, pointing to one side; then her accomplice too noticed just the type of rustic device that she would always assure sore and knuckle-sucking couriers when she eventually reached the doors of Great Donnington Manor that she would be getting soon. Lady Goldendawn pulled on the said museum piece and from somewhere within the vastness of Blackcroft, a faint tinkling sound was just audible.

The two friends waited for a few minutes, and then a few minutes more. "Try again," coaxed Beth, but her ally felt instinctively that such an intrusion would be unwise. Eventually a faint shuffling sound became discernible from within, making a slow, erratic but nonetheless steady progress towards the outer door. The visitors waited a little longer and eventually the mouldering structure swung inwards with a dull crack of the released latch and a creaking sound of its rusty hinges.

Before them stood the oldest man that either beholder thought she had ever seen. Nobody on the Hill knew for sure the precise age of Maj-Gen (rtd) Percival Forbes Arbuthnot Grenshaw, who now faced them. Some Hillites believed him to be more than one hundred years old, though Juliana guessed him to be in his mid to late nineties. Beth simply stared momentarily, before affecting a friendly smile so as not to appear disrespectful or rude.

"I'm ever so sorry to trouble you," began the lead supplicant as the grand old figure eyed them with a mix of curiosity and rather stern caution. "But something seems to be wrong with our car, and our mobiles aren't working either. I wonder whether we might trouble you to use your land line." Sensing, as she thought that the elderly householder might not be quite up to date on such innovations, Beth chanced another friendly smile over her friend's shoulder and counselled: "Telephone. Wants to call her husband."

The retired General responded with a look that though very tired suggested he had understood all along, before he said: "By all means, follow me." Then he noticed the disabled classic roadster on the driveway outside, and softened slightly for a moment. "Oh, I say," he responded. "Nice Aston! Is that the 1963 V8 model with the overhead camshaft?"

Its driver thought for a second then, not wishing to reveal that she didn't know, offered: "I'm not really sure. I'll check when I get home and let you know."

"It's the green one," added Beth, nodding a little in a further attempt at reassurance.

The enquirer's countenance suddenly became sterner once more, as behind it he resolved not to become so distracted again. "Follow me," he said. "We've been waiting for you for quite some while." The two women exchanged puzzled glances at such an assertion, but assumed that their host might have become forgetful with age.

"Seems friendly enough," whispered Beth. "Likes cars. What's an overhead cam wotsit?"

"Dunno," replied Juliana. "Didn't think they had naughty websites in those days."

The aged master of Blackcroft was a tad too deaf to hear his guests' hushed remarks, and the realisation of this made the visitors a little more bold. Their host was progressing so very slowly before them that the two women had ample time in which to take in their surroundings. "Wow! Have you ever been anywhere like this in your life?" sighed the fascinated Beth. Juliana recalled a childhood visit to the Castle Museum of Old Tork, on one of the few occasions when her parents had taken her anywhere, before they stopped doing so altogether.

There were suits of armour, ancient heraldic crests, stuffed hunting trophies, unpolished glass cabinets full of antique military weaponry, and many gilt framed paintings of bygone battle scenes or old, monochrome regimental photographs. But the furniture, curtains and carpets were all so infested by dust and black mould that the so *de rigueur* one time Queen of the Cybermall began to search out an open window in the hope of a breath of fresh air. Over everything there hung an all pervasive atmosphere of mustiness, punctuated by an only occasional whiff of moth balls; whilst dust covered cobwebs seemed to fill every possible nook and cranny, corner or recess, of which there were too many to count.

At one point, the village Mums espied a bright red 1960s or 1970s dial phone perched on a little table to one side of the route forwards, but still the weary Trust chair plodded slowly and agonizingly on, appearing not to notice it. "Probably doesn't work," offered Beth, noticing her friend's uncharacteristically nervous glance. "Hey, my Nan had one of those that she wouldn't let anybody change. I've never seen one since."

Eventually, General Grenshaw ushered his guests through the door to an oak-panelled chamber that appeared to the new arrivals to be set out like a mock courtroom; then their host locked the same door behind them with an action that neither visitor could fail to notice. Next he slipped the key into the pocket of his cardigan, that seemed to bear the testimony of countless past meat and three veg's, and shuffled ever onwards.

Along the wall opposite Juliana and Beth there was a mock judicial bench, complete with a raised dais on which were arranged a judge's wig, a small wooden mallet and a black cap atop a skull. Below it was a table on which various old, leather bound books were laid out; and behind which sat Edna Caruthers and Harriet Farquhar, the honorary and honourable treasurer and secretary of the Hogs Hill Preservation Trust. To one side, in what appeared to be an intended jury enclosure were seated the nine other worthies of that venerable body, who to a member appeared only a little less elderly than their leader himself.

On the wall above the bench was mounted the crossed sword crest of the English Fusty Dowdy Stuffy Society, of which all venerable Hillites were paid-up, lifelong members. The chair completed a painful progress up to his place of high office, then pulled on the maroon velvet and gold braided judge's robes that were hanging from the green leather seat behind it, the upholstery of which was split in several places. Then he slipped on the wig and seized the mallet from the dais before him, and with a double tap on the same structure pronounced: "Prisoners in the dock. You are hereby charged with violating the back way of the ancient and venerable sanctuary of Hogs Hill, and thereby on the second count of favouring change. How do you plead?"

Whenever General Grenshaw spoke it was with a rather breathless rasping sound that suggested to the younger hearers the action of a rusty old kitchen knife spreading butter on rather too soft but nevertheless burnt toast. "What, are you serious?" exclaimed Lady Goldendawn. "We only asked to use the phone!" But she only had to glance around the unmoving expressions on the faces of every committee member present to realise that the enquiry was uttered in vain.

"Mark that down as guilty, Farquhar," the judge instructed his colleague at the table below, since the assembled worthies always referred to one another by surnames only when on official Trust business.

Beth walked backwards and tried the door, but found that it was securely fastened, then she returned to her co-defendant's side and shrugged. "Better go along with it for now," advised Juliana.

"Giles Hatherington-Smythe, I appoint you counsel for the prosecution," rasped the judge, addressing one of the committee members who had many years' previously been a QC. Do you have your brief prepared?"

"Oh, rather," replied the worthy in question, attempting to steady himself on a shooting stick as he sought to rise to his feet. "Can't wait to get started."

The male committee members all appeared to be assisted by a variety of antique gentlemen's canes, shooting sticks or regimental staffs; whilst by the feet of all the ladies were placed neat wicker baskets in which were concealed a variety of essential personal effects. Then the judge turned towards Lady Goldendawn, and rasped: "Whom do you appoint as your defence counsel?"

The two prisoners exchanged glances, then Beth offered: "That had better be me. Can't see anyone else, eh?"

"Very well," responded the judge. You have fifteen minutes in which to prepare your case." Edna Caruthers nodded towards the door to an ante room and the village Mums walked through it.

"They're all mad!" exclaimed Juliana, as soon as she and Beth were alone together. "On trial for favouring change? I've never heard anything so ridiculous in my life! Just who do they think they are?"

"What are we going to do then?" her defence counsel enquired.

"Oh, I don't know; humour them I suppose. It's getting late and I don't want to find our way back to the village in the dark. But it's only a couple of miles. Let's play along with them, then high tail it out off here in the morning."

Beth agreed: "Yeah, they can hardly stop us, can they? They're all so old and decrepit that we could just push them over if they tried." Eventually there was a knock on the inner chamber door, and the village Mums filed back out into the courtroom.

"What is your name?" asked Giles Hatherington-Smythe.

"Juliana," came the reply.

"And do you favour change?"

"But of course. I mean nobody wants to stand still, do they?"

As he wobbled slightly on the point of his shooting stick, the counsel for the prosecution wished that he himself could do so. Teetering back towards the comfort of his seat in the jury enclosure, the former QC pronounced: "I rest my case."

"Oh come on Smythe old chap, you can't wrap things up that quickly," called a voice from within that area. Sir Peregrine Fortescue, the one time rake and scourge of the county's debutante parties in his youth, had spent the interval undressing both ladies with his remaining milky eye, the other being covered with a mouldy patch. "This is supposed to be a trial, man," he urged. "Do have a bit of sport with the fillies."

Edna Carruthers then moved a chair from the table into the space between the bench and the dock, and the prosecution counsel proceeded anew from a seated position. "What is your full name?"

"Juliana Beatrice Goldendawn."

"Beatrice!" snorted Beth to one side. "How sad is that? You've never told me."

"What do you mean? It's a nice name. What's your middle one then?"

"Haven't got one."

"Liar."

"Silence in the dock!" rasped the judge, with a tap of his mallet. "Proceed, Smythe … Come along man."

"Funny sort of name isn't it, Goldendawn?" resumed the prosecuting counsel.

"Well it's not my real name. It's a title. Lady Goldendawn of Great Donnington."

"A title eh? And how did you come by one of those?"

"Oh you can get them on mail order these days, ever since the King changed the old system."

"Quite!" rasped the judge from the bench above. "The reforming blackguard. Titles are an ancient and sacred privilege of the English feudal gentry and *not* to be traded by the common shop-keeping classes. Mark that down in evidence, Farquhar."

Juliana considered it best not to over antagonise her host. "It just seemed like a fun idea at the time," she offered. "I don't really take it seriously."

"Oh no?" thought Beth besides her. "Can't say that I've noticed."

The prosecution next pressed various lines of questioning concerning the defendant's husband's attempts to purchase properties on Hogs Hill, and her own generation of so much unwanted through traffic during her period of home cinema fame.

"You seem to know an awful lot about me," she protested. "You see when you're a celebrity people just all sort of want a piece of you. That's just human nature. It wasn't intentional, I assure you; and it was much worse down in the village where I live."

"Have you always lived there?"

"I have not."

"And where do you come from?"

"The other side of town, actually."

"Not that dreadful Lees estate where the milkmen and refuse collectors live?"

"No. Shottington, just beyond."

"Oh really, do you know the Brindley-Baxters at the Grange?"

Juliana for some reason that she didn't quite understand thought it best not to pretend, and so in an unusual display of humility, admitted: "Well I don't actually come from the village itself. I grew up in what they call the shanty town at the bottom of the hill. They didn't like to have a lot to do with us, up there."

"The caravan site," explained the judge, then he himself asked the defendant: "And why did you leave?"

"I didn't like it there. They were all so old and ... sorry, no offence. Anyway half of it burned down."

"And how did that happen?"

"There was this crazy girl there who everybody said was a witch. She was forever doing spells for people, but they always went wrong. Then she blew up the bulk gas tank by accident. I left shortly afterwards to work for the landlord, then I met my husband and we got married." At this revelation, the secretary and treasurer at the table below the bench exchanged sudden glances, and the judge himself began to scrutinise Juliana intently with a wholly different air to that of Sir Peregrine Fortescue.

Then he tapped his mallet twice on the dais and pronounced: "The court will adjourn for twenty minutes."

Juliana and Beth were ordered into the ante room and the jurors were allowed to take tea, while General Grenshaw and his two senior committee colleagues began to pore over certain of the old leather bound volumes that were arrayed on the table. Eventually, the court resumed and the judge himself took over the questioning, appearing to have lost all apparent interest in whether the defendant favoured change or not. As things progressed, the chair, treasurer and secretary all seemed to become more animated by the minute.

"Were there many trees at this caravan park?" the judge began.

"Yes, lots; or there were when I was little but people kept getting them cut down."

"And what sort of trees were they?"

"Oaks and ash mainly, or at least the old ones were."

"And why did people cut them down?"

"They didn't like having to sweep up the leaves or being pooped on by the Pigeons, and there was this man there who frightened them that the trees were all diseased and said they would blow over onto their caravans."

"What happened to him?"

"The witch put a hex on the five oaks outside her Dad's own caravan, so when he cut them down his goolies fell off, then another tree somewhere else fell on his head."

"Are you sure it was the witch? You said her spells always went wrong?"

"That one didn't."

General Grenshaw seemed to have acquired a growing new lease of life as this evidence was revealed, while Caruthers and Farquhar were by now scribbling furiously. "What happened after the gas tank blew up?"

"The landlord cut down all the trees that were left so that he could site big new park homes where the old caravans had been. Then I went to work for him at his country estate and a servant who was in love with me shot him."

The eager Lady Goldendawn knew not why she was being so forthcoming, or how she was selecting the particular answers to the honorary and honourable chair's enquiries that seemed to spring so involuntarily from her mouth in the language of a teenager. It was as if some primeval force that she did not understand had taken control of her tongue in this strange and ancient place, and that she was hearing her own youthful voice as if through a great mist of time.

Finally the judge asked: "How old are you?"

"Thirty-five," came the reply, "Just." Then the interrogator rested his case, and asked the defence counsel whether she had any questions of her own. Juliana's head immediately began to clear, so that she could barely remember what she had been saying moments earlier.

Beth had hardly listened to her client's cross-examination, having spent the time thinking up various questions herself with which to provoke what she regarded as these crusty old fuddy duddies. "Why are you all so against change anyway?" she began. "What's wrong with it? You should let outsiders up here and share what you have with them."

"Out of the question," retorted her opponent. "It never has been permitted and never will be."

Flummoxed a little by the equal brevity and finality of this response, the defence counsel thought again and offered: "Then why don't you offer some of your ways to the outside world? These gibbets that you have up here for instance. I think they're a really cool idea. They could become next year's must have garden accessory. I mean, nobody likes door to door salesmen, do they?"

"You know, this young lady might have a point there," piped up Mavis Trescott, the newest committee member who was not quite out of her seventies and also a closet reformer, though she dare not let her colleagues know. But the chair started to seethe a little, and his cheeks began to palpitate slightly as he rasped in an altogether unearthly tone: "Preposterous! The gibbets are an ancient and sacrosanct part of the original Hill lore, and only the most venerable of *all* Hillites are allowed to erect them."

Juliana and Beth exchanged glances, then the defence counsel enquired: "So what would happen if an outsider *copied* the idea ... without permission even?" At that, Edna Caruthers looked up at the intruder from her seat at the table and intoned contemptuously: "Why the bane of Barney's Tump would befall them of course. There can be no other outcome!"

"Quite!" rasped the General. "But don't be so free with your tongue, Caruthers. We do *not* share such information with outsiders."

The village Mums could elicit no further detail on the subject, but the local folklore that had been referred to told how any outsider who stole from the sanctity of the Hill in such a way as Beth had cited would inherit the undying legacy of the original great gibbet that was erected beside Barney's Tump in 1772, and which burned down in 1824. Thereafter, such usurpers were fated to greatly outlive all of their peers whilst slowly evolving into the most venerable of all Hillites themselves, until Hogs Hill ultimately reclaimed its own. Feeling it best to alter the subject, the defence counsel next asked: "What are you going to do with us?"

"If I had my way I'd hang you from the nearest gibbet right now, as an appropriate example," muttered the still fuming treasurer.

"My dear Carruthers," chided Harriet. "You know that we cannot do that. We would have to explain ourselves to the authorities outside and nobody would listen. They never do. They would just put the Hill out of bounds again like all those others."

But Edna was adamant: "No, no, no!" she insisted. "Some day

we *must* make a stand and people *will* listen. Don't be such a silly, Farquhar."

Seemingly insensitive to the utter seriousness with which the rebuke was delivered, Beth at this point issued a sudden snort of such force that it appeared to dislodge diminutive clouds of dandruff from the General's dwindling crown and bounteous eyebrows in equal measure; while various of the antique brass ornaments that adorned the room's many dark recesses were heard to rattle slightly in the gloom. Juliana, standing alongside her friend, could likewise hold it in no longer, and momentarily losing all apparent respect for the absurdity of the proceedings in which they had become embroiled, the two women collapsed into each other's arms.

The judge drew himself up indignantly in his chair, and with a rapidly darkening expression, leaned forward and thundered (if such a rasping delivery could be described as such): "You're not taking this seriously!"

"Sorry," returned Juliana, trying her hardest to recompose herself. "Just a little tickle in the throat." But then Beth snorted involuntarily for a second time, and only a little more softly than the first; and the defendants dissolved into a further fit of all too irreverent giggles.

Maj-Gen (rtd) Percival Forbes Arbuthnot Grenshaw, honorary and honourable chair of the Hogs Hill Preservation Trust, was by now attempting to rise to his feet and snatch up the black cap from the skull that lay on the dais before him. Just managing to do so, but nevertheless slumping backwards into the seat behind, he laid his left hand on the skull and with his right slipped the said accessory onto his bald and yellowing pate. The modest cloud of dandruff that had loitered in the air above him throughout this entire interlude began to descend anew and pepper the black felt headpiece with little white specks.

Then the judge rasped with an intent that seemed to defy his very frailty: "Prisoners in the dock. The jury will now retire, and if found guilty of the charge of favouring change you will be turned over on the morrow to the appropriate authority." Then he banged on the dais with his wooden mallet, and a man a little younger than Juliana herself entered through a side door, wearing a black jump suit and a blank expression. Lady Goldendawn visibly started:

"Mark!" she thought, upon immediately recognising Dellsey Manor's companion of her youth. "What in God's name is he doing here?"

The cyborg captain showed no sign of recognition, merely summoning four subordinates who grasped the prisoners by one arm each, with a rather bruising strength. The ailing judge commanded: "Take the prisoners away!", before starting a minor coughing fit and pouring a glass of stale water into a greasily streaked glass from the mould-stained decanter by his side. His two female cohorts nonetheless looked on in glowing admiration at this so potent affirmation of their revered Trust's enduring power over the unwelcome intrusions of the outside world. Juliana and Beth were led out of the room, through a maze of corridors and finally up a winding and increasingly narrow staircase to the top room in Blackcroft's tall central tower, where they were incarcerated for the night.

The exhausted Beth attempted to ward off a returning sense of panic, now that she and her friend were quite alone together once more (save for the cyborgs that guarded the far side of the chamber's door), by trying to focus on the funny side of their predicament. "Don't be such a silly, Farquhar," she repeated to herself, then snorted softly for that day's final time and fell into an uneasy slumber on a convenient *chaise longue*. But Juliana was still very wide awake, feeling deeply troubled as she pondered the sudden entry of five such young and bizarre players into the incongruous setting of the until then fusty old drama that had so strangely engulfed them.

Turning things over in her mind, she sensed the wider involvement of a far more worldly force than the Trust's aged eccentrics in what she began to feel certain was her own planned kidnap; and given recent events, the name of Emlyn Dellsey sprang uppermost into her reasoning. "Poor Beth," she thought to herself, looking down upon the sleeping form of her companion. "What have I got you into? ... If I'd let you drive, you'd probably have gone back by the top way. And it was only one of Alex's boys' toys, after all. I don't know what men see in cars like that!"

The guilty party retrieved a dirty old curtain that had slipped from the rotting pole above the west facing window, in which she covered her friend as best she could to protect her from the night's deepening chill. Juliana returned to the window and gazed out over the waning ranks of her own village's twinkling lights. Strangely, she thought, Great Donnington Manor itself seemed to be in total darkness at the spot where even at this height she knew instinctively to locate her marital home.

Then, upon realising that it was a clear and starlit night outside, the prisoner reached anew for the mobile that she had managed to conceal from her captors, and detected the merest trace of a signal on its display. She keyed her husband's code and somewhere in the vastness between the west-facing Hill and the escarpment in the far distance, a convenient mast that had not been sited in anyone's back yard or close to any local school transmitted a faint and flickering confirmation to the till then frantic Lord Goldendawn that his wife was indeed alive somewhere and attempting to contact him.

Alex had by this point at least ascertained that his wife had left their marital home that day, but still did not know whether or not she had returned. None of the neighbours that he quizzed could say exactly what had happened when the PPG attack occurred, though some recalled the sound of a helicopter. Eventually, somebody assured him that his wife had left home just before 2pm in a classic green Aston Martin. "That's my new one," the anxious husband thought to himself. "She wasn't supposed to know about it until I'd driven it myself." Later in the evening he called upon Beth's husband Paul.

The dressing gowned figure who appeared in the doorway beyond the wide brick patio recalled his wife "talking about a party in town and asking her friend Jules to go with her", but didn't seem over-concerned by her absence. Paul assured Alex that Beth was fond of the occasional "girl's outing", and that since she was usually a little the worse for wear before their end, he wouldn't expect her home until the morning afterwards. "We like to keep a little space in our marriage," he added with a twinkle of his eye. The caller briefly sensed the click of a bathroom door on the landing above, and a glimpse of retreating ankle, then Paul winked suggestively. It was none of his business, Alex decided.

A third reassurance came from Stanislav Miracek the driving instructor, who confirmed that the green Aston Martin had overtaken him in the open countryside between the village and town. He clearly remembered the two women within, since he had been able to cite a catalogue of driving test failing points to his young pupil. Alex returned to his parents' house just before midnight. At breakfast in the morning he persuaded his family that their mother must be away from home for a while to film a new HC show that the audience mustn't know about until it was actually screened.

"She will come back, won't she Daddy?" asked his young daughter; who had not been entirely convinced by the explanation as to why their house had disappeared.

"Course, love," her father replied. "Then I'll build us a better home than ever."

His elder, young teenaged son began to debate with himself how embarrassing his mother's latest planned excursion into celebrity might be, and whether he would ever live it down with his own friends. And after ferrying the children to their respective schools, Lord Goldendawn conceded to his parents on his return that: "If that bastard Dellsey harms one hair of her head, I'll kill him with my own bare hands if I have to pursue him to the ends of this Earth."

Chapter 10

Back in the court room at Blackcroft, a somewhat excited and apprehensive air marked the candlelit countenances of Harriet Farquhar and Edna Caruthers at the table beneath the dais. They watched and waited in tandem as their leader scrutinised an ancient leather-bound tome through a cloudy and pock-marked magnifying glass that projected a disquieting dance of dull radiance all around him. This was the master volume of the books of original Hill lore that had been invested in the successive honorary and honourable Trust chairs ever since that body's formation in 1824.

Minute after minute passed in an ominously charged silence, that was punctuated only by the patter of rodent feet from behind the wainscots and the occasional hoots of Blackcroft's resident Tawny Owls in the trees outside. Eventually the chair lowered his glass, stared into the middle distance before him, pursed up his lips and uttered a long, low sigh that suggested the overdue lifting of an almighty burden. The effort released a small cloud of dust from the food stained folds of his moth-eaten cardigan, that began to hover between and around the three aged worthies, almost with a celebratory air.

"Oh that my life's work should soon be done," he rasped almost exultantly. "And that soon I might shuffle off this mortal coil at last." Then he sighed for a second time, and the settling cloud of dust arose anew.

"Is it she?" enquired Harriet.

"Undoubtedly," came the reply. "Every detail of her testimony matches. The enchantress has for some time been resident amongst us in the dale below Hogs Hill Hall, as has the felon in the mystic glade on the lower town side. Now, at long last the legacy bearer has been returned to the Hill. The anciently ordained triumvirate of Squire Barney's will is complete."

Then the Trust chair exhaled for a third time with a suggestion of disappointment that briefly played about his so very tired but nonetheless deeply relieved features. "Three girls," he mused. "I had rather hoped that the legacy bearer might turn out to be a boy. Hoped for years it was that author chappie who re-named the vulgar new house in the glade ... but it wasn't to be." And then he sighed once more at the memory. "Pity. I rather liked him."

"She said that she was thirty-five," pronounced Edna excitedly.

"And to think that she calls herself Lady Goldendawn," chuckled Harriet in a glow of assurance over the eternal power of the revered ancient lore of the Hill. "How very appropriate!"

"Yes," rasped their leader in a burst of half renewed vigour, if such a weary assertion could be described as such. "And when we turn her over to the despoiler's whelp, the great conflagration will soon commence ... and after it the ancient and irrevocable ways of the Hill will govern this feudal land of England once again and forever!"

He then brought down his mallet with a moribund but nonetheless evocative thud that reverberated momentarily around the ancient panelled chamber, silencing even the tapping footfall in its darkest recesses. "Summon the others," he declared. "It is time to share at last the knowledge of the Trust's long appointed task."

Harriet and Edna left the candlelit chamber, returning soon afterwards with the nine remaining committee members, who resumed their seats in the mock jury enclosure.

"You read it, Farquhar" said the chair. "I have to say I'm feeling a little weary."

"Of course, dear," replied the secretary, laying her hand momentarily on her leader's frayed cardigan sleeve. "Don't tire yourself so." As the candles burned lower on their sticks, the light from them flickered ever more ominously around the wrapt faces of the gathered worthies, and Harriet proceeded to recount Squire Barney's ancient will in as modern day English as she could affect:

"This being the year of our Lord 1772, and I being Squire Barney Cockscomb, guardian of the ancient lands of Hogs Hill, and Shottington Ridge on the far side of the Isis, it is my unbreakable will that the ways of our lives herein should be preserved in the feudal land of England outside ever afterwards. To this end, three venerable gibbets must be erected in the grounds of my home of Hogs Hill Hall after my death, a central one of ash from my lands of Foulbury Coppice, flanked by two of oak from

Pincombe Thicket. Upon my decease, my body should be suspended from the great ash gibbet, while the felon Will Wayward and the enchantress Nan Chilswell are apprehended and hung by the neck until dead from the two gibbets of oak. Thereafter, my remains must be laid to rest on the Hill's highest point, and a burial mound raised over it to afford the best views over the Isis valley to the east. The two gibbets of oak and the bodies upon them must then be burned and the ashes interred beneath the great gibbet itself, to one side of the mound that should go by the name of Barney's Tump. This edifice will thereafter stand guard over the ancient sanctity of Hogs Hill, and defeat without exception the intentions of all outsiders or usurpers towards our lands."

At this point, Harriet lowered the great tome of original lore momentarily, and looking from one to another of the committee's nine lesser worthies, intoned with immense seriousness: "Fellow Trust guardians, this much you all know. It is only now that we three, your honorary and honourable chair, treasurer and secretary are permitted by the original lore to share with you the following." The bearer of this anciently ordained responsibility then took a brief sip of water before raising the leather bound volume once more and turning a page or two for brevity's sake, adjusting her spectacles on her by now slightly quivering nose with her free hand as she did so.

"Should the great gibbet be destroyed for any reason and at any time in the future, the guardian legacy of Barney's Tump must be transferred to my fields beneath Shottington Ridge to the east," Harriet resumed. "An equal number of ash saplings from Foulbury Coppice and oak from Pincombe Thicket should be replanted at that location, one for each year that the great gibbet stood. The remains of the felon and enchantress should at this time be re-interred beneath a group of five master oaks to guard over the sanctity of the entire enclosure. It is my, Squire Barney Cockscomb of Hogs Hill Hall's further unbreakable will that bad luck will befall anyone who damages those trees, and should any future occupant of that land be tempted to usurp the ancient power of the five master oaks, their own sorcery will be doomed to failure."

"Didn't the Goldendawn filly say something about that?" piped up Sir Peregrine Fortescue at this point.

"Yes, quite ... quite," replied the chair with an irritated wave of his wrinkled right hand. "Don't interrupt, Fortescue ... for Farquhar's sake."

"Yes, *poor* Harriet. Do continue dear," chipped in Edna Carruthers. The secretary raised the ancient tome for a third time and proceeded anew.

"At such future time that any landowner succeeds in destroying all of the trees of the Shottington copse, his family and fortune alike will become doomed to destruction in each succeeding generation. At such time a legacy bearer will also emerge from the enclosure and ultimately return to Hogs Hill, preceded by a new felon who will steal from the sanctity of our lands once more and incur the penalty ordained in this same will; and a new enchantress who will ultimately be banished anew. Upon this triumvirate being renewed and once the legacy bearer reaches the age of seven and thirty years, a great conflagration will engulf the outside world, after which the unchangeable ways of our lives on Hogs Hill in this year of our Lord 1772 will once more prevail throughout the feudal land of England. These things are final and irrevocable and may no man lay them asunder."

Harriet Farquhar then held up the page from which she had been reading in the fading candlelight, and the assembled committee members gasped as one at the sight of the unbreakable seal of Squire Barney Cockscomb of Hogs Hill Hall, beside a spidery signature in indelible ink that was dated 1772.

"There you have it," pronounced General Grenshaw. "As you all know, the great ash gibbet was burned down in 1824 by the grandson of Will Wayward. I have myself checked the Shottington Parish records, which prove that a copse of twenty-six ash and twenty-six oak was planted in the fields below the ridge at that time. That is where the caravan park in which this frightful Goldendawn creature grew up is now located. The new felon is that dreadful Day woman on the lower town side, who has long since committed the ordained crime by erecting that ghastly mock gibbet at the head of her own driveway. The enchantress is the d'Oriel wife with her appalling parties in the dale below Hogs Hill Hall, and now the legacy bearer has returned as well. You all heard her testimony earlier on this night. Every detail matches, and she is just two years short of her appointed time."

"Three girls, eh Grenshaw. Oughtn't at least one of them be a chap?" enquired the ever unsteady figure of Giles Hatherington-Smythe, the point of his shooting stick sliding slightly to one side on the jury enclosure floor by his feet. "What are we going to do with her?"

"I know what I'd like to do," chortled Sir Peregrine Fortescue with a twinkle of his remaining milky eye beneath its lazy lid. "And that other one. I've always favoured a filly that snorts!"

"Quite!" rasped the chair with an irritated tap of his mallet. Then he leaned on his bony elbows, set the fingers of both his gnarled old hands between each other and pronounced with a wry satisfaction: "This Dellsey fellow who wants her so much for his own purposes is the son of the landowner who felled the Shottington copse. She's already done for the father; I read about it back in 2004. Ruined his business, then that damned servant just walked in and shot the old boy dead. I've read about the son too in the newspapers and you know I'm sure he's up to no good with those funny foreigners. Doesn't escape a military man you know, that sort of thing. I think we should hand her over to him, don't you?" The assembled committee members of the Hogs Hill Preservation Trust agreed unanimously.

Juliana awoke early in the morning after an uncomfortable night of waking sleep. She walked over to the south facing window of the high central tower and attempted to take in the vast roofscape that was holed in many places below, and the broken gutters that cast cascades of the scene's all-pervasive moss and lichen downwards onto the mouldering walls beneath. Casting her eyes around briefly to see whether an old black hearse was anywhere in view, she beheld only a rotting Morris Minor Countryman that even from that great height appeared to be infested with large spiders; and the incongruous sight of a helicopter on the rising ground to the rear that she presumed to belong to the young men in black jumpsuits.

Looking southwards, the legacy bearer beheld what she thought must be a large pond, up from the surface mists of which faint cries of "gibbit, gibbit … gibbit, gibbit" appeared to rise in mockery at the prisoners' plight. Even the frogs of the Hill seemed to be on a separate wavelength from their counterparts in the outside world. Then an inquisitive Rook landed on the window sill outside, and Juliana asked: "Is that you, Mr Scrote? Be a dear and fly down to the village and tell my husband where I am."

The bird cocked it's head quizzically from one side to another. "Yes, I *know*," coaxed the prisoner. "If I don't let you kill those mice, the buggers'll be getting in my bed. What a little scaredy pants I must have been. I always was your little girl though, wasn't I you pussy cat?" But the Rook simply cawed loudly and flew off in the opposite direction; it hadn't been the ghost of Mr Scrote after all.

At the word "mice", Juliana heard a loud shriek from behind her, and turned around to see Beth standing on the *chaise longue*, casting her eyes anxiously around the floor squealing: "Where, where? Kill' em, kill 'em!" "Oh it's all right, Beth," purred Lady Goldendawn. "There's no mice. Just a funny old bird."

The legacy bearer then turned her eyes back towards the pond, and from out of the mist there arose a vision of three ancient gibbets in a line. The central one was unoccupied, but the beholder imagined that the dangling figures on the flanks were both beckoning to her as if in invitation to fulfil some primordial destiny. In that brief instant the phantoms seemed to uncomfortably resemble Gina Day and Elronda d'Oriel, dressed in the fashion of some long past century. Then it was Juliana's turn to shriek out loud, at which Beth regained the safe ground of the *chaise longue* and beseeched: "Where, where? You said there weren't any!"

More than ninety minutes passed after this, since the elderly committee members were unused to such late hours as they had kept on the preceding day; but eventually the door to the chamber sprung open and the cyborgs that re-entered it led the prisoners back down to the courtroom below. There was only one possible outcome. The defendants were both pronounced guilty on all charges, at which the impatient cyborgs manhandled the two women out to the waiting helicopter.

Emlyn Dellsey had agreed to allow the Trust committee to conduct the absurd proceedings of the trial in return for their complicity in bringing his hated quarry to him, reasoning that it would all contribute to the excruciating quality of his planned *pièce de résistance*. As the helicopter rose in the air above Blackcroft, Mark aimed a Tricron pellet at the classic green Aston Martin that disappeared in a little cloud of vapour. Then, once the aircraft was out of range, he unwrapped a Dellsey's own-brand chocolate orange from its packaging and lobbed it into the mansion's highest chimney pot. The mouldering old pile collapsed in a sea of grey dust, consigning the venerable worthies within to a long overdue re-appointment with their maker. And thus, all knowledge of the ancient and original lore of Hogs Hill perished forever, along with the sacred tomes that contained it.

Chapter 11

Emlyn Dellsey swung round in his chair to face the cyborg captain that entered his control centre. "So," he intoned dryly, rising from his desk. "You have brought me Lady Juliana Goldendawn. How do you find her? Do you still admire her, idolise her, worship and adore her? Would you *kill* for her again?" And with that final emphasis he pressed a key on his remote that sent the automaton into a triple back flip.

"I serve only you, oh great master," came the inevitable reply.

"Oh do cheer up Mark!" sneered the Gremlin; then he depressed a second key that caused the object of his bile to curl up in pain at his own feet. As the intensity control was tweaked, Mark clung to his master's ankles and kissed his feet for several minutes before the Gremlin saw fit to stop.

"Bring her to me!" the latter ultimately barked.

"What about the other one?"

"Bring her too."

The doors in the wall slid apart and the cyborg walked back out, returning a little later with the two prisoners. Their captor was sitting to one corner of his plasma screen with his right hand on the keypad console. "Welcome to my home, fair assassin," he began. "How do you find it?"

"It hasn't changed that much," came the reply. "This is new though, and I can't say I noticed any dungeons in your father's day. There's still lots of improvements that I'd make if it was mine, of course."

"Oh *really*?" sneered the interrogator. "And how do you find *your* home now?"

At that, an image of the moonscape that had once been Great Donnington Manor burst onto the plasma screen, and the presenter leaned forward and leered with a vivid flash of his platinum fillings. Juliana naturally started, and enquired in alarm: "Where are my husband and children?"

"Can't say," replied her tormentor. "Didn't check … Should I have done?"

"Who are you?" the Gremlin next enquired, fixing his malice onto the frightened figure to his quarry's rear.

"Oh, just a friend," offered Beth, falteringly.

"You really ought to keep better company then," the bully suggested. "Nice mess you've got yourself into now."

"What are you going to do with us?"

"Oh, I couldn't possibly tell you that ... her fate will be ... quite unspeakable ... and so will be yours."

Juliana had quickly recomposed herself during this interval, and determined to face down the son as she had the father. "You don't scare me!" she spat, fixing her adversary with an intense stare, and sensing that like his sire he was not entirely comfortable with being stood up to. "You're just like your father." Then she leaned forward and pronounced with a deadly venom: "All bluster! You'll *never* get away with this."

"Won't I now?" came the calm response. "I wouldn't be too sure about that. The authorities are all convinced it's the funny foreigners who've got you. They never suspect me of anything ... I'm far too clever, and they're so stupid!"

Emlyn tossed a copy of the Daily Mirror towards his accuser, that bore the headline: FUFO KIDNAP HELL OF MALL QUEEN JULES; then a rival Sun edition that simply screamed JAILIANA from its front page.

"You do so like to be in the newsprints, don't you, fair assassin?" the Gremlin next sneered, before enquiring: "How's that friend of yours, Bryony the Chair, and that absurd committee of hers? Still taking lots of pictures of sewage filled bath tubs every time that there's a little rain? ... Tsk, tsk. Caravan flotsam lives so disgustingly ... and there are no toilets in my dungeons. I expect that you'll feel quite at home in them."

Then the master of Dellsey Manor waved his hand at his black jump suited servant and commanded: "Take them away and prepare them for interrogation!" The doors in the wall slid apart, and an eager squad of Mark's subordinates burst in; then, seizing the women they manhandled them back to the dungeons where they tore off all their clothes and gave them only dirty blankets in return, with which to insulate themselves from the coming days' and nights' ordeals.

"I'm not sure you should have provoked him like that," suggested the disgruntled Beth, when the two friends were left quite alone together. "Look what he did to your lovely house." Fortunately, being cyborgs, their captors had displayed no naughty intentions towards them.

"Never mind the house," replied Lady Goldendawn. "Where are Alex and the kids."

Over the ensuing days in the dungeon, the village Mums were subjected to extremes of heat and cold, sudden plagues of hideous creepy crawlies that would as suddenly all expire, leaving a grotesque and clinging stickiness over all of the floor; many and various repulsive stinks that would issue at random from the grumbling ventilation ducts at the least expected moments; and ear splitting assaults of 1990s thrash metal music played by long overlooked Torkshire, Welsh or Latino zone rock bands. The meagre meals that would be thrust at intervals through the otherwise tightly fastened doorway were all clearly prepared from the most suspect of all Dellseys multimart own brand lines, but the need not to starve would nonetheless prevail.

Sometimes, dazzling lights would explode into life in the ceiling and be left on for hours so that it was impossible to sleep, whilst for other long and equally unpredictable periods the prisoners would be left in total darkness; and it was always then that the vilest of all creepy crawlies would begin to play around their bare ankles and entertain designs upon the innermost realms of their blanket cloaks. But the worst things of all were the noises from the adjoining subterranean chambers; the slashings and hackings and screams of souls in torment that suggested the visitation of the Gremlin's wrath upon unseen but no less unfortunate fellow captives.

At intervals, the door would open and the unfeeling figure of Mark would pronounce: "Master wants you," in an unerringly dull, blank tone. Then, as the detainees filed up to their latest examination at Emlyn Dellsey's hands, Juliana would beseech: "Mark, it's me Jules. Don't you remember me?" But the cyborg would never respond, though the supplicant noticed that it would turn an occasional glance upon her friend. She even resorted to squeezing her former admirer's hands or snuggling up to him during these excursions along Dellsey Manor's innermost corridors, and urging Beth to do so too; but the prisoners would always end up being ushered into the presence of their captor once more, who would attempt whatever sport he could extract from their predicament.

Beth soon wilted under the treatment, and the Gremlin quickly became bored with her; fixing his full attention onto his father's detested nemesis and attempting every possible tactic to break her. But as Lady Goldendawn's realisation grew that her adversary was intent upon a long drawn out process of psychological torment before progressing to any more grisly phase of his planned *pièce de résistance*, so she determined ever more deeply to seek out the son's weakness as she had uncovered the father's.

During these examinations, the Gremlin appeared fond of projecting the most gruesome possible images onto his plasma screen of the supposed ultimate fates of various past rivals. Upon seeing any of these, Beth would scream and cover her eyes, but still Juliana refused to flinch. On one particular occasion, their tormentor played the cult underground snuff movie: "Dinner with the Donspeakes".

In the opening sequence, the apron-bedecked figure of a spoof Grand Coalition Secretary of No Sense could be seen standing in the kitchen of his official residence in the apparent role of an HC celebrity chef, wielding a weighty meat cleaver in either hand. On the butcher's slab before him was arranged a headless and limbless carcass, that in the deliberately disturbing lighting employed by the director could have been that either of a dumb farm animal or a funny foreigner. The chef himself was of course not in the habit of making such trifling distinctions. Then he began to prepare that evening's minced beef casserole.

Hacking at the carcass wildly with both cleavers, the great world statesman commenced a frenzied denouncement of the worldwide forces of non-burger eaters who might not like to wear baseball caps; then he began to add the special ingredients of his particular recipe. "More beard! ... More *teeth*! ... More *finger*nails! ..." he chanted in a frenzy of hacking and slashing; as he gathered up and sprinkled in quantities of each delicacy with a demented zeal. Next he emptied a large pan full of mock gore that he had prepared earlier over the whole disgusting dish, then throwing himself atop it and turning towards a convenient camera with his trademark stare as he stirred the concoction with his bare hands, he pronounced: "And *lots* of extra spicy chopped tomatoes!"

The dinner party scenes themselves were simply too gruesome to describe. Suffice to say that the guests arrived to find the Secretary of No Sense surrounded by a squad of very large and heavily armed goons, and that after taking an apparent dislike to each guest in succession, he was the only person seen to eventually re-emerge from the building; though just one small splash of the intervening carnage had slightly stained a lapel of his sharp grey suit.

Through all of these mind games, though she knew not whether her husband and children were alive or dead, their target simply clung with all her strength to a resolve deep within her that her nearest and dearest had indeed survived, and so refused to entertain any possible alternative. For reasons that she could not comprehend, Lady Goldendawn felt aware of some primeval instinct that she was not entirely alone in this contest with the son of the father, which of course she wasn't.

So upon being presented with proof during one interview in the control centre of the unspeakable fate of a brilliant past French electronics techie whose disappearance she remembered well from the newsprints of it's time, the blanketed legacy bearer simply retorted: "Did your mother love you?"

The response was as measured and cynical as ever: "Oh, I expect so," Emlyn sneered with a platinum tinged curl of his lip. "Why don't I ask her and get back to you on that one?"

"God it stinks in here!" the returnee sighed, her face contorting in disgust on being thrust back through the dungeon door. "Telling me," the room's other occupant affirmed. "It's getting worse than Janet's house with all those nappies." Beth was lying forlornly in her by now familiar pose, looking utterly downcast and unmotivated on one of the fetid mattresses that served as the prisoners' only comfort in that foul chamber. Then she raised herself slowly onto one elbow, and sensing the onset of a renewed panic attack, began: "Did I ever tell you about ..."

Her somewhat distracted companion countered with a wave of her hand: "Yes, yes Beth. I've heard all your Janet's blocked toilet jokes. I really don't want to think about them in here. At least she's got a toilet of kinds, which is more than we have." Juliana had correctly sensed that her friend, in an effort to revive her own deflated spirits, was about to recount another of her favourite though rather tired repertoires. But the mattress' reclining occupant was not about to be deterred.

"No, silly," she rallied, raising herself a little further with a faint attempt at a smile. "About Janet and that courier. The girls who go to her parties all say that she'll only ..." But the interruption this time was a little sharper still: "And I've heard *all* your courier jokes ... *and* your Sharon jokes. I'm just not in the mood!"

At that, rebuffed and with a growing sense of panic welling within her, Beth snorted softly and nonetheless offered: "I wonder if Sharon's ever done it in the toilet with the bin men, like they say Janet and ..." She was not allowed to finish.

"BETH. Enough ... honestly!"

"Oh all right, grumpy boots. Have it your own way."

With her every effort at staving off the panic attack having been punctured, Beth clasped her arms about herself and began to quiver. "Oh, I'm scared!" she wailed, then her expression suddenly turned to one of outright horror. "Hey, Jules," she gasped. "There's something a little on the large side crawling right up where it shouldn't be!"

"Serves you right for bringing up Sharon," came the unfeeling response.

Beth's eyes were by now bulging a little, and she continued with a mixture of disgust and just a little hint of a purr: "Oh *no*. It's not going to ... It is!" At this point, the powerful loudspeakers in the dungeon's roof burst into renewed life, rendering all further conversation impossible. Covering her own ears as best she could, Juliana watched as her friend appeared to commence in the dimness a little boogie to the worst past excesses of Barnsley or Huddersfield's finest, as the panic stricken party attempted to shake off the attentions of her slimy yet unseen assailant.

Eventually the cacophony ceased, to be replaced immediately by the familiar cries and screams and gurgles of cruelly visited fellow inmates that filtered from various of the other chambers. As this crescendo grew ever more grisly in its suggestiveness, it became accompanied by the stamp of cyborg feet up and down the dungeons' central corridor. Then, in time with their rhythmic footfall, the guards commenced a chant that seemed no less threatening for its inevitably lifeless tone: "Obey, obey. For master will have his say. Do not resist. Desist, desist. There is no other way."

Beth covered her ears once more and lay stock still as she attempted to both shut out their predicament and control her terror, flinching only occasionally at the renewed onslaught of one unimaginable creepy crawly or another that all seemed to regard her mattress as home. But still Juliana refused to be swayed, and turned their limited options over and over in her mind in the hope of some inspiration. As the incantation in the corridor outside reached its own intimidating peak, the sickening thud of what suggested itself as an ultimate and deadly unseen hew of the Gremlin's wrath reverberated through his subterranean domain. Then an as unnerving silence prevailed for what seemed an age until the door swung open once more.

At the legacy bearer's next examination, the Dowager Dellsey herself was present, standing behind her adored only son with her so loving left hand laid upon his shoulder. With the right she would fondle his scalp as she fixed their quarry with an intent no less consuming in its malevolence than his own. Behind them on a table a large newsprint wrapped object was arranged, that the inquisitor would glance towards with a sardonic regard whenever he reached what he considered to be an especially excruciating passage of the proceedings.

Eventually, the widow exploded in an outburst of maternal fury: "Oh yes, I love him, fair assassin … Look at him! What a fine boy … What mother could fail to love such a son? … I loved my husband too. A *fine* father of a *fine* son … *Caravan* drainage!!" Next the doting Greta Dellsey was summoned, who issued such a stream of invective towards the object of the family's ire that even the worst past pronouncements of Kelly Pilkington were rendered mere Sunday school teachings by comparison. "Oh no, fair assassin," pronounced he who would rule the world. "Worm, informer … *agent* in our midst! You have no *possible* friends here."

Then Emlyn exploded the package to the rear of him that was designed to resemble a dubious Lees takeaway, and its hitherto concealed concoction of former EU offal mountain mince and recycled Bolognese sauce splattered the walls and ceilings for effect. But as the smouldering and hitherto inwardly turned front page fluttered to the floor behind the Gremlin's head, Juliana just made out the two line heading: " ...ndawn urged to withhold rans ...ldren go into hid ..."

"Take her away!" her captor then snapped towards the expressionless Mark; then he ordered two subordinates to "Get this mess cleaned up!" On being reunited with Beth in the dungeon, the excited partner shook her withdrawn and silent companion and shrieked: "Oh, they're alive, they're alive! ... Alex and the kids. I saw it in a newsprint in his office."

The exultant party managed to revive her companion a little, and the two women began to discuss anew how to effect an escape. "Look, it's obvious the men in jump suits are all robots of some kind that Dellsey controls; and the only one who ever comes in here is Mark," reasoned Juliana. "Now if only we can find his control panel, it should be possible to switch him off. Then he'll recognise me and help us get out of here."

"As simple as that," sighed the unenthusiastic Beth. "It could be anywhere. How do we find it?"

"We'll just have to seduce him," came the reply. "Next time he comes in, you grab him then I'll find it."

"Why me?"

"I think he likes you ... and anyway your tits are bigger than mine. I've seen him looking at 'em."

"Liar!"

"Honestly Beth, I think he fancies you."

"What? He's a robot!"

"Wasn't always."

"Thought he was supposed to be in love with *you*?"

"Oh, he was just a kid then. He's probably grown out of it by now," ... and such like. So in this way, Lady Juliana Goldendawn succeeded in steering her friend into the lead role in the planned seduction of the cyborg captain.

A seeming eternity passed before the dungeon door swung open again to reveal the emotionless figure of Mark, framed in the dull light without. "Master wants you," he began as always, but the prisoners did not rise at once.

"Oh Mark," cooed Beth in as sultry a manner as she could effect in her dishevelled state. "Don't you ever smile? What's wrong, dear. Don't you like us, or something?" Then the two women rose to their feet, allowing their blankets to fall to the floor as they did so. As they advanced upon their jailor, they cooed in unison: "You *do* like us don't you, Mark?"

The cyborg made no reply, but no movement either. Then Beth reached out and drew him into her ample cleavage, and still he made no protest so she tightened her embrace further. Juliana began to run her fingers through his hair and quickly found what she was looking for. Flipping open a small flap in the cyborg's skull, she peered inside and beheld a miniature trigital circuit board, to one side of which she identified a tiny switch that she just managed to flick with the broken point of her last remaining falsie before it too broke off. Then she blew the offending plastic fragment from within the cavity, closed the skull flap and wrapped her blanket about herself once again.

And so it was that the former travellers' waif and kitchen boy, and most brutalised of all recipients of the Gremlin's wrath, awoke from the twilight world of his years as a cyborg amidst an all enveloping soft collision that in that long drawn out and luxurious moment served to render his years of mistreatment at his master's hands a mere interlude. The returnee's immediate reaction was to tighten his own hold on Beth, who looking over his shoulder towards her co-conspirator protested: "Hey Jules, he's not letting go."

"Told you he liked 'em," came the mischievous reply, and still the boy clung on. "Hey come on Jules, stop him … I'm a happily married woman!" protested Beth, but her accomplice simply shrugged coyly. "You're not laughing are you … you'd better not be!"

"Course not."

Eventually Mark relented, and as his rescuer regained the comfort zone of her own blanket he turned around and started slightly. "Hey Jules, is that you?" he enquired, recognising his teenaged companion at last. "You've come back. Oh, thank goodness … Why did you go away?"

Within half an hour the at first bewildered returnee to the real world had largely recovered his composure, and then he began to assume a steady purpose. Fortunately, Juliana had succeeded in moving the tiny switch only to the position that disengaged Mark from his former master's central control function before the falsie had fallen off; so all of his various cyborg memory circuits remained intact but subject now to his own free will. "Do you know how his computer systems operate? Can you get us out of here?" pleaded Lady Goldendawn.

"Oh *yes*. I remember … I remember *everything*!" came the fervent reply. "Stay here and I'll go and get help. He's got back-up stocks of clones of all his captains. I'll activate one of them in my place so that he won't notice that I'm gone." Then he added rather enigmatically: "Be patient … I may be some time."

"Er, Mark dear," do you think you might find us some nice clothes before you leave?" piped up Beth at this point.

"Too risky," their new champion pronounced. "He's bound to notice. Just play dumb and compliant until I get back."

"Then at least get us some clean blankets!" protested his by now rather indignant rescuer. At that, Mark left the dungeon to return a little latter with a rather more wholesome assortment of the same commodity than had hitherto been available.

"Make sure you wear the dirty ones if you're taken up to see him," he counselled, before enquiring: "Do I get another hug for it?" of the grateful recipient.

"No! You've had one already," came the none too firm response.

"Oh, don't be so mean," sniggered Juliana. "You hug him!" retorted her friend, but Mark's adolescent loyalties had clearly shifted and ultimately he got what he desired.

Chapter 12

And so, the legacy bearer's accomplice made his escape from the private fiefdom of the Dellseys, to effect the long ordained destruction of the son as they had once brought down the father. But day upon day, even weeks passed without any relief from the renewed extremes of heat and cold, plagues and stinks, and deafening thrash metal that were unleashed with intensifying vigour upon the Manor's reluctant guests.

The substitute cyborg captain was naturally as emotionless as the original before him, and the examinations in the Gremlin's control centre became ever more unnerving. But eventually the original Mark reappeared in the dungeon's doorway once again, bearing a soft and comfortable Foremost cotton body stocking for each prisoner, with crisp new synthetic fibre track suits to wear atop them. "Well turn round then! ... No peeping," protested Beth as the village Mums prepared to put the garments on.

"Oh Beth, don't be so ungrateful!" goaded the giggling Juliana.

The three fugitives left the subterranean chamber for the last time, and as they made their way along the passage between the various dungeons, Juliana began to knock on the other doors, pushing open those that were unfastened and glancing inside. In response to her guide's quizzical looks she eventually asked: "So are there any more prisoners down here?"

"Don't think so," he replied. "But what about all those horrible torturing noises?" Beth then enquired.

"Probably just sound effects," came the bold reply. "That Dellsey's just a big Mummy's boy really. He can't stand the sight of blood."

"But all those hideous pictures on his computer?"

"Aah! He just downloads them from American porno websites. He's all bluster."

The legacy bearer now realised that her accomplice appeared to have acquired a great new self belief during his absence she knew not where, as if he too were not entirely alone in their joint venture.

"You see, you big softy. I kept telling you not to get so frightened," she then rather unkindly chided her friend.

Feeling suddenly a little peeved at being so she thought derided as a wimp, Beth pushed open another door and retorted: "Oh really? So what's all that blood and gore on the walls and floor in there then?"

"Oh yeah," Juliana casually observed over her own shoulder. By now they had reached the heavy iron door at the corridor's end and so began to ascend the stairway to the guards' quarters. When they reached the top, Beth turned to their liberator and spreading her arms slightly declared: "Now Mark, dear. You don't expect a girl to go out in this state do you? Where are the showers?"

The male collaborator at first protested that there wouldn't be time, but his new idol was insistent and Juliana too declared that: "It would be nice to smarten up a little." So their guide then led them to his own quarters and ushered them inside, fearful of being seen by any of the other captains who were all programmed to detect and report suspicious activity on the part of any colleague. His worst fears were realised as he beheld a fellow cyborg walking towards him with an enquiring expression.

"Master wants them fresh," he bluffed in his dullest monotone, and this other captain seemed convinced and walked away again. Then Mark himself slipped into his quarters and began to pace up and down, glancing impatiently towards the faint chorus of girly noises that were audible from within the shower room. Eventually Juliana emerged in her smart new tracksuit, suitably refreshed. Reading her accomplice's worried expression, she then shrugged and offered: "She always takes a little while to get ready."

Mark pulled out a satellite comms link and spoke to someone in a peculiar jargon. "Try and hurry her up a bit," he urged. At two or three villages' distance from Dellsey Manor, a statesmanlike figure flipped shut the cover of his own comms link, and declared with a sideways and irritated glance to his right: "Jeeze, Sylv ... *never* work with dames! They always keep ya waiting." Across the pond somewhere in America, a studio anchorman was announcing a little local difficulty before calling for a commercial break and then another slightly longer one; while Mark rapped ever more urgently on the shower room door with half a worried eye on his watch. "Minute!" invariably came the barely audible response.

Eventually the three conspirators emerged from a doorway opposite the parking area to one side of the Manor's great walled garden, and there as Mark had promised a pre-production model of Dreisler's planned ultimate competitor to the Jitsuhishi sat half concealed within the ranks of its assembled rivals and several older-style FWDs. "Wow, nice car. I'm *really* going to enjoy this!" proclaimed Beth, trying to take in its particular fusion of hugeness and sleek styling that belied the most sophisticated armour plating ever manufactured. Then she leaped into the driver's seat before anyone could stop her and locked on its safety harness.

"Er ... Beth. I think you should let Mark do that," protested Juliana. But her friend was adamant.

"No way!" she flared in a display of somewhat uncharacteristic firmness, not having forgotten being called a "big softy" by her friend in the dungeon corridor below. "If you hadn't got me tiddly in the first place none of this would have happened. You drove us into this mess. I'm getting us out!" ("And then let anyone back home tell silly jokes about my occasional little scrapes," she thought to herself, but of course couldn't say so out loud.)

"Is she any good?" enquired Mark.

"Oh ... I'm sure everything will turn out fine," came the none too confident reply.

An alarm sounded somewhere within the Manor's vast depths, then another and another. Realising that their planned escape had been detected, Mark climbed into the APC's back seat and urged Juliana to get in too. Weighing up her predicament's only two options, our heroine settled for the slightly less risky one. She climbed through the passenger door and locked herself as tightly as she could into the front seat's copious safety harness. "Quite right too!" chided her companion. "Now let's get this job done properly."

Squads of cyborgs were by now issuing from the Manor and heading for the Battlebusses. Beth threw the Dreisler's great engine into life then accelerated away and into the long driveway towards the estate boundary. She noticed a discarded free Daily Mirror TVD "Great War Movie Themes" lying on the dashboard and reached across to retrieve it. As she freed the disc from its plastic case and slipped it into the vehicle's player, the APC veered to the left, then back across to the right before the driver ultimately corrected its course and turned up the volume. Juliana glanced anxiously over her shoulder towards Mark, but he was talking intently on his satellite comms link and seemed unconcerned.

Upon realising that his father's hated nemesis was attempting to outwit himself too, the grand master and future ruler of the world Emlyn Dellsey became gripped by an all-consuming rage that could only be described as apoplectic. Its intensity immediately began to cloud his normally ultra-logical judgement, as he cursed himself for prolonging this queen of all enemies' mental torture instead of merely butchering her in his dungeons like her various predecessors on his personal A-list. He rushed to his arms cabinet and selected an appropriate array of weaponry with which to exact the only possible outcome that his mind envisaged to the upstart's insolence; then he hurried out to the parking area himself.

Seeing that the Battlebusses had all gone, the Gremlin opted for his personal mobile HUB (as its number plate proclaimed) to the control centre of his ancestral home; a sleek, gun metal grey Jaguar saloon that he had specially and fiendishly adapted in many ways. Not having seen the start of the chase, that as he strained his eyes now seemed engulfed in rising dust at some distance along the Manor's driveway, he knew nothing of the new Dreisler or from where it might have been procured. Emlyn assumed that the fugitives must have made off in one of his discarded older FWDs, and that therefore the contest's conclusion would be a formality. Then he activated the HUB's satellite location system and set off himself in hot pursuit.

By now the great iron gates were looming in the Dreisler's windscreen, but its driver showed no sign of slowing down. "Er, Beth ... do we know the exit code?" Juliana enquired, with another backward glance towards Mark. But her friend didn't hear.

"Now, if I remember correctly ... if I aim for that spot just ... *there* ..."

"BETH ... stop her Mark, Oh my God!!" The driver slammed on the brakes at the last possible second and the huge APC slammed into its challenger. As Beth threw the gearbox into reverse, the shuddering iron barricades catapulted open to their widest possible point, and as the victorious vehicle burst out of the Gremlin's domain into the wooded lane beyond, the gates' remains fell clanging into the path of the pursuing cyborgs.

"How did you know that?" asked the somewhat relieved front seat passenger. "Oh ... my father-in-law's had lots of gates like those," came the almost casual reply. "But he doesn't get them mended any more."

From the back seat where he was still talking into the satellite link in a jargon unknown to his female companions, Mark coached: "Great work Beth! Hey Jules, you said she was good. Try and get to open ground as soon as possible." The fallen gates had only temporarily inconvenienced their pursuers and the Battlebuses were catching up once more.

As the Dreisler raced along under the tree cover, the cyborgs in its wake began to lean out of their vehicles' windows and lob Tricron pellets at their quarry, but all of these bounced harmlessly into the air where they expired in little clouds of vapour. Beth turned up the volume again as her personal favourite great war movie theme began to issue from the in-vehicle entertainment system. Then the occupants sensed the louder thud of a PPG bouncing off the roof, and then another but still the vehicle remained unscathed. Looking ahead, Juliana noticed a mound of freshly steaming horse dung adorning the carriageway ahead of them at the point where a bridleway crossed. When the APC hit this particular obstruction at such great speed, it flew slightly in the air to the left and smashed fully broadside against a tree. Then it veered over to the right and similarly tested its opposite flank against a telegraph pole.

It was only at this point that a rather enlightening realisation dawned in the drivers' mind. Not a centimetre of bull bar was buckled, the headlamps were still intact, and not a single deep score mark adorned the length of either of the APC's sides. "Hey! ... I really like THIS car," squealed the excited Beth. "NOTHING damages it!" The Dreisler shot out from the edge of the woods and into open ground; then with a snort of such force that even the hitherto unflappable Mark ducked slightly to one side behind her, the driver steered it off road, and the jockeying Battlebuses all followed.

"Damn!" spat the irritated Emlyn Dellsey as, bringing up the rear, he too emerged from beneath the tree cover. The Gremlin's choice of vehicle had been his second major misjudgement of the day, after that of personally pursuing his enemy himself. Back at his family seat, platoons of Special Forces were announcing their noisy arrival along the driveway to his formerly untouchable realm, while more parachuted in from the skies above. But when the gung-hos burst into the Manor itself, lobbing stun grenades in every direction to many shouts of "Yo!" and "Let's kick ass!" they encountered only their intended quarry's startled staff.

Greta Dellsey had a little earlier escaped by a back route, seemingly unnoticed in one of the older FWDs and headed for the rendezvous point that was detailed in the Manor's evacuation plan. And after the specially placed sensors relayed that the enemy was indeed invading, the master computer in the control centre sent its daily back-up file to its secret Siberian duplicate then wiped itself clean. Ever watchful of the signal on his HUB's satellite location system, the absent grand master was forced to go round by the longer way and catch up with the chase when he could.

As the lead APC headed downhill across a broad field, scattering frightened farm animals in every direction, the Battlebuses behind it began to explode in clouds of grey dust and pink mist. They were easy targets for the squadron of Marauder Drones circling in the skies high overhead; the fabled remote controlled aircraft of the Grand Western Coalition that were used so effectively in precision assassination missions all over the Funny Foreign Zone.

"What's happening, Mark?" asked Juliana.

"We are not alone," came the rather enigmatic reply. "We have powerful friends. Keep going, Beth!"

The Dreisler reached the bottom of that particular field and smashed through a hedge into the lane beyond, since the driver could not locate any other means of egress. Glancing off an old, unmarked van in which a startled stand-in courier on the local beat was searching for an impossible to locate named house, the APC flew sideways and landed against one gate post of the field entrance on the far side that flew upwards into the air. The ruined and fallen gate itself splintered beneath the vehicle's bulk, before the opposite gatepost was likewise demolished and the intrepid threesome continued their progress down hill.

By now only three chasing Battlebuses remained. Then, in a crowning feat of bravado designed to score a few local points off the Coalition's renowned fighter-bomber pilots, the competing video games console operators at Grand Western Intelligence's Drone Control Centre in Langley VA, with whom Mark had been communicating all along, fired a final salvo that ricocheted off the victorious Dreisler itself and through the windscreens of its pursuers. "Yo! ... Yeehah! ... Better that you guys!" chorused the marksmen amidst an explosion of celebratory high fives. "That's some FuFo butt kicked!" Beth headed through a gate at the bottom of the second field, and Mark directed her towards a particular village.

"Sorry, Beth," purred Juliana. "I'll never doubt you again."

Her friend at first feigned mock seriousness, then beamed warmly and, just managing to suppress another loud snort, replied "Oh, don't be such a silly, Farquhar!" Then the village Mums exchanged their own exultant high five and sped on towards a date with destiny on the awaiting village's showground. As a by now rather seasoned celebrity, Lady Goldendawn was sensing the influence of some higher agency at work, and so casting aside her past aversion to her great friend's skill (or otherwise) at the steering wheel, waited in eager anticipation to see what that power might be.

The Dreisler finally screeched to a halt at the very toes of none other than the sharp grey suited, bespectacled and as always gallingly smug figure of Ronald P Donspeake himself; who had stared the APC down with such an air of unerring command that even Beth had felt compelled to slam on the brakes at precisely the right moment. At the Grand Western Secretary of No Sense's right hand, the slightly more squeamish looking, bright yellow countenance of Sir Sylvester Schwarzenorris had attempted to appear equally nonplussed, though the Supreme Commander had nevertheless visibly flinched slightly at the vital moment. All around the great world leaders were milling numbers of the burliest minders from Rick Nicey's Grand Western Security Corporation Plc, and many more American secret service agents who were all much larger still.

Slightly further away, the president of the Dreisler Automobile Corporation was awaiting his own turn on camera, flanked by two of his PRs who were bellowing into their mobiles and pummelling their palm tops. The contracts were already being prepared to sign up Beth to the planned new advertising campaign for their prized masterpiece, that would be rebranded the "Bethmobile" in her honour and ultimately achieve market dominance over the detested Jitsuhishi Battlebus. And all around the gathered ensemble the massed ranks of the Western media corps were filing reports back to their national HC news channels. Their inscrutable Oriental counterparts had not been invited, naturally enough.

The sound of the Dreisler's in-car entertainment system died, its doors sprang open and Juliana, Beth and Mark half staggered out into the media spotlight, to a chorus of cheers and applause from its assembled cohorts. Unbeknown to the two village Mums, the "Great Escape" sequence had been timed for live viewing on American east coast prime time HC, transmitted by the Marauder Drones' own remote cameras and a miniature in-vehicle one that Mark had been operating all through the preceding drama.

"Great work Jules," pronounced the No Sense Secretary, stretching out an immaculately manicured but totally trinket-free palm. "Ah guess ya've helped me save the world one more time."

"Me too!" exclaimed an indignant Beth. "I did the driving!"

"Yeah, we'll be sending ya the bill for the Dreisler," quipped Ronald, before turning momentarily towards the cameras as he always did upon cracking one of his driest asides. Poor Beth! It seemed that even at such a moment as this she was doomed to be the butt of all the driving jokes.

"Yeah ... Great work too," the smirking Secretary conceded, then he enquired: "Er, what did ya say your name was?"

"Me too?" Sir Sylvester next chipped in from the immediate right, flashing his trademark double row of immaculately crowned white tombstones. But the master of glib simply slapped his junior partner's bright yellow wrist and turned back toward the cameras himself.

Suddenly, a ripple of excitement disturbed the crowd as a seemingly demented figure rushed up behind the village Mums and their male accomplice, Mark. Upon realising the irreversible enormity of this unplanned implosion of his personal grand world vision, the former master of Dellsey Manor must have abandoned all reason. As he attempted to lob his last remaining tricron pellet at the Grand Western Secretary of No Sense, Emlyn the Gremlin was hit squarely between the eyes by a precision shot from one of the Marauder Drones that were still circling overhead.

The younger Dellsey was seen by HC millions to expire in an explosion of pink mist, that roundly splattered many of the assembled players but nonetheless only slightly stained one lapel of the resplendent Ronald P Donspeake's sharp grey suit. The Secretary of No Sense then drew himself up to his full height, and turning towards a convenient camera uttered his most celebrated victory cry: "Fellow Americans and Grand Western Coalition partners everywhere … We got him!" Deafening applause burst forth from the crowd, and the three heroes Juliana, Beth and Mark turned towards it. Opposite them the seasoned world statesmen likewise milked the acclaim for their own maximum effect.

Then a lone, chirpy voice from somewhere within the milling throng was heard to enquire: "Er … are you forgetting anything, love?" Lord Alex Goldendawn next thrust himself onto centre stage through the massed ranks of the ever watchful security agents, closely followed by Beth's Paul. The adored wives flew into their husbands' arms and the dripping pink mist that still half-covered both women seemed intent on bonding the reunited couples as never before, while the massed ranks of news channel cameras transmitted their long and immensely relieved embraces to a spellbound Western Zone-wide audience.

Back in town, the Goldendawn's two younger children were watching the live broadcast proudly at their nan's house. "I like this programme," said their little daughter. "Mummy's so clever!"

Her older brother, sitting besides her piped up: "Hey look, Dad's in it too. Eugh … they're kissing. That's disgusting!"

Then the door opened and the elder, teenaged son walked into the room. Shutting down the video game on his new trigital palm top he glanced towards the HC screen and casually observed: "Oh no, is Mum showboating again? … Parents! … They're *so* embarrassing. I'll just never live this down."

Chapter 13

The celebrity that had engulfed our heroine on those two previous occasions in her life was as nothing compared to the trans-Atlantic fame that took over both village Mums' lives following these momentous events. The Daily Mirror declined to serialise Juliana's story for a third time, since its readers had far less interest in affairs of world order than the outcome of HC reality shows; but the broadsheets nevertheless competed vigorously over the abundant pickings. The government persuaded the King to waive the politicians and rugby coaches precedent once more, and the Goldendawns were able to tear up their mail order titles and bask in the glory of the real thing. But Paul shared the reigning monarch's view of such things and so declined the same honour for himself and Beth, settling for various new and lucrative non-executive directorships instead.

The three heroes of the "Great Escape" were flown to America at the personal invitation of the president of the Grand Western Coalition himself, on his own official jet; then they embarked upon a tour of the sole world superpower's major cities. Millions turned out to applaud the bashful and blushing Brits as the latest blast, plague and stink proof, glass-topped Dreisler stretched limos paraded them slowly through the streets of those teeming metropoli.

Mark nevertheless bowed out of the proceedings at an early stage, having previously agreed to be recruited by Grand Western Intelligence; leaving Juliana and Beth to complete the round of major HC network chat shows. Upon his earlier liberation at Lady Goldendawn's hands from Dellsey Manor, the male conspirator had headed straight for Whitehall from where he had been flown out to Langley VA to undergo extensive debriefings that had revealed his former master's great conspiracy to the Grand Western Coalition.

At one point, the fascinated American scientists had moved the master switch on the cyborg control panel in Mark's skull into the off position, at which the all-knowing informer had totally lost confidence and begun to ask for packs of super strength, imagining that he was back in the early morning rush hour queue at a Dellseys multimart off licence counter. But when his interrogators moved the switch back to the position at which Juliana's last remaining falsie had fallen off, the formerly abandoned travellers' waif and kitchen boy had immediately re-acquired the abundant self-belief of an all-conquering superhero.

Mark went on to become one of the most celebrated of all Coalition special agents, seeing service in the ensuing years' most daring operations behind FuFo enemy lines. When the turncoat cyborg-lite eventually fell, his body was laid to rest in the Heroes Cemetery at Langley VA; then a plaque was raised in his honour in the memorial garden of Instant Makeover Square in Lower Manhattan where only the greatest of all Coalition icons were commemorated.

But through all of the various debriefings that punctuated his further heroism and laid bare his former master's evil empire, the ex-Gremlin's former captain somehow failed to reveal the existence of the cyborg stocks in the Dellseys multimart cellars, over the pond in the faithful offshore subsidiary of Britain. It was only years later, after the apocalypse, that a new post-mortem on the cyborg's remains exposed the microscopic sliver of falsie plastic that had corrupted that particular memory circuit in all that intervening time.

Back in 2023, the village Mums' American tour culminated in a grand state banquet at the seat of government in Washington DC itself. The live HC news channel broadcast revealed Juliana seated at the top table to the president's right, with Beth to his left. On Juliana's own right was Coby Shaman, general secretary of the Divided Nations Insecurity Council, who being a career diplomat could converse both fluently and with the greatest apparent interest upon any subject that a fellow guest might choose to raise. Lady Goldendawn found him to be a most charming man, whilst remaining unaware that her friend was finding things a little less to her liking on the far side of the president.

It seemed to the less seasoned celebrity Beth that almost all of the many and frequent splashes of extra spicy Bolognese sauce from her own left, even though everyone else was enjoying the most exquisitely prepared Alaskan salmon mornay, seemed to be united in the all too obvious purpose of attacking the very expensive new frock that she had purchased that day especially for the occasion. The few exceptions appeared to display an equal intent towards that afternoon's blonde rinse at the capital's most exclusive salon. But as ever, by the end of the course just one tiny splash appeared to have slightly despoiled a lapel of the Secretary of No Sense's own sharp grey suit.

The great world statesmen on either side did their apparent best to entertain the rather incongruous figure between them, but it seemed to Beth that neither was very interested in clothes, shopping or children; and eventually she was seen to yawn roundly. The five second delay that was the norm for all live news broadcasts in America succeeded in editing the incident out, but the pirated copies that inevitably proliferated throughout the Oriental zone replayed it over and over again to the great amusement of the inscrutable locals.

For some time the recognition had been growing in Beth's mind that her friend inevitably seemed to get the better deal and the greater share of the attention, even though she herself had played the more heroic role in the "Great Escape". The five second delay had also edited out that moment when Juliana had wimped out at Dellsey Manor's gates. This apparent imbalance was in some part due to the subtle influence of the Dreisler Automobile Corporation's PRs, who mindful of the American multinational's need to maintain its position in FuFo zone reconstruction markets, were all too aware of the double edged sword that their new standard bearer represented.

Though all too eager to capitalise upon Beth's "Great Escape" performance in emphasising their master APC's indestructible qualities, they likewise did not wish to draw attention to the same product's potential for wreaking havoc in the wrong hands; a side of things that also naturally concerned Beth's own husband. So while his wife was engaged in her first major brush with celebrity, the canny Paul negotiated a highly lucrative agreement whereby the couple would receive a long term retainer in return for the adored but accident prone party never herself being allowed to drive the vehicles in question.

Back at that grand state occasion, Beth's was not the only mind entertaining hostile thoughts concerning Lady Juliana Goldendawn. Towards one end of the top table, the flashing double rows of immaculately crowned tombstones that tried desperately to catch the attention of some camera or another masked a bitter resentment towards the usurper of "his seat" at the president's right hand. And within the bright yellow facade of Sir Sylvester Schwarzenorris' outwardly animated countenance, plans were forming of a fitting vengeance.

At the banquet's close, Ronald P Donspeake's aides invited both village Mums to a private dinner party at the Secretary of No Sense's official residence the following evening. But there were limits as to what the two heroines were prepared to endure in the role of world saviours, so Juliana politely cited an unavoidable prior commitment, whilst Beth pleaded that she had absolutely nothing to wear. Then they headed straight for the airport and caught the next plane home.

Somewhere high above the mid-Atlantic, the pair fell out. Once again the throng of American admirers in the first class cabin, who all asked for the women's autographs, ordered them drinks and enquired whether they knew their own relatives in this or that provincial city of the little offshore subsidiary; all seemed to be paying more attention to Juliana than Beth.

"Why is it always you?" the wounded party eventually demanded. "Oh don't be silly, Beth. You know it's not like that," her friend replied.

"Oh no? Great work Jules, guess ya helped me save the world. We'll send ya the bill for the car, wot's yer face," protested the neglected partner, mimicking the Secretary of No Sense.

"Well it's not deliberate, I assure you. Come on, don't be so jealous. That's not like you."

At that point an American businessman walked back up the cabin and handed Lady Goldendawn an invitation to a private function some days ahead at his corporation's London offices. "Let us know if you bring that friend of yours," he added. "We'll take down the gates for the evening."

Besides the recipient, Beth began to turn as red as the splashes of Bolognese sauce that still tainted her blonde rinse. "What! Am I invisible or something?" she fumed.

"Oh come along ... he was only joking." Then the row started.

"It's always you. You, you, you! You got to sit next to that nice general secretary, while I had to put up with that grisly Donspeake who ruined my lovely new frock. You always steal all the limelight for yourself!"

"Oh *really*? … I suppose that nice fat advertising contract with Dreisler doesn't soften the blow then."

"You wimped out!"

"Only at the gates."

"Yes, and they edited it out of the broadcast. Paul told me so."

"We'd never have got out of there in the first place, if I hadn't found Mark's control panel."

"Only because he liked my tits!"

"Oh Beth, really! You were a quivering jelly in that dungeon most of the time. It was me who held us *both* together, *and* stood up to Dellsey … I didn't even know if my husband and children were alive or dead."

Faced with the seeming inevitability of a losing argument, Beth then stormed to another seat at the back of the first class cabin and began to attack the glasses of champagne that the women's on board admirers had bought for her. Juliana settled down to watch the in-flight movie and hoped that her friend would get over it. But when the plane touched down in London there was still no reconciliation. A by now rather hurt Juliana attempted to intercept her former ally at the exit from the airport terminal, but though still a little unsteady on her feet, the indignant Beth simply swept loftily past and out towards Paul's newest Jaguar saloon that was parked in readiness across the four disabled bays.

"What's wrong with her, love?" enquired Lord Goldendawn as he took his own Lady back into his arms.

"Oh, she's got the hump," came the reply. "You know how fame affects people."

Chapter 14

Lady Goldendawn returned home to find that work was already well advanced on the building of the bigger, better "Greater Donnington Manor". Alex had sited two modern day Donningtons in the former garden, in which his family could survive until the work was completed. Through the windows of these childhood throw backs, Juliana would watch daily as the new proper house rose from the ashes, and calculate what further little extensions and improvements might be required before things would all be quite right; as well as what the various furnishings and fittings should be. The replacement marital abode thereby acquired a cerise room, a coral room, a sunrise room, an aquamarine room and assorted other chambers decorated and furnished in all of the most fashionable tones of the day; though for some reason Juliana could not bring herself to include anything in that year's most must have shade of Bolognese.

There was even a bright yellow room, a small utility area to the rear of the property in which a light fingered decorator had opened a little package that he had found delivered to the back door. The would be thief bore the new complexion that had been intended for his patron's wife forever afterwards, whilst the coating on the walls and ceiling resisted all attempts either to remove or paint over it. In the end, the Goldendawns hung a double row of tombstones mural on the wall opposite the home laundry and dry cleaning system, and mounted a sign over the inner door bearing the motif "Schwarzee's Revenge" with which to both amuse their dinner party guests and excuse this unfashionable anomaly in their otherwise most *de rigueur* of abodes.

When the seat of the intended future Goldendawn dynasty was finally complete, a grand house warming was held, to which everyone who was anyone in the village and town were invited. The Niceys and Tillers were all there, naturally enough; as were Sam's family and the Days, and many other special friends. Even the d'Oriels arrived, fashionably late, and stayed for over an hour before politely citing a further pressing engagement; since Juliana had for some reason felt prompted to attach a note saying "Let's be friends" to her arch competitor's special invitation. Elronda, appreciating that she could hardly hope to derail this latest celebrity bandwagon, had decided to accept and so bask a little with appropriate grace in the international heroine's reflected limelight.

Elronda was also seen to display a particular interest in Gina Day, who she knew of by reputation as the Hill's only other moderniser but had actually seen only rarely in the past. Before leaving, Elronda invited both Juliana and Gina up to the Dale for a long girl's chat, and the threesome afterwards became firm friends. As the parties to this fated alliance searched for early common ground upon which to build good relations, they embarked upon a campaign of misinformation with which to entice the new committee of the Hogs Hill Preservation Trust; who the subtly scheming *femme fatale* of d'Oriel Dale had at once identified as their natural mutual enemy.

Those replacement worthies, who to a member were only a little less advanced in years whilst no less fusty, dowdy and stuffy than their venerable predecessors; were thereafter fed a sporadic diet of spicy innuendo concerning various shameful threats to the Hill's very sanctity that would have to be snuffed out at all costs in the time honoured manner. Imagine the committee's mortification for instance, as they became convinced that the site of Blackcroft had been acquired by a megalomaniac Antipodean actor who planned to build a permanent shrine there within which to indulge his personal and all consuming messiah complex.

The spoof copies of the Town Times that the co-conspirators' young agents would deposit in the variously rusting and hitherto derelict mailboxes along the Hill's most foreboding and unvisited byways, would pronounce that this most monstrous of all ghastly intruders had even submitted planning proposals to widen the back way, so as to afford his legions of American and Oriental followers easier access. But little did the mischievous reformers appreciate in what they were meddling, or that the final and irrevocable legacy of the Hill was as ever working towards its ultimate goal.

Back at that grand house warming, Juliana and Sam had overheard Gina declaring to a mutual friend: "I have to say, this white goods millionaire who's trying to buy the next property to us has clearly got an awful lot of money. But I can't say that he matches it in the taste department."

Though still not appreciating what the reference during her trial at Blackcroft to the "bane of Barney's Tump" had been all about, Lady Goldendawn yet confided in her old friend: "You know ... I'm somehow never quite sure about Gina ... I can't help wondering if she might not be a closet Hillite ... or at least, the longer that she lives up there ... Hmm."

The diminutive town Mum wasn't quite sure what her hostess was referring to, but nonetheless affirmed: "Reckon she needs watchin', me darling." Later in the evening the furniture tycoon's wife was heard to protest: "But of course I give them all a Christmas tip. These *trades* people provide a very valuable service."

A great party was enjoyed by all, but Juliana always regretted that Beth and Paul had cited an "unavoidable prior commitment", since it appeared that her fellow heroine of the Grand Western stage still had the hump. The only other invitees to decline were the Bates', since Janet had found out that children would be present and hence considered the risk of infection to be altogether too great. In her absence, Lady Goldendawn overheard some rather surprising snippets of village tittle tattle as she circulated amongst her guests, such as: "Well they do say that Janet will only ... you know" ... "That's why her husband doesn't ... you know, any more" ... "I have heard that it's always blocked" and "Not even that courier, the naughty but nice one who she couldn't keep her hands off, would."

"Well I never. Who would have thought it?" the hostess smiled to herself. "I do seem to recall Beth saying something about that." This new hot topic could in part have been due to the also missing Sharon having some time previously left the village upon succumbing to an illicit pregnancy. When her husband found out, he had obtained a quickie divorce, then as quickly remarried a nuclear physicist who would always be working too. Finally he sent his children away to boarding schools and erected a Wild West-style gibbet by his gate, just in case any still cruising cowboys might not have learned of the altered arrangements within; though he could never recall quite from where he had got such an idea.

Sharon was in time re-housed in the "Smelly Stairwells of Great Heath", the most run down single mother block in town; but she missed her older children dreadfully and found it difficult to feel true love for the new arrival. This strange, altogether rough infant had been born tattooed from head to foot, and his hair steadfastly refused to grow beyond a number one cut. Whenever he cried, which was often and lustily, the mother would imagine that brick and plaster dust was issuing from his mouth and ears; as if to scold her for her own very infidelity and the jealous sentiments that had first given rise to it. In due course the child was taken into care, and Sharon was transferred to Great Heath NHS Mental Healthcare Trust. There she spent the remainder of her years plotting the downfall of Greater Donnington Manor's mistress with her room mate, who would never say anything about herself except that her name was Kelly, and she had once been famous.

On the morning after the grand housewarming, Juliana sat cross-legged before the HC screen on one of the several brand new sofas in the lime reclining room. She was watching a Sunday arts review programme in which her friend James Lee Patience was being interviewed about his newest blockbuster novel that had just topped the national best-seller charts. "I suppose ... what I'm saying ... is that ultimately ... we're all the same," the raconteur, wit and all round good egg was intoning; with a half-vacant stare over the interviewer's shoulder.

"Oh no we're not, James Lee," our heroine mused to herself, as the pale, diffused sunlight that was shining through the room's leaded glass windows cast merry little patterns onto the walls and ceiling. "Because, despite everything ... I rather suspect that you still live in a caravan ... and I've got a big house. So there!"

Outside, somewhere in the village, three ladies in nurses' uniform were enquiring whether the party had finished yet and if there was any drink left. Just up on the Hill, a line of ponies passing between the rival great iron gates of d'Oriel Dale and Hogs Hill Hall shied nervously at a distant baying of formidable dogs that signalled a hung over straggler from the party's mistaken incursion into the back way. Over on the town side, Trevor Day was busily fitting a lately discarded sharp suit to the dangling effigy that as ever guarded the entrance to his long driveway. As he did so, he pondered whether the idea might catch on if it were marketed as a must have garden accessory through his furniture warehouse chain, "Triffs". In town, at Sam's Beauty Emporium, the weekend cleaners were sweeping up the lopped curls and discarded falsies; and consigning polystyrene bottles to recycling boxes before the Monday morning collection.

In the salon's elaborately traffic calmed street, gangs of local authority workmen were repairing the various footways, raised brick obstructions, chicanes and traffic humps; ahead of the forthcoming week's APC visitations. Contrary perhaps to some readers' expectations, life on The Lees continued much the same as always; since the author had at no stage clarified whether Cuylee McGrouse's last two tins of red kidney beans had been of the ring pull variety or standard issue. Business was brisk at the compulsorily requisitioned Dellsey Manor Theme Park, where long lines of vehicles were queuing for their excited occupants' tickets. And, somewhere out in the frozen wastes of Siberia, a furtive squad of inscrutable Oriental cyborgs was unpacking the back-up stock of Gremlin clones and preparing them for reactivation.

"No, James Lee, we're not all the same," Juliana thought to herself once more. "Because I'm special, and one day I might just save the world again." Her reverie was interrupted by an incoming trigitext alert on her mobile comms link. "You'd never have done it if you hadn't let me drive," the message read. "Course Beth, you're special too. We still friends?" our heroine text'd back. "Course," came the reply. Then Lady Juliana Goldendawn flipped the device's display cover closed and turned her eyes back towards her home cinema screen.

PART 3

The Tins and the Time Capsule

Chapter 1

The low autumnal sun that shone through the haughty west-facing glass screen of Hogs Hill Hall cast a curious pattern on the great oak table of that primordial pile's revered parliamentary chamber. At the antique edifice's head the Dowager Day, prime minister of the feudal land of England and most venerable of all Hillites, sat flanked as always by Nigel Scroatley-Browne the chancellor and Sir Nicholas Coverlet the home secretary. A cabinet meeting was in progress and the prime minister was perusing a list of supplicants from various emergent nations of the post-apocalypse mainland alliance, that were attempting as was their habitual but somewhat futile custom to establish trading relations with the little offshore fiefdom whose aged and eccentric leaders were gathered therein. From the wall above the threesome, the formidable likeness of the Hall's builder Squire Barney Cockscomb surveyed the proceedings loftily from within the grand gilt frame of an eighteenth century painting, while various other revered past Hillites of note displayed a similar and unflinching disdain from the chamber's antique panelled sides.

The large, lucid eyes, hooked nose, full lips and slightly deformed jaw of the bewigged face in the founder's portrait conveyed a certain intellect and vision, yet still more than a suggestion of a cruel and unyielding nature. The red-coated squire's right hand was depicted resting upon a skull, while from the left there dangled a noose that fell below his ample breeches to play sinisterly about the buckle of one ornate dress shoe. The other foot appeared to be engaged in the act of extinguishing the life of some insignificant yet wayward wild creature, and between them these various symbols served to impart a dire challenge to any beholder of that enduring image in oils to defy the original's will at their own considerable peril. No such insolent confrontation suggested itself from the table below those all seeing eyes on this day however, as the assembled senior representatives of Hogs Hill's most revered lineages huffed and puffed, yawned and blustered their way through another session's affairs of state concerning the peculiar domain over which these assorted, elderly worthies now so pompously presided.

Eventually, the Dowager lowered her small assortment of papers then her cloudy spectacles in turn, and demanded a little testily: "Why, tell me am I seeing the Russian ambassador second? The Hill lore on such matters is quite plain. Ruskies are *always* third." The chancellor leaned forward and intoned softly and with just a suggestion of candour: "This one paid us two hundred million groats to *let* him be second, ma'am." At that revelation the prime minister thought for a moment and her wrinkled nose twitched slightly as she considered how though her colleague was not in the habit of being entirely forthcoming over the fullness of the fiefdom's coffers, the sum that he had cited was none too trifling.

"Very well," she pronounced. "I shall make an exception, just this once." Then she enquired, with a sharpness that rather belied her greatly advanced years: "And I trust that you have not put any of it to one side ... for *yourself*?"

At that, the chancellor and home secretary exchanged knowing glances, then protested as one: "Perish the thought, ma'am!" whilst the foreign secretary, Douglas Hay-Wain also shuffled slightly with a hint of discomfort in his own split leather seat.

The prime minister next examined some further papers, and then enquired of the last named: "Have the south coast ports been secured against all comers?" At that, various of the assembled holders of high office either exhaled slightly or shuffled their own papers while the foreign secretary himself prepared to face down this, in his view rather too consistent pre-occupation for the he knew not what-teenth time. Though all of the fiefdom's cabinet members were selected from the most aged and venerable of Hillites as was only fitting, the ultimate and implacable venerability of their leader could nevertheless still exasperate some of them more than a little at times. Whilst nobody present was especially enamoured with Frenchies, Spicks, Ruskies, Huns, Ities, or the ever restive Jockos and Provonians even closer to home; the prime minister and certain of her most aged cohorts' position could nonetheless seem a little trying at times to certain of the younger, mere octogenarians present.

174

"One really shouldn't be quite so concerned, ma'am," the foreign secretary ultimately countered. "I would personally direct more attention to our northern and western borders. Those frightful Celts are becoming quite restive again."

But the prime minister thought for a few moments and then pronounced: "No … double the night watch in the southern ports. Have we got any more information on that awful Antipodean messiah person?"

"Yes ma'am," and "No ma'am," her cabinet colleagues variously responded, realising the futility of attempting to reason with her, and the meeting dragged on until early evening.

Nobody amongst the ruling elite knew the exact age of the Dowager Day, but what was undeniably without doubt was that she was the most venerable of all Hillites and hence the only possible choice as prime minister. The one-time furniture tycoon's wife, Gina of the early twenty-first century now sat at the head of a family dynasty spanning five generations. The only remaining member of her own generation, she had also outlived all of her peers, becoming ever more venerable with her advancing years; and her sons, grandsons and great grandsons now exerted influence over significant areas of the fiefdom's more lucrative, though undeniably parochial commerce.

The offshore fiefdom of England had suffered especially badly during the early part of the apocalypse. At that time, previously undetected, remotely activated and fiendishly upgraded cyborg hordes had at intervals emerged from multimart cellars across the country's south to raze vast urban areas with untold loss of life; whilst the migrant workforce of the north's park home estates had wrought a similar retribution upon that remote, rainy and windswept industrial belt. But throughout, the ancient sanctuary of Hogs Hill itself, above the west bank of the great River Isis, some forty miles upstream from the former capital London, remained untouched; and all over the fiefdom a peculiar phenomenon began to be observed.

In the two years prior to the global catastrophe's onset, Gina Day's now dear departed husband Trevor had marketed garden gibbets through his furniture warehouse chain Triffs as the must have accessory of that time. Upon these the purchasers would like to suspend effigies of their own choice with which to deter unwanted visitors or cowboy tradesmen, or provoke near neighbours with whom they might be in dispute. Gina had got the idea herself from the practice of some of her most venerable Hillite contemporaries of that time, and her husband had eventually recognised its market potential. Little could those upwardly mobile settlers on the Hill have dreamt how all of those then fashion followers who had erected a "Triffs Garden Gibbet" on their land would not only survive the apocalypse itself, but afterwards proceed to live to a great age whilst gradually and inexorably becoming ever more Hillite-like in the process; just as the now Dowager Day was fated to do. And so, as Squire Barney Cockscomb himself had foretold in his irrevocable will of 1772, the unchangeable ways of life on Hogs Hill in that distant century once more came to prevail throughout the feudal land of England.

As a consequence of Gina and Trevor's then inadvertent meddling in the original gibbet lore of that historic locality, the bane of Barney's Tump that was anciently ordained to befall any such outsider who might steal from the sanctity of Hogs Hill had thus spread like a virus throughout the fiefdom. But nobody at that time or since was actually aware of Squire Cockscomb's undying and unbreakable legacy, as all knowledge of it had perished with the collective and untimely deaths of the then Hogs Hill Preservation Trust committee in 2023. By the time of this renewed drama, the moneyed population of the feudal society that emerged anew following the worst ravages of the apocalypse had therefore become more Englishly fusty, dowdy and stuffy than at any time prior to those events; whilst not to mention more exploitative of have nots at the expense of the haves.

When the afternoon's deliberations at Hogs Hill Hall eventually drew to their close, the prime minister requested that her personal carriage be summoned to take her back down to her private residence in the mystic glade on the lower eastern side. "I really couldn't spend tonight in that ghastly, vulgar boarding house," she informed her closest cabinet colleagues, before adding with a sigh: "I seem to have been feeling so very … fatigued just of late."

Sir Nicholas Coverlet, Nigel Scroatley-Browne and Douglas Hay-Wain variously replied: "Of course, ma'am," "Try not to tire yourself so," and "I'm sure that's very wise;" before the carriage drew up before the Hall's majestic, gold embossed doors with their neat arrays of Hillite family crests. Once the various footmen had made their equally grand and so very aged charge comfortable within, the carriage drew away once more and the chancellor, home and foreign secretaries were left to their own dark devices away from their venerable figurehead's own scrutiny for another shadowy and secretive evening at the seat of power.

The property now known as "The Boarding House" was situated in the dale below the Parliament building itself, immediately across the narrow and ancient thoroughfare of Hogs Hill's middle way. It's pre-apocalypse owners, the then fashion magnate Armando d'Oriel and his beautiful wife Elronda, had abandoned the fiefdom for the Italy of the male partner's forebears as soon as the new Hillite ruling elite ascended to power. Having, like the younger Days ever been considered "ghastly *nouveau riche*" by their various neighbours, the d'Oriels now considered their position to have become untenable, and so opted to resettle their family in a land where their own deeply cherished values of style and good taste would be so much more generally appreciated.

Selling the house was naturally impossible, since no Hillite would be likely to contemplate the great "vulgarity" of inhabiting a dwelling that had been extended and modernised. "If the blighters can't be bothered to have 'em built big enough and right in the first place, then what do they think they are doing here?" had always been the prevailing, more "well-bred" attitude.

The then chancellor Hugo Scroatley-Browne, grandfather of the present incumbent, had therefore requisitioned the building and its rolling grounds at a fraction of their true value, while his Hillite peers exulted at this long overdue banishment of those most unwanted of usurpers from their own so venerable midst. Afterwards, the house in the dale became used for accommodating the rare emissaries from abroad who might actually be received on the Hill. Having usually been identified as possessing something or another of value that could be plundered for the common local good, all of these unwise guests would end up being made away with during the night in the time honoured Hillite tradition of hospitality where outsiders were concerned; never to set foot in their home countries again. But most recently, and as the prime minister's own contribution to government had lessened with her advancing frailty, the house in the dale had become an ideal location for the out of hours' deliberations of the chancellor and home and foreign secretaries, once the more elderly cabinet members could prolong their own days' travails no longer. Though they still held their leader in the utmost Hillite esteem, it seemed plain to this threesome that her own time was surely drawing nigh. And being themselves mere octogenarians, they entertained slightly less of an antipathy than most of their colleagues towards the comparative modernity of the surroundings in which they would meet nightly to plan the succession.

As the Dowager Day was conveyed downhill along the broadening middle way, she began to turn over in her mind the many years since she and her late husband had first selected Hogs Hill as their home. She momentarily thought again of how very weary she seemed to have been feeling just recently, and as reflection upon reflection of gnarled old oak, dense conifer and acidic rhododendron danced about the antique carriage's ornately patterned glass windows in the fading evening light, her mind turned back to a distant time just prior to the apocalypse itself. There, through what now seemed an immense nostalgic haze and to the comforting hoof-fall of the horses all the while, the centenarian matriarch recalled her thirty-something equivalent sitting in the great and exquisitely planted conservatory to one side of the house in the dale below Hogs Hill Hall, with her then dear but now long lost friends Elronda and Juliana.

The figures in this vision were busy putting the final touches to the various arrangements for the lavish party that was planned in the village to the Hill's immediate west to celebrate Juliana's thirty-seventh birthday. As they went over the buffet menus for one last time to check that everything would be just perfect, two of the friends suddenly glanced at one another, seemingly trying to suppress a smile. "What's wrong?" Gina at once enquired. "I didn't just sound like a Hillite again, did I?"

Juliana left it for Elronda to respond, since the latter could always be relied upon to put such things so very nicely: "Well … maybe just a little bit."

"Oh dear, it seems to be happening more and more often. I really don't know why."

"Well, Jules and I do notice that too, Gina dear, and you have asked us to point it out when it occurs … I'm sure it's nothing."

Seeing the slightly troubled look that crossed her friend's face, and in order to change the subject, Juliana next enquired: "Are the garden gibbets still selling well?" At this, the apparition of the furniture tycoon's wife brightened once more and replied that they seemed to be as popular as ever, before asking her companions whether they themselves had bought one yet. Juliana answered: "We'll be getting one soon", as was her custom whenever anyone might mention something that they had which she didn't have. The phantom Elronda next assured her friends with the original's customary tact that the Triffs gibbets were a charming idea, but that in the fashion world it was important to always try to stay one step ahead, rather than to follow the must have trends of the moment. The third spirit Juliana visibly grimaced at that, though Gina herself remained as ever unconcerned at this sign of the one-time deadly rivalry that had existed between her two friends, and which still seemed to simmer just beneath the surface.

As the prime ministerial carriage reached the junction of the middle way and Hogs Hill's broader main way that led back towards the mystic glade, its passenger tapped on the roof with her staff to signal to the coachman to rest awhile. The Dowager looked out over the land of Poets' Meadow, that fell away steeply to the east and afforded one of the most spectacular vistas of all over the wide Isis valley below. The beholder recalled the once famous skyline of the former town, with it's various historic churches and other grand buildings that from this same point had inspired not only poets, but many an art society outing sitting at their carelessly arranged easels on warm summer afternoons, and even more mere dog walkers or ramblers who had simply felt so at peace with the world at this spot. And as the last vestiges of evening light faded in the skies overhead, the carriage's occupant began to feel suddenly less akin to the most venerable of all Hillites as she had somehow become, and imperceptibly more like that far younger Gina of the distant memory that had played itself out in her mind moments earlier. Her reverie then moved on to Juliana's thirty-seventh birthday party itself, a few days after the final planning session in the conservatory.

This celebration seemed on course to eclipse even the birthday girl's most lavish past extravaganzas, until at 8pm prompt the familiar church bells rang out all over the country, summoning the population to its compulsory viewing of "Eastenders". The government of the day had introduced this measure so as to reinforce the dominant position of its broadcasting corporation's flagship soap opera at the head of the national curriculum, and hence fend off his majesty's opposition's habitual carping over declining educational standards. But on this fateful evening, not one monosyllable of argumentative cockney gruff could be detected on any of that age's 563 available home cinema channels; not even BBC Soap 24. Almost all of them, save for perhaps one or two shopping or auction channels, appeared to be united in presenting the same and terrible moonscape images. In the end, Juliana's husband Alex had been obliged to announce to the uneasy ranks of their assembled guests: "Ladies and Gentleman. It would appear that London and Washington DC simply aren't there any more."

Still the weary Dowager's troubled reverie moved onwards. On the morning after those momentous attacks, an old unmarked van had swept through the open rustic gateway at the head of the house in the glade's long drive, past it's ever present guardian effigy dangling from the Triffs' original and the small square notice proclaiming "SALESMEN KEEP OUT" on the gallows pole beneath. This mail order courier was bringing the latest offering from Gina's favourite range of expensive children's clothes, that coincidentally also enjoyed some favour amongst the younger Hillites of the time who had inherited properties from their more venerable forebears. The van's driver always enjoyed his long chats in the glade if its mistress was not too busy; though he too couldn't help but notice how she seemed to be growing more like her neighbours with the passage of time.

Meaningful conversation was such a rare feature of this lone wanderer's working day, amidst the more usual round of endless and inane observations about the weather, the finer points of ladies clothing sizes, a peculiar science whose meaning ever evaded him no matter how long he remained in the job; and the perennial complaints of fanatical "Foremost" brand loyals whose love-hate relationships with the object of their addiction always seemed to focus upon him personally. That market leading catalogue's call centre operatives in Bombay, New Delhi or Rawalpindi were all briefed to exploit this strange but enduring local nuance to the maximum advantage, language difficulties allowing; and the slavish devotion of Foremost's customers always seemed to endure no matter how much they might complain about wrong goods received and unmet delivery deadlines. On this particular morning, the kindred spirits chatted for a little longer than was their habit about the terrible events of the preceding evening, until Gina ultimately pleaded that she really must tend to her children's ponies and the visitor headed back downhill towards the town in the Isis valley below.

< The Courier's Last Round – an anecdote >

Back in 2025, it was beginning to rain as the courier reached town on what would prove to be his last ever round, and his first call was at a well-known doggy kafuffle stop. In an attempt to lift his mood further after seeing such a favourite customer as Gina Day, he rapped a little more loudly than usual on the door in question, and the excited yapping of the miniature but highly excitable terriers within announced themselves as ever to the outside world. Next a chorus of: "In … In! … In!!" became audible from somewhere inside the suburban semi, and the courier looked to heaven for the umpteenth time as the familiar drama of dogs and owner chasing themselves up and down the hallway and in and out of various doors played itself out before him. "Stupid animals … I'll kill 'em," the albeit temporary victor pronounced upon eventually opening the door.

"No you won't," the figure without thought to himself, before daring to venture: "Terrible what happened yesterday, wasn't it?" But at that point, a hyperactive terrier burst anew from within the inadequate prison of the lady's front room, and snatching up a half-signed manifest to a renewed chorus of "In! … In!!", the courier retreated to his idling vehicle.

At the next stop there was no reply, so the courier walked part way around the house and placed the delivery by the side door, before returning to post his calling card. It was raining steadily now, and just as he reached the gate a familiar sound of hand striking glass commenced to his rear. He turned to see an anxious looking old man standing behind the window holding a curtain aside in one hand, while with the other he waved the calling card above his head instead of reading it; then the courier gestured "round the side". Still the supplicant did not seem to understand. The courier took two further steps towards his van but the banging on the window became more frantic still, so he retrieved the parcel and returned to the front door yet still it did not open. Eventually a shadow was discernible within, fumbling with the latch, but the mortise lock was tightly fastened.

"Hold on a minute!" called a voice. The courier then proceeded to spectate with a mixture of exasperation and pure amazement, counting the passing minutes as his customer searched first the kitchen and then climbed slowly upstairs and back down again on a futile quest to locate the mislaid key. Eventually the elderly gentleman walked around the corner of the house, since the side door had been unlocked the whole while, and pronounced: "Well you might have brought some decent weather with you."

Biting his lip, the courier merely proffered his manifest, trying to keep it dry as best he could below the open porch. Nothing irritated him more than being attributed with "bringing weather", and he wondered as so many times before whether he must be the only person who ever came to some of these customers' doors. "Sign and print there please," he invited in as polite a manner as he could muster.

"Wot, 'ere? ... Where? ... Print it," the old man proceeded to mumble to himself, holding the board and its tightly clipped sheets of paper back out in the falling rain as he tried to locate the correct place on the sheet that had twice been clearly pointed out to him. When the ballpoint pen failed to make its mark upon the by now sodden paper, the customer concluded: "It's got no ink in it." Then the courier dared to offer: "Terrible what happened to London yesterday, wasn't it?"

"Reckon this rain's setting in for a while," came the inevitable reply. "Can you arrange some better weather next time you come?"

The day's third call was a collection from a regular customer who never seemed to keep anything that she ordered and had left a message to say the items would be hidden behind her bins. The recipient retrieved the returns, then wrote out the receipts as usual before venturing back towards the letter box, wondering if he might for once manage to escape the attentions of the neighbourhood watcher across this particular street. He wondered in vain: the second old gentleman in question was already stumbling towards him, calling: "Do you want me to take that?"

"It's OK, it's a collection," the courier explained.

"Do you want me to sign?"

"It's not a delivery, it's a collection."

"Here, I'll take it for you."

"It's a *collection* ... she's sending it back!" A hint of understanding at last seemed to dawn in the assailant's eyes, then the courier chanced: "Wasn't it terrible what happened to London yesterday?" The elderly neighbour looked at him blankly for a moment, and then declared: "Not a very nice day, is it?"

The downcast hearer began to walk away, and on reaching his van just heard the inevitable last offer of: "Don't you want me to take that?" As the courier drove away up the road, the image in his rear view mirror that was staring after him with a perplexed expression and with one arm still raised in the air, eventually faded from view. "Oh well, at least it's stopped raining," he consoled himself.

After several more calls, the old unmarked van drew up at another notorious terrier location. This diminutive Old Torkie specimen became immediately visible leaping three feet into the air and back down again behind the glazed part of the front door even before the courier managed to reach it. Then he knocked with his bare knuckles at precisely the right spot to send the animal into paroxysms of crashing against the door's inner side and snapping at the letter box, whilst yapping wildly the whole while. Would the owner for once in his life shut the dog in somewhere before answering the front door, the visitor wondered.

He need not have done: the said barrier swung inwards and the middle-aged man before him began his customary dance, kicking backwards with both his heels and shouting "Get back, get in there!", as his canine soul mate darted first to one side of the flailing feet and then the other, lunging at the courier and occasionally trying to snatch the parcel from his grasp, before retreating behind its protector once more. "It's all right, he won't hurt you," the customer then as ever pronounced. "He's all noise."

"Hurt me?" the courier mused to himself. "I could squash it under my boot, more likely!"

Then the agitated terrier spotted the front garden gate that the caller had left deliberately ajar so as to prolong the entertainment, and immediately bolted for it closely followed by the owner. As man and dog chased each other wildly around the street outside bringing various passing vehicles to an abrupt halt, more neighbouring men's best friends of varying size commenced their own hullabaloo of yapping, barking and howling that was quickly augmented by the habitual shouts and curses of their owners. As one or two more uncontrollable pets managed to effect an escape into the street and their various minders inevitably followed, the courier abandoned all hope of obtaining a signature and sauntered back to his van. "Wasn't it terrible what happened to London yesterday?" he called out upon reaching it. Nobody answered, except for one lady of advancing years who called across from a nearby garden: "Are you coming in to read my electric too?"

"My God, the whole world's about to erupt and these people all carry on just the same as they always do," the lone daily wanderer thought to himself. "Do none of them have an inkling about what's going to happen out there?"

Then there came a rap on his passenger window. "Need it signing for?" the customer offered as he clung onto his still yapping and snapping little charge by the collar, dragging the tiny dog back towards his open front door. The man inside the van simply couldn't resist: he wound down the window, passed the clipboard through, and as the owner seized it the terrier propelled itself once again into the nearest doggy-owner kafuffle whilst various similar ones played themselves out up and down the thoroughfare. And so the courier's morning passed as it always did, from one doggy drama to another uncomprehending elderly encounter, while he clung to the hope of one or more of those bath towel or scanty moments that might just serve to somehow lighten the tedium.

The van driver had thus far remained aware that given the previous day's events, the normally absent ranks of addicted Foremost commuters whose unvarying complaints via Bombay, New Delhi or Rawalpindi were intercepted and then erased by his home answering console late into each evening, would probably not be working as usual. Eventually these worst fears were realised as a smartly attired and not unattractive, but even so much too intense woman in her late twenties, waved one hand in the courier's face as she came to her door; whilst with the other she frenetically key-padded a palm top computer that was supported by a broad strap around her neck. Under her chin was tucked a mobile comms link, into which she was assuring someone that she would "speak to my people and get back to you on that one." It seemed that no matter whether London might still be there or not, appearances nevertheless needed to be kept up.

Eventually the waiting visitor was permitted to proceed with delivering what this one-time commuter had ordered, at which she proclaimed: "Is that all? Haven't you got anything else for me?" The courier briefly considered his stock response of "Not unless you want a hug," that was popular on various parts of his round; but on this occasion he considered it very, very briefly indeed. Then the customer announced: "I was expecting them yesterday."

"No doubt. I didn't get them until this morning," her adversary informed her. "But I specifically asked for them to be delivered yesterday," the young executive emphasised a little more shrilly. "I didn't get them until *today*," the accused party repeated, showing her his manifest to prove it; at which the complainant threatened: "I'm really going to have a go at them this time. I'm expecting much more than that."

Then the courier enquired a little provocatively: "Do you think it could possibly have something to do with London simply not being there any more?"

"That's no excuse," came the immediate response. "*I'm* still working!"

The hearer by now could take no more: "Oh really?" he retorted with as much irony as he could inject into the highly charged atmosphere on this particular doorstep. "I thought for a moment that you might simply be making a lot of pointless noise!"

As this barb struck home it's recipient fixed the offender before her with an affronted look and demanded frigidly: "Give me your name! I'll have you removed."

"By whom?" came the calm reply. "You needn't suppose there's a queue of people waiting to take *this* job off me?" Former London commuters never seemed to realise that. Then the wrongdoer walked away, leaving the frustrated woman fuming on her doorstep and preparing to rant and rave at customer service.

The next Foremost devotee to be dealt with that morning was

a least a friendly one, though the deliverer often wished as with so many other regulars on his round that this lady might occasionally manage to talk about something other than clothes, shopping and children. He rang the doorbell and the familiar figure of Jodie presented itself, holding a small child in her arms while two yet tinier members of her copious brood commenced to play about her ankles whilst staring up at him and smiling the whole while, as small children do. "Oh hello, I thought that would be you. They said most of it was in stock, though one or two were on delay; but they said Friday," this customer began.

"Wasn't it terr…" the caller attempted to interject, but Jodie barely drew breath before continuing: "Oh, and I've got a return. I ordered a size twelve and they sent an eleven. I can get into an eleven some of the time but a twelve's safer, though their elevens do fit me more often than most people's. I went to the shop and they had an eleven, but I'd already ordered the twelve …"

"Wasn't it terr…"

"My kids'll only dress in Foremost, won't you poppet … mwah. It's such good quality, isn't it? I wonder if the man's brought your new jumper, hey. Oh she will be pleased. We love our Foremost jumpers don't we, sweetheart?"

It was no use. The bewildered male caller simply could not inject any morsel of his own into this non-stop maternal monologue. He had never quite managed to work out just how many children Jodie must have, but judging by the eager faces that would peer around door frames and seemingly from any nook and cranny behind their overworked but uncomplaining mother, double figures did not seem an unreasonable estimate. And since Jodie did not appear to be quite out of her twenties, he puzzled at how she could possibly have produced so many in such a limited span of years, or indeed how the time for the bodily functions involved could have been set aside amidst her ever burgeoning domestic commitment. Once, when the courier had been invited inside, the whole house appeared to be piled from floor to ceiling with ironing in various stages of completion; whilst partly consumed meals of one kind or another seemed to cover every flat surface.

With the previous day's events still playing on his mind, he eventually took a deep breath and blurted out: "Terrible what happened in London and Washington DC yesterday, don't you

…?" But before he could finish a loud crash and a louder scream were audible from the kitchen, above the constant back-drop of bickering infant voices and the whirr of spin and tumble driers. The mother retreated from view to investigate, then the man at the door wrote out a receipt and didn't wait for Jodie to pronounce her verdict.

The courier had saved up that day's call in town that he had most been looking forward to until last. And as he edged past the badly parked ranks of giant smart Mums' vehicles that were engaged in their daily contest with the elaborate traffic calming measures and parking restrictions to either side of Sam's Beauty Emporium, his heart began to beat a little faster. He drew to a halt besides the towering new Dreisler Bethmobile that was parked at the craziest angle of all in front of the salon itself, switched on his hazard warning lights and then announced his arrival at the door.

All delivery men and postmen, indeed most male callers fell for Sam because she was such a darling and such a dish; and this courier was no exception. The object of his admiration burst into view before him and grabbed at his manifest and pen, managing as always to stroke his hands slightly as she did so. Then she leaned in close to sign the sheets and as he placed his own hand on her far shoulder and effected a little squeeze, they beamed momentarily into each other's faces. Sam chattered as always about what was in each of the familiar pink Foremost bags, who it was for and what she was expecting next; while the caller tried somehow to get a word in edgeways.

Suddenly, the beautician glanced backwards over her shoulder towards what appeared to be some kind of commotion within her salon, and the courier managed to offer: "Don't you think it's terrible what happened in London and Washington DC yesterday?"

His idol tilted her head back slightly and shouted: "Yeah, that's right! … Cheers me darlin'," and with that, as quickly as the tiny bundle of energy had appeared in the doorway it was gone again. Things were always that way with Sam. The courier pressed his eyes close to the glass door and beheld what appeared to be a cat fight between two salon juniors, who were tearing at each other's hair and eyes as they rolled around locked tightly together on the floor before the ranks of cheering customers. The proprietess had gained a position atop a chair from where she was calling out the odds and chalking them up on a little blackboard as the excited punters placed their bets. "Such minor local disputes," the outsider ultimately consoled himself; and then he wound his weary way homeward.

Once he had regained the safe haven of his own park home, this lone daily wanderer turned on his HC system and tuned to NBC War 24, that was beamed in direct from America. Switching immediately to multi-screen mode, the viewer attempted like many more concerned contemporaries on that apocalyptic morning to take in the scenes of devastation from various locations across the Atlantic, and the images of equally distant funny foreign vistas that were burning in retribution for those most insolent and unjustifiable of attacks. In one lower corner of the screen, the animated image of the newest Grand Western Secretary of No Sense, Arnold T Numveldte III, sporting the familiar white cane and slightly stained lapel of all his assorted predecessors, was analysing the finer points of the action just as those others had always done. Across the length and breadth of what had once been London, burly men in ridiculously bizarre and over-inflated protective suits were wielding highly comical arrays of equally ineffective equipment in a doomed attempt to locate any, just any possible application for the government's long vaunted major incident action plan. Then the multimart cellars on some of the south of England's worst housing estates began to disgorge their long hidden and deadly legacy, after which the retaliatory air strikes commenced in earnest.

✧ ✧ ✧

The Dowager Day's carriage eventually turned through the ruined gates of her private residence on Hogs Hill's lower eastern side, past its somewhat decaying guardian gibbet and along the tree-covered drive that was pot-holed in many places, to draw up by the house itself. Prior to the apocalypse, Gina and Trevor had been as notorious locally as the d'Oriels for daring to modernise and extend this same property, attracting the undying disdain of their gentrified neighbours in equal measure to those other "so very vulgar" favourers of change in the shadow of the Hall itself. But many, many a long year had now passed since the sound of trowel upon brick or hammer upon nail, or the scrape of shovel mixing cement or mortar had echoed around the mystic glade. And the Dowager's private domain had hence come to present a similarly mouldering air of faded grandeur to all of the many other venerable ancestral relics that adorned each and every one of Hogs Hill's favourable vantage points, and various lesser locations besides. The sole exception where relative modernity was concerned now remained the much maligned if necessary in its way edifice of "The Boarding House".

Sitting a little later beside a blazing wood fire with an assortment of blankets wrapped about her legs, and once the butler had taken the supper tray away, the grand matriarch summoned her housekeeper to say that she would rather like to be left alone on this evening since she had much to think about. Her reverie next turned further back in time to when she and Trevor had first purchased the run down property of an old Hillite bachelor with no heir himself, but who had displayed a liking for the company of authors, artists and such other frightful threats to the Hill's very sanctity in the eyes of his neighbours. She recalled the welcoming party from the Preservation Trust, the three rather stout and formidable ladies of a certain age who had beaten a path to their door, each dressed in a tweedy suit and carrying a neat wicker basket on her arm. How those worthies had recoiled upon learning that the newcomers in their midst were *shop keepers*, before beating an immediate retreat, never to darken the offending door again.

In the ensuing years, when time allowed before the children had arrived, the inquisitive twenty-something Gina had taken to exploring the many footpaths and bridleways that criss-crossed the geological feature of the Hill. The locals were known to tolerate visitors on foot or horseback a little more readily than offending through traffic, since public rights of way were after all a historic and peculiarly English eccentricity that was worthy of upholding in their eyes, within limits. And on one such excursion, the young outsider had first beheld those mysterious gibbets whose erection, then unbeknown to herself, was the ancient and sacrosanct privilege of only the most venerable of all Hillites. Quite why her youthful counterpart had decided to adorn her own gateway with such an imitation edifice, the reminiscing Dowager could somehow not now recall. After all, door to door salesmen were hardly in the habit of plying their business on the Hill, no more than any other species of door knocker. But the said edifice had nevertheless survived until the present time, and the sleepy prime minister suddenly felt that she would rather like to draw back the curtain and gaze towards it once more if only she could summon the strength to raise herself from her fireside seat.

The hoot of a Tawny Owl was just audible from somewhere in the glade outside, then an answering call from a little further afield, as the Dowager's reminiscences next turned to the long years of the apocalypse itself. At a fairly early stage in the global hostilities, as the town in the Isis valley below was obliterated along with urban centre upon urban centre the length and breadth of the country, the realisation had dawned amongst the Hillites that their own ancient and sanctified lands appeared to be displaying a peculiar immunity. And so the leading families all called in their descendants from far and wide to sit out and survive within the confines of their own crumbling yet copious ancestral homes, the progressive destruction of civilisation in the world without; and all of the lesser families naturally followed suit, including those local anomalies the Days and the d'Oriels. Nobody knew quite why Hogs Hill should have been rendered such a safe haven, but the more senior ranking amongst its gathered residents naturally relished the opportunity to plan their own eventual accession to power, once the Grand Western vanguards of freedom and the rampaging robotic and funny foreign hordes of the enemy had finally run out of people to slaughter and places to destroy.

Year upon year of global conflict passed, yet still the Hillites' inheritance remained immune. It seemed a logical assumption to these assembled, old-moneyed and in some cases landed dynastics that they might well be the only such interests to survive in any numbers what Squire Cockscomb himself had long foretold as the "great conflagration in the world outside". And so they stood firm, sat tight and looked forward to the future date when the rightful privilege of the English feudal gentry would once more be reaffirmed as was only fitting, and the offshore fiefdom of their vision would be secured for ever against the incursions of unwanted outside or foreign influence of any kind. And as time ground on, the sheltering family in the mystic glade seemed to become less and less distinguishable from their peers amongst the

Hill's now younger cohorts.

In contrast, the d'Oriels were roundly scapegoated by the newer settlers: "Don't be so naughty, Toby. You sound just like one of those d'Oriels," "Eat up your greens or you'll turn into a d'Oriel," or "Don't stay out late or the d'Oriels will be after you," the newer generation Hillite mothers would variously chide their errant offspring when appropriate. But as the bane of Barney's Tump pursued its inescapable course, it became rarer and rarer for any young offender to suffer unfavourable comparison with a Day.

"What's a d'Oriel, Mama?" an occasionally bold or inquisitive child might dare to enquire. "Why those frightful, vulgar outsiders who live in the dale below Hogs Hill Hall," they would then be informed. "And we don't have dealings with the like of them, do we now?"

And so, as these children grew, they would become fond of mounting raiding parties to throw stones or launch assorted other missiles at these dreadful d'Oriels; or poison the rabbits, squirrels and assorted birds of ill omen in the immediate vicinity that in these times of hardship became something of a staple diet even on Hogs Hill. But the great iron gates to "d'Oriel Dale", and the razor sharp anti-intruder measures that adorned all of its boundary fences, served as effective barriers against the first of those annoyances; whilst unbeknown to their tormentors, that other and most maligned of all sheltering families had their own particular sources where sustenance was concerned, and very fine fare it was for the most part. In time and as they approached adulthood, the growing young d'Oriel entrepreneurs also came to control the Hill's native Duck and Pheasant resources, which was perhaps not unsurprising given their seemingly enduring talent for staying one step ahead of the game. This particular harvest was only supplied to the world outside, naturally enough, with the exception of their mother's old friend Gina and her own relations over on the lower eastern side.

The Dowager began to feel a little more chill despite her fireside repose, as the late evening elements outside conspired to effect their habitual designs upon what with the passage of time had ultimately become her rather draughty abode. She rang the bell to summon the butler who stoked up the fire just a little, and then she announced that she would really like to retire before long. More staff were then despatched to prepare their mistress' bedchamber as the grand matriarch mused on.

She next thought briefly of the sudden and seemingly spiteful retribution that the enemy had exacted upon the village to the Hill's immediate west, that had reputedly wiped out its entire population. None amongst the ruling elite ever ventured down on that side now, though rumours still reached them from time to time concerning a strange cylindrical object at the former settlement's centre that by repute would resist all attempts either to remove or render it asunder. But the Hillites paid no attention to such an idle notion, dismissing it as being beneath their consideration. Then, as an errant shard of blazing wood carelessly tumbled from atop the glowing fire and against the blackened guard by the hearthside figure's blanketed feet, she began to retrace in her increasingly troubled mind that most recent half century since the apocalypse had ultimately played out it's calamitous course.

Whilst the d'Oriels had seen fit to relocate to sunnier climes abroad once an albeit uncomfortable peace resumed in the world outside, the family from the mystic glade on the lower eastern side appeared to acquire a growing acceptance in local society. As the senior Hillite order consolidated its grip upon governance, land, property and commerce in equal measure amid the re-emergent social order of Squire Cockscomb's ancient feudal vision, the once despised Days' influence was likewise seen to grow and grow. And as that newest of Hilllite dynasties expanded in numbers and wealth through two further generations, the ultimate and implacable venerability of the grand matriarch at its head grew ever more unquestionable with each passing year.

So thus it transpired that at well beyond her own ninetieth year, the Dowager Day was nominated by her peers from all of those historic lineages to become their prime ministerial figurehead. "Oh the burden of office, and the loneliness of command!" the figure by the fireside now cried out in her solitude, unseen and unheard by all of those dear and always fleeting players of her own expansive past, and ultimately unloved by the available companions of her so unnaturally extended dotage.

The door then opened and the butler entered to enquire: "All is prepared now for ma'am to retire. Is one quite ready, perchance?" The Dowager nodded with a seemingly consuming lethargy, and more servants were summoned to convey their aged charge to her bed chamber and make her comfortable for the night. All the while, the evening's various reminiscences continued to play upon that waning and troubled mind as if to present a certain reality. "I *cannot be* a true Hillite," the sufferer at length murmured to herself, once she was left quite alone again; "So how, tell me how have I become the most venerable of them all?"

As the figure in its lonely bed gave vent to this ultimate anguish before the eyes closed and the head inclined to one side on the sleeper's assortment of pillows, the guardian gibbet by her home's outer gateway quivered slightly, and then slipped by four or five more degrees to the vertical. And just at that moment, a peculiar trick of the moonlight within the mystic glade suggested to a watching wench from the kitchen the faint and ghostly form of a man dressed in the habit of an eighteenth century squire moving noiselessly amongst the ever whispering trees.

"Hush yer talk, or I'll box yer ears for ye!" scolded the housekeeper, pulling this scrawny girl away from the window. "It's there. Oy juss seen 'im, missus!" nonetheless came an excited protest. "All buckles, an' breechuss, an' big black 'at. Oy tell ye, 'e's out there!"

Then one of the prime minister's offduty personal attendants rose from the kitchen table with its adornment of variously wholesome leftovers, walked to the same window and drew back the curtain to carefully survey the scene outside for himself. "Lord a mercy on us!" this guardian at length exclaimed out loud, falling back into a convenient seat and commencing to wipe his of a sudden somewhat paler brow. "It be 'e ... the ow'ld squoire 'isself. The same as be in the paintin' above 'er seat at the 'all."

The various staff of the great Hillite families mostly came from long servant lineages themselves, and liked to compete with one another over affecting the best rustic dialects. "Young Ned" the septuagenarian gardener, who claimed to be descended from one of the oldest of all servant families, next looked up from his seat to one side of the crackling fire, and stuffing a little more weed into his clay pipe pronounced: "Oy do reckun uss 'ow 'e eff coom to zee 'er orf ... They do zay uss 'ow he do appurr win 'ere the owldust in a faarmlee be reddee to shuffle aarf the coyle."

"And enough of yer own talk too Ned Beaseley, if I could unnerstan' a word ye say," the housekeeper scolded anew. "I've never heard such nonsense in me life! An' oy don't bileeve yer from an old serving family at all. Children's entertainers more loyke!" But as one or another growl of troubled dog or sinister shy of nervous horse nevertheless suggested themselves faintly from here or there in the ominous realms of the haunted air outside, this woman felt a sudden compunction to ascend to her mistress' bedchamber and check upon the welfare of the sleeper within.

From a high window of the ante-room to one side of that same resting place, the prime minister's on duty personal attendant was also surveying the mystic glade beneath through a brass spyglass, trying as best he could to focus upon the ever shifting shadow that suggested itself first from here and then over there in the uncertain moonlight as it filtered through the tree cover. But in time his gaze settled upon the guardian gibbet at the gate itself, and the beholder gasped as he beheld the newly dangling form of an eighteenth century felon. Then, smoke began to rise from this ramshackle edifice that together with its last tenant began to smoulder spontaneously; and so the roving spirit of Squire Barney Cockscomb evaporated into the gloom.

The attendant watched no longer, but burst into the neighbouring bed chamber at just the same moment that the housekeeper entered from the door in its opposite wall. The bane of Barney's Tump had released it's hold over Gina at long last; and the centenarian Dowager Day, most venerable of all Hillites and prime minister of the feudal land of England, was seen to have finally and very peacefully passed away in her sleep. The Russian ambassador was thus destined not to be seen second after all, as the so astute and suddenly rather more wealthy Hillite triumvirate in waiting of Nigel Scroatley-Browne, Sir Nicholas Coverlet and Douglas Hay-Wain had anticipated to their own mutual advantage all along. And when the dawn mists rose on the morrow, only a small mound of cooling ash by the mystic glade's entrance and a few charred patches on the rotting gate that the last falling embers of its perennial overseer had yet failed to ignite, served as a final testimony to the departed occupant's youthful folly in having so unknowingly stolen from the ancient sanctity of her adopted Hogs Hill domain.

Chapter 2

At a few leagues' distance beyond the east bank of the Isis, amidst the bombed out and never rebuilt ruins of what had once been The Lees estate on the former town's far flank, three girls aged about fourteen years or so sat around an open fire over which the skinned and gutted carcass of a rabbit was roasting on a makeshift spit. On one side, the flames played about a fair skinned and freckled yet nonetheless somewhat wizened countenance that was framed in a tumbling mass of dirty, bright orange hair. This urchin, named Gail led that locality's foremost fighting clan; and through the flickering firelight glowered back her soiled and surly lieutenants Sami and Beka, who both appeared to be in the early stages of pregnancy. All three girls were a little too tough and battle hardened to be described as pretty, yet still they exhibited a kind of allurement submerged in a brutalised lost innocence that might be considered engaging in its way, had anyone less savage than themselves been present to behold it.

Further afield, many other carelessly assembled groups of adolescent urchins, both male and female lounged around their own fires and cooking pots, amongst and between the random disgorgement of makeshift shacks, covered hollows, and remains of past giant four wheel drives or touring caravans that served as their meagre dwellings. It being evening, this pitiful populace was winding down the day by idly inhaling from small bags whatever lingering solvent substances they might have been able to extract from the rubble and rubbish of fifty years vintage that sufficed as their only inheritance.

Here and there, other groups of worn out young women in their twenties were variously engaged in washing and cooking, quarrelling and skirmishing. And far and wide around all of these forsaken denizens, their teeming brats played out a futile daily existence of mere survival in this most marginalised of all post-apocalypse communities. Though the town had been quickly consigned to Tricron (or was it Quadron, Cinquon or whatever?)

dust by the enemy, some kind of shelter had at least been possible thereafter in the more conventionally destroyed environs that had once surrounded The Lees' own multimart cellar; so here these desensitised descendants of the then war orphans now eked out their daily existence.

All of these urchins became sexually active immediately upon reaching puberty and thenceforth went at it like the rabbits on which they habitually fed, and few people who inhabited the site of the former bad estate now managed to live much beyond the age of thirty. So their rampant, rabid and highly belligerent little progeny were doomed to a continuous round of acrimony and aggression as they sought out their own future pecking orders in this most bleak and unyielding of settings. Since nobody neither knew nor cared very much which children actually might belong to whom, the countless brats were mostly organised into large, anonymous crèches; though the more able bodied of the older women did attempt at least to feed and care for them as best they could.

As they grew, all of the strongest children, both male and female became set aside for fighting; whilst the weaker were allowed to either disappear in the night as frequently occurred or succumb to the many causes of premature mortality that nobody bothered to question. And the struggle for supremacy between the perennially warring clans of The Lees inevitably became the defining purpose of this underclass' so blighted young lives.

Hogs Hill's ruling elite paid scant attention to what it regarded as such irrelevant flotsam and detritus of their inherited post-apocalypse order. The exception was when the raiding parties of the Office for Trade and Industry would sweep through The Lees or similar former bad estate communities here and there, to procure child labour for the mills, mines and industrial units of the fiefdom's north, or the farms and forests of the more genteel south. And given the rate at which the underclass was seen to reproduce, not to mention its typical life expectancy, the human harvest proved to be largely self-sustaining and another convenient source of revenue for the Hill's own holders of high office. All of the fighting urchins were smart enough to avoid capture during the usually nocturnal forays, and in their ignorance they seemed to look upon this purging of the weak almost as their pre-apocalypse forebears might welcome their own regular refuse collection.

"They say Kowlea's dug up some magic stuff," Sami informed her leader, speaking in the urchins' curious dumb patois.

"Wot sort of magic stuff?" came the at first only half eager enquiry.

"Cupla tins a somethin', as oy 'eard."

"Wot's magic about 'em, then?"

"Can't be opened or dented, so they say. Reckon we should bash up Kowlea's lot agin and get 'em off 'er," suggested Sami, who was the more aggressive of Gail's two companions. These three waifs liked to style their following the "Golden Urchins", after Gail's own hair colour, and Kowlea's clan were their principal local rivals.

"Don't sound very magic to me," then spoke up the always less passionate Beka. "Oy 'eard those park kids 'ave got a noo chief called Greta, an' they wanted to come over 'ere and bash us up but she stopped 'em."

"Oo told ya that, then," Gail at once enquired.

"That kid Leigh, 'oo all the other boys call 'girl's name'. 'E goes over theer some a the time an talks to 'em, 'cos no-one 'ere loykes 'im much, besoyde me. Ya know 'ow 'e's always moochin' about."

The small and isolated vagrant band of the 'park kids' inhabited a strange little wooded enclosure below Shottington Ridge, about a mile east of the one time Lees, and they were looked down upon roundly even by the lowest of their neighbouring underclass' low. Squire Cockscomb's original plantation of 1824, that had somehow regenerated itself since the apocalypse, was still referred to locally as 'the park' though nobody knew nor cared exactly why.

"Reckon we should get them tins off Kowlea, then challenge the park kids to teck 'em off us," Gail at length pronounced. "Then we'll bash 'em up proper, once and fer all and show that Greta 'oo rules round 'ere."

At that, Sami produced a stained and slender wooden flute upon which she blew a reedy rallying call, and numbers more scruffy urchins descended upon the fire-lit encampment from various sides while the roasting rabbit on its spit was cast carelessly aside. Then, as the council of war commenced, the forlorn figure of the boy named Leigh crept into his customary position on the periphery, behind a convenient pile of rubble from where he listened intently and waited doggedly as ever for the opportunity to stake his claim to some kind of place in urchin society.

The time honoured bad estate tradition of spelling children's names in any way that the parents pleased had survived the apocalypse, at least in the phonetic sense; as had the elsewhere rather fleeting turn of the twenty-first century fad of naming new babies after the places where they had been conceived. Kowlea therefore remained a fairly popular appellation locally, having been handed down from the original war orphans through successive urchin generations; and large numbers of boys on the former Lees estate were naturally named Lee, and girls Leigh. These children would therefore become identified amongst themselves by some prominent physical characteristic or notable trait; such as spotty Leigh, big knob Lee, fat gut Lee, lug 'oles Lee, burping Leigh, and almost inevitably where children of all ages are involved: Lee the farter.

Just one unfortunate boy urchin had somehow managed to acquire the identity of Leigh for himself, and so was doomed to be the scapegoat of all his male peers. Since none of these children could have any notion of reading or writing, never mind of spelling, the girls all wondered how their male counterparts could tell the difference. But children no matter how savage or marginalised, as ever demanded their objects of scorn; and since the unfortunate boy named Leigh had become so undeniably different by being identified as such, nobody dared to take his part.

"Wot ya want these magic tin things off Kowlea so much fer anyway?" enquired the one exception Beka, as Gail set about outlining the Golden Urchins' newest attack strategy upon their arch rivals. "Cos she's got 'em, an oy ain't!" came the fierce reply. "Need oy 'ave asked?" the ever less enthusiastic lieutenant thought to herself, though she could not say it out loud to her leader.

Gail habitually coveted anything belonging to others that she saw or heard about but did not have herself, only to as quickly lose interest once she actually possessed it. And so the battle plans were laid and on the morrow hostilities were engaged; and on the same afternoon that the passing of the Dowager Day was announced in Hogs Hill Hall across the Isis, the victorious Golden Urchins brought their trophies home in triumph. As grand a feast as the destitute community could muster was prepared that evening by the older non-fighting women, and the available solvent supplies were distributed for the assembled fighters to enjoy.

All urchins of the underclass displayed a seemingly inborn fondness of digging and burrowing in the rubble of their ruined environment, not only in search of edible morsels or intoxicating substances, but also for buried treasure; the dream of which served as a comparative motivation to the pre-apocalypse national lottery. And thus it was that the defeated Kowlea had most recently excavated from, unbeknown to herself the site of her distant forbear Cuylee McGrouse's one time larder, the two small cylindrical objects that were to change the course of the feudal land of England's late twenty-first century destiny.

The retaliatory attentions upon The Lees of the Grand Western Coalition, back in the 2020s, appeared to have had a curious effect upon these long lost artefacts; because not only had it become impossible either to open or damage them, but the original design of the paper wrapping seemed to have been fused indelibly onto the metal itself. And there for all to see, had these urchins who now so coveted their prize any idea of such things, the words 'Red Kidney Beans' proclaimed themselves beneath a once familiar early twenty-first century logo: 'Dellsey's *Fresh*'.

"Go on, Kyle. Troy an open 'em. Oy dare ye," a rather light headed Sami challenged a burly for his age and by reputation bullying boy that many of the others looked up to. "Look see, theer's sum kinda ring thing on the top. Reckon that's 'ow ya do it." But try as he might this boy could make no impression upon the mysterious objects. Certain of Kyle's variously intoxicated male peers then similarly grasped the opportunity to prove their pubescent machismo, but as the boy named Leigh as ever watched from somewhere in the middle distance, all failed in that ambition.

"Told ya they was magic," Gail of the golden hair then announced a little exultantly. "An' it's that noo Greta bitch at the park that oy'm challengin' next. 'Oo's wiv me?" The roar of affirmation was probably audible from the mysterious enclosure beneath Shottington Ridge itself.

"Someone'll 'ave ta go over theer an' challenge 'em fer me," Gail next announced, since in such a flushed with success and intoxicated state she would like to imagine a little formality to match her enhanced sense of importance. "'Oo wants ta be moy emissary?"

"Yer wot?" immediately queried Beka.

"Moy *emissary.*"

"Wot the 'ell's an emissary?" chortled Sami, before assuring the younger boy next to her: "She allus cum's out wiv them big words when she's stoned." Both Sami and Beka knew full well that when the time came, the Golden Urchins would creep up upon and surprise their enemy, just the same as they always did.

But Gail for now informed her lieutenants with a little loftiness: "Someone as goes fer me instead of me doin' it meself, stoopid! 'Oo wants ta?" At that the skulking Leigh suddenly thrust himself forward, sensing an opportunity to make himself useful, but the chorus of condemnation was as instant as it was savage.

"Yaaah! ... Get lost! ... Get 'im! ... Bash 'im up!" all of the fighting boys variously began to yell, with Kyle's the loudest voice of all. Then, while some of these boys commenced a mocking chant of: "Girl's name, girl's name, girl's name!" others pelted the intruder with dirt and stones and any other missiles that they could lay their hands on until Leigh made his customarily hasty retreat.

"Stoopid girl's name!" the glowering Kyle spat once the banishment was effected. "Oy'll bash 'im up proper if 'e duss that agin."

A faint chorus of muttering from assorted other boys: "Yeah, bash 'im up ... Smash 'is 'ead in ... Kick 'im in the nuts ... Roast 'is goolies," and such like eventually died on the night air and the grumbling protagonists resumed their places by the feast fires.

"Woy d'ya all 'ate 'im so much?" Leigh's sole friend Beka then dared to ask.

"Cos 'e's got a girl's name," came Kyle's surly reply.

"Wot's wrong wiv that then?"

"Nuthin' if yer a girl, but 'e ain't," and with that the speaker's tone and facial expression both affirmed that he had rested his case. Kyle was almost thirteen, and planned before long to either challenge Gail for supremacy or form his own rival clan; but for now those were ambitions that he kept close to his own chest.

Eventually, the boys and those girls who were not already too heavily pregnant began to pair off, wandering away to their various hovels for the nightly round of love making, if such a savage and unfeeling pastime could be described as such. Sami chose the burly and belligerent Kyle as her mate on this occasion, while the more sensitive Beka wandered off to find and comfort her unfortunate friend the boy named Leigh. Gail, being the clan leader was above consideration by any of her male subordinates, and so as ever saved herself for the day when a male child of equal stature might emerge to claim her as his own. Sex and solvents were the only comforts of this underclass, and before long the air became filled with the customary faint chorus of murmuring, groaning and heavy breathing that characterised each Lees' night.

Then a far louder discord of beating hooves and barking dogs announced itself, and the air became lit with many torches. The fighting urchins all made themselves scarce, as was their wont whenever the procurement squads of the Office for Trade and Industry rode in, to watch from a secure distance as that fine body of men went about their own particular business. This raid was led by Algernon Fortescue himself of that most lecherous of Hillite lineages, the head of procurement for mills and mines.

As was typical during these sorties, all of the non-fighting boys were quickly subdued by rod, lash or musket butt; before Fortescue's foot soldiers commenced to round up and avail themselves of the more wholesome girls, or indeed any that they could lay their hands upon who were not overly afflicted by off-putting spots, sores or lesions. None would protest as that band of brigands set about reaping the perks of their livelihood, since none had ever experienced any greater refinement in such matters; while a few of the invaders were seen to select a boy or two of their choice as well.

All the while, the commanding officer strolled amongst the flailing urchin limbs and the pumping buttocks of officialdom with a voyeuristic and lascivious glee, until a minor palpitation at length played itself out within the hitherto barely functioning realms of his breeches. At that he momentarily coughed, gasped and spluttered an acknowledgement of his own ultimate satisfaction at the sordid scene that surrounded him, before blowing a sharp note upon a whistle; and the rascals and ruffians in his employ rose from their labours once more. Finally, two large ox carts were summoned and that night's harvest was herded aboard, to be carried away to a future life of daily hard labour and nights of nourishing the whims of the mill and mine owners who sated Algernon Fortescue and certain of his venerable relatives' ever extended palms. So the following day, there were fewer mouths of the underclass to feed, once again though not for so very long, and life on the site of the former Lees estate continued in just the same way as always.

Chapter 3

With the passing of the Dowager Day, the Hillite triumvirate in waiting of Nigel Scroatley-Browne, Sir Nicholas Coverlet and Douglas Hay-Wain were able to consolidate their own grip upon power. All of the most eminent Hogs Hill families were represented in the cabinet: amongst them the military Grenshaws, the distinguished Bayworth-Hamels, the great legal dynasty of the Hatherington-Smythes, the rakish Fortescues, the conceited Caruthers', the pedantic Bagdalen-Spellwrights, the rather more straightforward Smiths; and last but by no means least the Farquhar's who were forever doomed to be lampooned by their peers from almost all of those other great lineages as "the Sillies".

The most entrenched and implacable amongst the holders of high office had invariably aligned themselves with the late prime minister in applying the strictest possible interpretations of Hill lore to all manner of policy issues that could have filled the geological feature's various vaults and counting houses with many times more plunder than had actually been extorted from the fiefdom's downtrodden subjects to date. But never before had three such relatively young and able politicians filled the top three cabinet posts of chancellor, home and foreign secretaries at one and the same time; and so the present incumbents set about extending their collective interest as never before, whilst continuing to line their own pockets all the while.

Their task was greatly facilitated by the only possible choice as the new prime minister. The most venerable of all Hillites was now the centenarian Sir Cuthbert Pincombe, who spent most of his time in the debating chamber gently dozing in his own bath chair. And since this particular worthy had a marked tendency to nod in his variously fitful slumbers, and rarely realised where he was if he might on occasion fully awake, it would therefore be the simplest of matters to secure his casting vote upon whatever points might be in contention at any time. The Pincombes hailed from the vast even by the Hill's standards and as ever crumbling pile of 'Arden

Propley', that was set within it's own estate at roughly the same distance to the south-east of Barney's Tump as Hogs Hill Hall lay to the south-west.

The present Sir Cuthbert himself had achieved national notoriety as a young man, early in the twenty-first century, as an activist for the then English National Spanking Federation of which his father and grandfather were both presidents. That most genteel of gentrified body's annual championship had been held at the Pincombes' own, appropriately named family seat at the height of each summer throughout the latter two decades of the twentieth century. Each year, large numbers of 'squires' and their selected 'squeakers' as the noble practitioners of the art and the young objects of their fancy were respectively termed, would be welcomed from far and wide to the Hill's highest environs to enjoy the fun of the festival's three day duration. Even though the event was seen to generate large amounts of normally reviled through traffic, most of Arden Propley's near neighbours tolerated this anomaly since privately they rather enjoyed that sort of thing themselves. Even the exceptions amongst them did not wish to deny what they viewed after all as another peculiar, old-moneyed eccentricity and hence one more cherished right of the English genteel class that should not be supplanted.

Then, just before the turn of the century, some sixteen years of previously comfortable patrician complacency became swept away with the election of the first government of the eventually to be re-branded Sylvester Schwarzenorris. The ancient and most dignified gentlemanly pastime of wench spanking immediately assumed a high priority on the wish list of the reforming city dwelling zealots who guided the new prime minister before his attention turned ever more exclusively to matters abroad. And through the successively re-elected administrations led next by Alasdair Handelson and then Milton Lawson, the policy makers of that period sought to outlaw more and more long enjoyed rural pursuits such as Otter sluicing, Muntjac bottoming, Hog's bladder hurling, stoned Crow shooting, and a practice involving soon to be slaughtered Snipe and a series of diminishing rotations that was rather too excruciating even to be described quite plainly in parliament.

This had nothing to do with the then fashionable arguments of child or animal welfare; it was out and out class warfare. The Hillites of that day, together with their gentrified counterparts across the country, all knew that however much the politically correct Islington smart dinner party set at the new heart of government might like to decry their own long cherished sporting traditions as cruel, elitist, sexist or degrading; the real aim was to wrest control of the English nation's countryside heritage away from the age-old order of its feudal gentry, and with it any claim to continued governance itself.

After all, was it not this same body of intellectual, middle class opinion that had already declared what it termed the unutterable "C-word" as demeaning of women's image of themselves and very position in society, whilst granting the gentler gender continued *carte blanche* to decry their male counterparts by whatever slang names for genitalia they themselves might chose, and just as often as they might like to. And there were abundant "plonkers" or "dick-heads" within the elder echelons of public life after all; whilst the outlawed term had surely become the lingering preserve either of lowly public house footie screen audiences, or occasional media award winners who might have had a little too much to drink. "Just which has the more damaging potential, I ask you?" became an oft heard protest at Hogs Hill and similarly gentrified dinner parties of that day.

The traditional juxtaposition of popular rump and gentrified knee was clearly coming under threat as never before. So thus it was that the latent force of Squire Cockscomb's ancient legacy, that was final and irrevocable and which no man might lay asunder, in his own words of 1772; that had since lain dormant beneath the original's burial mound of Barney's Tump on the highest point of Hogs Hill above the west bank of the great River Isis, became stirred once again in defence of the hallowed institutions of his own formerly ruling class. And thenceforth the unseen power of that unyielding past landowner, who himself had been one of the foremost local spankers and Otter sluicers of his day, became bent fully upon guiding the course of events that would realise the conditions set out in his ancient will, whereby a legacy bearer would return to Hogs Hill, preceded by a new felon and enchantress.

All the while, endless appeals, challenges and attempted

amendments on the part of the older order grumbled on ever more tediously through session after session of the early twenty-first century parliament. The rural lobby would posture that if the proposed legislation were to be passed, numbers of comely, plump and as the national federation liked to at least assume, virginal village wenches would be condemned to less rewarding careers as shop assistants or fast food operatives. They likewise argued that even more Otters and Muntjac would have to be destroyed in a considerably less humane fashion than the traditional, genteel 'sluicing' or 'bottoming' of the concerned sporting gentry; and that uncontrollably larger populations of Snipe would be doomed to the comparative lethargy of life on artificially recreated wetland nature reserves, only to have their eggs predated by similarly enhanced numbers of rather too *compus mentis* Crows.

Eventually, the urban elite countered by actually daring to ban the surely benign annual national Pooh sticks championship that took place each summer a little to the south-east of Hogs Hill at that point where the River Isis flowed beneath the twin hillocks of Wittering Humps, a local landmark. Upon this location, large numbers of green-wellied gentlefolk would descend for just one weekend of the year to churn up the river's banks with their giant off-road vehicles, before the excited occupants and even some of their children proceeded to drop twigs off one side of a particular footbridge, then dart across to see which emerged from the other side first. It was a pursuit so trite in its simplicity that surely only the English genteel class could possibly have considered indulging it, yet there lay the criterion and so the urban reformers by stealth closed in once more. And in response to this most ultimate of slights, the incensed landed gentry embarked upon the hitherto unthinkable course of a campaign of civil disobedience, and the youthful Cuthbert Pincombe rose to his then five minutes of fame.

Imagine the public amusement and tabloid headlines when an outraged party of Hillite bucks, prominent amongst whom were the youngest Fortescues of that day, actually invaded the debating chamber of the Palace of Westminster. Then, and during prime ministers' question time, Cuthbert's storm troopers dared to bare their own buttocks not just in full view of the ever present home cinema cameras, but in the direction of the mortified lady Speaker of the House herself. Various co-conspirators who had taken up position in the public gallery above were seen simultaneously to bombard the prime minister, on a rare but nonetheless all too anticipated visit to the same chamber, with an array of brightly coloured, messy, sticky substances that almost succeeded in obscuring several sewn on patches of the great statesman's then trademark kitbag and rucksack. Cuthbert himself managed to snatch up the Rt Hon Member for Barking's favourite Kalashnikov assault rifle from its familiar repose against the despatch box and wave the said weapon in the air, before ultimately being wrestled to the ground by the bodyguards in black tights who up until that point had been so comprehensively outflanked.

All this was to no avail: the time-honoured tradition of wench spanking eventually became outlawed, to be driven underground along with all of those other revered rural recreations. And so the slap and tickle of the squires, and the squeals and giggles of the squeakers seemed set never again to be carried on the balmy high summer air during those three days of the year beside Hogs Hill's middle way. But the irrevocable power of the Cockscomb legacy moved ever forward, and through that part of this history in which the youthful legacy bearer brought down the landowner who had felled all the trees of the Shottington copse, then the new felon and enchantress settled on the so unwelcoming Hill, the unknowing Sylvester Schwarzenorris abandoned his ruling party's new vision of home society for more and more foreign adventures that would ultimately bring about the long foretold "great conflagration" of Squire Barney's bidding.

As Cuthbert Pincombe's own years advanced, he rather distanced himself from his family's past predilection, though the Fortescues remained aware of whence they might partake of the pastime, naturally enough. And now the one time rebel was to sit out the remaining days of his dotage dozing in the new parliamentary chamber of Hogs Hill Hall, himself having inherited the office of prime minister of the feudal land of England.

"Oh come along, Grenshaw old chap," the elder statesman might hear if only he could manage to stay awake. "You know the Frenchies always say that they didn't see what happened. It's just a way that they have with them. One really shouldn't be so concerned." Or perhaps: "Antipodeans? Perish the day that they might effect an entry upon our shores." And maybe, thirdly:

"Certainly not! Their ambassador paid us nothing like such a sum."

Through the five post-apocalypse decades of Hillite rule, no attempt had been made to repair the once proud country's shattered infrastructure, since it was this course of total inaction that most admirably suited the purposes of the emergent governing class. Given that all of England's major urban centres had been wiped out, and along with them that most galling of previous ruling elites with their constant inroads upon the time honoured ways of their rural betters, it became a relatively simple process to re-impose a village and market town economy and social order upon the surviving and for the most part formerly middle class Triffs garden gibbet purchasers who constituted the new human resource.

The pre-apocalypse financial institutions had likewise been liquidated as the former capital London was consigned to Tricron (or was it Quadron, Cinquon or whatever?) dust; and thus it was that the first Hillite chancellor Hugo Scroatley-Browne inflicted his master stroke of calling in and then ceasing to grant all credit. The downcast population of the long re-awaited fiefdom of Squire Barney's feudal vision was thereby immediately and irreversibly enslaved, after which the vulgar, new money pound that had itself rebuffed for so long the most ghastly foreign intent of the egalitarian euro, was abolished in favour of the genteel and gentrified groat of centuries long past.

Such was the new government's success in imposing it's total control, that had a free press survived its tabloids would no doubt have dubbed the plunderer of the people's purses 'Hugo Groatley-Browne'; but Scroatley he and his successors most shamelessly remained as they succeeded in becoming the most accomplished personal profiteers in all Hillite history. The Hill's by the time of this narrative's leading financial dynasty had themselves been regarded as a relatively unsung entity until the final decade of the twentieth century when the exploits of one Richard Scroatley-Browne had succeeded in elevating his then somewhat struggling family firmly into local prominence.

The young Richard displayed the slightly reddened and wrinkled complexion, prematurely receding hairline, mousey curly hair and rather long nose of all his male lineage. And as if the family name was not sufficient in itself to fire the adolescent imaginations of his schoolfellows, these inborn physical characteristics doomed the unfortunate youth to be lampooned most savagely by his bedfellows of dorm and competitors of rugby field as 'Richard Head'. Upon graduating with an upper second in financial mismanagement and malpractice from the University of Any Part of England that Hadn't Already Got One (formerly Brackley, Northants Technical College), and in order to gain his revenge upon the wider world, the said whizz-kid had thus set up the 'Richard Head Foundation for Aspiring Billionaires' that relieved untold thousands of mug punters of their life savings, redundancy pay-offs, small inheritances or suitably large credit card advances on either side of the millennium.

First, this most august yet totally bogus financial institution targeted that era's former career pen pushers of advancing middle-age who had been winkled out of their long and closely guarded corners in salaried and pensioned employment by the downsizing squads of the then large London accounting firms. Secondly, albeit in an untypical Hillite manner, Richard turned his attention abroad to the western European mainland and its numbers of bored and homesick expatriates who might be relishing the opportunity to return home to enjoy anew their beloved lost pleasures of bubble and squeak, mushy peas or pickled gherkins. And next, the foundation turned it's corrupt intent upon the new markets of eastern European émigrés who then as ever afterwards were attempting to gain a lucrative toehold into offshore English society. Americans, inscrutable Orientals and funny foreigners remained beneath the consideration of even this most forward thinking and financially creative of Hillites, naturally enough.

Eventually, Richard Head's great scam had been exposed for what it was and this model for all future clever and devious Scroatley-Brownes embarked upon a lengthy term at a London high security prison, where he perished in the opening enemy onslaught of the apocalypse. But such had been the simplicity with which his family had concealed their youthful protégé's ill gotten gains, that none of the countless dispossessed victims were ever able to recoup their losses. For years the investigating teams of the large London accounting firms milked vast pools of public money in attempting to unravel what they assured endless, expense-laden parliamentary sub-committees must be the offshore banking and creative accounting networks involved. But nobody in government ever thought to look in the great cellar beneath the family's ancestral pile somewhere along the closed world of Hogs Hill's back way where the loot was actually concealed.

Since the long years of global conflict had tested the financial resources of all the most senior Hillite dynasties to the extreme, the previously middle-ranking Scroatley-Brownes were thus able to emerge into the post-apocalypse polity with some financial clout. This family had been more than prepared to undergo a certain amount of privation throughout their particular sojourn in return for preserving a substantial proportion of Richard's ill gotten gains with the specific intent of securing future prominence. And now, Hugo's grandson Nigel had further enhanced their hidden fortune with his share of the Russian ambassador's groats, that since the currency was non-negotiable in the international markets to which all of his subjects were denied access, had actually been paid in gold.

Chapter 4

Sitting in his counting house on the evening after the immediate past prime minister's grand funeral, the chancellor reflected with satisfaction upon the thoroughness with which he and his colleagues the home and foreign secretaries had mapped out the future economic and social stability of the fiefdom that was now their inheritance. In his right hand a glass of vintage cognac rested atop a pile of gold ingots. On the floor at his feet, the bottle from a very fine case that a French envoy had not seen fit to bestow upon his Boarding House hosts, but which after his inevitable decease therein they had purloined anyway, cast in the candlelight a strange silhouette upon various other arrangements of embezzled bullion that Nigel Scroatley-Browne gazed upon with a covetous warmth. "The largest amount ever raised from an overseas ambassador, and him a Ruskie too," the mean spirit mused to himself. "Better not let old Grenshaw's clique get an inkling of it. They're absolute sticklers for the blighters always being third."

The swindler then raised his glass to his lips and chuckled to himself as he turned over in his mind the perennially tedious positions and prejudices of his late leader's closest cohorts. "Hah! Devious Frenchies, cheating Huns and Hollanders, Spicks forever after our fish I ask you? Let them all come, let them all try to establish trading relations. The Hill's vaults and cellars aren't half full yet, never mind the Boarding House crypt. What was those fools' latest complaint? Antipodean messiah, that was it. What poppycock! This is the feudal land of England, for heaven's sake and we the Hillites are the finest of its gentry, the natural rulers. Let no outsiders entertain designs upon our sacred shores if they are not prepared to pay for it in kind. And pay for it handsomely they most assuredly will for so long as I am chancellor."

The following year would see the fiftieth anniversary of the inauguration of the first Hillite parliament, to commemorate which event a grand summer festival was planned locally; and the beneficiaries of Squire Barney's will had certainly been more than successful in ensuring that the home population had paid most handsomely throughout the intervening period. Once Nigel's ancestor Hugo had called in all the credit, the southern half of the fiefdom was organised into a genteel parish network of village estates surrounding its mostly surviving smaller market towns. The still all too necessary if rather "vulgar" mills, mines and industrial units of any functioning economy were once more confined out of the sight of polite society in the rainy and windswept north, where an understandably less refined feudal order likewise came to prevail under appropriate southern supervision.

Competition to establish their places in a social and governing hierarchy was immediately fierce amongst the new ranks of provincial Hillites that the bane of Barney's Tump had spawned across the length and breath of the south, and those with the means to best buy favour with the ruling great families of Hogs Hill itself quickly rose through the ranks. A parish master was set up in the biggest house in each village to oversee the daily lives and labours of their smallholder or tenant subjects. At first, some of these local grandees were called squires, others sheriffs or perhaps wardens; but in time they all became known in the common idiom as the "Triffs bearers" after the symbols of authority that adorned the entrances to every one of their private domains.

The numerous other garden gibbets dating from the mid-2020s were all confiscated from their now lowlier purchasers and eventually destroyed, whilst erecting one carried a capital sentence that nobody dared to invoke. And for every Triffs that guarded each village's "big house", one or more tithe barns would lie behind, and an appropriately large receptacle beneath to consume the proceeds once the estate produce had been converted by whatever means into cash.

The Triffs bearers all reported to local magistrates who presided over their own courts and municipal staffs in the market towns. There, the original eighteenth or nineteenth century public buildings that might variously have gone by the name of town, corn or shire halls, assembly rooms or market houses, were all re-converted for use as the new seats of local authority; and the cellars and vaults beneath those splendid edifices came to match the structures above in terms of size, grandeur and most of all content. These grand old municipal piles became the settings for a regressive system of petty sessions and quarterly assizes that dispensed local governance and justice in equal and sacrosanct proportion, and new great gibbets of oak and ash from Hogs Hill itself were erected before them all as a symbol of the ultimate provincial power that was invested therein.

Tithes were levied upon village small holders and tenant farmers or artisans for the lion's share of just about everything that they produced. The petty sessions also oversaw a selection of additional parish charges: for maintenance of roads and drains, autumn leaf sweeping, tree lopping and control of messier avian species. No-one in the village communities could ever recall any of these amenities actually being provided, and all complained obsessively amongst themselves concerning their ever unfortunate lot; but still the parish charges ate up that smaller proportion of their meagre incomes that wasn't taken by the suffocating tithes themselves. And just as the Triffs bearers soaked up most of the day to day produce of their own estates, so the greater share of that plunder would in turn be claimed by the market town magisterial class for re-sale to their own local populaces at a suitably large profit. The lower echelons of town dwellers, such as shop keepers, crafts and trades people were all taxed as stringently as their village brethren, needless to say; as all the while the bulk of local produce filtered upwards through the layers of officialdom and was variously creamed off at every stage.

As the bane of Barney's Tump ensured in its ancient and irrevocable fashion that the dual strata of local office holders outlived their peers and grew ever more venerable with their own advancing years, the authority of the expanding ruling dynasties became more and more implacable and their justice ever more fierce. With no formal banking system upon which to draw loans, the lower orders had no means to improve themselves, and the unbreakable dominance of the Triffs bearers and magistrates simply grew and expanded in proportion with the steadily burgeoning contents of their personal vaults and cellars.

To ensure that the village and market town economy was accountable to central government, the magistrates were mostly second or third generation members of those great Hogs Hill lineages whose most senior representatives held office in parliament itself; except for a small number of trusted provincial cohorts who might have possessed the unusual means necessary to purchase such power for themselves. A similarly intense competition to that which had established the Triffs bearers played itself out amongst the middle echelons between the magisterial ranks and mere townspeople. And nothing either in the public, polite or proletarian life of the fiefdom escaped the all-pervading attention of the fabled "Winklers", the universally feared Hillite equivalent of a secret police force.

Double dealing was endemic to the entire system, between the Triffs bearers and the Winklers, that latter unregulated civil force and the seedy staffs of the magistrates; and the town officials back to the parish masters. Local governance was rife with what its practitioners regarded as a gentlemanly and hence excusable deceit, since all the parties to it would endlessly fabricate whatever alleged misdemeanours they could muster in every lower tier of the pecking order to their own; to develop commerce as best they could in the proceeds. These tendencies had undergone a particular expansion during the reign of the immediate past prime minister, as the influence of the newest Hillite dynasty grew and spread into the provincial polity. In line with their family's latterly acquired seniority, the third and fourth generation Days secured many a position of authority in monitoring the actions of the market town administrations and ensuring that Hogs Hill Hall remained fully appraised of the fullness or otherwise of the provincial public vaults. And as time passed, they also became particularly influential in guiding the activities of the dreaded Winklers, and turning them to their own greatest advantage.

Towards their more venerable peers these ever more devious Days would feign the utmost Hillite pomp and reserve, but amongst themselves they liked to dress in 1960s sharp suits and converse in the London gangland accents of that time, since the family name had that certain rhyme to it after all. Amongst the oldest moneyed Hogs Hill lineages, however the memory had never been extinguished that these more latterly respectable and acceptable Days had once upon a time been mere shop keepers; and notwithstanding the indefatigable influence of the bane of Barney's Tump, therein lay the distinction that could never be altered. The ever resourceful Nigel Scroatley-Browne played upon that lingering prejudice most skilfully, and thereby established his own network of informers who ensured that the official channels of communication back to Hogs Hill as represented by the objects of his scrutiny were by no means the only ones.

The Days, most prominent amongst whom were the third generation brothers Barnabus and Columbus, had thus felt the expediency of submerging more and more of their wide-ranging protection rackets, trade in stolen goods and groat laundering operations conveniently out of sight within the more commercially orientated, less landed society of the fiefdom's north. Considerable fortunes were raised through an extensive web of double dealing and extortion involving those rainy and windswept regions' hardly less corrupt mill, mine and industrial unit owners; and the richness of the southern family's various northern manor house vaults became the subject of considerable local repute, not to mention envy. None of this booty found its way back to the great cellar beneath the house in Hogs Hill's mystic glade on its lower eastern side though, since none amongst the Days would dare to provoke the unholy row that would surely have resulted from their dynastic head the Dowager herself discovering that her descendants were now engaged in *changing* the way in which they were so readily accumulating *new wealth*.

The current chancellor, and hence his colleagues Sir Nicholas Coverlet and Douglas Hay-Wain knew all along what their former leader's family was up to; and the two factions enjoyed a mutually distrustful relationship. Barnabus and Columbus liked to assume as best they could that the chancellor was under their own influence, and given Nigel's unmatched personal talent on the make the Day brothers would refer to him between themselves as the "grand warden of the fiefdom". But all the while, their adversary's all too transparent intent was to add the Day family fortune to his own lineage's carefully concealed coffers, to swell the bounty first raised by his ancestor Richard. That was until the Boarding House conspirators were approached by the Russian ambassador, with the latter's hitherto unimaginable resource of English groats convertible as it was into gold. Thenceforth the shop keeping Day family's mysterious local promotion and more recent good fortune had paled into irrelevance in the triumvirate in waiting's future vision, even if it meant breaking an inviolable tenet of Hill lore by allowing a Ruskie to be *first*.

Tithe day in the southern villages became an unchanging monthly ritual that was played out on each first Friday when the downtrodden smallholders, tenant farmers and artisans would be obliged to trudge up to the big house with their barrow loads of requisitioned produce, and bagsful of groats to cover that month's parish charges. None amongst them would dare to voice their perennial complaints about the state of the roads and drains, the ever present threat to their meagre dwellings from overhanging branches, having to sweep up autumn leaves themselves, or the uncontrolled attentions of pooping Pigeons or incontinent Crows. All knew that agents of the Winklers would be mingling with them to fulfil in this as so many other ways that fine institution's defining mission of winkling out all dissent. Nobody was allowed to leave the big house grounds until the slow and tedious process of checking all the tithes and payments against the ordained rates, then entering them into the Triffs bearers' copious books had been completed. Then the dispossessed would be herded before their lords' and masters' guardian gibbets to witness the afternoon hangings that served as an appropriate example to all present.

Fellow villagers despatched at these solemn parish proceedings might be those who had fallen behind with their payments, or other minor miscreants: guilty perhaps of offences such as letting their crops grow to more than the regulation height, making unauthorised alterations to their dwellings, burning the wrong type of fuel in their enforced poverty, or flying a kite without permission. More serious dissenters who might be deemed culpable of, for instance setting aside produce for personal gain, answering back an estate official or approaching a better's wrong door, might be referred to the petty sessions; whilst anybody winkled out for the most serious of all charges of "favouring change" would be condemned to face the full wrath of their market town's quarterly bench. And on those most austere of occasions, large and vocal crowds of first stone throwers would assemble from far and wide before the great oak and ash town gibbets to witness as so many times before the ultimate affirmation of Hillite power. The fiefdom's justice was always this final, since Hogs Hill Hall showed no inclination for the unnecessary expense of a prison population, and transportation was hardly in keeping with Parliament's inherent distrust of all places overseas, not to mention its seemingly growing aversion to Antipodeans.

A certain pomp and ceremony came to surround the life of the market town courts as their presiding officials competed amongst themselves through ritual and banquet to demonstrate their relative wealth and social standing. Thus it was that the social life of the new provincial Hillites also came to revolve around the one-time assembly rooms and corn halls, since those public buildings' provided an appropriately grand setting for the country dances of what became the summer season. At these events, through the months of June and July, the more upwardly mobile of Triffs bearing families would aspire to their daughters of marriageable age catching the eye of a middle ranking town family's son; whilst the latter class would similarly hope for the favour of a future magistrate.

This social activity, if such a joyless ambience could be described as such, became the remit of the greatly rejuvenated English Fusty Dowdy Stuffy Society that organised the summer season with an unremitting zeal. Only those daughters who most constantly and steadfastly demonstrated those qualities of the Society's own time honoured title were permitted to marry and thus ensure an appropriately austere succession. Any young female who might be deemed capable of spontaneity, wit or spirit would be instantly identified by the Society's ever present adjudicators, who fulfilled the same role at the country dances as that of the Winklers in society at large. Having shamed their families in this manner, such unsuitables would thereafter be assigned to a life of service in the employ of their positively vetted betters. And any who did not even then curb their rebellious tendencies, which needless to say was almost all of them, would be granted appropriate terms of sporting correction at the ever eager hands and across the equally receptive knees of the once more swelling ranks of the spanking 'squirearchy'.

That most gentlemanly body's National Federation would place its own young bucks at all of the season's foremost social events. There these agents would pick out any bright young things that they might identify as "ripe for the squeaking" in the sport's particular parlance, and whilst both sides' elders sat politely analysing whether the tunes fitted the dances, covertly encourage the so frowned upon traits. No such display would escape the scrutiny of the all seeing adjudicators, and though warned most sternly of the dangers and consequences in advance, a certain number would always fall from grace. And thus the Federation was assured a rich recruiting source, since the offending wenches would invariably be the most comely of each season's crop, naturally enough. The Federation and the Society were in league with one another, of course since the arrangement also served to uphold the latter's position as the foremost guardian of the fiefdom's morals. For heaven forbid the situation whereby a provincial Hillite daughter might not reveal a proneness to spontaneity, wit or spirit until after her nuptials had been sealed.

All of the other sporting traditions of the English gentry enjoyed a similar revival under Hillite rule. And so the country dances of the market town summer seasons came to enjoy a shared association with the grander meets of the revitalised rural Otter sluicing, Muntjac bottoming, Hogs bladder hurling, stoned Crow shooting, and something unspeakable to do with Snipe fraternities; not to mention whatever other distortions of nature's original intent the gentrified imagination could conjure. Even the annual summer Pooh sticks championship at Wittering Humps enjoyed a renewed popularity, though due to its rather frivolous nature only under strict parliamentary licence. In the first week of August, these assorted facets of the social calendar would culminate in a grand festival on Hogs Hill itself, at which the season's various betrothments would be announced and the ever assured sanctity of the fiefdom's provincial succession would thus be celebrated.

To mark the forthcoming golden jubilee of this social and political order, the most genteelly grandiose of all festivals was in the planning, and sitting in his family counting house at the time of this narrative, Nigel Scroatley-Browne reflected upon the intervening five decades with a certain smugness. As he did so, the autumn wind that disturbed the trees overhead provoked a rustling chorus of "ownleeee the fusssstiessst, dowdeee and ssssstuffffeeee.... essst". At that the chancellor glanced upwards in affirmation of the turbulent testimonial, with an especially self satisfied air. This most able of plunderers of the proletariat now controlled the dominant faction in parliament, the new prime minister was a mere puppet of his particular preferences, his arguably most potent rivals were all set to be sidelined, and he himself now presided over the greatest fortune ever to be amassed in a single Hillite cellar, notwithstanding the slight indelicacy of where it might have come from. "To the future," he mused to himself, raising his glass of cognac in the air and swirling its contents with a certain complacency.

But in that instant a further and particularly furious gust seemed to suggest a growling reproach of "Furrrrssssttt?" as if it had somehow been dredged from the deepest and most affronted well of all ageless Hogs Hill tradition. Closer at hand the chancellor half heard a subtly chilling whisper playing about his ears of: "Vulgar new wealth, you know ... be careful with your meddling, old chap." And as he rather involuntarily fidgeted a further time with the glass in his hand, sensing a faint outline that implied itself in the reflection so cast upon the opposite wall, the rebuke resembled the once redoubtable tones of the newly freed dowager. "Pah!" the momentarily nonplussed plotter muttered under his cognac enhanced breath. "It wouldn't be the end of the world, would it?"

As if in response to that protest and to suggest at least not for the time being, the wind suddenly died and so the trees ceased to sigh, though one or two formidable dogs in the vicinity nonetheless seemed prompted to bark and yowl their own eerie discord. Certain Hillites were undoubtedly becoming, by the standards of their most venerable forebears, perhaps a little too innovative for the collective good in their pursuit of personal gain; and the ancient domain of Hogs Hill itself was hardly the setting in which to gloat over such excess. For even the mouldering fabrics of that place's many primordial piles exerted a certain scrutiny of their own, and nothing either conceived of or committed therein could hope to escape the judgement of the lingering souls of countless residents past.

The revitalised feudal culture of Squire Barney Cockscomb's final and irrevocable legacy of 1772, which no man might lay asunder, had as its half century approached never been more insular in its suppression of the home populace and rigid rejection of all foreign influence. But unbeknown to the future architect of Hillite and especially his own personal prosperity that Nigel Scroatley-Browne assumed himself to be, a somewhat strange outside entity had come to land upon England's sacred shores and so the seeds of rebellion were set to be sown.

Chapter 5

Greta knew not who she was or from whence she came. She remembered awakening on a southern shingle beach of the land that was now her home, within a newly opened cylindrical object; and then wandering, wandering, ever alone before feeling irresistibly attracted to the wooded enclosure of the Shottington copse where she now passed her morose and troubled days. Further back she sensed uncertain memories of an unhappy childhood in a distant land, and an unfeeling mother also named Greta, who had spoken of her moody daughter's fifteen identical fathers in various parts of the then war ravaged world.

Whether or not any of these bizarre sires still lived or where they might be was also a mystery to Greta, as was the exact duration over which she had remained in suspended animation within the time capsule that had carried her across the seas. But the noise in her head, the constant chatter in her mind that imparted the most conflicting and confusing of notions within this tormented young woman, suggested that a father of kinds might indeed be attempting to communicate with her and conveying some vital purpose. For given the peculiar nature of Greta's parentage, the brain of the park urchins' new chief was a cruel cocktail of human tissue and partially functioning cyborg circuitry. And though she often wished to be relieved of her mind's inner discord, whenever it did temporarily relent she would at once feel so utterly alone.

After walking ashore, this strange and sullen girl who had an air of around seventeen summers had for some months wandered at will around the Hillite fiefdom's southern reaches, observing with a mixture of distaste and envy the corrupt and exploitative feudal order of the Triffs bearers in village upon village, but always evading capture by the dreaded Winklers. On occasion she would mingle with the baying crowds to witness the fierce justice of the quarterly assizes in one market town or another, or observe from the outside the so stilted and stifling social procedures that set in place the provincial gentry's succession.

Eventually she had approached the proud geological feature of Hogs Hill itself from the west, and upon encountering an object not dissimilar to her own most recent tomb immediately beneath the slopes on that side, the babble in her brain had become almost unbearable. Still the discoverer felt a compunction to investigate, but try as she might she could effect no entry nor discern any door. And so this Greta wandered onward and upwards, determining to return one day to free what she felt certain must be that second time capsule's encased occupants.

For a while the interloper concealed herself within the Boarding House, where she would eavesdrop upon the nightly deliberations of the chancellor, home and foreign secretaries. And there the mysterious and undetected emissary from abroad soon decided that she did not care for these Hillites or their fusty, dowdy, stuffy customs; and so vowed that if this geriatric gentry did indeed govern the absurd domain in which she now walked, she would not rest until she herself had become the instrument of their demise.

In time she descended the Hill's eastern slopes to cross the great River Isis below, and after taking up residence in the enclosure still known as 'the park' her new found purpose deepened further. For there amongst the regenerated ranks of oak and ash, Greta sensed not merely the influence of a more distant forebear than her absent and longed for father, but a far older and latent power that detested the ruling Hillites with an intensity that rendered her own newly dawned dislike ineffectual by comparison. For here were preserved the twice defiled remains of the felon Will Wayward and the enchantress Nan Chilswell, who had both been murdered in 1772 according to the funeral rites of Squire Barney Cockscomb.

Greta now lay in a familiar pose, resting upon one elbow amidst the multiple trunks of what must originally have been a group of five oaks. It was here that the ancient power that she sensed would speak to her most clearly inside her head, just as it had once called to itself another, turn of the twenty-first century favourer of that same spot. And always when the spirits of Will and Nan talked within Greta's troubled mind, the ceaseless electronic chatter that tortured the human-cyborg hybrid's very soul would clarify a little and render her momentarily more at peace with herself.

All around the reclining figure and as far as her eye could see, more multi-trunked protrusions of oak and ash and just one weeping willow appeared to have long since thrust themselves anew through the broken and scattered slabs of flat concrete that lay everywhere within this mysterious enclosure, in a now potent reaffirmation of the power of nature. In the near distance, the scarce ranks of the park kids whom Greta now led were going about their own daily round of cooking, washing and squabbling; though no brats were to be found here since this small vagrant band observed a strict social order that tolerated neither children nor pets.

Of a sudden, the peace of the afternoon was rudely shattered by a chorus of shouting and jeering as the invading Golden Urchins announced their own wilful and warlike intent, which was symbolised by the magic tins of red kidney beans that were raised, tied to poles above two impromptu standard bearers' heads. But the startled park kids merely stood upright in an outward facing circle with their arms spread wide, a gesture that according to the urchins' code of honour signalled that they did not wish to fight.

"Come on, foyte! ... Wot's wrong wiv ya! ... Cowards! ... Stoopid scum bellies! ... Gippos! ... Foyte, me owld boots ye!" their antagonists variously goaded.

But one amongst the park girls simply replied with a new found serenity that was not known on the neighbouring Lees: "No. We'll not foyte ya. Greta's forbidden it. Go 'ome in peace an' foyte no more."

The ever vociferous Kyle then thrust himself forward and sneered malevolently: "So wot's wrong wiv 'er then? Call 'erself a chief! Cum on, stoopid poo in yer pants park kids. Foyte or we'll bash yer up anyways."

The commander in waiting cared for no code of honour but his own, and that was most dishonourable indeed; but the object of his aggression faced him down with a still more serene stare of her own and admonished: "Please don't speak to us loyke that, agin."

Kyle was becoming more agitated by the second, and so spat back: "Woy? Ya sum kinda Torkie or sumthin', as must na be called names?"

"Wot the 'ell's a Torkie?" Sami demanded, to which Kyle imparted: "Them cissies as lives up north an' must na be called nuthin' by no-one, an' squeals if they is, stoopid;" though for the blighted young life of him he knew not from where such a notion came or what indeed it could mean. "Wot?!!" came the collective and very loud protest from almost everybody present, and at that even Kyle assumed a momentary air of embarrassment.

At length the peace making girl informed her adversaries: "Greta says we must foyte among oursel's no more, an' all our koynde should unoyte aginst the 'Illites. Join us or go on yer way. We'll not foyte ya nor no other urchins no more."

"Oo the 'ell's the 'Illites," the ever enquiring Sami at once interrupted as her own mind balked at such a sudden profusion of hitherto unknown species. The park was the furthest that any of the urchins of The Lees had ever travelled from their own locality, so none of them knew anything about life in the wider world.

"Them toffs as live across the river over theer," the park girl replied, gesturing westwards but only to be brought up short again by a further collective enquiry of: "Wot's toffs then?"

The golden haired Gail herself then drew herself up to her full height and demanded: "Torkies? ... 'Illites? ... Toffs? ... Wot the 'ell's 'appenin' round 'ere fer me owld boots' sake? Explain yersell's or foyte us anyways!" And so it was that the park kid peacemaker, though unbeknown to herself at that precise moment, rather wisely imparted: "People as 'ave got lots a stuff that you ain't."

Given that rather more readily comprehensible assessment, Gail's own interest was immediately and inevitably aroused, and so she signalled to her own troops to rest easy. "Reckon we moyte foyte 'em wiv ya arter all then," the leading urchin of The Lees then replied. "Teck us to see this Greta."

"Welcome. I've been expecting you," the hybrid local head pronounced from her position beneath the five master oaks. She looked into the fascinated faces of Gail, Sami and Beka in turn, and as Kyle paced impatiently about in the near distance muttering invectives under his breath towards any park kid that he could still attempt to intimidate, the three Golden Urchins returned Greta's gaze with a curious intent of their own. "She says ya wants us to foyte the 'Illites wiv ya," Gail began. "Don't think we knows 'em though, so reckon ya oughta tell us 'oo they are."

Greta grimaced slightly in her familiar fashion as some fleeting assault of electronic chatter flickered about her own mind, and then she replied: "Reckon you know them well enough. It's they who come in the night, not to mention their own breeches so the boy Leigh tells me, and carry off the weaker amongst you to a life of slavery."

"Of wot?" Sami inevitably interjected at this point.

Her leader's expression became a little fiercer, and flaring slightly as she faced the newcomer down Gail then declared: "Them kids ain't no use to us anyways if they can't foyte. Woy should we troy to keep 'em? Tell us wot the 'Illites 'ave got that oy ain't."

Greta could see that converting these nearest neighbours to her own cause might well take some time and effort, but still she bid them stay awhile and proceeded to entice Gail in particular with a careful selection of ideas that she felt from her past discussions with the boy named Leigh might produce the desired effect. And in response to Greta's subtle promptings, the golden haired girl began to feel possibly for the first time in her short life a thirst for new knowledge to match her habitual lust for any material trinket that others might have that she did not yet hold herself.

After an hour or so, Gail bid the still hyperactive Kyle to cease his own hostile rantings and take the recently mustered fighting force from The Lees back home. Her own head reeling with such a welter of new ideas and words of varying degrees of bigness, the impatient Sami decided to leave too; but Beka remained. Then, once the departing Golden Urchins were safely out of sight and mind, a further new convert joined the group beneath the five master oaks as Leigh himself emerged with his customary stealth from the shadows and snuggled up to his hitherto sole friend under the approving gaze of his new mentor.

The four teenagers sat talking late into that evening and when Gail eventually rose to depart, such was her preoccupation with the many new concepts that had been so skilfully planted into her hitherto undeveloped mind that she completely forgot to take her so recently acquired and most prized tins of red kidney beans with her. Once Greta was quite alone again, a sudden and particularly savage burst of electronic discord of her ever dysfunctional cyborg circuitry immediately drew her attention to the discarded objects; and when that anguish came to rest upon them the resultant din within her skull seemed set to cause her entire being to explode. "Is that you, father?" she called out in her torment; but as ever in these moments of maximum malfunction, no reply came.

One of this strange, lost girl's fifteen identical sires had indeed survived the apocalypse. Faced with the inevitability of stalemate, that last remaining Gremlin clone had blasted off into outer space from an unseen Siberian location, together with its' most brilliant of inscrutable Oriental associates; their mission to develop a final solution of harvesting giant asteroids to propel back towards Earth and finish the job once and for all. Clear contact between distant father and discarded daughter still awaited the perfection of that most fiendish of all technologies, though in her as yet enforced solitude the ill-fated Greta instinctively sensed a vital importance for those only surviving 2020s Tricron bombs as the two tins most undoubtedly were. And so she concealed them for safe keeping within the gnarled and protruding roots of her adopted oaken shrine in the strange copse below Shottington Ridge that was now her altogether comfortless abode.

Through the ensuing winter weeks, a string of puzzled prospects of Greta's nascent cause would gather at intervals with Gail beneath the park's five master oaks to try to take in as best they could the newcomer's teachings. Sami's own shortest of attention spans ensured that she attended but infrequently and even then under protest, though Beka and Leigh became active in attracting representatives of various other Lees fighting clans, including Kowlea herself to these assemblies.

Though only too aware of her potential converts' lack of wherewithal and intellect, Greta nonetheless felt that since this urchin underclass was possibly the only sector of society that the governing Hillites' all-powerful scrutiny chose to overlook rather than oversee, it must represent the best available starting point from which to foment any future unrest. And so, through seemingly endless external onslaughts of: "Wot?", "Fer me owld boots sake!" and "Ow many more big words?" that competed in equal measure with her mind's eternal inner distress, the educator attempted to impart some knowledge of the world beyond her pupils' immediate environs and the corrupt command of its rulers;

with a hope of somehow, some day effecting change.

Kyle naturally took advantage of his leader's frequent absences to enhance his own local standing, and Sami increasingly aligned herself with him. That warlike pair commenced to lead their clans people on a fierce new round of "bashings up" across The Lees, to bolster the leader in waiting's sought for dominance. But this preoccupation of the foot soldiers' and their would-be future chiefs suited Greta's own purpose as all the while she groomed Gail and Kowlea for greater things.

When the time was eventually right the teacher led her two foremost pupils to the nearest Triffs bearers' villages, there to observe in secret those feudal overlords' unjust order for themselves. Then, and as Greta had intended all along, upon beholding such a hitherto unimaginable abundance of things that she as a local leader did not enjoy for herself, Gail's entire education up until that point became irreversibly focussed upon her tutor's so carefully crafted mission; and Kowlea likewise did not wish to be outshone by her own so recent rival.

Thus it was that on one wild and windy mid-winters evening, a local victory feast of the Golden Urchins was interrupted by an incoming and most solemn procession led by the returning and newly joined Gail and Kowlea, with various other Lees' clan leaders in their immediate rear. "Golden brethren," the lead pair proclaimed to the fire lit gathering with such a purpose that any routine cries of "Wot?" died straight away in the various callers' throats. "Foyte among our own kind no more. From this day forth (to more faint protests) we all unoyte agsinst the 'Illites.'"

To both appease and flatter the immediately blustering Kyle, and according to Greta's own counsel, the bully was on the spot put in command of the new campaign; and realising that it could hardly compromise his own future claim to leadership of the unified force, that most belligerent of boys at once rose manfully to the task. From her briefings with Leigh and Beka, Greta had sensed that the next nocturnal visitation of Algernon Fortescue's procurement squads could not be too far distant, but she intended that when it came a very different outcome must await them.

Never before had caring for or protecting the less forward or more vulnerable of their community been a consideration for the underclass, but now at the end of each day the non-combative urchins of The Lees would all be shepherded to safety while their fighting peers mounted a nightly watch for the new foe. Several such sojourns passed without incident, but eventually the familiar sounds of hoof fall, whiplash, baying dog and lustful human intent became borne once again on the late evening air. But this time there was no careworn welcome from the cowed and compliant crèche of the invaders' anticipation; merely a loaded silence that played all about the flickering camp fires around which the usual harvest would normally have been scattered.

Several seconds passed, during which horses shied, hounds fell silent and the noble band of procurement officials eyed one another tensely, glancing in every direction all the while. Then a stinging slingshot slammed into the sweating temple of Algernon Fortescue himself, and the commanding officer toppled from his mount. Of a sudden the stillness became supplanted by the jeering catcalls of Kyle's onrushing fighting elite and the targets of their assault, having no stomach for an even contest, scattered in all directions to save their own skins, abandoning their oxcarts as they went.

Seemingly insensitive in his stunned state to the enormity of his predicament, the head of procurement for mills and mines next attempted to haul himself upright to be at once grasped by two of the most well built youths present, while a third loosened the intruder's belt. The quarry then shook his own head a final time and stared in sudden terror as he found himself being approached by a blade wielding boy whose look of fixed intent he could in no way find it within himself to return. And so with a deft swipe of the said weapon and an as careless casting aside to the most convenient canine recipient, Kyle signalled to his subordinates to inflict their own worst devices upon the so recent molester in chief. In the morning, Gail and Kowlea conveyed the corpse, trussed atop its one time mount, down to the ancient ford across the River Isis, from where they sent the animal on its way to the hilltop of the immediate west. But yet it transpired that in her ignorance, Greta had not chosen the best possible bait with which to draw the enemy on.

"Damn these oversexed Fortescues," Sir Nicholas Coverlet muttered in the direction of his deputy Soames Hatherington-Smythe, as the battered and mutilated body was uncovered before them. "Where had this one been dipping his infernal wick, I wonder? He'll not be the first of that accursed lineage to suffer such a fate."

There was hardly a family on the Hill that had not been embarrassed at some time past by the time-honoured sexual predations of one Fortescue or another; and this rather prudish home secretary felt little aversion to any comeuppance that might still from time to time transpire.

Indeed the most rakish of all amongst the line in question had always looked upon such mishaps as an occasional kinsman's "slicing-off", as fitting testimonial to the enduring reputation of their own particular pedigree. And so the name of the most recently "lost member in both senses" was added to the Fortescue family's special roll of honour that was toasted at one or another of their own disrespectful dinner parties or significant anniversary gatherings. Algernon's remains were laid to rest within the mausoleum of the applicable ancestral pile along Hogs Hill's back way, a no less lecherous cousin was promoted into his place, and the functioning of the Office for Trade and Industry continued largely unabated.

When no retaliation came, Greta felt something of a dilemma. She reasoned that word must no doubt have got back to the raiding party's superiors concerning the unusual resistance that had been encountered at The Lees, but equally that Hogs Hill itself appeared to remain largely unconcerned. She dared not yet encourage her unsophisticated followers to mount attacks on one nearby village or another, for fear of overwhelming reprisal that might nip their rebellion in the bud; but she likewise feared that having so enlightened Gail and Kowlea as to the apparent rewards of village rule, the headstrong creatures not to mention the even more impulsive Sami and Kyle might take matters into their own hands and thus court disaster.

Still many leading lights of the local underclass would attend the park seminaries at which Greta would attempt to imbue her particular philosophy whilst urging restraint the whole while. But in the absence of actual Hillites to do battle with, these adolescents who had never known any way of life but conflict inevitably began to lose the hitherto carefully implanted plot, and so they started to at least skirmish amongst their own kind once again.

What the revolutionary most needed was some means of subverting the establishment from within, but as her new disciples ultimately wavered in their allegiance the foundling from foreign parts could think of no way within her means to achieve that most difficult of objectives. And all the while Greta's tortured intellect became ever more gloomy and depressed as the unceasing babble and chatter within it could summon no solution, while she longed as never before and as if her own heart would break for the guidance of some semblance of normal parents.

"Don't suppose ya've seen moy magic tins of stuff, 'ave yer?" Gail enquired upon rising from beneath the five master oaks to make her own final departure, leaving only Beka and the boy Leigh behind. "Oy think oy fergot to teck 'em 'ome that other toyme."

"Nah," replied her so recent mentor. "Can't say that I have."

Chapter 6

Upon one momentous dawn in late winter, the park kids and their near neighbours of The Lees were as one awoken by the onset of a fierce electric storm, that having blown in from the west appeared to regard Shottington Ridge as a barricade that it somehow feared to cross. Greta was immediately laid low as bolt upon bolt of lightening set her chaotic inner circuitry singing with sensations that might be described as ecstatic were it not for the agony that tortured every tingling nerve end in her hybrid human-cyborg body. So while her subjects proceeded to evacuate their home for fear of falling boughs, their leader could only stagger wildly about, unable to see where she herself was heading and losing all sense of where she might actually be. Eventually Greta struck her head against the upturned edge of a slab of concrete that stood at a high acute angle to the ground, and as the blow caused her senses to momentarily clear she crawled in her rain soaked confusion into the dank shelter that the cavity beneath the slab offered.

Whether she actually saw what happened next, or whether the cocktail of her brain was playing out some invention of its own in her semi-conscious state, the fallen figure could not tell. As Greta looked back towards the five master oaks, a jagged shaft from the ink-black sky above struck the highest point of that particular trunk beneath which she had buried the two tins of red kidney beans. As that stream of natural energy reached earth it seemed to assume an even more magnificent intensity upon meeting the man-made power within the hidden Tricron bombs, and the entire shrine became lit up for several seconds with a luminescence that seemed to suggest the almighty meeting of two almost mutually respectful forces. Though hardly able to endure at that moment the renewed affliction inside her own head, the buzz and crackle of the watcher's inner circuitry nevertheless became soothed in equal measure by a lilting female voice that as if filtering through an unseen void of time and space beseeched: "So cold, so cold ... and oh so very dark ... foul murder ... unholy burial ... no life, no death ... just space between ... imprisonment ... eternal incarceration ... so wicked, so unjust, and why? ... Let us out ... oh let us out!"

Then, as the firmament framing the group of multi-trunked trees ultimately faded, Greta imagined the illuminated outline of two ghostly figures, one male and one female, stretching their arms out towards her. And in that brief moment before unconsciousness engulfed her, the enigmatic emissary from she knew not where felt sure that the latent force that she had sensed beneath those trees ever since having become drawn to them herself was in the act of being given earthly renewal. When the beholder of this odd vision eventually awoke, the thunderstorm had subsided and she could hear the familiar voices of Beka and Leigh calling out for her. Greta then crawled out from her place of concealment and her two friends rushed up to her, but though scratched and bruised, afflicted by creepy crawlies and shivering in her still sodden state, this chief was a resilient soul and so bid her lieutenants not to fuss.

"Sumthin' a bit strange 'as 'appened," Beka then announced. "Oy think ya shud cum an' see over 'ere."

The three teenagers walked back towards the five master oaks where the entire ranks of returned park kids were conversing in hushed tones whilst staring as one in the direction of two faint human forms that appeared to be engaged in arguing with one another close by Greta's own most favoured spot, though no sound of voices could actually be heard. The clearer to define of these two apparitions was that of a slim and hauntingly beautiful, raven-haired girl of around nineteen summers, who was attired in the serving costume of some century long past. The object of her apparent chagrin, that seemed somehow to be more difficult to discern, was a tousled haired fellow in his early thirties, wearing scuffed leather breeches and a brown tweedy waistcoat atop a billowing white blouse. This outfit was topped off by a rustic cap and a red patterned neckerchief that served to add a dual hint of mischief to its wearer's altogether irreverent, indeed cheeky manner and lazily defiant body language. No adornment offset the dainty neck of his opposite number, however and so the gawping urchins could all plainly identify the vivid red abrasion that there disfigured this girl's otherwise exquisite fair skin.

Of a sudden the female spirit became aware of her audience,

and as she turned towards them her attention was drawn by a brief burst of energy within their leader's own head, and so the two girls' eyes met. The first then bid her own companion be silent, while also attempting to slap him in response to some disrespectful quip on his part; before looking searchingly all about herself. Her eyes eventually settled upon what appeared to be the remains of an antique caravan park gas meter, the stanchion to which was still embedded in the ground nearby; and with a glance the girl bid Greta to follow her. Next this spectre seemed to enter into the hard metal object, at which she immediately assumed a more solid and less ethereal hue; before starting something akin to a curious game of charades, though still she appeared unable to actually speak. As Greta watched, she could feel that the presently vaporous creature was appealing for some kind of more suitable, hard inanimate object through which she and her fellow spirit could take on corporeal form.

In response to that entreaty, the inner noise that so afflicted the hybrid suggested most strongly some piece of such a purpose as it had been trying to impart for so long. The recipient walked back to the group of trees and began to dig with her bare hands beneath the blasted trunk of that morning's maelstrom. Then upon raising the objects that she excavated from therein, she held them out towards her visitors and offered: "Here, try these". And thus it was that the long undead guardians over the sanctity of Squire Barney Cockscomb's eastern lands, in whom some part of his ancient power had been invested for so long, became transformed upon their renewed earthly existence into walking, talking Tricron bombs.

The show now being over, various of the gathering were sent away to prepare food, while Beka, Leigh and some other more senior park kids settled down to talk with their new guests. Given the despair that Greta had discerned in the allegedly defiled and undeniably imprisoned voice that had so moved her through that brief vision after her favourite oaks had been struck, the rescuer couldn't help but notice how the two figures that now sat before her seemed not to be so traumatised after all by their two and a half centuries of confinement underground. Perhaps it was the opposite pole of the so potent force that the cans of their new found corporeal strength contained, but as the ensuing conversation unfolded the original felon and enchantress came to exhibit an immediate and all too apparent confidence that more than a little belied their own past mistreatment.

"Tell us who you are and where you come from," Greta began at which the tousle-haired man at once retorted: "Tell me who you are, darlin' and I might do the same!"

The girl at his side then slapped his wrist and scolded: "Pay him no regard. He has no manners, and thinks of nobody but himself." Then she continued: "I want to first tell you that we know a little of who you are, Greta; for I have felt the pain and torment that you suffer since you came to this spot. Imprisoned as we were within the earth beneath these noble old oaks, where I have been forced to endure this rough, coarse fellow as my only companion neither in life nor death for so long, we could feel your own dislike of the Hillites. But that is nothing compared to our own loathing, for it was the great Hogs Hill landowner of that long past time when we actually lived who had us murdered on his foul whim and then interred without due rights at first one spot of his choosing and then this."

Her pronouncement being over, the speaker then nudged the man at her side, and prompted: "Go on then. Tell this kind rescuer who you are."

"Oh you've finished 'ave yer? … The name's Will … Will Wayward," the strange and somewhat sardonic new visitor replied, with a touch of his cap. "I was a felon, that's to say a thief, burglar, vagabond … an' I was always pinchin' things off them 'Illites, until they did me in fer it. That's pinchin' as in nickin', stealin', robbin' … not like pinchin' girl's bottoms, though I liked to do that as well. All of them 'Illites knew what I was doin, an' 'ated me fer it, but they could never catch me at it, nor even see me a lot of the time … which was not to say that they was Frenchies or nuthin'. I was just too clever fer 'em."

"So ow'd they get to do ya in then?" interrupted Beka. "Ya couldn't 'ave bin that smart … 'Ere, where's 'e gone?"

"Over 'ere."

"Where?"

"Now 'ere … or maybe 'ere … ya see what I mean?"

"Wot's goin' on wiv 'im?" the confused Lees urchin demanded, whilst various others glanced agitatedly all around themselves as well.

"Ere I am again," the felon then teased. "Or maybe I ain't. 'Oo knows? Bet ya can't see me now?"

Will Wayward had the particular and none too infuriating knack of never allowing himself to be seen quite clearly, which after all was something of an advantage for a felon. "Sorry," he informed this new and hence rather bemused audience. "Just practisin' me favourite Faustian poses."

"Yer wot?" Beka at once protested.

"Me Faustian poses. All of us Faustians do 'em," came the teasing reply.

"Wot's Faustians, then?" came Leigh's own puzzled enquiry, to which Will responded: "People as do a deal with the Devil, of course." The eighteenth century smart Alec was momentarily nonplussed by the next post-apocalypse urchin enquiry of: "So 'oo the 'ell's the Devil, then?"

But Will Wayward briefly considered the unintended contradiction, before offering: "Old Nick, Beelzebub, the Prince of Darkness ... Him that stitches up clever little bastards who no-one ever unnerstands, never minds sees quite clearly ... what's the matter with ye all?" No-one responded, though the dark haired girl shot Greta a glance that seemed to suggest: "Just humour him."

"I met the Devil once," Will carried on regardless. "Or at least he said he was the Devil."

"Oh yeah? What'd he say to ya then?" Greta herself at this point challenged, whilst still feeling uncertain over what the rather exotic newcomer might actually be talking about.

"He said: 'Copy my poses, why don't ya?' and so I did," the felon informed his new benefactor. "And so I 'ave been doin' ever since. Yer unnerstand?" Nobody responded for a second time. It was becoming plain to Greta that this Will Wayward had more than a capacity for being extremely irritating if encouraged. Had he been cast in any early twenty-first century reality home cinema show, he would almost certainly have been the first to be voted off.

Then the gathering turned their attention to the female figure by Will's side, and Beka asked once more: "Oo are you, an' where d'ya come from?"

"My name's Nan ... Nan Chilswell," the raven-haired beauty began. "I came to live upon Hogs Hill in the year of 1767. I was an orphan. And a distant cousin of my dear lost father, for my mother had long since died too, had offered to take me in. His own family was very large, and so we all had to work very hard to keep everybody fed. And if some of the work was not to the girls' greatest liking then we just had to do it anyway, if you sense my meaning." With that last memory the speaker puckered up her dainty nose a little and turned her head to one side, looking towards the ground.

"Yes, I think I get the drift," Greta affirmed. "After all," Nan continued. "We had once had servants ourselves when I was small, before my dear mother died and then my poor father took to drink and lost all his money. So to become a serving wench myself was quite a shock to me."

"Oh, I see," said Greta, realising the hastiness of her initial assumption. "How did your father lose all his money?"

"Oh the poor dear man fell in with a bad lot who would prefer to lay wagers on the Badger baiting, and Toad throttling or fawn rogering, rather than partake of an honest day's toil. And the rogues and ruffians who organised those foul sports always made sure that nobody ever profited but themselves."

"Really? How very unfair," Greta sympathised.

"Yes," whimpered Nan with a further pucker of her nose. "And so I went to work for the Bayworth-Hamels, one of the most distinguished families in the locality, and at the yearly feast of the Hill's noble Otter sluicing meet I caught the attention of the great landowner, Squire Barney Cockscomb."

"What happened then?" Greta enquired, hoping for a rather more spicy response. "Oh, he would use me most cruelly!" the other girl obliged. "From that day forth I would be taken to him once a week, and the Squire would have his way no matter what. For I was far too weak to resist him and none would ever come to my aid, such was their fear of him."

"Seems these Toffs haven't changed so much," Greta thought to herself, recollecting the visitations of the procurement squads, before offering: "Poor lamb! And you being so young and innocent as well."

"Indeed, and so alone and friendless," Nan sighed. "He was not a man to be denied. Sometimes my ripe young cheeks would be so pink and stingy afterwards that I could barely sit down again!"

Greta suddenly felt a little taken in. "Oh, is that all?" she next rather scoffed. "I thought you meant that he …" but she was not allowed to finish.

"Oh *no*," Nan sighed for a second time. "Everybody on the Hill knew that the Squire had a problem in *that* direction, which was why he was so fond of spanking young wenches in the first place, quite apart from having no heir. But his game keeper's apprentice Billy was a *wonderful* lover."

Then, as her own countenance brightened considerably with the recollection, the sylph-like figure continued: "Oh, many was the night that we would lie together beneath the stars within Foulbury Coppice or upon Pincombe Heath, and Billy would take me with him to paradise and back again. I did love him so … or at least until his accident …"

Though sensing her own dwindling interest in this narrative, Greta still enquired: "What sort of accident?" And Nan responded: "My darling Billy was shot in his own bottom during the annual duck harvest of Foulbury Lake. I think the Squire arranged for it to happen himself because he knew that we were lovers. But anyway, Billy always walked with a limp after that, and some of the pellets that had lodged in more awkward places couldn't be removed. And so … well he … wasn't so *good* at things any more, and I came to think of him more like I would a brother. Anyway, Ben the blacksmith's boy was very handsome, but oh so clumsy so I didn't do it much with him. And then there was Wilf the ploughman, and Chas …"

"What?" spoke up Will Wayward at this point. "Who are all those others? You never let me nor my brother Ted touch ya once!"

"Oh, you're still there are you?" an only slightly embarrassed Nan countered before drawing herself up in a rather affronted pose and scolding: "I should think not, you rough felon. Look how dirty your hands still are!" But Will chose to ignore this rebuff, and so instead teased: "Couldn't see me, eh?"

"Don't start all that again!" cut in Greta. It had become clear to the last named that the "young and innocent" party of her so recent estimation had indeed been something of a prize in the locality of her own day. "What was happening with you and the Squire while all this was going on?" she next enquired.

"Oh he would use me most cruelly," Nan sighed for a third time.

236

"Yes, I think we've established that. Get to the point girl!" But the admonished party barely heard, and so continued: "Whenever I got back to the servants' quarters at my own employer's house, all of the other wenches would insist upon examining my poor bruised rump. Then they would announce their verdicts upon the Squire's performance and settle the wagers that they had made amongst themselves. They were all jealous of me of course, because I was the fairest wench by far on the Hill, as well as having the cutest bottom. And *they* all had spots and some of them even had boils, *yeuk!* So the Squire paid no regard to them, even if Will here and his brother probably knew every one of them at one time or another."

With that barb, the speaker glanced all around her, but did not seem able to locate its target. "Over here!" he eventually called, but Nan hardly cared whether she could see him quite clearly or not.

"Oh, it was all so trying," this mistreated and misunderstood girl then resumed. "My employer was naturally enjoying the Squire's favour, as indeed were my own relatives. Even my step brothers and sisters would all poke fun at me and call me 'Muntjac' ..." and that was as far as the rather vain creature was allowed to proceed.

"No ... really?" interrupted Greta. "Even though that particular species didn't become part of the native fauna until escaping from Woburn Park in the latter half of the twentieth century?"

Nan suddenly looked a little confused, and so offered: "Well, I expect that you can see my point. What's Woburn Park?"

Her opposite number indulged herself with a wry smile of satisfaction and then responded: "Dunno. Some kind of caravan place I expect. I just wanted to stop you from going on about yourself so much, and that was the best I could come up with on the spur of the moment."

Though Greta's normally chatter-filled mind remained at relative peace in this present company, she began to wonder which she might ultimately prefer as company: her familiar electronic torment or these equally irksome returnees that she had somehow roused from the realms of the undead. It seemed plain that if encouraged to talk about herself, the female player could be more than a little prone to self-absorption, and so Greta demanded: "Tell me how you got to be beneath these trees for so long, and be quick about it!"

At that, Nan pouted a little and drew herself up in a gesture of affront once again, but nonetheless obliged: "As I grew, I became strong enough to stand up to Squire Cockscomb, and so informed him that I would endure his vile attentions no longer. And thus he had me denounced as an enchantress, and since so many people were envious of me already I was made an outcast. Then, when he died the rogues and ruffians in his service murdered me on his orders, alongside that rough felon here ... er, over there? ... well never mind."

A faint call of "Yoo hoo" seemed to play momentarily about the ears of the small assembly beneath the five master oaks, as Leigh at this point piped up: "Wot's an enchantress, then?" All of those present had sat enthralled throughout the preceding narrative, since none amongst them had ever in their short lives encountered any being quite like this strange, rather dreamlike and so well spoken Nan Chilswell.

"A witch ... soothsayer, sorceress," Nan then very politely attempted to explain, but anticipating a collective cry of "Wot?", Greta interjected in the urchins' own patois: "Someone as does magic stuff," and the audience understood.

238

Chapter 7

The better that Greta got to know Nan Chilswell, the more she realised that despite her initial judgement of the girl as vain and self-absorbed, the original enchantress could as a woman scorned become a most effective agent through whom to gain an insight into the hitherto shrouded workings of the Hillite power base. But all the while the plotter at the park came to entertain a healthy distrust of the felon Will Wayward, who she felt sure would be out for no-one but himself in any venture that he might himself care to take on. What most suited the aspiring spymaster's purpose was that these spirits of her recent acquaintance seemed to experience no difficulty in freeing themselves from the sealed tin cans of their corporeal substance, and then as easily re-entering them whenever they might chose to do so.

It was thus a simple matter for the ghostly entities to waft across the Isis valley and on up to Hogs Hill, there to go about any business either of Greta's bidding or their own choosing, and then return to the Shottington copse to reclaim bodily form once more. The spirit felon unsurprisingly took maximum advantage of his now near invisibility to irritate the Hillites of his traditional scorn, in one trivial way or another, even more than he had in life some three centuries previously. But the raven-haired and retributive enchantress, upon walking the locality of her former life once again, quickly came to share the park chief's desire to be an instrument of her former abusers' overthrow.

On Nan's first unseen incursion into Hogs Hill Hall, the nonagenarian minister of defence Piers Grenshaw was engaged in bickering, as was his so frequent custom with the foreign secretary Douglas Hay-Wain. "My dear Grenshaw," the latter declared, while the spook looked on from the sanctuary of the rafters high above the debating chamber; "How many more times do I have to tell you that my counterpart in Paris assures me the situation with this Benson fellow is quite under control."

"Then what did I tell you?" the opposite number next

protested. "I've always suspected that damned Frenchie sees a lot more than he admits to. I don't trust the man. My own contacts have informed me by today's Pigeon post that this accursed Antipodean, Matt Benson has by now established large colonies in several mainland locations and intends to advance as soon as he is ready to. I trust those damnable former road and rail tunnels are still well and truly blocked at this end, nonsense that they always were."

While the prime minister as always nodded in his slumber at the head of the chamber's great oak table, Sir Nicholas Coverlet then came to his colleague's aid, declaring: "You seem to be developing an obsession with this so-called messiah, Grenshaw. My Winklers in the southern ports would deal with any of his kind as soon as they might dare to step ashore, besides which my Spanish counterpart, one Carlos Grandavia has pledged that their own fleet would intercept any attempted crossing."

But the minister of defence's countenance merely blackened on being so enlightened and he barked: "So you're in league with those blasted Spicks now are you, Coverlet?" while Sir Cuthbert Pincombe himself half awoke for a moment at this point and was heard to splutter: "What? He'll be after our fish!"

"There, there prime minister, don't alarm yourself," the home secretary then countered with a reassuring wrap of the blankets that as ever insulated his chair-bound figurehead's knees. "No fish. Just the prawns around the Provonian coast that the good people over there don't like to eat themselves." And so the debate ground on in the void below the eavesdropper, eventually to be settled as so often by the prime minister's casting vote and in the foreign and home secretaries' favour.

Of all the world's denizens, the Antipodeans had survived the apocalypse in the greatest numbers, and subsequently migrated to Europe in hitherto unprecedented numbers at least during the barbecue season of the summer months. The said Matt Benson had once been a movie star, prior to developing an all consuming messiah complex and thenceforth acquiring a mass following; first amongst the war-wearied populations of re-emergent America and the former Oriental zone, and then the as traumatised European mainland. An even more massive flow of donations had needless to say been forthcoming from his legions of adoring devotees, so to entertain special designs upon the eccentric offshore fiefdom of England hardly suggested itself as a logical next step. But the most entrenched amongst Hogs Hill Hall's cabinet appeared to be little different from any of their pre-apocalypse counterparts in government in imagining that such an ambition must be uppermost in this as all potential foreign invader's ghastly plans.

For their own part, the chancellor, home and foreign secretaries remained sceptical, though they nonetheless presumed to play upon certain of their colleagues' fears in any way that might produce further advantage for themselves. The bargain with the Spanish was a case in point, though that country's fishing fleet was as ever helping itself to much more than the stated quotas of unloved and hence surplus Provonian prawns.

On the spirit enchantress' next unseen foray into parliament, more parochial concerns appeared to be in contention. "I really think one ought to address the grammar of that particular statement," Leticia Bagdalen-Spellwright, the under-secretary with special responsibility for the succession was admonishing a more senior spokesman. The various members of her revered lineage were sticklers not only for grammar but pronunciation in relation to spelling, and peculiar English preciseness in all its forms. Through successive generations prior to the global conflict, family representatives had always sought election as councillors of the former town in the Isis valley, with the express aim of naming after themselves as many of its buildings, streets, bridges or institutions as was possible. Thus they were assured of endlessly indulging their undying passion for denouncing the great stupidity of England's wider population in not appreciating that "Bagdalen" was in fact pronounced "Baudlun" locally. Employees both of the local authority and the so-titled institutions had for years all been expressly forbidden from spelling that spoken name to any outside correspondent or would be visitor, and so the time honoured pedantry of the Bagdalen-Spellwrights endured. From a vantage point to one side of Squire Barney Cockscomb's grand portrait, the interloper yawned as so many others had before her.

Day upon day, Nan Chilswell would conceal herself about Hogs Hill Hall's many rotting rooms and recesses, to snoop upon the deliberations of one or another Parliamentary sub-committee, as well as the proceedings within the grand debating chamber itself.

Prompted by Greta's own counsel, she would also waft across to the Boarding House of an evening to similarly scrutinise the after hours deliberations of the central cabinet cabal. Being a somewhat astute spirit, the one-time serving wench was fairly quickly able to assess the various factions and rivalries of the ruling elite, whom it seemed to her were barely different from their so pompous, tedious and overbearing ancestors of her earthly self's own long distant lifetime; which of course they were not. She came to feel an almost equal contempt and fascination for Harold Bayworth-Hamel, the heir of her own girlhood employers, who though she could never figure out exactly what office he might actually hold would always introduce any contribution to government that he cared to make with: "Speaking on behalf of the most distinguished families present ..." In response, the assembled Hillite worthies would invariably proceed to cough amongst themselves, fidget with any small object that might lie conveniently close to hand, and rustle their papers as if in respectful variance with their haughty colleague's hereditary self-esteem; but Harold himself was never, ever deterred.

By contrast, Nan came to almost pity Jolyon Farquhar, the minister without portfolio who it appeared to the unseen observer always seemed to be searching for something useful to do. But whenever this rather junior late-septuagenarian seized the opportunity to thrust himself forward for one assignment or another, his cabinet colleagues would counter with such well worn responses as: "Not a task for an idle Farquhar like yourself, I would have thought," "What did that useless Farquhar just say?" or "Really, how silly!"

Upon all of these instances, the entire assembly would momentarily descend into barely suppressed merriment at their traditional object of fun's discomfort; since it was a longstanding point of honour amongst themselves to compete over the best Farquhar puns. Only Edward, the current representative of the Caruthers' dynasty, ever seemed to miss the point of this most venerable of all Hillite in-jokes.

Such skirmishes were mere minor manifestations of inter-family enmity, however. It became abundantly clear to the hidden or hovering listener that the most festering schism at the heart of Hogs Hill authority was that between the squabbling cliques led by the oldest moneyed Grenshaw's, Bayworth-Hamels and Bagdalen-

Spellwrights on the one side; and the chancellor, home and foreign secretaries whose pedigrees had rather more recently made a more pernicious progress through that most bizarre of all pecking orders. "Two hundred million?" Sir Nicholas Coverlet's barrister-like tones boomed around the debating chamber during one particularly fierce exchange. "I can only reiterate that the immediate past prime minister, God rest her soul, had become a little prone to wandering in her mind towards the end; and that so you must have been misinformed. The two hundred *thousand* coins in question are stored safely within the Boarding House vaults where they might be inspected by any interested party at any time."

The three highest office holders had indeed surrendered the said sum of groats from their collective family coffers, for the exact purpose of fielding just such hostile enquiry as they were currently facing; but still their opponents were not to be swayed. "Speaking on behalf of the most distinguished families present, I feel it is our duty to emphasise that this sum you state, Coverlet is still the highest ever raised from a foreigner," Harold Bayworth-Hamel was next heard to argue. "And that given the nationality of the envoy in question, such acceptance constitutes a clear violation of Hill lore. Might I remind you, once again that Ruskies are always ..."

But at this point the apparently ever more self-satisfied Nigel Scroately-Browne chose to interject: "Oh for heaven's sake ... that would hardly bring about the end of the world, would it?" And the spying Nan Chilswell, in common with every object of her study present, thereupon experienced the strangest of sensations that none save the spirit enchantress herself could afterwards clearly recall.

As if in answer to the chancellor's careless *faux-pas*, the habitually uncertain light that competed with the debating chamber's lofty west-facing window of a sudden dimmed; banks of trees immediately without seemingly united in a windswept chorus of rustling and whispering, various of their tenant Crows cawed in the most clear-headed of manners, and one or more distant barks of Muntjac became carried from afar on the momentarily anxious afternoon air. And with that ultimate bottoming out of these assorted portents, some sense of a low yet lugubrious forewarning from within the depths of the ground on which Hogs Hill Hall stood groaned about the hallowed monument's very fabric, which was felt by everyone within to shudder slightly on its foundations.

The first to recompose himself was Piers Grenshaw, who leaning forward and fixing his adversary with a sickly stare, intoned with deathly calm and as if through the deepest of recesses that excluded all at hand: "Be careful in your creativity, Scroatley dear boy. The ways of our lives on Hogs Hill in this day as through all time past must *never* be altered. And that ultimate authority through which we are each here now may yet have no regard for any of us."

Notwithstanding their appropriate Hillite staidness and reserve, the elder faction were more than a little prone to superstition. Some concept of the original Hill lore, as had been set out in the ancient tomes that were destroyed along with the Grenshaw family seat of "Blackcroft" back in 2023, had nonetheless passed down through successive generations of that most respected lineage. For the ancient power that Squire Barney Cockscomb had drawn upon in formulating his legacy of 1772: that was infused in the very bedrock beneath Hogs Hill Hall, Arden Propley, the former Blackcroft and every other crumbling ancestral pile of the Hill's great families, was the essence of English feudalism itself.

Thus it was that the eighteenth century landowner had risen to such local eminence in his own time, thus the same power had become reincarnated at the close of the twentieth century, and thus it had overseen the renewed growth and prosperity of its favoured gentry ever since. But what nobody amongst the late twenty-first century polity could know, and which the current chancellor, home and foreign secretaries appreciated least of all, was the final judgement ordained within that same original Hill lore should its unstinting cause of stifling change be abandoned. Such expansive stores of vulgar new or even more offensively, foreign wealth that were now boasted by the Scroatley-Browne, Coverlet and Hay-Wain back way cellars were thereby doomed ultimately to implode, together with the fortunes of those who had been guilty of amassing such ill gotten gain. And it had similarly been ordained, just as a triumvirate of felon, enchantress and legacy bearer would set in play the conditions for a Hillite return to prominence; that a vengeful quartet of bizarre and unearthly outsiders would in the event of transgression become the instruments of that irreversible demise.

Chapter 8

All the while that the original enchantress was so usefully engaged in espionage on behalf of Greta's cause, the second spirit Will Wayward pursued its separate and careless agenda. The returned felon could no more reform the habits of his past earthly life than the testy targets of his renewed mischief could consider change themselves, and thus a steady stream of valuable trinkets and family heirlooms mysteriously came to be missed in one ancestral Hogs Hill pile or another. Initially the bandit banshee would carry these trophies back to the park of an evening, there to indulge in a repertoire of "now you see them, now you don't" tricks whilst attempting to show them off; but none amongst its supposed new found friends cared to be so impressed.

As he came to realise that those Shottington copse companions were set upon a rather more solemn campaign against the targets of his own scorn, Will briefly considered whether such revolution might represent his best personal gain and quickly decided not. So the self interested party one night walked away from the eastern enclosure of his and Nan Chilswell's past long confinement, within the latterly acquired tin can that he somehow cared not to discard, never again to return. By sun-up the tousle-haired thief had trudged all the way over to the grand geological edifice beyond the Isis' opposite bank; and thus for the first time since the courier's last round in 2025, Hogs Hill reacquired the most idiosyncratic of lone daily wanderers.

Roaming at will indeed became the wayward spirit's wilful purpose, while it's personal treasure trove grew in parallel with the rumour that spread concerning an invisible entity in the Hillite midst. And with such spreading unease a superstitious dread began to take root within local high society that all could no longer be well in regard to the ancient and once unshakeable order of its observance. For a base the unwelcome guest chose the site of Blackcroft, that he reasoned lay conveniently off the beaten track of even that least travelled thoroughfare of Hogs Hill's back way.

The owning Grenshaws themselves had long abandoned the place, refusing to contemplate the great vulgarity of a new house becoming their family seat that rebuilding would inevitably involve. So they had relocated to the neighbouring and suitably rustic retreat of Foulbury House that skulked within the coppice of the same name on the far side of the listless lake that lay between the two estates. No human foot ever trod the longest of all the Hill's many long and often winding driveways now.

Within this sanctuary Will Wayward lighted upon the ruined remnants of an outhouse that gave access to the old mansion's extensive cellars, which the discoverer at once foresaw as a most suitable place of containment for the future riches of his illicit intent. Those underground chambers remained variously clogged with the dust of this place's past demise, and when the surviving Tricron bomb in the new tenant's trust came into contact with its creator's one-time handiwork, a supercharged energy seemed to arise about the entire location. And thus the mischievous phantom became aware of a notion of some vital force that was invested in itself, and then another idea that the tin of beans in its keeping should be retained for wise use at a critical future juncture. So though the felon would have little immediate use for that object of his corporeal substance, he kept it carefully hidden within his lair in readiness for whatever purpose might emerge.

The spirit Will also quickly discovered that he was by no means the only bizarre life form to dwell within the former Blackcroft's ruins. Particularly during the warmer days as spring turned to summer, the old estate would become infested with very large numbers of even larger, hairy spiders that seemed to emanate from the long corroded hulk of what had once been a Morris Minor Countryman. The car in question had long ago been the pride and joy of one Phylogenies Grenshaw, who having been boffin rather than top brass material had invested much of his working life in developing the stuff of arachnophobiac nightmares.

Eventually this government biologist succeeded in hybridising the two most fearsome spiders known to late-twentieth century science: the Great Andean Hairy and the Giant Botswana Brown; under contract from the then Ministry of Defence to develop spiders for military security applications that were even scarier than large, fierce dogs. Then a third and even more alarming species came somehow to corrupt the cross-breeding programme, ostensibly by accident but just as possibly by design, and orders were made for the project to be abandoned and all of the spiders to be destroyed. But Phylogenies himself had come to nurture such a devotion to the creatures of his creation, that upon his forced resignation he conveyed in his vehicle of choice to the unvisited Grenshaw family seat a small number of prize specimens, that ever since had multiplied and further mutated far from either the enquiry or sight of spider fearing society.

Will Wayward could hardly believe his good fortune upon discovering this hidden resource. As a youth in the eighteenth century, the future felon had been an absolute terror for dropping worms or slugs down the necks of girls' dresses. Still he would delight in provoking the local ladies through sudden encounters with one or another large creepy crawly or small furry mammal; quite apart from the more than occasional, unanticipated pinch of younger Hillite daughters' bottoms and similar assaults upon one or two more mature examples besides. Now the lone daily rover carried a bag of the hairy scary arachnid brutes with him wherever he went, to plant them behind various items of bathroom furniture, at the bottom of linen baskets, under piano lids and pillows, or within the fruit bowls and jewellery boxes of one Hogs Hill household or another. And thus through the early summer of the Hillites' golden jubilee year, ahead of its planned grand festival, all of the most positively vetted daughters in residence would become prone to the most extreme displays of spontaneity, if not wit or spirit, whenever such a concealed and slumbering eight-legged agent might be by chance reacquainted with the light of day.

The supercharged dust of Blackcroft's one-time grandeur was also host to a teeming population of vigorous ants. Whilst the slothful spiders wiled away their own time in the balmy summer air outside, these far smaller counterparts remained intent upon their own power plays in anticipation of that time when they too might one day rule the world; or turf wars with their deadly local rivals, the teeming and unseen hordes of house dust mites that infested each and every Hillite home. And through the peculiar energy that permeated the cellars of their shared existence, the lingering felon found that he was able to communicate quite readily with the tiny creatures.

The various warlords of this highly organised insect society each seemed to resemble the ruling Hillites in one distinguishing trait or another, and thus the newcomer became acquainted with, amongst others the oh so clever Brill Y Ant and its closest lieutenants Domin Ant and Signific Ant, the highly patrician Intoler Ant, the under utilised Applic Ant, the sexually rapacious Devi Ant; and last but by no means least Belliger Ant, for whom spelling had never been a strong point.

Those commanders' miniscule platoons proved to be the most valuable of intelligence gatherers, particularly given the ants' highly complex networks of informants and double agents within the bountiful house dust mite community; and through these associates Will Wayward was able to map out the locations of all the most well-filled vaults and counting houses in the vicinity. And hence the original felon also became aware before so very long of those great gold bullion hordes of the chancellor, home and foreign secretaries, that were so at variance with the doctrine of the original Hill lore.

As the summer progressed, and given the disquiet being generated across the locality of Hogs Hill through the mysterious and unpredictable phenomena that daily issued from the one-time bastion of Blackcroft, the spying Nan Chilswell carried frequent bulletins concerning the residents' unease home to her guru Greta at the Shottington copse. The two enigmatic female entities came to almost approve of the male defector's separate agenda, since it seemed to be serving their own purpose of destabilising the seat of power rather more effectively than they might have imagined.

Greta and Nan had by this time become the firmest of allies, and the sylph-like spirit would report back regularly to the dysfunctional semi-droid upon all that she herself gathered either in Hogs Hill Hall by day or the late-evening preserve of the Boarding House. Thus the campaign mastermind learned of the ruling Hillites' great aversion to all foreigners, but that the one they most distrusted was an Antipodean named Matt Benson who was said to be a messiah. The plotter at the park likewise came to appreciate the potential of the equal unease felt within certain factions of government over the intent of the restive Celtic races on England's northern and western borders; and the apparent rift that had arisen out of the Hill's highest office holders acquisition of rather more foreign funds than would enjoy their more conservative colleagues' consent.

Greta at first reasoned that fashioning alliances with the outside interests in question must surely represent the logical way forward, but before she could work out in just what way she might do so, the entire course of events took another twist when one evening, roughly four weeks ahead of the Hillites' golden jubilee celebrations, Nan Chilswell returned to the shade beneath the five master oaks with a new companion. The young woman in question went by the name of Cayte, and though clearly some years older than her late-teenaged hosts, she herself would only describe herself as "ageless". That quality could most certainly be applied to this newcomer's particular attractiveness, whilst her ultra-alluring personality captivated almost everyone of wit or spirit who encountered her. Cayte in return had always felt a partiality for the most exotic of companions, and so when the spirit Nan had stumbled upon this other riddle roaming Hogs Hill's highest environs with apparent designing intent, the two had at once sensed the strongest of bonds. And now, as soon as she too beheld this rather curious new creature, the equally puzzling Greta was likewise drawn into similar communion.

Cayte was actually a space alien who had been sent to Earth by her own race some time after the apocalypse to assess the ravaged planet's potential for colonisation, but since she would always forget whatever it was that she was meant to be doing no sooner than she had started to do it, she was hardly the best possible choice for such an assignment. Her secret identity had been that of a foundling child who would be received by a middle ranking Hill family, much like Nan herself in her own past time; but as she had grown this girl came to display such an inclination for the subtlest and most captivatingly spontaneous traits that her adoptive kin had not even dared subject their charge to the summer social season's judgement. Years below stairs and the most unyielding terms of sporting correction had all been to no avail, and eventually Cayte simply walked away from the realm of her restraint one day, ever since to spend her time travelling on the European mainland or even further afield if opportunity allowed. But each summer the refugee would return to Hogs Hill ahead of the celebration of its succession, to enlist the support of more recent fallen daughters and hence inspire those unfortunate servant girls to disrupt the annual proceedings as best they might.

Dark rumour concerning "Cayte the festival wrecker" had long circulated in the more superstitious sectors of Hillite society, just as its same members had most recently become anxious over notions of thieves in the night, a sinister spider master and the new threats so posed to the sanctity of their preferred unbending order. Over the years the festival kitchen and serving wenches had always been cautioned most carefully as to the penalties for collaborating with the returning rebel, but no such links were ever proven and certain of the special ingredients that Cayte had a particular talent for accumulating on her foreign journeys would always find their way into one ritualistic recipe or another.

As a result, most of the more solemn summer festival banquets or ceremonies had become subject at one time or another to sudden descents into most un-Hillite like behaviour that would remain the subject of below stairs hilarity throughout the interval between one celebration and another. All of the serving ranks' least correctible veterans would relish every opportunity to so discomfit each season's carefully selected targets, and every year new incidents would embarrass the normally so staid and dreary festival goers as never before.

Now, upon becoming acquainted with the long scorned Nan Chilswell and grimacing Greta who had sailed ashore from she knew not where, that same past tormentor of polite custom at once elected to pool her particular talents with these new allies. And with Cayte's enlistment to the cause there thus became ranged against the common ruling interest a malfunctioning human-cyborg amalgam, two barely perceptible returnees from the spirit world of the undead, and an ageless and artful if absent-minded space alien: a vengeful quartet of bizarre and unearthly outsiders if ever there was one.

Chapter 9

Whirr and hum, crackle and fizz: through so often crippling and intermittently painful onslaughts of electronically induced seizure and distorted yet no less deafening feedback, the corrupted circuitry of Greta's daily discomfiture persisted in its attempts to aid the lost girl in her search for further enlightenment. "Where are you, father? ... Speak to me, dear! ... What is it that you want from me; is there something? ... Can I never please you?" she would variously cry out in her bewilderment; but still the confused creature could gain no clear insight into whether indeed that absent yet so longed-for sire might entertain any special purpose for her in whatever scheme she felt convinced must be her mission in the locality where she now dwelt.

Through all these contradictions, the park chief retained a fascination for the frequently vacated bean tin that she had given to her friend and ally Nan Chilswell, since it seemed to somehow chatter with the inner workings of her own troubled mind in a way that at least suggested clarity of a kind. And just as Will Wayward had become infused within his Blackcroft lair with the notion of some future use that these mysterious objects must be saved for, so the remaining tin in Greta's keeping seemed to convey to her a special purpose amongst the random riddles of her constant reflection.

The peevish past purchase of Cuylee McGrouse, in the Lees' Dellseys multimart of 2023, had in fact been two samples from a limited developmental batch of Tricron bombs that indeed were programmed to be detonated only at a critical future juncture of their carriers' calling. Thus it was that the young, bad estate mother had at that time been unable to open these ring pull cans, just as all those others who had most recently tried would similarly fail. And thus they had been consigned rather irritably to the most rubbish strewn recess of the Lees larder in which they had remained mislaid yet still intact until their chance exhumation and transfer to the park years later.

When the research project in question had ultimately been abandoned by the Tricron technology's inscrutable Oriental creators, all of the known inventory had been recalled and scrapped, yet due to the unknowing action of an eager to please new shop assistant on that distant day, just two examples survived. Now it seemed that, irrespective of any intended communication or otherwise from outer space, the abandoned artefacts were acquiring a will of their own in influencing their current keepers to fulfil the purpose of their own original manufacture.

Nan and Cayte were by now busily engaged in rallying the below stairs fallen females of Hogs Hill society to the cause of upsetting the course of the soon to commence summer festival as never before. As a space alien, and therefore being prone to feeling spaced out for much of the time, Cayte experienced little difficulty in wafting across the Isis valley with the phantasm of her recent alliance on their daily excursions. There the ethereal pair became reacquainted with many enthusiastic partners in the annual returnee's previous campaigns, all of whom warmed to the presence of the ghostly past servant girl Nan, and new plans were laid to infuse the conventional festival fustiness with unpredictable and embarrassing incidents that would match the most grandiose ever proceedings to come in fitting proportion. It was never very difficult to outwit the resident Hillites and their many staid and unspontaneous guests in these ways, given those opposite numbers' own unfailing lack of imagination and insufferable assurance in their so stuffy social status.

"Poor Greta. What is it that ails you, dear?" the soothing tones of Nan Chilswell played in the semi-conscious mind of the park chief upon its half-waking from one particularly furious inner assault. "I just wish that I had had normal parents," the latter replied with a downward glance as painfully longing as it was so bleakly lost; but then as ever upon such careless moments of accidental introspection, this hardy soul recomposed herself.

"So what have you two been up to today?" Greta rallied with a shake of her fast-clearing head, and then both friends knew at once that further enquiry as to the third's inner torment would go unanswered. The enchantress was on this evening, as usual upon regaining the subtly sombre shade of the five master oaks, resettled within her own bean tin; and once Cayte had wandered absent mindedly away, the spirit felt the compunction to unburden herself of the designs that the device had been distilling.

"This metal cylinder that you so kindly gave me for a body talks to me in it's own way," the Tricron tenant began. "Does that seem strange to you?"

"No, not at all," came the eager reply. "It chatters to me too when you're not here. And it's often the only time I can make sense of a lot of the stuff that I grapple with all day. What does it say to you, then?"

Nan Chilswell's so beautiful face next seemed to acquire an especial evocativeness and a lilting refrain played about Greta's ears, as if through all the distance between the other girl's past earthly and renewed existences, imparting: "I know it has some tremendous destructive power that has been bequeathed to me by a force that I cannot understand, and which I must use very wisely. And so I know why it is that I have been reborn and what my task here must be."

Then with a glance to the west in the direction of her past Hogs Hill abode, the spirit added: "And just what the moment of my so careful choosing *will* be." The two girls then sat conversing intently for some time until they were interrupted by the return of Cayte, alongside whom were the excited figures of Leigh and Beka.

"Gail an' Kowlea are dead," the first of those urchins announced. "The 'Illites 'ave 'ung 'em, an' in the mornin' Kyle's gonna start bashin' up all the other Lees clans to show 'em oo rules there now."

With that news, Greta stared into the short space between herself and the dishevelled messengers, and with a grimace sighed simply: "The fools." Similar bulletins had reached her over the previous two weeks concerning how the headstrong leader of the Golden Urchins had indeed assembled a fighting force which had marched off to the village that Greta herself had first shown to Gail. Kowlea, not wishing to be outshone, had decided to join her former rival but the cannier Kyle had remained behind with a sufficient following of his own with which to establish future control. The expedition had been doomed to failure, it's leaders captured and their subordinates all carried off to servitude; and now the most final justice of that village's market town masters had been the unwise Gail and Kowlea's inevitable fate. It would be

Kyle and his now permanent mate Sami who would hold sway on The Lees from this day forth.

Greta sat up for a little longer that night once everyone else had retired, ruminating upon how her nearest neighbours would now be forever beyond any schooling such as she had once sought to bestow; and that given Nan's earlier revelations the ambition that she had assumed for herself upon her own arrival in the fiefdom had been transferred to the safest of keeping. And thus, to the gentle sighing of the multi-trunked trees all around and calls of the copse's feathered night foragers, the oft-tormented being drifted into a reverie. The park chief had, since meeting Cayte often quizzed that wanderer abroad as to what life was like on the European mainland, and now her own imagination took over.

The lost girl imagined herself standing at the site of the former town in the Isis valley's transport terminus, Worcester Place. From there, prior to the apocalypse and a little outside the usual conventions of British reserve, a network of 'naughty buses' had ferried the uncomforted to the flesh pots of Europe for a mere thirty pounds return if booked a month in advance. But now just one stagecoach a week departed, conveying occasional Hillite officials with the appropriate clearance to the south coast port of Yolkestone where their crossing could be effected by the furtive flotilla of Spanish trawlers in Sir Nicholas Coverlet's special service. But in this vision, it was not such a clandestine agent of the ruling cabinet cabal who waited at the staging post but Greta herself, in readiness for seeking out and then joining that mainland force for ultimate enlightenment that was the messiah, Matt Benson.

< The Flight of the Naughty Bus – Greta's dream >
Onward ever onward: rattle and crash, lurch and wobble; through the eight day scheduled journey time to Yolkestone, the bruised and battered Greta would question most fervently why she had ever left home. The fiefdom's roads had undergone virtually no upkeep through fifty years of Hillite management, just as in the total absence of ghastly foreign oil imports, rail and air travel had been consigned to their so very vulgar places in history. The ruling class had long considered lack of mobility to be amongst the most effective means of keeping the proletariat in its rightful place. Thus,

in just the same way that the pre-apocalypse population had commonly campaigned for traffic calming in their own villages or urban streets, before acquiring four ton, four litre 4x4s in which to run down the equivalent measures whilst speeding themselves and their children in safety through everyone else's locale; so in the early years of the present fiefdom local officials had all demanded passage through each other's patches whilst seeking to restrict access to their own. And so the outcome was that England's decrepit road infrastructure became strangulated by an ever more complicated and universally corrupt system of turnpikes.

At every parish boundary, the local Triffs bearers would be entitled to variously devious arrays of backhanders of their own devising, whilst stopovers at the route's strategically located coaching inns were only a little less risky than nights spent in Hogs Hill's infamous Boarding House itself. "Oh yes, we have rooms. Many fine rooms," one most macabre of all the innkeepers who were tasked by parliament to apprehend unauthorised travellers leered in response to Greta's enquiry, his sinister tone being barely audible above the background metallic scrape of a meat cleaver being sharpened. "That will be just for *one* night, I presume?" Having grown so used to sleeping out of doors during her sojourn at the Shottington copse, the prospective escapee of this dream at once decided against altering those most recent habits.

At every stage of this grinding, gruelling journey, the traveller would observe the pitiful lot of the smallholders who toiled on one village estate after another, and be touched anew by their lack of reward just as when she had first walked ashore so many months previously. And given her constant buffeting and battering, Greta often wondered how the fiefdom's great and good managed to find their way around so readily on their own business of governance: either they had access to a superior class of carriage or the author was as ever being a little selective in his portrayal of such things. Eventually though, the stagecoach drew up in Yolkestone before the once eminent edifice of the long sabotaged entrance to the 'Continental Tunnel', at which the passenger was forced to surrender her last few groats should she wish to disembark. She had no means now with which to bribe her way aboard a cross-channel trawler, but at least in this reverie beneath the five master oaks that predicament proved to be no stubborn obstacle.

Inspired perhaps by her turn of the twenty-first century predecessor Sheralee, the sudden sorceress of Greta's vision simply raised her arms aloft and spoke for a few moments in a curious tongue; but no unplanned side effect transpired. Instead and at once, the untold tons of earth and rubble that clogged the one-time marvel of late-twentieth century engineering burst obediently outwards, and through the exit so revealed there emerged a gleaming, silver-coloured, high-speed locomotive drawing wagon upon wagon of naughty buses that were scheduled for every conceivable mainland destination.

The exultant emigrant then walked along the line of railcars until she beheld the name in electronic lights of the French town close to which Cayte had told her the messiah could be located, before climbing aboard the luxury coach concerned. And with that the train re-entered the temporary gloom of the tunnel, whose gateway imploded anew behind it, eventually to re-emerge on the other side. But when it did so, dreams being curious and unpredictable things, the clock had become turned back some three quarters of a century.

As far inland as the eye could see, the path of the now crowded naughty bus of Greta's choosing was blocked by a choking confusion of vehicles bearing ranks of returning Brits, all patiently queuing to politely nod and agree their way through the bastions of bureaucracy that blocked their own passage home, without anyone daring to commit the unpardonable indiscretion of "making a fuss". Long years after the first twentieth century London government to do so had committed its offshore and insular land to membership of a unified and hence deregulated Europe, the archaic institution of 'daylight saving time' had been preserved for the express purpose of moving homeward travellers through border controls that came to prevail nowhere else on the mainland, thence to emerge at around the same local time that they had first entered the tortuous process on the far side.

It was only the dutiful legions of rule-conscious little Englanders who were ever so inconvenienced of course, since although their continental cousins would all sign up to the same protocols the Spanish would as always proceed to ignore them to their own advantage, while the Germans and Dutch would continue to cheat their way around them; and the French would simply glance to one side with a certain *"je ne sais quoi"*, affecting not to notice that such constraints existed at all. Of course reams of regulations needed to be formulated for whatever purpose, in order to keep the ranks of Euro-bureaucrats in expense accounted and pensioned careers, but it was only the union's most reluctant and complaining member that ever seemed to implement any of these measures, and then always to its own populace's eternal disadvantage. But as one after another English village shop would be closed down by squads of inspectors under Whitehall's own jurisdiction, and successive, early twenty-first century administrations heaped the blame for endless indirect taxes of their own invention at Brussels' door; at least the electorate remained suitably fearful of the ever present threat to its traditional, island way of life that the mainland's so much fairer and classless system must surely pose. And thus the ultimate purpose was served of keeping the foreign invader at bay: had things really changed so much over the ensuing three quarters of a century?

"Oh, get on with it!" the impatient figure of Greta eventually shouted, and with that protest this vision took another twist and the naughty bus carried her forward into a veritable modern day wonderland. Wherever the traveller might look there sped sleek cars, serviceable vans and doughty trucks; whilst high-speed trains rushed by on rails parallel to the well maintained highway and aircraft roared in the skies overhead. In every direction she also beheld smart houses with instantly made over gardens; offices, schools and factories; that all bore ample testimony to the pace of some fifty years' reconstruction that had been denied the so downtrodden denizens of the land she had left behind.

On, on flew the naughty bus, past shopping malls, entertainment complexes, comfortable hotels and wholesome eating places; and in all these locations there were banks of money trees, as post-apocalypse cash dispensers were styled, at which huddles of beaming consumers jostled one another for ready access to unlimited credit. Greta would gaze in wonderment at the affluence that seemed to announce itself from wherever her eye might dwell, whilst trying also to take in the omnipresent advertising hoardings that extolled seeming miracles of post-apocalypse technology to the untrained eye of this observer; until at length she reached her journey's end.

The newcomer trudged around that French regional town for much of the day, becoming steadily more frustrated as she enquired of one local after another: "Have you seen the messiah?"

"*Mais, non,*" always came the subtly ambiguous response. Poor Greta: no-one had ever counselled her as to the futility of such a line of questioning in the country where she now trod. Eventually the disheartened semi-droid lighted upon a supermarket, outside which two fair haired, well built and very sun-tanned young men were loading value packs of continental beer atop a large pick-up truck. Reasoning that they might indeed be Antipodeans she walked over to them and asked: "Can you take me to the messiah, Matt Benson?"

"No worries, mate!" came the laid back reply. "Come with us." Then the supplicant climbed atop the vehicle, settling as comfortably as she could amidst the hum of its several refrigerators, and was whisked away from that town to the future calling that she so sought.

Eventually the passenger beheld a large compound that lay in a deep gully of a brooding geological feature named the *Ardonne Massif*, which was famous in French cuisine for it's gourmet patés and sizeable spicy sausages. As the vehicle drew up in an outer courtyard, on every side busy representatives of what appeared to be many nationalities were variously engaged in stacking cans of beer into banks of refrigerators or cleaning the carelessly strewn garden barbecues that cluttered the entire area.

"Follow us," one of Greta's escorts announced: "Nah, what did ya say ya name was?"

"Greta, what's yours?"

"Ivor," the young man replied. "Ivor Horniman, and this is my cousin Brett."

"G'day Greta," offered the second, broad shouldered and muscular Antipodean, with a no less broad smile. "We're kinda senior guys around the gaffer. Us 'Hornies', as we're known to our mates, get to do a lot of the best work around here." Then, feeling a little intrigued as to what exactly this Brett might be referring to, the new arrival followed her new acquaintances through a succession of doorways, rooms and corridors that eventually gave way to the messiah's inner sanctum.

"Hi, great to have ya aboard," the figure on the throne before the visitor proclaimed, stretching out a hand and squeezing that offered in return by Greta with an all too apparent suggestiveness. "Ya come far?"

"England actually."

"Bonzer. Don't get too many in from there, heh heh. Bit of a difficult place to get in and out of, as I hear. But as soon as I'm ready I'm gonna advance over there anyway."

Matt Benson was dressed in flowing, all enveloping robes, the colour of which he would change according to the days of the week and their particular courses of enlightenment. At this moment he was clad in black, and though to Greta he appeared undeniably good looking and a deal charismatic, she thought him on first impressions to be a little on the short side for a messiah; which indeed was a widespread rumour amongst people who had not met him.

Turning back to Ivor and Brett, Matt then invited: "Nah why don't ya fix up this little lady with a beer and show her to the guest quarters. Then …" he added, turning upon his recruit a twinkle of the eye that was unmistakeable in its meaning: "Ya can freshen up hey, an' you an' I can get a little better acquainted, heh heh."

Being a former movie star, Matt Benson was never slow to exercise his messianic privilege of "getting a little better acquainted" with all new female converts to his cause. The cousins then led their charge through more passageways and eventually across another courtyard to a block of studio apartments, where they showed her to her lodgings.

"Nah Greta," Ivor then counselled, taking both her hands into his own and looking seductively into her face. "The gaffer's a regular fella and a real bonzer messiah, don't get us wrong. But it's kinda known amongst us senior guys that a second comin' durin' a single enlightenment ain't that likely, if ya get my meanin'."

"Well I never, who would have thought it?" Greta flirted a little in return, never having been used to such a degree of male attention as she was suddenly commanding.

"Yeah, an' just between the three of us here," Ivor continued.

"Mmmm?" came a second tease. "I don't think ya should really expect things to last too long at all."

"Oh dear, and me having travelled so far as well."

"That's right. So if after gettin' a little better acquainted with

Matt ya still don't feel quite enlightened enough …"

"Yes?" teased Greta once more, gazing back into the bronzed Antipodean's liquid blue eyes. "Me an' Brett live just over there."

"Thank you, I'll remember that," the new guest assured her guide, and then she was left quite by herself.

The habitually so troubled young woman of this vision could never remember feeling so at peace with the world as during the next hour or so that unfolded in that apartment. The main room was but sparsely furnished, with a bed, chair and small table, atop the last of which there lay a single volume of the thoughts of Matt Benson. But the billowing lace curtains that fluttered in a balmy breeze that blew off the *Ardonne Massif*, to filter cheerful birdsong and aromas of scented wild shrubs through the slightly open casements, served to create a most soothing and refreshing atmosphere that was augmented by the soft and comforting hum of the inevitable refrigerator that occupied one corner of the room. Even more revitalising were the warm and healing waters that flowed from above Greta's head and gently caressed her skin, as the road soiled traveller exulted in the soapy luxury of an *en suite* shower room. Eventually, after such an invigorating interim, the emigrant emerged, naked and renewed to envelope herself in the all consuming luxury of the simple bed's soft and compliant white linen, lying back on the verge of a sleepy delight to await the moment of her forthcoming enlightenment; and at length this dreamer felt the warm and reassuring sensation of a hand touching her shoulder.

※　※　※

"What's that big smile on your face for?" the careless tone of Cayte chided as she casually shook the slumberer awake. "Have you been at my stuff? … I can't find it anywhere." It was indeed morning, and the three female parties to the vengeful quartet seemed set to play out once more what could be a thrice or more times daily ritual.

"Sorry Greta," Nan Chilswell's rather more melodic voice next sung. "Cayte thinks she's lost her stuff again. We gave it all to the kitchen girls on Hogs Hill, silly. That was the plan, remember?"

But the anxious party nonetheless asserted: "No, not that stuff.

My stuff!" at which Greta rubbed her own eyes and tapped the space alien's hind quarters, producing a metallic resonance and scolding: "Do you think it could have something to do with that bulge in your back pocket?"

"Oh yeah," replied Cayte, glancing gratefully downwards and recovering a half crushed tobacco tin. "Thanks, I forgot. See you in a minute."

As the ever spaced out entity then retired to some convenient shade, the spirit enchantress excused her with: "It's always in such an endearing way though, isn't it?" And though still feeling a little irritated at having been denied the albeit dreamland opportunity to discover whether Matt Benson was indeed a little on the short or even quick sides for a messiah or not, Greta could not help but agree. Before so very long Cayte returned, upon which Nan ghosted upwards and out from the tin can of her confinement once again and the pair wafted on across the Isis valley for another day's mischief making. And as the ruling elite of England's golden jubilee drew ever nearer, Greta was left alone with her troubled deliberations once more.

Chapter 10

The first week of August duly arrived, and all of Hogs Hill's various monuments became decked in rather tired bunting and their entrances guarded by straw effigies of Otter, Muntjac and various other native mammals, but most abundantly great Hogs themselves as symbols of the traditions invested in the upcoming festival. The week long climax to England's summer social season always opened on Friday evening with a grand country dance at which all of the newly betrothed and their immediate families would be present. There, the positively vetted cream of young feudal society would be tasked with competing with one another in demonstrating the particular preciseness and etiquette that the English Fusty Dowdy Stuffy Society demanded of all participants in the social customs of its so stern remit. It had always been Cayte's greatest ambition to inflict her special arts upon this austere and sacrosanct occasion, yet to date she had always been thwarted since only the most trustworthy of kitchen staff were ever selected to cater for an event that was viewed as a barometer of the Hillite social order's enduring vigour.

What most suited the festival wrecker's purpose was that at the commencement of proceedings, the dutiful daughters were each allowed to partake of one small glass of sparkling wine and a special ceremonial truffle. And since the first of those indulgences was often these young women's first experience of alcohol, Cayte fully realised the potential for plunging the ceremony into unplanned pandemonium if only the truffles themselves could be suitably enhanced. Now, in the golden anniversary season, it had fortuitously transpired that one of the space alien's most mischief making yet outwardly discreet veterans had somehow been allocated to the preparation of the delicacy in question. All was set for a grand opening evening *extraordinaire*.

The event was held in the great ceremonial hall of "The Old College", an immense pile set close by the junction of the Hill's middle and back ways. This decaying expanse had been, as its name rightly suggested an academic institution prior to the apocalypse, but now its facilities were reserved for the more splendid social functions surrounding the most noble local sporting meets, and of course the summer festival itself. As the great and the good of polite provincial society gathered therein once more, the ball gowned betrothed daughters and their penguin suited and white tied future husbands mostly mingled and practised their steps in the centre of the hall, while the older generations of their various families seated themselves around numerous tables that lined both the long side walls. At a top table above the small musical ensemble of the evening's dance band, were gathered the EFDSS social committee members themselves, together with the leading luminaries amongst the festival's organisers, and two special guests.

Since all of the dancers present had been positively vetted over the preceding two months of one market town calendar or another, it was not deemed necessary for the Society's adjudicators to officiate further at this most exalted of occasions. Two of the most senior and revered men from the ranks of those overseers, bald Ned of Gloucester and Ned the pillock, were nonetheless present in a purely ceremonial capacity, since due to their own past excesses the Society had come to consider that granting them such honorary and honourable status was the best way of keeping them under control whilst avoiding any loss of face of its own.

Over his greatly advancing years, the first of these two gentlemen (it seemed that many of the male adjudicators went by the name of Ned) had come to exhibit an all consuming zeal for condemning tunes that did not fit the dances; this being a constant topic of small talk amongst purist participants in the practice concerned. And so this adjudicator had increasingly abandoned the common mission of identifying unsuitables for the Hillite succession in favour of winkling out musicians who in his own estimation dared to offend in the said respect. At one stage of his personal crusade, so many fine players had been led to bald Ned's own garden gibbet that the continuance of the summer social season itself became threatened by a shortage of willing dance bands. And so the zealot was eventually elevated by his peers to the higher whilst restraining plane of his current calling, though he was still invited to attend events such as the opening night of the Hogs Hill festival at which it was deemed even the best bands should be kept on their toes.

In contrast with the religious fervour of his bald colleague, Ned the pillock would simply bore people to death. He considered himself to be the fiefdom's single greatest authority on English country dancing and would pontificate endlessly to anyone within earshot as to the fine and exclusive definitions that he alone applied to that same social art. In truth, nobody ever actually listened to him, but this most opinionated of worthies nevertheless loved to circulate between the polite smiles and inane nods that charted his progress around every event that he attended, ever impervious to whether his so freely and frequently offered views were actually valued or not. Beneath the gaze of these two elder statesmen and their assembled social committee hosts, a master of ceremonies eventually called the expansive gathering within Old College Hall to order. Then as the band played a brief and most fitting introduction, a small procession of serving wenches brought forth trays laden with glasses of sparkling wine and the most especially prepared, traditional chocolate truffles.

Nobody amongst the assembled upholders of the fiefdom's moral fibre appeared to heed the knowing glances from the twinkling eyes of these servant girls as they circulated amongst the eagerly outstretched, laced gloved fingers of this season's social successes. And through the evening's first two dances the occasional indiscreet flash of ankle or shoulder, or sudden unusual palpitation of normally restrained breast tissue went similarly unnoticed. Then, early in the third dance and from some anonymous location within the ubiquitous ambience of frozen smile, glazed gaze and endless etiquette; a first faint snort became audible, then another rather louder one followed by one or two more. Next, from somewhere to the rear of the hall, something akin to the neighing of a horse announced itself; followed by a passable imitation of a braying donkey from within the front rank, exhibition set itself. Over the next ten minutes or so the Society's foremost caller came to struggle against a growing chorus of animal and bird impersonations as one normally prim and proper daughter after another descended into a deepening disorder that soon enveloped the entire dance floor. At the same time, their embarrassed male opposites became afflicted by a series of slaps, nudges and playful tweaks that implied the welcome of an even more flirtatious response that was nonetheless not forthcoming.

The relatives who lined each of the old hall's sides continued to converse politely on the caller's excellent choice of dances and how very well the tunes were fitting them on this prestigious evening, whilst doing their utmost to hide the growing discomfiture that every one of them felt. Eventually the music ceased momentarily and the entire female line of one set from fairly near the top end of the hall broke ranks to run down to a large table that was positioned in readiness for the laying out of the interval buffet. There, some of these seemingly intoxicated young women climbed onto that barrier before commencing to raise their ball gowns and strut around in a squatting position, flapping their elbows and cawing like Crows, shouting: "Poop, poop! ... Poop, poop!". At the same time, various similarly excited fellows pointed their own arms and still gloved fingers in imitation of mock shotgun fire, crying: "Zap! ... Pow! ... Gotcha!" like characters from a twentieth century comic book. From a viewpoint behind the high window above the hall's entrance, Cayte casually informed the by now enthralled spirit at her side: "Hey, I forgot it did that. I wonder if we put a bit too much in?"

"Where did you get it from?" Nan then asked.

"Can't remember," came the inevitable reply. Then the space alien shrugged, and counselled: "Keep watching, this should be good!"

Worse was indeed to follow: shortly afterwards a female voice from a further set even nearer to the band demanded in a tone as suddenly indiscreet as it was loud: "Does anyone know what sort of noise a Snipe makes?"

A first, even more reckless reply then enquired with a snort: "Is that beforehand, or during what happens to it?" while a second added with a careless cackle: "And we all know *what* happens to them, do we not?"

Various other girls were then seen to nudge one another and giggle at such a suggestion, while the line in question proceeded to play out the required series of diminishing rotations; but even the most swan-like neck present was unable to effect the so impolite contortion that had been alluded to. Elsewhere in the hall, one dancer in a bright yellow ball gown had succeeded in gaining a position atop an ornate plant pot stand, where after sending its former adornment crashing to the floor she started to squeal excitedly: "Little bit of bread and no cheeeze!" Upon a nearby windowsill, a second bird impersonator, clad in a pastel green number was chanting: "Chiff chaff, chiff chaff, chiff chaff!"; but was cut short by one of the regrouped Crows who scoffed: "Lawks, not a lot of poop to be had out of one of those, hey?"

All the while the milling miscreants' assorted parents, aunts and uncles, and grandparents continued to face down the unfolding chaos with a steely reserve worthy of an English colonial dinner party under fire from revolting natives. The past exploits of Cayte the festival wrecker were uppermost in the thoughts of every more mature family member present, but none was prepared to commit the indiscretion of actually giving voice to their concerns. Instead, as the figures at the top table debated how order might best be restored, they merely persisted with their habitual banal small talk, whilst aiming an occasional nod or other blanking gesture at the roaming figure of Ned the pillock who still blustered and bored his way endlessly between one seated group and another.

By now a large number of coyly smirking serving wenches were also circulating amongst the gathering, offering trays of one delicacy or another, all of which would be politely refused. And through every available window or open niche, numbers of kitchen skivvies were competing for the available viewing space with which to witness the unfolding slapstick for themselves. Eventually the master of ceremonies made an appeal on behalf of the caller for correct dancing to resume. But his own rolling tones were immediately interrupted by the strident voice of Wellingtonia Bagdalen-Spellwright, a tall, buck-toothed Hillite daughter with a deserved reputation for putting her foot in it. "Tabitha Trescott," she announced to the best friend at her side. "You are a Muntjac and I am a big, fierce hunting poodle, and now I am going to properly bite off your ..."

She was not allowed to reveal what: "Wellingtonia, please! ... Your grammar!!" came an instant and booming reproach from the top table.

The split infinitive had stood no chance of escaping the all-enveloping radar of this debutante's Great Aunt Lymphoma, one of the Bagdalen-Spellwright's most senior matriarchs and secretary of the EFDSS social committee. Given such a lamentable *faux-pas* on the part of the newly betrothed representative of that so revered lineage, the band was finally ordered to cease playing and upon the formidable secretary's personal insistence the hallowed institution of the grand opening dance was called off. The young men all drifted off in search of whatever port or brandy they might be able to locate, whilst all of the temporarily dishevelled daughters were taken home to recuperate in their own time. Only Ned the pillock remained within Old College Hall until the event's scheduled end, still pontificating out loud to himself and apparently unaware that anything untoward had transpired at all, or indeed that everyone else had left.

In retrospect, both Cayte and Nan appreciated that such a spectacular success as they had enjoyed so early in the festival was unlikely to be repeatable. On the Saturday morning, large numbers of Winklers were drafted onto Hogs Hill to police the seven days to come. Nothing could be proven once more against Cayte's culinary accomplices, but all of the kitchens were searched most thoroughly and a variety of suspect substances removed for resale by the Day brothers in the more seedy locales of the fiefdom's north. And from that day forth, the festival kitchen and serving girls were all kept under the severest scrutiny, on pain of far harsher penalties than the usual terms of sporting correction. The two would-be mischief makers in chief nonetheless continued to drift largely undetected around the periphery of various festival events, seeking out opportunities to further annoy their unwilling hosts wherever they might find them; and in this respect they soon discovered that they had a rather unexpected ally.

The regularity with which huge hairy spiders were seen to suddenly materialise, at vital stages of so many ceremonies where ladies of particular sensitivities might be officiating, proved to be a continued riddle that was beyond even the most seasoned of Winklers to solve. Numbers of male dignitaries similarly came to be afflicted by unexpected eruptions of ants that seemed to display a peculiar talent for carrying off essential props or trinkets at the critical stages of one sacred ritual or another. It seemed that Will Wayward had his uses after all, and Nan Chilswell once more appreciated how though her long companion of subterranean times past was as ever pursuing his own agenda, it did seem to be in sympathy with the common goal. Indeed the felon appeared to be matching Cayte's enduring flair with "culinary herbs" with a new found talent for clever tricks with animals, the most notable of which transpired as a daring deliverance of the festival's specially bred brood of Otters.

As from far and wide the fiefdom's august sluicing fraternity gathered for their own golden anniversary gala on Tuesday morning, the entire crop of soon to be mistreated mammals were found to be well and truly blocked by a spider's web-like substance in all of the more vital orifices; rendering true sluicing in accordance with the proscribed protocols impossible to perform. Then after the reprieved creatures were quarantined to await inspection by the rather overworked Winklers, they were all spirited away by the ant armies of Blackcroft and released around the bridge beneath Wittering Humps. There on that same afternoon, the festival's most frivolous fringe event became similarly sabotaged when the newly liberated Otters proceeded to chase all of the Pooh sticks that were dropped from above upstream, and then chew them into little pieces.

As all the while the enchantress saved up her own great design for the festival's final evening, she indeed felt grateful for her fellow phantom's assorted contributions to the gathered gentry's disquiet, particularly since she was by now losing a little faith in Cayte. The longer that Nan spent in her new friend's company, the more she noticed how the space alien could never remember what it was that they were meant to be doing, and seemed to display in her total spontaneity a complete inability to actually be in any specific place or know where she was going until she arrived there; so much so that the spirit wondered how such a disorganised fellow entity could possibly have conjured up so many little triumphs against the Hillites in the past. Yet still Nan would always concede to herself that her companion was no less loveable for all of her many more inexplicable qualities and so could never think ungenerously of her.

On the festival's fifth day, Nan and Cayte ghosted into the grounds of "Arden Propley", the ancestral seat of the prime ministerial Pincombes where just as in the late twentieth century, the revived annual championship of the English National Spanking Federation was shortly set to commence. Whilst sundry groups of gentlefolk stood engaged in polite conversation here and there, a large gathering of "squires" from all over the fiefdom was busily mingling with and sizing up the season's selection of new "squeakers" who had been winkled out during the year's market town social calendars. The male contestants were always granted a little time immediately prior to the tournament, in which to pick out those wenches that they would most like to be paired with and lay wagers between themselves as to the likely quality of sport that each might offer.

The noble practitioners of "the most gentlemanly art" were all clad in the checked tweed suit with plus fours of their umbrella body's informal uniform, and most exhibited a certain colouring of face that belied their collective predilection for pink gin. Many were adorned with monocles, handlebar moustaches, gold watch chains, floral buttonholes and such other symbols that suitably conveyed squire-like status; while all past winners of one competition or another either here or in their own locales would sport the relevant medals from coloured ribbons above their breast pockets.

The ancient and genteel pursuit of wench spanking was in fact governed by a very firm code of etiquette, so hence the squires were always most fastidious in their attentions upon that part of a lady's anatomy which so captured their particular fancy, whilst it was rare for a female participant to actually suffer such indiscretions as might in occasional hushed tones be termed a "wandering of hand" or other such covetous advance. Any lapse upon the part of the so tempted that might in the Federation's own eyes be deemed to constitute the "unsporting correction of a squeaker" would result in the most severe of all penalties of excommunication for the perpetrator, which was a scandal that almost every self-respecting squire felt unable to endure.

A number of rogue practitioners had nonetheless managed to slip through the net of the Federation's jurisdiction in the recent past, though their existence was most forcibly denied in polite circles. Thus, with the co-operation of a creamed off group of willing and suitably rewarded below stairs veterans, a second, more clandestine wench spanking circuit came to flourish in "unsporting correction dens" that were mostly controlled by the Fortescues and certain mill, mine and industrial unit owners from the north; all under the inevitable protection of the Day brothers and at the latters' usual percentage.

No such dubious ambience had ever tainted the blue riband tournament of Hogs Hill's summer festival however, since this was where each season's debutant squeakers were introduced to that particular aspect of their future careers in service, and hence where the largest congregation of regular squires was guaranteed to gather. On this occasion, as every year, a post horn eventually sounded and the milling crowd that covered Arden Propley's rear lawn fell silent. At this summons, the squires regrouped beneath a raised stage below the house's grand but inevitably crumbling south façade, while the wenches of their recent appraisal were all guided into a small marquee to one side. A copious tray of pink gins was then brought forth, and the well-filled glasses of that beverage were passed amongst the contestants until all were so fortified. Finally a small brass ensemble played an introduction, and the noble ranks of gentlemen spankers, their chests thrust outward in pride, burst lustily into a hearty rendition of the Federation's revered hymn:

Here at Arden Propley in the summer when it's hot
We gather each season to smack wenches on their bots
Lots of comely, nubile, plump young rump across the knee
What a most splendid and efficacious remedy
Spank them all prop'ly, spank them hard
Make their rumps ripe, pink and stingy here in our back yard
See the wriggling gigglers shriek and whoop and squeal with glee
Smacking wenches' bottoms is just wonderful to me

Watching from the cover of a convenient shrubbery, Nan and Cayte'e own past sullied rumps ached at the memory. They looked at one another as if to agree: "Yes, these ridiculous old farts actually seem to think that we enjoy it," though they felt no need to exchange that sentiment in words. All the while, the once more prim, positively vetted younger members of the invited audience indulged their own damning delight at the inescapable plight of their future underlings. That group's recent close encounter with collective infamy had in the end merely served to strengthen their common bond. And since all of these still betrothed young women were aware that the Winklers suspected the complicity of past years' still rebellious recruits in what they themselves now dismissed as "the unfortunate incident of the truffles", these fledgling fusties dowdies and stuffies were all looking forward to their own future guidance of this season's disfavoured daughters with a peculiar relish.

Then, as the brass band rounded off with a musical repetition of the hymn's final line, and the rousing refrain ultimately died upon the air, the gathered squirearchy raised their glasses as one in the traditional toast that signalled the onset of competition proper: "To the squeaking!". And so the gentlemen practitioners repaired to two seating enclosures on either side of the stage, while the spectators took their own seats to the front; as did the judges on a podium above. After a brief pause, the first three squires took their positions atop as many plain wooden chairs that now occupied the centre of the platform, before placing their gins aside, rolling back one sleeve and initiating a brief series of arm flexing exercises. And lastly, the first three blushing and bashful, but no less blooming beauties who had fallen from provincial family grace through displays of spontaneity, wit or spirit were ushered falteringly forwards.

Imagine the assembled moral guardians' collective horror when the bottoms of their traditional scapegoats, upon being bared for inspection were each found to exhibit a livid pinch mark from some other hand to that pertaining to the knees over which they all three now lay prostrate. Nan and Cayte exchanged an exultant salute in the shadows: the felon Will Wayward, with his own fondness for certain attentions upon girls' hind quarters, had come up trumps again. The Federation rule book laid down very precise definitions on matters such as the allowable trajectory of hand towards rump, the maximum force that might be applied, and fine distinctions between the most sporting slaps and tickles and points deductible blows, strokes or caresses. Pinching was a clear foul that could only result in instant disqualification, and when every wench amongst the festival pool of squeakers proceeded when summoned to exhibit the same defilement in the crucial area, truly sporting contest was deemed impossible to proceed with. Never before had such a pandemic of prior unsporting correction been recorded; and so the most sacrosanct of all events in the Hillite sporting calendar had most shockingly, and just like its social equivalent the grand opening country dance, upon this most prestigious golden jubilee occasion, to be abandoned.

Chapter 11

Given the enormity of what was at once viewed as the most outrageous assault upon genteel tradition since the most gentlemanly art's temporary outlawing some three quarters of a century previously, all amongst the most senior Hillites could now entertain no doubt that the acceleration of recent disruptive and unexplained happenings was reaching crisis point. An emergency cabinet meeting was called at once but nonetheless decreed, and as usual upon the prime minister's casting vote, that the week's events should proceed to their traditional finale. But afterwards, a fringe meeting chaired by the minister of defence Piers Grenshaw, and attended by the cabinet level representatives of the Hatherington-Smythes, Caruthers', Bayworth-Hamels, Bagdalen-Spellwrights and various other oldest-moneyed lineages unanimously passed a motion to gather the evidence with which to collectively de-frock the rather too creative chancellor, and reforming home and foreign secretaries on charges of favouring change.

Even Jolyon Farquhar, the uninvited minister without portfolio, decided to show his face at the summit since he hoped that his support might at least afford an opportunity for his own kin to be viewed as a little less idle, useless or silly; but that particular grievance was one facet of Hillite inter-family culture that never, ever altered. "Get the Farquhar out of here!" the chair ordered as soon as Jolyon appeared, to a familiar chorus of venerable chortles on the parts of his otherwise most deadly serious fellow plotters.

So the culmination of the golden anniversary festival drew on, but amidst an atmosphere of such nervous tension as had never existed before. As she floated through the crowds Nan Chilswell positively exulted in the palpable unease and growing superstitious trepidation that she detected all around her, only barely beneath the surface of the continued stubborn ambience affected by the stiff upper lips and frigid countenances that were set upon seeing out the celebrations at whatever cost. But the enchantress could not fail to also notice how Cayte, having been relieved of both the tools of her trade and her past years' allies at such an early stage, appeared to have lost all interest for another year.

Thus it was that as dusk drew in on the Wednesday evening, the returned local beauty from a past century laid her hands upon the space alien's flagging shoulders, gazed into that friend's enigmatic eyes and beseeched: "Now Cayte, dear; I must leave for a while now. Be sure to meet me at Hogs Hill Hall for the closing ceremony on Friday evening," knowing that to be the best way of ensuring this freest of wanderers would by such time be long gone. Then Nan Chilswell wafted on back to the Shottington copse to say goodbye to Greta, after first appraising the park chief of all that had occurred in the interim and recovering something that was rather essential to her own purpose.

The final day of the fiftieth festival was uncomfortably humid. The grey, overcast daytime skies yielded little by way of windy respite, yet by late afternoon a brooding breeze at length blew up that served to lower a rustling and whispering final curtain upon this date's social and sporting series of closing ceremonies. As Hogs Hill's now unusually animated tree cover came sinisterly to match the fearful sentiments that challenged all who strode that setting to stand firm, long years of surly suppression of spontaneity, wit and spirit came under challenge as never before. It was as if the very essence of English feudal values that had for so long issued from the ground beneath so many wary footfalls, was indeed and at last wavering in its once irredeemable intensity.

By evening, the heavens bulged bellicosely with a deepening menace, yet still no rainy reprieve would lighten the load that weighed upon every mind present. As they did each year at this same time, the great and the good gathered beneath the gilt-framed portrait of Squire Barney Cockscomb in the debating chamber of Hogs Hill Hall itself, to hear the traditional address of the most venerable of all Hillites. All of the great dynasties had called home on this climactic evening their scattered relatives from whatever provincial positions of power they might normally occupy, and in pile upon ancestral pile across the so apprehensive locality the members of each and every family were now assembled in a most obdurate readiness for their various revered and senior members to return home with the prime ministerial blessing of perpetual governance. A simultaneous series of banquets was then scheduled to commence within every ancestral seat, that no matter what must serve as the continuing affirmation of the local gentry's assured succession.

There was one Hillite who remained oblivious to the now ubiquitous unease and malign trepidation that had spread like a cancer through the proceedings of the previous eight days. As over that period Sir Cuthbert Pincombe had been wheeled around in his bath chair between those certain ceremonies that required a prime ministerial input, he had really not taken in very much at all. On every one of those occasions one or another senior proxy from his lineage had officiated at his gently dozing and ever nodding side; but he was the most venerable of all Hillites and the inviolable protocol governing the closing ceremony demanded that no matter how elderly or infirm the incumbent might be, they would be tasked with still making the prime ministerial address as best they might be able. At the appointed hour, a reverential silence therefore fell upon the gathering as the freshly spruced up and dusted down figurehead was wheeled into view, and numbers of Pincombes proceeded to almost fall over one another in fussing about and attempting to rouse their senior patriarch to the call of duty.

Just how many minds in that hall might have considered a parallel between the ensuing series of snoring, gasping, wheezing deliveries that in no way substituted for a speech, and the suddenly so fading standing of the Hillite social order it was impossible to say. Certainly many must have yearned for the rousing rallying calls and celebrations of past achievement that had been so unfailingly delivered by the doughty dowager of immediate past office and many more distant premiers still; but no-one present dared to show their feelings, and even less voice them.

At length the figure in the bath chair could prevail no longer, and various relatives proceeded to wrap blankets about the ailing Sir Cuthbert's lower limbs whilst waving smelling salts beneath the elder statesman's yet slightly trembling nose. And thus it fell upon the so distrusted home secretary to act out one further break with hallowed tradition, as he pronounced a little too readily in his revered leader's place: "Ladies and gentlemen. It remains for me to request, according to our time honoured and unalterable custom on this most exalted of evenings: Are the Snipe prepared?" And despite the low esteem in which he who uttered those words was held by so many present, a stirring avowal still reverberated around the parliamentary chamber.

At the summons of a post horn chorus from the minstrel's gallery above, a procession of flunkies then brought forth a covered silver platter that they laid with great pomp before the impromptu master of ceremonies, Sir Nicholas Coverlet. But notwithstanding the week-long attentions of the so feared Winklers, the Hall's long sullied yet still spirited kitchen skivvies had succeeded, albeit with a little supernatural assistance, in subverting the intended ceremony before making themselves immediately scarce. And thus, when the lid of the incoming offering was raised, the audience gasped as one upon beholding not the traditionally arranged yet a trifle impolite to truly discern, eventual outcomes of avian bill and diminishing rotation; but a single tin of red kidney beans.

As the gathering fell into shocked silence, a fair skinned and raven-haired, yet vaporous vision of a somewhat affronted looking, eighteenth century serving wench was seen by all present to issue from the same unfamiliar object and ultimately recompose itself in direct sight of the authoritarian gaze of the founder's portrait itself. "Damn and blast your new fangled meddling, Coverlet and your infernal colleagues," the voice of Piers Grenshaw was next heard to admonish from somewhere within the assembly. "Creative accumulators of vulgar new wealth and favourers of change! What unholy retribution have you brought upon us all now?"

Upon this protest, the chamber's haughty west-facing glass screen was suddenly blown inwards by an almighty and unearthly gust that suggested just such a vengeance as the minister for defence was citing. And as the assembled members of the present establishment and supposed beneficiaries of its hitherto unyielding system became showered by falling crystal shards, the so long scorned passion of the original enchantress was heard to play eerily about the ears of all present: "Murderer and abuser! May nature's intent never again be distorted, nor womankind debased upon your own foul whim. I, Nan Chilswell, in whose defiled remains you first invested guardianship over the ancient sanctity of Hogs Hill in the year of our Lord 1772, and thereafter your lands below Shottington Ridge for so very long, declare the reign of your subjects ... over!"

At that, the wavering voice of none other than Jolyon Farquhar piped up: "Er, hang on. These things are meant to be final and irrevocable, and no man might lay them asunder?"

"I am not a man!" the feisty reply echoed around all of the mortified and recoiling old Hillites present, various of whom grimaced and exchanged glances as if to suggest: "Whoever could have come up with a line like *that*?"

"Not me, that's for sure," the soul of the author who had once renamed the house in the mystic glade on the lower eastern side mused to itself. "Though at least none of them are casting themselves into pits, or fleeing to hide in holes and dark lightless places far from hope."

The apparition then elevated itself to the highest point in the rafters above, before fixing its full will of a woman scorned upon the tin of red kidney beans beneath, that nobody present had seen fit either to snatch up or expel. The critical juncture of Nan's choosing was indeed nigh, and as the gawping patrician ranks looked on in ghastly trepidation that object's ring pull finally flicked upwards, the lid peeled back and Hogs Hill Hall crumbled into clouds of dust; as at once did every one of the ruling order's aged piles across that historic locality, while all of those monuments' occupants were rendered lifeless. The spell of Squire Cockscomb's ancient legacy was broken at last, and across the fiefdom the garden gibbets in village upon village likewise evaporated in puffs of vapour, along with the great oak and ash symbols of authority in all of the market towns.

Many of the Triffs bearers and magistrates, their own lives having been so unnaturally extended by the bane of Barney's Tump, simply expired on the spot upon being released; while the younger generations of the same families and all of their erstwhile subjects mostly reverted to 2020s type and immediately turned their attention to re-acquiring unlimited credit, giant off-road vehicles and instant garden makeovers. Even some long-forgotten mail order deliveries reappeared in their original and unacceptable locations to the rear of properties, through cat flaps or beneath front garden pampas grasses; and had England's infrastructure been rebuilt in the interim, distant call centres in foreign lands might no doubt have sprung into contact once more, feeding customer complaints back to their grey market, moonlighting home workforces as of old.

Only two houses still stood across the yet proud geological feature of Hogs Hill's length and breadth: those eternal anomalies in the dale below the Hall and the mystic glade. To the first of these the spirit of Nan Chilswell repaired, her own mission having been accomplished, there so she intended to linger ever afterwards. Upon taking up residence, the original enchantress did however find the available haunting space to be a little crowded, given the many ghosts of executed foreign envoys that already dwelt therein.

On realising the irreversibility of the fate that had befallen all of the district's families, the second spirit Will Wayward immediately set the great ant armies of Blackcroft to work in transferring the contents of so many vaults and counting houses to his own copious cellars. Then he left the plundered fortune under the guard of the estate's resident scary spiders and set himself up as the new master of the house in the mystic glade. Lastly the particular militia of the warlord Belliger Ant carried all of the Russian ambassador's gold back to that residence's own great cellar, being for some reason the only ones of their insect kind who felt at home in the new location. And from that day forth, the foolish felon coveted the poisoned chalice as his own, just as the now despatched chancellor, home and foreign secretaries had before him.

Further afield, a spontaneous uprising engulfed all of the parish estates and market towns as the latterly so subjugated locals sacked the big house cellars and public building vaults in their clamour for ready cash. The northern manor houses of the mill, mine and industrial unit owners suffered a similar fate as their recent masters were mostly cast out to fend for themselves in the future; though the racketeering Days managed to secure their own strongholds for a little longer. And when the competition eventually subsided, those who had succeeded in grabbing the most immediately set themselves up as money lenders, to satisfy and so exploit their less nimble fingered peers' renewed and insatiable appetite for easy credit. But, perhaps most miraculously of all, as the antique environs of Hogs Hill had ultimately dissolved into long overdue oblivion; so the past town in the great Isis valley below was seen to re-materialise in all of its former glory, and thus became the only conceivable future capital of post-Hillite England.

Chapter 12

While Greta, Leigh and Beka strode into the town centre to witness the miracle of its reincarnation for themselves, pick-up truck loads of Antipodeans were already pouring into the transport terminus of Worcester Place. To the east, that threesome's one-time neighbours of The Lees would as ever persist in their own so hostile, parochial and pointless pursuits. Yet here the newcomers were immediately setting about laying claim to the best public buildings and housing complexes, ahead of the nearer market town residents eventually forgetting their renewed and rapacious greed for the means to material wealth and waking up to that same ambition themselves. Everywhere the Antipodeans went they proclaimed the imminent coming of their messiah Matt Benson, which as if to emphasise the reach of the now vanquished essence that had infused the ancient bedrock of Hogs Hill for so long, had first been predicted in a spoof newspaper distributed there by the new enchantress, felon and legacy bearer back in 2023. Now everything was being prepared for the very event of that same distant stratagem.

Just as in Greta's recent dream, the gateway to the Continental Tunnel had opened spontaneously and anew upon the fall of the English fiefdom, and for day after day the constantly returning railcars disgorged ever more pick-up trucks laden with refrigerators, garden barbecues and many, many joyful followers of the great man himself. Lastly, upon his own triumphant entry to the town in the great Isis valley, some forty miles upstream from the one-time capital London, Matt Benson immediately set himself up in its grandest civic edifice: Bagdalen Hall, in Bagdalen Street, close to Bagdalen Bridge and just across the way from the former Bagdalen Institute. From there his entourage lost no time in filling their offshore conquest's temporary political vacuum; as all the while new female converts to the cause would confirm to the enquiring glances of the messiah's minders: "You're right, that was quick!" upon being shown out from Matt the inveterate movie star's newest inner sanctum. And given the numbers of formerly fallen females of spontaneity, wit and spirit who flocked to the new capital from all around, there were many willing recruits to this path of enlightenment indeed.

The Antipodeans were not the only outsiders to entertain designs upon the newly unfettered fiefdom. When news of the fall of the Hillites reached the far flung Celtic realms of Chilly Jockoland to the north and the western island Republic of Provonia, the gangster barons who controlled both former British provinces immediately decided to mount invasions of their own. And so the ancient barrier of Hadrian's Wall, that had stood firm through the five preceding decades was ultimately breached once more, and thousands of vengeful Jocko clansmen commenced to rampage through large swathes of northern England; burning and pillaging and converting the womenfolk after their own fashion in the manner of their ancestors since time immemorial. Almost simultaneously, the private army of the foremost Provonian mobsters, the brothers Terry and Mervyn O'Phanneaghness, mobilised its own belligerent intent; the nose tip tufts of the foot soldiers fluttering in the breeze as they were conveyed across the Welsh sea in a flotilla of Spanish trawlers that had been hijacked specifically for the purpose.

Since those chiefs cared to regard themselves as politicians first and hoodlums second, they always observed a deal more ceremony than their chilly Jocko counterparts. Thus this invasion force was led by an eighteenth century sailing ship, on the poop deck of which the brothers themselves stood resplendent in their full dress uniform of green military parkas and black balaclavas. Over one shoulder of each man was slung their choice of ceremonial firearm, newly oiled Uzi sub-machine guns of early twenty-first century vintage that might just have once passed through the infamous garden shed within the Shottington copse itself; whilst upon either hip they toted an array of their favourite electric drills. It was of no concern to these returning heroes of the Provonian cause, statesmen even in their own estimation, whether an electricity supply had ever been restored in post-apocalypse England: the moment of their personal destiny was nigh.

These disgruntled nationals had cherished such a revenge upon the English ever since that distant century when the colonial forces of Oliver Cromwell had dug up all of their potatoes and force-fed entire rural communities on prawns in order to secure their compliance. From that day hence, the Provonians had loathed their one-time conquerors with an intensity previously reserved for the tiny, pink crustaceans themselves. Now the long-coveted ambition of so many predecessors was Terry and Mervyn's to achieve within their own gangster baron prime, and so they sailed onwards, their chests thrust out in pride to the tuneful pipes and beating bodhrans of their personal bodyguard. All the while their own tufts of nose tip fur bristled through the holes in their balaclavas, dyed with the bright green and white hues of the republic's flag especially for the occasion.

Eventually the flotilla entered the murky industrial port of Scousepool, the traditional point of ingress for all Provonian migrants, and thence onward along the conveniently preserved inland waterway of the Mancheatster Ship Canal. As it progressed, those on board would detonate locks and bridges in their wake, for no better reason than they had always been used to blowing things up. And when they announced their noisy arrival in England's north-west industrial heartland, through a marching pipe band that proceeded to parade up and down the quayside of their landfall, the Provonians wasted no time by O'Phanneaghing about. They quickly seized control of several of the best mills and industrial units in the immediate vicinity, burning out some of them simply to make a point; just as their past Cromwellian tormentors had once despoiled all of their ancestors' choicest potato patches. And thus a fitting challenge was laid down by Terry and Mervyn to their English opposite numbers: those other brothers Barnabus and Columbus Day.

The Dynasty of the Days had in their entirety absented themselves from Hogs Hill's golden anniversary festival, nominally out of respect for their departed senior matriarch, and thus had survived the fate of all their one time neighbours. More to the point, the family had known that with the Dowager's decease it could never enjoy such forbearance in the old locale again, given the long memories that the late chancellor and his closer associates delighted in playing off so skilfully against their own interest; and thus the collective decision was taken to relocate permanently to their northern manor house strongholds. Upon the grand implosion of Hillite rule, and supported by as many former Winklers as they could relocate from the south, the dominant brothers and their most senior kinsmen had naturally intended to boost their own future fortune through controlling the greater share of local commerce within the new economic order. Now they found themselves arraigned against the even longer memories of the newly arrived Provonian partisans, and thus swung into motion the fiercest local conflict to grip the rainy and windswept north of England since the Great Park Homes Turf War of 2023.

For week upon week into the ensuing winter, the bleak and still much ruined streets of Mancheatster, Scousepool and the smaller but no less grimy towns of the belt that lay in between, would resound to the daytime sound of small arms fire and ride-by shootings as the two sides sought out a new pecking order; or the occasional louder pronouncements of improvised ox-cart bombs. And by night, the parochial torture chambers of the Day and O'Phanneaghness brothers alike would conceal their own foul secrets from all but the unfortunate captives within. Given their personal delusions of political grandeur, Terry had come to style himself as the Provonian minister of culture back at home, while Mervyn had assumed the title of minister for education. Now these statesmen of their own estimation wasted no time in educating the jockeying parties of the north-west's post-Hillite power struggle as to the culture that they intended for that region in future. All the while, the rampaging Jocko hordes continued to attack the interests of other senior Days or their local associates even further north and across the mining regions of Old Torkshire and Jordiland on the far side of the Pennine range; while Terry and Mervyn O'Phanneaghness sought out their own alliances with the clan commanders concerned.

Though the far northern aggressors of Chilly Jockoland had long shared their Provonian cousins' great partiality for despoiling all things English, the tartan clansmens' driving force had always been viewed as one possibly of jealousy in London's pre-apocalypse corridors of power; rather than any deeper or more ingrained political impasse. Whilst ever willing to thrust their "Jockoness" forward for the approval of all who might care to be so impressed, this volatile Celtic race had likewise habitually displayed something of a touching vulnerability that their southern adversaries would seemingly always feel it their duty to pander to in return. Hence, throughout the past heyday of the British Broadcasting Corporation, its London weather forecasts had invariably begun with the most awful extremes that the far northern province could conjure. Generations of prospective footie pools winners had likewise been kept in weekly suspense while the Jocko results were recited in their most minor league entirety each Saturday evening, even though none who dwelt to the north of Hadrian's Wall ever cared two hoots whether such a southern nicety was observed or not. And in just the same way, pre-apocalypse English rock or movie stars who might have boasted a Jocko ancestor, no matter how tenuous that link might have been, would somehow always feel compelled to overstate the chilly connection from the comfort of their rather more clement, adopted American abodes.

Through much of the twentieth century, the "Jocko problem" had been successfully contained through the staging of a biennial footie match at the former capital's old national stadium. Thus, for an entire twenty-three and three-quarter months out of every twenty-four, the restive Celtic hordes would tolerate the drudgery of their lowland distillery and factory jobs, or dutifully tend to the great highland golf courses and national parks, with the sole motivation of saving up for the next excursion south; there to witness the dream of beating the "auld enemy". Through this system and aided by appropriate backhanders from Whitehall, the Jocko gangster barons of those times became willing accomplices in subjugating the entire provincial workforce through an all-embracing system of payments to "Wembley clubs", that reclaimed the greater share of the provincial economy's wage bill and ensured that nobody but the barons themselves ever enjoyed the means to stray very far from home.

For just one week ahead of the sporting fixture in question, the various ancient crossing points along Hadrian's Wall would be opened anew, allowing the grey or blue cheeked, red eyebrowed and orange wigged Jocko hordes to pour southwards; there to engage in a brief orgy of urinating on London's pavements and shouting in their unintelligible accents at passing traffic for no apparent reason, in anticipation of the so coveted victory. No Englishman ever dared to attend the footie match itself, since a rolled up newspaper would be the only facility known to the visiting army after seven previous days of roving debauchery; and the consequences of responding to verbal challenge and so revealing oneself as a "Sassenach" were even more unimaginable. But in these ways the tartan bedecked tourists were always indulged and the sums involved in relaying the old stadium's turf and erecting new goals should the Jocko team occasionally win were likewise viewed as acceptable expenses by the governments of the day.

Such a *status quo* prevailed until the advent in the mid-1980s of the great reforming mayor of London, Benjamin Dreadlock. That second generation Caribbean émigré was dubbed "Blue Ben" by the contemporary tabloid press, since until his election he had cultivated the most fervent revolutionary persona, only to subsequently display a revenue raising zeal that roundly put to shame his patrician peers in Parliament itself. First the new metropolitan council of his bidding banned all vehicular traffic from the capital's streets before issuing licences at a fee to anybody who would pay, which needless to say was almost everyone whose business took them into the exclusion zones concerned. No elasticised bank note ever duped the warden or wheel clamping agents of Blue Ben's special revenge upon the pillagers of his particular ancestors' colonial past. Hitherto unrivalled totals of twentieth century tithes flowed into the authority's "worthy causes" pool; to be siphoned off to fund councillors' luxury holiday homes abroad, expenses paid "fact finding missions" to the world's more disadvantaged regions, and resultant unprecedented speculation upon international "reconstruction markets".

Following the success of the London traffic tolls, similar levies were next imposed upon doing business itself within the same exclusion zones, and eventually the biennial Jocko invasion became targeted with a clean-up tax. All involved steadfastly refused to consider this slight upon their long granted freedom in each twenty-fourth month to pee at will upon the streets of London, which the inebriated Jocko hordes viewed as an inviolable right that reflected their own suppressed superiority. And so the old national stadium was ultimately demolished, and all the fixtures of its former calendar save one became relocated to the rather more compliant province of wettest Wales, subject to a suitable percentage payable to London's ever opportunistic Dreadlock Hall that squared up to Parliament across the great River Isis all the while.

By the time that the first government of the new, late 1990s urban elite swept into power, the tried and trusted past means of containing the Jocko problem were deemed rather too unfashionable. And so, where once the dual condescension of weather forecasts and footie results had suffices, devolution of provincial rule became the preferred solution. Thus the gangster barons were able to expand and consolidate their own local power base as never before. The Wembley clubs of old became superseded by racket upon racket that similarly stitched up the local economy, while the vice-like influence of the iron bar and razor squads of those at the tip of the provincial pyramid discouraged all dissent.

Now the distant policies of both "Blue Ben" Dreadlock and Sylvester Schwarzenorris himself were coming home to roost, since no matter how much freedom from southern scrutiny the barons might have enjoyed for so long, their inborn hostility towards the "auld enemy" had never, ever waned. And so the Day brothers' resistance movement was eventually defeated, and on being driven out of their adopted locales, Barnabus and Columbus headed back to their southern roots; where they reasoned the logical step was to elicit the assistance of the messianic pretender to government, Matt Benson.

Meanwhile, out in the asteroid belt of the solar system, the last remaining Gremlin clone and its inscrutable oriental associates, were testing their instruments over and over again as they attempted to unravel an unplanned conundrum. The gargantuan propulsion system of their most cataclysmic ever invention was by this time almost ready to activate, and the asteroid homing pods that they had transported to Earth some years' previously should by now have been distributed from the original Siberian landfall site to all of the scheduled impact points across the planet. But no trace could be detected of the most super-functional ever squad of cyborgs that had been programmed to carry out that task, and scan upon distant scan was revealing a somewhat surprising, single concentration of the pods in question at a rather unlikely location. And all the while, the mysterious time capsule at the former village site beneath Hogs Hill's western flank kept its own counsel as to its eventual relevance or otherwise to this narrative.

Chapter 13

Swinging around in her secretary's chair, Greta eyed the tousle haired visitor before her with a deal of suspicion. "You're losing your touch, Will," she goaded. "I saw you coming plain as anything."

"Yeah, well I meant ya to see me," came the testy reply. "Didn't want to scare yer gaffer now, did I?"

"What do you want?" the messiah's new personal assistant then challenged. "Mr Benson is a very busy man, and he's preparing for an important meeting in just under thirty minutes time?"

In response the indolent individual before her revealed a little loftily by his own past standards: "My staff up on the 'ill inform me that he's just a bit keen to get 'is 'ands on a stock of two 'undred lost gold ingots. I know where they are, an' it ain't up there. So tell 'im that and then see if he'll find time to see me, or maybe I won't let 'im quite clearly, 'oo knows?"

"Your staff!" Greta interrupted. "I suppose you mean all those spiders and ants that Nan told me about." Then she rather scoffed: "Talk to you now, do they Will?"

"That'd be tellin'," came the tantalising reply. "Maybe they do, maybe they don't. There's more things goin' on round 'ere than you know about, that's for certain." The secretary could tell plainly that this unfortunate past acquaintance had lost none of his more irksome qualities since their respective paths had separated, though he did seem on this occasion a little glum.

"Ok, I'll try to get you ten minutes, and no tricks mind," Greta ultimately conceded, before protesting: "Hey, where's my best pen gone?"

A faint taunt of: "Would, I ever?" next played about her ears as she walked through to her new employer's inner sanctum only to find the object of her irritation already seated therein.

"Oh Greta, how ya doing? Didn't quite see ya coming for a moment there," said Matt Benson. "Could ya get this gentleman a cup of real Italian coffee and a jammy dodger?"

Will Wayward was indeed no longer a happy felon. Being now deprived of Hillites to annoy in general and steal from in particular, his renewed earthly life had descended into boredom; and as he idled away his days in the mystic glade with only his chattering bean can for company, the commodity that he now so wished to discuss was exerting an influence in tandem with that last remaining Tricron bomb. Just as that latter object had become so animated in response to the supercharged dust of Blackcroft's cellars, it seemed also to feel a communion with the hidden bullion horde of the new location; and all the while the evolving notion of a vital purpose that it imparted to its reluctant keeper tested this spirit's criminal intellect and played upon his covetous mind. Through his brief interview with the messiah, Will therefore managed to persuade his host that having been a game keeper in the former foreign secretary Douglas Hay-Wain's employ, he had himself seen the Russian ambassador's gold carried away in an ox cart to a secret northern location, far from certain political rivals' suspicion; and thus the felon hoped this deception might safeguard his own keeping of the poisoned chalice for a little longer.

Eventually Greta re-appeared in the inner sanctum's doorway, to announce: "Messrs Barnabus and Columbus Day are here to see you now, Mr Benson." Having seen just what Nan Chilswell had achieved with the first tin of red kidney beans, and indeed experienced its promptings for herself, the former park chief naturally felt a little concerned at the second device remaining in such irresponsible hands; not to mention whether the clarity with which Will Wayward was allowing himself to be seen meant the so volatile bomb was indeed here in her own and her boss's presence.

"Aah, enough of that pommy formality, just call me Matt like everyone else," the messiah answered with a wave of his hand, before turning back towards where his guest had been. "Well thank you Mr Wayward, that's been most ... hey, where's he gone?" And that latest trick of the light at least reassured his secretary that the potential for destruction in the spirit's keeping must still be safely up on Hogs Hill somewhere, and thus that no critical juncture for its detonation had yet been selected.

Two burly, sharp grey suited men next appeared behind Greta, and once the introductions had been effected, Matt Benson shot them a laid back smile from his throne and invited: "G'day gents, great to meet ya. I hear you'll be needing my help with a little local difficulty up north." The Day brothers, having been freed from the twin constraints first of an indomitable family dowager to answer to, then Hillites as a whole to conform with, were by now cultivating their 1960s London gangland personas as never before; and so they would conduct any negotiations that they entered into in the most intimidating cockney gruff that they could muster.

"Yeah. We're having a bit a trouble on our patch with Jockos and Provonians," Barnabus thus began. "They ain't got no respect. They think they know better than us, don't they Col?"

"Yeah, that's right," responded the second brother. "Ain't got no respect at all, Barn, and we don't like it do we?"

"No, we don't like it at all. We ain't used to it, and they need to be taught a lesson, don't they Col?"

"Yeah that's right Barn. They need to be put right back in their place."

"And that's where I come in, is it?" Matt Benson suggested at this point. "Oh, nice gruffy banter by the way fellas. If I'd crossed ya myself I'd be feeling quite scared by now." Then he asked: "Say, what exactly is your business up north?"

"Oh, banking, insurance, general trading, medicinal herbs, that sort of thing," Barnabus replied, at which his opposite number's expression brightened a little.

"Medicinal herbs, hey? Have ya got anything that can slow a fella down a little in the … you know department? In all my years as a movie star and now a messiah, it's something I've never quite managed to master."

"No," the first Day brother responded abruptly, before his sibling as bluntly observed: "Aren't you a bit on the short side for a messiah as well?"

At that even Matt Benson's habitually relaxed demeanour became a little ruffled, and he admonished: "No need to get personal fellas. Will ya be wanting my help or not?"

The three men conversed for a little longer and then the Antipodean ventured: "Say, I don't suppose ya've seen a store of gold ingots around your patch, as ya call it. I lent 'em to the Hillites a while back and have it on good authority that they were all transported up north just before what happened here." In his customary messianic confidence, Matt had revealed far too much of his own hand at once, and the brothers saw an opportunity. They knew of the rumours that had circulated in provincial society of an illicit foreign fortune having been secreted on Hogs Hill, and the rift that it was causing at the seat of governance; and of course hoped to get their own hands upon the loot sooner or later. Now they at once felt intrigued by this newcomer's assertion that the infamous donation had been made in gold and that he himself had been its source. They also knew for sure that the hoard had not been moved anywhere; and so they led their opposite number on.

"Oh yeah. The Jockos have got it all right," Barnabus began. "We offered to look after it ourselves, but that Scroatley-Browne geezer just wouldn't listen. Never listened, did he Col?"

"No Barn, never ever listened. Just called us shop keepers, and we didn't like that did we bruv?"

"No Col, we didn't like that at all. That Scroatley-Browne just wasn't a sensible geezer."

Then the first brother asked: "So where did you get it from in the first place then?" and once more Matt Benson was far too forthcoming with the information he revealed.

"Oh ya see, when you're as big a messiah as I am ya tend to accumulate a lot of ready cash from donations and that sort of thing," he began. "So I decided to put some of it into portable property and turn it into an offshore investment. I did a trade with this Russian fella on the mainland, then one of my guys left it with the Hillites for safe keeping. We'd heard how difficult it was to get in and out of England, and how tight with their own money the government was, and figured we could get the gold back once we advanced over here anyway. My own emissary posed as a Russian ambassador, heh heh. Never came back though … don't know what happened to him."

"How many ingots are there, then," Columbus next enquired, and Matt revealed: "Two hundred, and my guy should have told the Hillites they were worth a million English groats each."

"How much are they worth then?"

"Oh, much more than that, heh heh," came the for once cagey reply. Then the messiah looked suddenly startled and glancing towards his robe stand by the side wall, protested: "Hey, what's that first fella doing back in here?"

Greta was next summoned and assured her boss that Will Wayward had indeed been shown out, but Matt nevertheless bid her stay to keep an eye on things. Then, this messiah having quickly recovered his momentary loss of composure, the three men began to discuss a deal whereby the Antipodean would mobilise his mass following against the Celtic invaders in return for being able to recover his mislaid investment.

Once agreement was reached, Matt Benson produced a satellite telephone from the drawer of a writing table to one side of his throne, and keyed a number: "Hi, Ricardo?" he chirped. "It's me, Matt. G'day. Say, can ya send me over two hundred thousand pizzas … nothing fancy: margheritas, pepperonis, that sort of thing. And fifty thousand catering sized cans of extra chunky vegetable soup, enough ovens and cooking pots to heat it all up with in a battlefield situation … oh, and thirty thousand prawn cocktails. Bonzer, you're a mate!"

The speaker then put down the phone, and flashing another smile at his audience announced: "Ricardo d'Oriel, heh heh. Best little wholesaler on the mainland. He can get ya anything." And in response to some rather bemused expressions he enlightened those before him with: "That's the way to deal with those Jockos and Provonians. They won't know what's hit 'em."

"You don't seem to have much of a regard for them," his secretary next spoke up, only to be informed: "Nah, where I come from they always finish third. Mind you that is kinda written into the pay per view contracts."

"Isn't that a little unfair?" Greta next ventured, being ever a champion of the underdog.

"Not where the Frenchies are concerned, or that fella who traded me the ingots," her boss imparted. "Now I'll be needing to build some great engines of war to fire all that stuff at the bastards with."

And so Greta offered: "There's lots of trees where I used to live that I don't suppose anyone wants. You could make them out of those." And Matt Benson, the megalomaniac Antipodean messiah of long past prophecy and great present renown, fell for that means to his own downfall hook, line and sinker.

Whether or not any anciently bequeathed power still lingered within the Shottington copse, or there had indeed been any intent in Greta's proposition, all of that enclosure's multi-trunked oak and ash were thus felled for a second time. As the great engines of war of the messiah's bidding took shape, the Day brothers' own gruff messengers conveyed challenges back to their former northern strongholds and a date was set for a grand showdown at Wotfud Gap, the time-honoured gateway through England's north-south divide.

What none of the southern parties to the arrangement could know however, was that the bullion that had prompted the scheduled battle was in fact not gold at all. It looked sufficiently like gold to have fooled first Matt Benson and then the late Nigel Scroatley-Browne, Sir Nicholas Coverlet and Douglas Hay-Wain; while the mysterious Russian businessman who had brought the horde out of Siberia in the first place had at least appreciated it's likely lack of value. But what nobody knew was that the commodity that Will Wayward now so desired to keep for himself, that Matt Benson wanted back and the Day brothers wished to acquire, was in fact the last remaining Gremlin clone's lost store of asteroid homing pods.

Even after the apocalypse it seemed that mysterious individuals were still prone to emerge from the frozen wastes of the devices' landfall, armed with huge fortunes with which to dupe their western contemporaries. The particular plunderer in question had also sold the squad of most super-functional ever cyborgs that had accompanied the pods to Earth, to the pay per view barons of Oriental home cinema as an almost impossible to beat footie team. The ever inscrutable population of that zone, being a most functional and efficient race themselves, actually appreciated that sort of thing; so once their new sporting heroes had settled into the millionaire lifestyle thus afforded them, they had come to completely disregard their original programming. But out in the solar system's asteroid belt, those same cyborgs' creators were now in no doubt as to where their homing pods had ended up, and so were searching for a suitably large projectile that could do the required job with the single impact that would now be necessary.

Chapter 14

As the morning sun climbed in the skies over Wotfud Gap, it's rays lit up a teeming scene of battle preparedness. Prior to the apocalypse, this same location had been a motorway service area, and had assumed its present misspelled title on account of the large numbers of children named "Wotfud" who had been conceived during illicit north-south liaisons in its several motels. And through some four decades leading up to the millennium and twenty-five years afterwards, this refuelling, shopping and eating place complex had watched over the traditional crossing point of England's most enduring social barrier with an unwavering dedication to duty.

In direct contravention of the ubiquitous chips and cola with everything culture of those times, the frontier post had at one stage become celebrated for introducing separate restaurant menus on either side of the artificial boundary in its guardianship, that had even attracted the attention of certain culinary critics. But the northern foods, washed down as they were by properly mashed Old Torkshire tea, "Nukey Broon" or an even more mystifying concoction to the southern consciousness that went by the name of "Mild", would always suffer unfavourable comparison or even be roundly lampooned as the bias involved never ever wavered.

The near impossibility of successfully negotiating England's north-south divide had been most aptly demonstrated early in the twenty-first century when that era's leading northern supermarket chain "Jimbo's" had bought out an ailing southern counterpart. No matter how comprehensive an array of *de rigueur* dinner party lines the new entrant's shelves might be stocked with, and despite even re-branding itself as "Jimbrose" to foster a more sophisticated southern image, the only product lines that proceeded to sell in any quantity were black pudding and mushy peas. Upon entering the stores, the southern shoppers would invariably head straight for those same two items, and upon locating them would break into loud conversations containing many an "Aay, champion!", "Ee bah goom," or "Ay oop moother!". Then they would proceed to the checkouts to similarly mock the staff with: "Eeee, tha's a reet bobby dazzler lass," or such like before demolishing all the traffic calming measures of the car parks outside in their giant off-roaders, then making their triumphant and self-satisfied way home.

The situation had hardly been helped by the media of the day, which had talked in terms of nothing but black pudding and mushy peas since the moment that news of the intended takeover first broke. Then, on the day of Jimbrose's southern launch, one tabloid had published free cardboard cut out cloth caps and mufflers for every reader; while a rival had printed its inner pages on luminous green or livid lilac paper with instructions on how to convert them into authentic Mancheatster flares, complete with over large outside pockets on either thigh. Attempt after attempt to woo the southern consumer were all rebuffed, though in fairness what most confused that audience was the new chain's seeming fascination for bathroom line promotions: "Buy three tins of Borlotti beans. Get a free sponge" – "Half price cream bath with two packs of sun dried tomatoes" – or "A free electric fan heater with every £50 spent," and so forth.

The prejudices concerned were by no means a one-way phenomenon of course, since no southerner could dare to so much as speak north of Wotfud Gap without immediately being challenged with "Cockney, eh?" no matter where in the south they might actually reside, "We talk to one another up here you know;" or "There'd be an R in it if you said it like that!" The stubborn barrier of the north-south divide was forever insurmountable, and so Jimbrose's descent into bankruptcy was swift, its guiding entrepreneur, Jimbo himself was found electrocuted by one of many unsold fan heaters in his own bath tub; and all of his erstwhile stores were either absorbed or closed down by the dominant southern supermarket chains, both of whom continued to stock black pudding and mushy peas amongst their own multitude of product lines without drawing comment. Those competitors, being major tabloid and home cinema advertisers, had of course played a part in prompting the campaign of ridicule against their northern challenger all along, notwithstanding their own in-store promotions; and had as naturally found no lack of uptake for the undying stereotypes that they had drawn upon so effectively.

Now it was two aspiring forces to future unification, albeit after their own unfamiliar fashions, who were gathered at the divide's crossing point to do battle for control of England as a whole. On one side, atop the most strategic locations amongst the ruins of the service area buildings, numbers of bronzed and beaming Antipodeans were manning their great oak and ash engines of war; whilst within easy proximity yet out of sight of their foes were arranged the pizza ovens and cooking pots of the coming conflict. Despite the early spring season, the men were typically clad in the same three-quarter length strides, vests and similar attire that, due to the inner warmth of their special enlightenment, had sustained them through the intervening English winter as well. Now they were mostly wise-cracking amongst themselves from beneath broad-rimmed hats in their customarily laid back style, while their female peers were likewise smiling, possibly in recollection of a recent course of guidance by their great leader; though here and there newer English converts to the cause were no doubt wondering whether their own next turns might be a little longer lasting.

Opposite, all along the higher reaches of what had once been the far motorway embankment there were massed thousands of leering, stamping, shouting and swearing, fist waving Jockos; who whenever the whisky-induced call of nature so prompted them would relieve themselves in the direction of the "auld enemy" in a fair impression of their footie-mad forebears on the urine-soaked streets of London so long ago. Here and there, atop the level concrete foundations of fallen motorway signs, stood the Jocko clan commanders, all attired in ceremonial plain grey Macintoshes that denoted their high status, and tartan dress berets topped off with extravagant bobbles in varying shades of red, yellow or blue.

On either flank were grouped the rather less showy Provonians, their dyed green tufts of nose-tip hair poking out from their black balaclava masks above their camouflaged battle fatigues; one brigade under the command of Terry O'Phanneaghness and the other answering to Mervyn. These western island partisans were variously equipped with one or another firearm, whilst at certain strategic points mortars or surface to air missile launchers had been set up. But the much larger mass of marauders from the chilly, far-northern province indulged themselves with no such weaponry; for in their primitive pride those bristling "Bravehearts" intended to prevail in the confrontation to come through naked Jocko aggression alone.

The best placed vantage points of all were adorned with certain spectators equipped with a comparatively incongruous array of outside broadcast cameras and similar technology, for the event was being screened live on Antipodean home cinema that followed the exploits of its favourite son Matt Benson wherever he went. To reinforce the pom stereotypes so preferred by the home audience, a look alike of the celebrated past BBC war reporter, Phil le Clerc could be seen filing his report from atop a grassy knoll that must once have been a parking area landscaped feature.

"After the break we'll be announcing our great competition," the moustachioed, denim shirted figure of 'Necro Phil' as he had been known in the journalistic circles of his day, was saying. "And for all you fellas at home there's the chance to bed the BBC foreign correspondent of your choice." Then the actor in question shot a quizzical glance towards his producer, from beneath his own receding hairline and furrowed brow, as if to enquire: "Is this the way wars are really reported down under?"

As if in affirmation, millions of HC screens across the region of Matt Benson's birth became filled with the images of four mannish females, whose ghoul-like features and mid-Atlantic accents had nightly on either side of the millennium, along with 'Necro Phil' le Clerc himself, filled the pommy living room with images of death, destruction and despair from wherever in the world they could be dredged up. "Nah fellas," a studio anchorman next announced: "These sheilas might look a little past their prime, but they're built to last like a brick gunny house and they go like the proverbial door in the wind. If ya don't believe me, just ask Phil there. Heh, heh ...he's been with all four of 'em!"

Antipodean HC news channels certainly appeared to have a reporting style all of their own. "But ladies, there isn't so much choice for you I'm afraid," the presenter continued. "Answer this question correctly, heh heh ... and you get me. So come on girls, get on those phone lines. I'm hot and I'm horny, and you won't have to dig me up first!" It did seem that this competition was rigged a little in the anchorman's favour.

When the programme turned its attention back to the serious

business, the figure of Matt himself was seen to ascend to the elevated position of his command post, flanked at either shoulder by the pommy Day brothers, Barnabus and Columbus. First the messiah called on his satellite phone England's foremost weather forecaster, who after consulting all of the other paraphernalia that cluttered his own garden shed reported that there would be blizzards in the far north of Jockoland and rain in Mancheatster, but otherwise the outlook was dry and bright with a freshening breeze. With that reassurance, Matt disappeared for a moment into his personal robe tent, before emerging anew in his most resplendent purple with gold braiding. And then he delivered a rousing rallying call to his troops, with various endorsements of the live broadcast's assorted sponsors; and to many return cries of "Bonzer!", "No worries!" or "Good on yer, mate!"

After another, rather long commercial break in which all of the sponsors featured, the order was given for battle to be joined, and a first wave of screaming, gesticulating Jockos announced its fierce bloodlust. Forward they most forcibly charged but only to be stopped in their tracks by a salvo of splattering, squelching margheritas that singed those warriors' red eyebrows and leering lips before making a sticky descent over the tartan clad areas beneath. As the Antipodean audience on the opposite side of the planet sat enthralled to the accompaniment of a rousing orchestral refrain, their heroes at once reloaded and the enemy's second rank was similarly repelled by a blistering barrage of pepperonis that not a single Provonian mortar shell or surface to air missile could successfully intercept.

Given the haste with which his large order had to be prepared, and a shortage of the traditional ingredient of Ricardo d'Oriel's native Italy, the supplier concerned had actually topped these pizzas with a sliced sizeable substitute from France's most renowned source. But where generations of Frenchman had been roused upon sating themselves of the same spicy delicacy to return their wives' or more often their mistresses' sultry gaze and murmur: "*J'ai un ardonne massif, mon chéri*"; the so less refined Jockos merely descended into impotent rage that was quickly drenched in a scalding shower of superheated, extra-chunky vegetable soup. All the while the furtive Provonians on either flank were being picked off before they could fire their arms in anger by well-aimed prawn cocktails that sent them scurrying for cover, their once green nose tip tufts dripping with pink seafood sauce as they fled. And so, these frustrated fighters of both Celtic persuasions were ordered to retreat and regroup.

An uneasy lull then played itself out as the Jocko clan commanders gathered in a huddle to discuss tactics, their hands thrust deeply into their Macintoshes as they glared all about themselves in irritation. Reinforcements were called up from the rear but it was the O'Phanneaghness brothers' troops who were the first to mount a renewed advance, to counter which Matt Benson revealed a shock strategy of his own. From behind the grassy knoll where the spoof Phil le Clerc was still attempting to gain a war reporter's ultimate accolade of being felled himself on camera, there arose a strange chorus of seemingly submarine sounds; then an altogether bizarre, pink-outfitted battalion scrambled atop and across the same area of raised ground. And upon beholding the quivering multiple legs and antennae, and armoured crustacean shells of the messiah's elite squad of prawn troopers, the Provonians scattered again in all directions with a mixture of long-held loathing and outright terror. Pizza after clinging, sticky pizza and cooking pot loads of scorching vegetable soup still smacked into and splashed all over their own targets as the Jockos supported their western cousins with a great push of their own, only to be left cursing into thin air in their unintelligible accents and shaking their fists once more.

"Where'd yer get that idea from then," gruffed Barnabus Day, as his brother stood open mouthed to one side.

"Aah, it's nothin' really," the commander in chief replied a little modestly. "The pay per view fellas back home pull that sort of stunt on 'em all the time!"

By now the blue-dyed, grey or red cheeks, orange wigs and tartan tunics of the furious jockos were all virtually indistinguishable from the slithering and dripping mess that covered every protagonist present; and the order to draw back was issued for a second time. The three men atop the messiah's elevated position nevertheless eyed their enemies suspiciously, upon then seeing the mobsters Terry and Mervyn move across to join their Jocko counterparts in planning the next move. And being all too aware that their stocks of soup and pizza could not last indefinitely against the expansive Celtic hordes who were all spoiling for a renewed assault on the opposite slope, the joint Antipodean-English command knew that this coming engagement must be the decisive one.

No such combat would be joined, however as instead the events took a turn that none save the curious interloper who next entered the fray could have foretold. Suddenly, in the centre of the battlefield and in a way that none present could have seen coming, there appeared the indistinct figure of a tousle-haired man wearing a red neckerchief and pert grin; who proceeded to saunter to one side with a languid defiant gait. When it reached the threesome of its intention, this somewhat sardonic vision suddenly evaporated into thin air, leaving in its place a small tin can; while a lingering sigh: "Just practisin' me Faustian poses," wafted around that command post.

"Red kidney beans, heh heh. Wasn't that that gamekeeper fella again?" chuckled the unperturbed Matt Benson, picking up the discarded object and summoning a nearby lieutenant. Then he pointed a little too confidently towards the opposing ranks and suggested: "Nah why don't ya pour these all over the biggest thin and crispy pepperoni ya can find and fire it right at that big, blue cheeked, bristling bastard over there. Just look at him, heh heh … could almost be me in another role, hey?"

That casual conceit proved to signal the movie star messiah's all too brief death scene, as his adoring home audience saw him carelessly flick open the last remaining Tricron bomb's ring pull, at which their HC screens went immediately blank. The Antipodean networks at once substituted the live broadcast with their own "Neighbours 24" channel and consulted their sponsors, while the air of the distant battle scene became filled with billowing pink mist that soon condensed, stained variously with vitriolic splashes of blue, grey or red into a viscous lagoon. Here and there the former nose tip hair or beret top bobbles of those so consumed floated briefly as a fluffy flotsam on that liquid expanse's shimmering surface, to be snatched up for nesting material by swooping swallows or simply become scattered in the wind as the rancid remains of the so recently warring armies eventually drained away into the broken concrete and overgrown topsoil of what had once been Wotfud Gap.

The island gem of England, that other Eden and demi-paradise of past poetic praise, was free from all foreign invaders once again; and it's latest deliverer Will Wayward, the critical juncture of his own choosing having thus passed, glided away again to covet anew the large store of asteroid homing pods within Hogs Hill's mystic glade. Was this felon really so different from that district's past objects of his self-centred scorn?

Chapter 15

As Greta, Beka and Leigh made their way down the west-facing slopes of Hogs Hill, the English rural patchwork of the wide vale between that noble landmark to the rear and the rolling escarpment on the distant horizon was bathed in the sunshine of a new spring season, as if in exultation at the island realm's release. Across the panoramic vista that had for centuries past uplifted all who had similarly trod the same tracks, compact concentrations of white moving cloud cast passing shadows over a lush tapestry of fields, hedgerows and scattered clumps of trees in complimentary shades of colour that yet defied in its pastoral plenty the worst past intent of any great conflagration of Squire Cockscomb's or whosoever else's bequeath. And despite those recent ravages and the years of neglect that had followed, throughout this verdant landscape there were scattered numbers of still characterful, grey or yellow stone cottages or as reclaimable brick built houses that simply ached for restoration. In one scenic setting or another, run down farms or battered one-time barn conversions made their own particular appeals; whilst at certain points historic church towers or spires competed over reclaiming the visual high ground from ruined grain silos or the remains of cellular network masts that insisted in thrusting their own redundancy skywards.

Word of the incredible climax to the battle of Wotfud Gap had reached Bagdalen Hall during the previous day, at which Greta had known for sure that such an outcome could only have been of Will Wayward's design. Recalling all that had transpired since making her first resolution to destroy the former Hillite fiefdom, the lost seafarer had decided that with both bean tin bombs having attained their ultimate purpose and their carriers now returned to the spirit realms from whence she herself had played a part in resurrecting them, she must either seek out some new calling in this England of her landing or else set sail once more. So, with the Antipodean settlers all gone, their erstwhile leader's assistant had at once resolved to leave the now mostly empty capital in the Isis valley to the attentions and desires of its next wave of colonisers from one market town or another; and rather than go back to the ever squabbling wasteland of The Lees, that secretary's office juniors had elected to accompany her to whatever home they might next find. First, though there was one last local matter that Greta had long since resolved to attend to.

Now, the song of skylarks tumbled from the air high above the descending threesome, while on all sides the buzz, clicks or assorted chirps of newly hatched insects filled the long grass that brushed their knees or succumbed to their footfall as they advanced towards the location of their intent. And since certain quantities of many and various reconstructive goods had been brought in by the Antipodeans up until their recent demise, the soothing sounds of nature were supplemented from here and there in the middle distance by the as busy hum of mowers mowing and strimmers strimming; and the rap, tap and scrape of so many recently obligatory, old fashioned cottage gardens disappearing anew beneath slabs and gravel, railway sleepers and blue weatherproof decking. In various locations, louder reports of dwellings undergoing refurbishment similarly announced themselves, as the western vale's more ambitious inhabitants entertained renewed notions of prosperity that had been but vain hopes for so very long.

In line with this widespread rejuvenation, the dawning, post-Hillite and now post-Benson culture was likewise none too averse to exploiting appropriate commercial opportunities; and so in the continued absence of imported road vehicles to adorn with personalised plates, a similar trade was emerging in must have house names. Already, ever popular and more conservative favourites such as certain tree or animal burrow names, "The Gables", "Dunroamin" or "Bron-y-Aur" were being selectively short supplied in equal measure with the most fashionable new flavours of the moment: "Barney's Slump", "Fair Wind Past" and "Triff No More"; whilst anything associated with an author who had once renamed a still surviving property on Hogs Hill itself was guaranteed to drive up prices across the market as a whole..

Inspired by this sunlit scene of rebirth all around her, Greta was in expansive mood: "My work here has hardly begun!" she commenced to regale the loyal urchin lieutenants at her heels, with barely an electronic interruption from within her usually so disordered mind. "I will not rest until I have created a fair and equal society for all, in which it only rains during the night, bark chippings really do stop the weeds, unlimited access to sun hats is the birthright of all small children, and nobody but *nobody* is allergic to house dust mites. A truly enlightened society in which everyone loves to eat fresh fruit and vegetables and obesity is unknown; where disposable nappies are a renewable energy resource, and ... what else? Oh yes, more than ninety per cent of people know the correct way to brush their teeth" ... and such like.

All through this burgeoning soliloquy, a rather lost looking Leigh would glance to one side as if to enquire: "Wot's she on about?" while the equally bemused Beka would simply shrug her shoulders in return. But eventually the seeming visionary of a renewed future nanny state fell silent, upon seeing that the more immediate task that she had set herself appeared now to require no outside input.

About the once defiant but now defunct cylindrical container of the time capsule that had for so long stood at the former village site where Greta herself had first come across it, were seated a family of five, two golden retrievers and a marble statue of a cherub; all of whom, apart from the statue, appeared to be in the act of devouring something akin to freeze-dried mountaineering rations. "Juliana!" the assembled group of characters exclaimed as one. Then Beka, who after all was a futuristic reflection of our earlier heroine's one time companion Beth, lost her urchin accent and asked her old friend: "So that's where you've been all this time. What happened? You've not been in part three at all, except in flashback right at the beginning."

"Oh, he said I wouldn't be, because he thought I couldn't be bothered even to read part one," came the unconcerned response. "If you can *believe* that? And me a busy village Mum as well, without a moment's spare time in my day. The chance would be a fine thing!" Then the so put upon party nonetheless saw fit to prompt: "Is it an international best seller yet?" At that the players who were gathered before her commenced to shuffle their feet, clear their throats and gaze vacantly over one another's shoulders.

"Oh well, not to worry ... Does the world need saving again?" the returnee next enquired.

"Naah," – "Too late," – and "Done it already," her audience variously informed her; at which Juliana proclaimed: "Oh well, I suppose I'll just have to inherit it then!"

"Blessed are the meek," thought Greta; then Leigh, who wasn't a futuristic reflection of anyone, piped up: "Where'd ya git that magic metal tube thing from, then?"

"Oh you could buy them on mail order back in 2025, but nobody else thought it would happen, so we got it as a clearance line," the boy urchin was informed. "It was guaranteed though: won't open until all hostilities finally cease, or a full refund. Mind you, we had to send two back before we got one that didn't have a dent in it."

"So how did you know yourself then?" Beka next enquired.

"I *think* it's something to do with being a legacy bearer," came the reply. "You know the sorts of things that he makes up, bless him."

By now the speaker's husband had finished rubbing his own eyes, and was attempting to take in the scene of comparative emptiness that lay all about them. "Blimey, love," he at once spoke up. "That's an awful lot of houses that'll have to be rebuilt."

"Now first things first, dear," admonished his better half. "We'll be needing the biggest and best one for ourselves before you start!"

Then suddenly, the air all around the group cooled and the daylight dimmed as an immense and seemingly Earth-bound object partially obscured the sun. "What's that?" gasped Juliana, glancing skywards; while at the same time Greta's desperate entreaty of: "Father … is that you?" died in her own throat.

THE END